T0304441

ADMIRAL

About the author

Julian Stockwin was sent at the age of fourteen to the TS Indefatigable, a tough sea-training school. He joined the Royal Navy at fifteen before transferring to the Royal Australian Navy, where he served for eight years in the Far East, Antarctic waters and the South Seas. He was awarded the MBE and retired with the rank of Lieutenant Commander. He now lives in Devon with his wife Kathy.

Admiral is the twenty-seventh book in the Kydd series. Julian has also written a work of non-fiction, *Stockwin's Maritime Miscellany*, and two standalone historical novels, *The Silk Tree* and *The Powder of Death*.

JULIAN
STOCKWIN

ADMIRAL

**HODDER &
STOUGHTON**

First published in Great Britain in 2024 by Hodder & Stoughton Limited
An Hachette UK company

2

Copyright © Julian Stockwin 2024

The right of Julian Stockwin to be identified as the
Author of the Work has been asserted by him in accordance
with the Copyright, Designs and Patents Act 1988.

A CIP catalogue record for this title is available from the British Library

Hardback ISBN 978 1 399 71676 5
Trade Paperback ISBN 978 1 399 71677 2
ebook ISBN 978 1 399 71678 9

Typeset in Garamond MT by
Palimpsest Book Production Limited, Falkirk, Stirlingshire

Printed and bound in Great Britain by Clays Ltd, Elcograf S.p.A.

Hodder & Stoughton policy is to use papers that are natural, renewable
and recyclable products and made from wood grown in sustainable
forests. The logging and manufacturing processes are expected to
conform to the environmental regulations of the country of origin.

Hodder & Stoughton Limited
Carmelite House
50 Victoria Embankment
London EC4Y 0DZ

www.hodder.co.uk

If it had not been for the English I should have been emperor of the East, but wherever there's water to float a ship we're sure to find them in our way.

Napoleon Bonaparte, *St Helena*

Those far distant, storm-beaten ships, upon which the Grand Army never looked, stood between it and dominion of the world.

Alfred Thayer Mahan, *Naval Strategist*

North
Sea

3°E

52°N

London

Portsmouth

Brussels

Waterloo

Plymouth

Paris

Ushant   Brest
Iroise   Brittany

Nemours   Fontain

Auxe

Ushant

4.7°E

Penfeld
River

Grande
Minou

Chenal
du
Four

The Goulet

Brest

Rade de
Brest

48.3°N

Pointe du
Toulinguet

Les Vieux
Moines

Iroise   Le
Sea   Corbin

Brittany

Atlantic
Ocean

Roche
de Lion

Napoleon
Route Bac
to Power

0   5

nautical miles

Tévennec
rock

Chaussée
de Sein

Raz de Sein

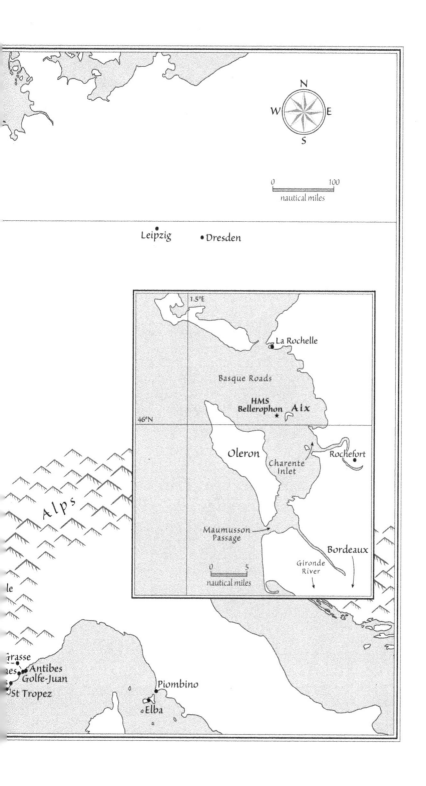

N
W E
S

0   100
nautical miles

Leipzig
• Dresden

1.5°E

• La Rochelle

Basque Roads

HMS
Bellerophon   **A i x**
★

46°N

Oleron

Charente
Inlet

Rochefort

Maumusson
Passage

Bordeaux

0   5
nautical miles

Gironde
River

Alps

Grasse
Antibes
Golfe-Juan
St Tropez

Piombino

Elba

Dramatis Personae

fictional character

*Sir Thomas Kydd, captain, HMS *Thunderer*; made admiral into *Centaur*
*Nicholas Renzi, Earl of Farndon, former confidential secretary to Kydd

Thunderer, ship's company

*Ambrose	Second lieutenant
*Binard	Manservant to captain
*Clinch	Fourth lieutenant
*Clinton	Captain of Royal Marines
*Craddock	Kydd's confidential secretary
*Doud	Quartermaster's mate, friend of Stirk
*Gubb	Purser
*Halgren	Captain's coxswain
*Joyce	Sailing master
*Lawlor	Gunner
*Martyn	Third lieutenant
*Opie	Boatswain

*Pinto	Petty officer, friend of Doud
*Roscoe	First lieutenant
*Stirk	Gunner's mate, long-term acquaintance of Kydd
*Upcot	Carpenter

Centaur, ship's company

*Bayley	Captain's coxswain
*Cawley	First lieutenant
*Chace	Fourth lieutenant
*Clare	Sailing master
*Dicken	Admiral's secretary
*Lovett	Flag lieutenant to Admiral Kydd
*Mathews	Second lieutenant
*Moore	Third lieutenant
*Sankey	Manservant to admiral
*Tippett	Flag captain, *Centaur*

Others

Adye	Captain, HMS *Partridge*
*Amillet	French colonel engineer under Moreau
*Appleby	Housekeeper to Kydds
*Bazely	Captain, *Topaze*; old friend of Kydd
Berthier	French grand marshal and chief of Imperial Staff
Brisbane	Captain, with Kydd in Curaçao
Cambronne	Military commander at Napoleon landing
Campbell	Colonel, British commissioner in Napoleon's exile in Elba
Carnot	Major, in charge of fort on Aix
Castlereagh	Secretary of state for foreign affairs

Corbineau	French sergeant engineer under Moreau
Croker	First secretary to the Admiralty
Dalesme	General, French garrison on Elba
Decrès	Minister of marine, Paris
Duke of Clarence	William, future king and having a naval past
*Essington	Admiral, first promoted Kydd to quarterdeck
*Fookes (Prinker)	Parliamentary under-secretary and man-about-town
Fouché	French minister of police, secret service
*Francis	Kydd's son
Franklyn	Envoy of Britain to court of Louis XVIII
*Garsen	Mrs, fortune teller
*Hoskins	Colour sergeant, old acquaintance of Kydd
*Jenkins	Proprietor, London Inn, Ivybridge
Keith	Admiral and commander-in-chief, Channel
Lord Liverpool	Prime minister
Louis XVIII	Brother of guillotined Louis XVI, restored to throne of France
Maitland	Captain, HMS *Bellerophon*
*Malone	Wealthy landowner
Marchand	Napoleon's valet
Maria Walewska	Countess, Napoleon's mistress
Melville	First lord of the Admiralty
Metternich	Austrian chancellor
*Moreau	Adjutant commandant of Napoleon's engineers and confidant

Murat	King of Naples, brother-in-law to Napoleon
Ney	French marshal and army commander
Oudinot	French marshal
Palmerston	Secretary of state for war
Pauline	La Principessa Paolina Borghese, Napoleon's vivacious sister
Philibert	Captain, frigate *Saale*
*Picheur	Admiral and French commander Brest region
Schwarzenberg	Austrian supreme army commander
Sidney Smith	Admiral, often contentious in his actions
*Simon	Drummer boy, of Kydd's earlier acquaintance
*Soper	Clerk of court, Exeter Assizes
Soult	Marshal of French Empire
Taillade	Captain, brig-sloop *Inconstant*, only vessel in Elban Navy
Vandamme	French general
Vansittart	Chancellor of exchequer
Wilberforce	Fiery anti-slavery campaigner

Chapter 1

1814, HMS Thunderer, *the English Channel*

'Our pennants, manoeuvre well executed.' The signal lieutenant of HMS *Thunderer* tried to conceal his pride, as
he relayed this to his captain, standing legs a-brace on the
quarterdeck of the venerable ship-of-the-line.

Very good. Do acquaint Lieutenant Ambrose of my appro-
bation of his conduct,' acknowledged Sir Thomas Kydd.

It had been intelligent and timely work at the staysail by
his second lieutenant's fo'c'sle division taking up on the
new tack. In the fluky calms the rest of the squadron had
missed stays.

Admiral Cotton had been insistent that his command
should exercise regularly, which Kydd put down to a need to
reduce boredom as much as operational necessity. His own
seamanship after long service in a fighting frigate was
unmatched, in no small part due to his origins as a sailor
before the mast.

One by one the other ships took the wind. Kydd had
sympathy for the captain of the ponderous flagship *Culloden*

trying to keep with the sleeker third-rates. Still, it was a measure of the man that the admiral had publicly acknowledged *Thunderer*'s achievement.

The breeze gave a playful lift and the seas chuckled under the 74's forefoot as the line took up on the fresh tack – and a new signal leaped up *Culloden*'s mizzen halliards.

'Our pennants, sir, and "Proceed in execution of previous orders."'

It was a welcome hoist, requiring *Thunderer* to make for port to spend a week refitting after the gales and general unpleasantness in the Channel during the autumn. And shore leave was to be granted for the seamen after their long blockade duty.

Kydd wasn't going to let them off so easily, however, and once out of sight of the squadron the decks thrilled to the heavy rumble of gun trucks. One side of the three-ton thirty-two-pounders competed against the other in the hard exercise of drill, the mock serving of the monster creatures and running them out before hauling in for a 'reload'.

There was a chance for the losers to regain the honours: Kydd had carefully hoarded his allowance of powder and shot in order to put in some live firing, always appreciated by the crew, who enjoyed the smoke and concussion after the tedium of long days of peace and order. The target was an old painting scow fitted with an inverted V mast between which a worn red blanket made a serviceable sail and firing mark. It was streamed astern, bobbing jauntily while *Thunderer* wheeled around at a half-mile's range.

Kydd wanted to see the action on the gun-deck. He knew that his presence would indicate serious interest in the proceedings and he clattered down the ladders to the gloom of the gun spaces.

Martyn, the lieutenant of the lower gun-deck, stiffened.

He was as much under eye as the gun crews. 'Honoured to have you with us, sir,' he said carefully. 'Times from you?'

'No. Do know, sir, I'm not here and you'll have your timings from the quarterdeck.' His first lieutenant, Roscoe, would be up there, conning the ship as if in a battle to 'rake' and 'harry' the hapless punt. Kydd would watch from the sidelines.

As the preparatory orders rapped out he quietly surveyed the row of guns. With the fleet-wide hunger for men there were not enough to man both sides fully so to keep an element of competition every second gun was manned. It gave them more room to perform the deadly ballet that was play at the guns and, at the same time, scope for speed, which would stay with them when fighting a single but full side of guns.

The din of bellowing gun captains, growling quarter-gunners and peremptory officers' calls died away. The crews were tense and ready.

Then Kydd noticed a thick-set, broad-shouldered figure standing still and watchful in the centre of the deck under the gratings: gunner's mate Stirk, a warrior of legend and one to whom Kydd owed so much of his formative early years as a young seaman.

He'd personally trained the gun-captains and his critical eye would judge them far more harshly than Kydd. Nervous glances at the figure were more numerous than those towards their noble captain.

'For exercise – larboard, five rounds.' The relayed command was piped at the hatchway and Martyn rapped the order that had the gun crews snap to alert. As a drill only there would be no firing but the side of the violently heaving three-ton iron beasts was no place for the faint of heart.

Five cycles of 'loading', 'running out' and 'firing' were exercised as Stirk stood impassive. This drill was commonplace, at most evening quarters conducted as routine. A flick of his finger indicated that the starbowlines were winners. They could now laze and watch the larbowlines sweat in a round to see if they could claw back a victory.

Then there was a lull, which Kydd knew was Roscoe bringing *Thunderer* around to bear on the target, seeming a far smaller mark through the gun-port than from the open deck. It gave time for the crews to gird for action – gun pouches of spare flints, quill tubes for taking the spark from the gun-lock to the main charge, slow-match gently glowing in the match tub and training tackle ranged free.

'Open fire t' starboard in five minutes!' squeaked a midshipman messenger at the hatchway. Ready loaded, the massive pieces were run out in a deep martial rumbling, their muzzles questing over the restless seas.

Kydd squatted, squinting through a gun-port at the far-off red blob. This would not be broadsides, which were used only at close quarters to terrify an enemy at the height of an action. Instead, each gun would fire alone so that fall of shot and therefore accuracy could be made out.

Stirk moved behind and in line with the muzzle of the first gun. He kept clear to allow the gun-captain room but had the same sight picture.

There was work with the crow to lay the gun more precisely – Roscoe knew to keep the ship unwaveringly on course – and more at the quoin until the gun-captain, back curved over the gun to see down its length, was satisfied.

The man paused a heartbeat to have the lazy heave of the ship lower the muzzle on target. Then his hand on the lanyard to the gun-lock whipped back. With an ear-splitting bellow and instant smother of gun-smoke the black monster slammed back, its shot taking seconds to reach out and send up a leisurely white plume fifty yards short but well in line.

Stirk padded over behind the gun-captain. Words were passed and the man nodded vigorously. The gunner's mate resumed his position, and even from this distance Kydd could make out the dark glitter of Stirk's eyes – he was satisfied with the performance.

It wasn't that the gun had missed. It hadn't. A real opponent would loom many times larger and the present shot would most certainly have taken it well in the centre of its bulk. It was more that the first ball from this gun had been so effective from the start. If the rest of the gun-deck was like that then any sudden close action would be lethal to the enemy.

No more than two rounds per gun were permissible in the miserly allowance but they made the most of it. With the setting sun came the crash and roar of guns. Then it was rest, the welcome benison of grog and the evening meal.

Chapter 2

At the other end of the ship the wardroom had invited Kydd to their dinner. Together they toasted the taut man-o'-war in which they found themselves and happily joined in the old catches and glees so revered over the years.

> *'I'm here or there a jolly dog,*
> *At land or sea I'm all agog,*
> *To fight, or kiss, or touch the grog;*
> *For I'm a jovial midshipman,*
> *A smart young midshipman,*
> *A veeeery little mid-ship-man . . .'*

Sung by Ambrose, the mature second lieutenant, it brought roars of laughter.

The more nostalgic third lieutenant, Martyn, offered:

> *'Aboard of my true love's ship I'll go*
> *And brave each blowing gale;*
> *I'll splice, I'll tack, I'll reef, I'll row*
> *And haul with him the sail:*

In jacket blue, and trousers too
With him I'll cruise afar,
There shall not be a smarter tar
Aboard a man-o'-war . . .'

Kydd sighed and relaxed with his brandy, regarding his officers with affection. Such warm, enjoyable evenings were what it was to be an officer at sea in these long wars. The French were not abroad and it was becoming increasingly unlikely that they would be caught up in a grand fleet action in the near future, but if they were, *Thunderer* was ready.

His eye caught Craddock's. His confidential secretary never drank more than guarded sips but was an agreeable messmate.

'Dear fellow,' he called, above the happy din, 'do tip us something of the evening.'

Craddock raised a glass in acknowledgement. The man had witnessed hideous scenes in the Adriatic but service in *Thunderer* had brought him through to the other side.

'I'd rather I had the sea cant to add to your merriment – but I don't. Should Mr Shakespeare serve, I should be glad to oblige.'

'Do carry on, old trout.'

Craddock stood, and imperiously declaimed:

'In cradle of the rude imperious surge
And in the visitation of the winds,
Who take the ruffian billows by the top,
Curling their monstrous heads and hanging them
With deafening clamour in the slippery clouds,
That, with the hurly, death itself awakes?
Canst thou, O partial sleep, give thy repose
To the wet sea-boy in an hour so rude?'

To his evident surprise it was rapturously received, if some-what glassy-eyed by some.

'*Henry the Fourth, Part Two*,' he added apologetically. 'The third act or so, as I remember.'

The moment was saved by Kydd, who expressed a pressing desire to unburden himself of a somewhat saltier ditty – and the evening progressed to the early hours.

Chapter 3

Approaches to Plymouth Harbour, Devon

'Great Mew in sight, nor'-east, seven miles, sir.'
In hours Kydd would be back in the inexpressibly
dear surroundings of Knowle Manor and would know the
love of Persephone, his wife. He levered himself out of his
cot, letting Binard, his valet, set up for his morning shave.
A daybreak sighting was good navigation by the quarterdeck
and there, further inland beyond the triangular rearing of
the island, was all he held dear. And he would be in time
for the evening repast.

A little later the big man-o'-war's anchor plunged into the
mud of Cawsand Bay and, for all intents and purposes,
Thunderer had made her way home. Dutifully, Kydd took boat
for Mount Wise to make his number with Garland, the port
admiral.

'Weren't expecting you, Kydd. Weary of North Sea
pastures?' The man looked tired and more than a little hunted,
and Kydd wondered what impossible task had been laid on
him.

'As it may be, sir, Admiral Cotton did send me here for the fettling.' It had been thoughtful of his commander to specify Plymouth instead of the nearer Portsmouth dockyard, making casual excuse of a current build-up of work there.

'I'll get it under way with the master attendant, then. You'll need victualling – powder, shot?'

'It's been quiet in our parts, sir. No need, really.'

The admiral looked up gravely. 'You'll have heard that Boney has got himself an army of size again, of course. How he does it, God knows, but what we can be sure of is that he'll be on the march again presently and we'll all be pitched into a new wrangle.'

'And we'll serve him in the same way,' Kydd said stoutly.

Garland gave a thin smile. 'If you saw things from where I'm sitting you might have your apprehensions, I believe. Know that three parts of four of our fleet is all the seven seas over preserving our empire and I'm to find the means to keep 'em there.' He slumped. 'And muster hulls enough to face up to Boney here if he gets uppity.'

'A long war, sir.'

'A devil of a long war – but pay no mind to me, Kydd. You make the most of your liberty ashore. I heard you now have a youngling in tow?'

Chapter 4

Knowle Manor, Devon

The evening sun gilded the leaves of the trees, achingly poignant before the autumnal winds turned them bare. Kydd was at the heights of happiness, however, for he and Persephone had young Francis toddling round and round the lawn as dinner was being prepared.

'It's all so ironic,' Kydd reflected.

'What is, dearest?'

'That here I am, as contented with life as any man alive – with my true love in mine own estate and a modest sum to keep us in our aged years.'

'So you deserve it, my dear.'

He stopped and looked at her fondly. 'Have you ever considered that, wicked as it is, if it were not for this endless war I would still be . . . of the common folk? No hob-a-nob with the King, prize money, the respect of the people, a thousand men to do my bidding. I owe it all, Seph, to a bloody war.'

'You'd succeed whatever you chose in life, Thomas. Your

country needs you at this time, you've answered, and that's all there is to it.' She glanced fondly at their son. He was visibly tiring and they retired inside.

The next day Kydd decided to ride with Persephone to the snug Ivybridge alehouse, the London Inn, to meet his neighbours and tenants in that pleasant setting. The ostler came out to take their horses and they entered the dark, brassy interior to scattered greetings, but there was a distinct pall in the air.

'They've had a dismal harvest this year, the second in a row,' Persephone whispered, as they took up their favoured high-backed bench near the fire.

Kydd felt for them. Early to rise, toil and care every day of their lives – and in the last act a failure for all their efforts.

'Not so dimber, the yields this year, Daniel,' Kydd called to a shrunken man in a worn smock, nursing his beer. 'Shall you join me in a pot?'

He was rewarded with a mumbled account of storm-beaten wheat fields and a stubborn murrain in the cows before others came to add their tales of grief. One or two tried to say something about Kydd's war but the gulf between this ageless rustic existence and the majestic heave and menace of the ocean was too great.

The gloom was almost palpable and, in Kydd's heightened mood of delight at his return home, it was dispiriting. He caught Persephone's eye, and they took their leave.

They picked their way homeward in silence, the clopping of the horses' hoofs loud in the afternoon stillness. After a space Persephone said lightly, 'Thomas, my dear, should you oblige me in a small matter, I'd be so grateful.'

Her horse whickered as if adding its encouragement.

'Why, of course, my darling. What's it to be? The orangery or London for the Season?'

'Not so arduous at all, my love.'

'Well?'

'My dear, have you ever wondered what life holds in store for you?' she said softly, avoiding his eyes.

'Often!' Kydd laughed. 'A mariner in anything of a blow has his views, you must believe.'

'I meant more . . . our future, my dearest.' The tone had become more troubled and Kydd felt a wash of misgiving.

'Is there . . . Have you anything as vexes you, Seph?' he asked.

'Thomas, there's a lady in the village I'd like you to meet.'

'Er, if you wish it.'

'She's of a certain reputation.' At Kydd's puzzled look she went on carefully, 'Well known as being out of the ordinary . . . fey, as you might say.'

'As claims to see into the future?' At sea he'd encountered lower-deck trouble-makers, who'd unsettled the crew as they darkly foresaw certain shipmates being swept overboard or suffering some other dire fate. Or disclosing who would not survive a bloody conclusion in an action against the enemy.

Persephone went on, 'She knew that Eliza Mortimer would not see her eighteenth birthday and forecast that George Broadley would lose his farm before the end of the year. Not only that but—'

'No.'

'Thomas. Mrs Garsen is a respectable widow who has the gift of prescience. It wouldn't do you harm to hear what she has to say, now would it?'

'I don't believe in such catblash, Seph.'

'You did say you'd oblige me in this small thing,' she said, lifting her chin.

It would not be an easy matter for Kydd to dismiss.

Chapter 5

The little cottage was set back from others, and as soon as they set foot inside, Kydd was oppressed by its gloom and the faded furnishings of another age. Mrs Garsen was a short but pert individual of some years but with uncomfortably sharp eyes.

They were shown into a small front drawing room with a diminutive bay window.

'And what can I do for you, my dears?'

'Ah. I met Mrs Bampton in the market the other day,' Persephone said, 'and she recommended your services in the matter of advice in respect of . . . of the future.'

Both women ignored Kydd's snort.

'I see. Well, please to sit. I won't be a moment.' She returned with a single candle in an elaborate Oriental holder, which she placed carefully on the table between them. It was scented with a vaguely eastern aroma that reminded Kydd of the harem of Pasha Djezzar, the Butcher, in Acre.

Moving shadows were cast all about the dimness of the room.

'May I know to whom I'm speaking?'

That it was Captain Sir Thomas Kydd and his lady did not disconcert her and she sat primly, hands in her lap. 'This is upon a question concerning a decision of sorts, perhaps.'

Persephone glanced at Kydd, then replied steadily, 'Not as who should say, Mrs Garsen. I'm rather more interested in my husband's prospects.'

Kydd was startled. She wanted to know his prospects? She knew well enough their holdings in Consols at three per cent and—

'I see. Then I find it will be necessary to know more of the gentleman. Do present your right hand, Sir Thomas.'

'This is ridiculous, Seph. How can she—'

'Sir Thomas. You know nothing of my profession yet object to its practice. It is, may I point out, the result of many years' study and experience and owes nothing either to witchcraft or the diabolical. Kindly oblige me.'

'Do as she asks of you, Thomas, I beg,' Persephone muttered.

Reluctantly, he obeyed. The seer cradled his hand and peered closely by the light of the candle, then looked up sharply. 'A very interesting study – most interesting. This is not the hand of the common sort, yet neither that of the gentle-born.'

She studied it further and leaned back. 'I see . . . much pain. A rope – no, many, together. I do not know what this can mean,' she ended wonderingly.

Kydd felt the creeping unease of the unknown invade his soul. How could she know that the knight of the realm before her had once been flogged with the cat-o'-nine-tails on the deck of a man-o'-war?

'Never mind that, Mrs Garsen. What does the future hold for him? Will he . . . will he live to see his grandchildren, for instance?' Persephone cut in, her voice both brittle and troubled.

Then Kydd understood. She was trying to find out if he would survive Bonaparte's murderous war.

The woman darted an appraising look at Kydd and said flatly, 'In these times, my lady, the threads of existence are not easy to trace. The stress and vexations of war do distort the decrees of Fate that are laid down for an individual and are hard to realise by mere mortals.'

She paused and then said in a businesslike tone, 'I believe we must look to the cards. I favour the piquet variety in this delicate matter. Have you any objection? No? Then I will ask when it was Sir Thomas received his existence.'

'When I . . .?'

'He was born in 1773, the month early January.'

'Capricorn – thank you.' She began slowly and carefully shuffling the cards, laying them down one by one in front of her, peering intently at them as she did so. 'Yes. As I feared. A sad moil of strife and striving.' She looked up directly at Kydd, and in the single candlelight her expression was chillingly bleak.

'Your profession is one of hazard, I see. There have been occasions when your continuance on this earthly plane has been despaired of and I must advise that I find these will not cease in any wise.'

'Can you not . . .?' He heard a catch in Persephone's voice but in the face of such could think of nothing to say.

'I will try.'

To his alarm she sank back with a moan, her eyes rolling up out of sight.

'The line of time I can see is not long . . . not long, and my vision is obscured – so much din and furore on either hand and it is difficult to distinguish, to understand . . . Ah, I see now a road, which we comprehend as the highway of life.' She mumbled something. Then, collecting herself, said more loudly, 'I must tell you, it does not extend for so far –'

Persephone gave a small cry, her hands to her lips.

'– for all is veiled in an evil fog that swirls to and fro in a vexing manner.' She swayed, her look of concentration fierce as she strove to see more clearly. 'It is causing me distress to penetrate further but for your sake I shall try to do so.'

In the absolute stillness she contorted and writhed, then gasped, 'The fog lifts just for a moment – and there ahead I perceive that the highway does not end. I see it forks. There are two roads now that go in their two directions. This then is a point in your existing where a deciding must be made in a great matter, in which you must not fail.'

'What is it? Do tell, please.' Persephone was now openly wringing her hands.

'I – I cannot go on, the pains, the agitation it is causing me,' she said faintly, her features suddenly old. 'I must cease and withdraw before . . . before . . .'

The session was at an end.

Chapter 6

Outskirts of Bautzen, Germany

A movement caught Adjutant Commandant Moreau's eye. A slight dip in the landscape, shadowed in the failing light, was strewn with bodies after a particularly vicious clash at arms. The stink of squalid deaths and reek of gun-smoke hung in the chill of dusk, redolent of the piteous desolation and waste of life that was war.

His horse picked its way nervously through the corpses as he returned to Napoleon Bonaparte's campaign headquarters. He had made a foray into the forward lines to verify the condition of the bridge over the Hauptspree, which had so lately been in enemy hands.

Movement again. This time he caught sight of several ragged individuals who were robbing the corpses and his mind erupted into a blazing rage. He wrenched the horse's head around and urged it over, hurling abuse at the scattering figures but one crouched low, yanking at a dead officer's waistcoat. Moreau tore out his heavy service pistol and blindly loosed off a shot. The pilferer dropped on to his victim, writhing spasmodically. The colonel of engineers who was with Moreau said nothing, falling in behind as they rode on.

Lanterns were flickering into light in the distance towards Bautzen but nowhere was as bright as the complex of tents and carriages that was Napoleon Bonaparte's Grand Quartier Général Impérial. The emperor would probably be at his desk in the larger tent at the centre and it would not take Moreau long to make his report.

But the tent was alive with noise and laughter, filled with the glitter and splendour of officers of every high rank. Champagne in hand, they were loudly extolling their part in the recent victories that had made Bonaparte's name feared again in the land.

It had been a remarkable recovery. From the months since the calamitous retreat from Moscow, swift and heroic measures had been taken that now saw the army at something like its original immensity – more than half a million under arms, their numbers growing rapidly as younger conscripts joined the ranks.

In the artillery parks at least a thousand guns awaited action, and with Napoleon Bonaparte in personal command, it seemed the grand retreat was over. In only the last weeks the situation in Germany had been transformed. A brilliant engagement resulted in the capture of Dresden followed by the ejection of the Allies from Hamburg, a major strategical coup. Then it had been hard-fought battles, at first Lützen, then lately Bautzen, that had seen the courageous but bull-headed Blücher and his Prussian Army of Silesia fall back in disarray.

It could be only a matter of time before the emperor's troops made a strike against the Allied horde that would leave the roads to Berlin, Prague and Warsaw, even to the Oder, open to re-conquest.

The noisy gathering quietened and eyes turned to the swirl of activity at the entrance – the emperor.

In his old-fashioned white breeches, field grey and plain tunic, with a single star, he was the centre of attention, moving slowly while still dictating to a secretary and affecting not to notice the press of officers. Processing to the centre of the capacious tent, he stopped and looked around in surprise.

'*Mes braves!*' he murmured, with affection. 'My loyal and ever-victorious band of warriors. We who have stood by our country in its gravest adversity and now gather to rejoice in success-at-arms. I salute you – I salute you all!'

He neatly relieved a nearby officer of his champagne and theatrically toasted them, bowing politely at the roared response.

'And I bring you news that shall set all true hearts of France a-beating.'

He now had absolute silence.

'The enemy are seeking terms for an immediate peace, an armistice, and I'm minded to oblige them.'

Gasps of astonishment met his words for surely it couldn't be so. Arrayed against them were three monarchs at the head of their armies – Tsar Alexander of Russia, Francis of Austria and Frederick William of Prussia – the mighty hordes that followed bent on revenge. That they'd been brought to this pass was incredible.

'A measure of the fear and respect that is now commanded by the French Empire, I believe, and a dramatic portent to our destiny,' Bonaparte added. His tone was not triumphant, or exalted, but one of certain conviction, acceptance of logical inevitability.

Moreau shook his head as though to clear it. He of all on the Imperial General Staff knew the wider situation as adjutant commandant of the *corps des ingénieurs géographes*, an engineer responsible for the vital strategic service of providing the staff with the maps and enemy assessments so necessary for war planning.

By any metric the enemy had little reason to lay down their arms, if only for a period. With their lines of supply safe-guarded by an invincible Royal Navy, and the vast masses of Russian peasants endlessly streaming out to join the horde, it would appear the end was inevitable.

Were it not for one thing: this was not a host acting as one under the direction of a single mind. The Allies were fractious, bickering, opinionated and divided among competing leaders and they'd been out-manoeuvred by the greatest military genius that ever was.

He'd leave the head-scratching until later. For now, with rising spirits, Moreau joined in the general mood of jubilation.

Chapter 7

The armistice was granted, at first merely three days, then some weeks, and months into a blustery autumn. The Allies seemed to have recoiled to lick their wounds and all the while the Imperial Headquarters was in a ferment of activity. Bonaparte set to, preparing energetically for his grand advance, securing adequate stores, powder, clothing, making proclamations to the regiments, organising reviews and awards, martial display, pomp.

'I'd wish for space to repose, I swear,' Colonel Engineer Amillet said quietly, his eyes closing. The process of reproducing artillery-ranging diagrams for the regiments was not moving ahead at the speed his chief, Moreau, would be happy with.

'What's that, Gérard?' Amillet hadn't known Moreau was standing behind him, distractedly leafing through yet more demands from Grand Marshal Berthier and his general staff.

Amillet opened his eyes and surveyed the pile of diagrams. 'As I fear I'm drowning in paper is all, sir.'

Throwing down his documents, Moreau gave a gusty sigh. 'Shall we not flee to my quarters for stolen refreshment, do you think?'

The cognac went down well and the two friends visibly loosened.

'To more grand blows in the old style,' Amillet breezed.

'The old style,' Moreau agreed cautiously. But he knew things that were being deliberately concealed from the common herd. Bonaparte's judgement had been in question in more than a few instances. Now he seemed not to realise that his old empire of men and resources was no longer his to order about at whim as it had been in the glory days of conquest.

There was also his apparent obliviousness to the huge shortfall in horses after the colossal losses of the Russian campaign. This was bad enough in battle – no matter how brilliant the action, it was Bonaparte's practice to throw overwhelming cavalry at the losing enemy to turn victory into a crushing rout amid great slaughter. But in the engagements at both Lützen and Bautzen the Prussians had been able to withdraw in good order to fight another day.

And cavalry was needed to range across the vast frontage of the facing enemy to bring back regular reports of their forces. Without this knowledge every strategic decision risked a blunder in the darkness of ignorance. In addition to the loudly trumpeted triumphs, there had been, within days, three lost battles fought by the emperor's less gifted subordinates, one at the cost of an imperial eagle with its commanding general, all for want of intelligence.

'As long as the temper of the rank and file is up to the call,' Amillet responded, not catching Moreau's eye.

'Quite, old fellow. You know the figures as well as I, but ours is not to question the means.'

To conjure an army on such a scale it had been necessary to conscript near-children and the long-retired. The veterans that Bonaparte had led to stand proudly astride Europe were now few, and famous regiments were formidable in name only.

Amillet was not down-hearted. 'But, sir, it secures us the numbers. If we count those standing ready in garrisons as well, we can field close to a full million under arms this very day.'

Moreau sighed but remained silent at this further indication of Bonaparte's fading powers. Those garrisons, relics of the time when the whole continent was subjected to the French Empire, were under orders to remain in their fortresses. They were intended to act as impassable threats to the progress of the Allies' armies. Instead, they'd been contemptuously bypassed and isolated by the advancing troops and now lay starving and forlorn far in their rear. It was a sad misjudgement that effectively halved Bonaparte's numbers.

Yet, as had been shown so recently, given a straight fight, the emperor could still bring cunning and energy to the fray to produce an undoubted victory. And, Moreau reasoned, his master's overall strategy should result in success in the longer term. After all, in the past he'd beaten each and every opponent that now faced them. He knew their strengths and weaknesses, and his strategy was simple. Given their absurd desire to act independently, Bonaparte would take on each separately and inflict defeat by bringing to bear overwhelming numbers under a single command.

A stony-faced orderly interrupted the pair with dispatches. From the expression he wore Moreau knew it brought bad news and quickly tucked the pack into his waistcoat to read later. Probably another misstep by Marshal Ney facing the Prussians.

'I mislike that we're to sit in idleness while Germany lies at our feet,' Amillet said, helping himself from a dish of sweetmeats.

'You dare to question our emperor, sir?' Moreau said, in mock horror.

'Oh, well, I thought that—'

'Time to return to work, I believe,' Moreau said abruptly.

In a private corner he turned to the dispatches. It wasn't just bad news, but a series of merciless hammer blows. First, the Austrians had broken the terms of their alliance with Bonaparte. They had moved to be counted among the Allies in coalition against them, a wily manoeuvre by Metternich, their Machiavellian chancellor. It would now take fiendish efforts to counter the torrent of fresh troops pouring into the field.

The rest was worse. Encouraged by this shameless act, the Allies had unilaterally broken the armistice, and the rest of the dispatch set out specifics of a bold line of advance by Blücher out of Silesia while the other columns were apparently on the move in the direction of Leipzig.

Moreau crumpled the paper. Damn their lack of horses and reliable reconnaissance! His dispatch was only a copy, of course, and by now Bonaparte would be pacing to and fro, then make some lightning decision that would send army divisions at speed to confront the threat. This was where the master strategist would be in his element.

On the featureless plains of central Germany the two titanic forces would confront, then fall to the brutal killing and destruction of one another. An unimaginable spectacle of at least a million souls locked in lethal combat in a single stretch of countryside. And they had to be supplied – meals brought to them each day, powder and shot, clothing and shelter, hospitals and surgeons. There was no end to the immense demand, which in turn required skilled staff.

It was complicated in that different elements of the military formations would be marching this way and that to head off a thrust here, take advantage of a situation there. If the movements of the commander on the spot were not relayed back at once to Headquarters the vital supplies would end up at the wrong destination. And it was Moreau and his department who maintained the battlefield plot. They would be responsible for ensuring its accuracy and timeliness in this and Bonaparte's sweeping strokes of strategy.

As if that was not enough, as an engineer his duty was to ensure river crossings by bridge or pontoon: hundreds of thousands would tramp over them in advance or retreat, or even over marshes that required passage by heavy guns. Failure could not be entertained.

Chapter 8

The vast Allied armies, manoeuvring only by forced route-marches for days at a time, began to coalesce in their positioning. And it became ominously clear that Leipzig might not be the intended objective.

'Give me that!' Bonaparte grated, at a sweating messenger bearing news of the latest developments in the field. 'Moreau!' he barked.

'Sir?'

'Your assessments are *pas bon du tout*, you rogue. What am I to make of this, that Field Marshal Schwarzenberg is heading for Dresden, not Leipzig?'

His hair was tousled and thinning, the sunken eyes gleaming with a demoniac energy.

'Sire, my sources – such as they are – do indicate Leipzig as the objective with—'

'Rat shit. This is naught but a clumsy ruse. It's Dresden they're after. And there I shall make it a hell on earth for the beggars.'

The town was at least seventy miles south of Leipzig, some days' march, rendering unrealistic any notion of recovering forces sent there, should there be a determined assault on

Leipzig. This would be one of Bonaparte's famous gambles.

'I'll take the bulk of the army with me,' Bonaparte continued. 'Should amount to two hundred and fifty thousands. Place 'em both sides of the Elbe before Dresden.'

He didn't raise his head from the staff map as Moreau carefully pointed out the risk to Leipzig, throwing out, 'Don't worry, Old Crow. I've a wicked surprise in mind for Blücher.'

The campaign headquarters rapidly struck camp, the practised result of countless occasions, and a quarter-million men set out to tramp the long miles ahead.

Moreau had several matters to attend to and delayed leaving. He was about to depart when a flustered aide hurried up with urgent intelligence. It didn't take him long to grasp its grave implications.

Captured dispatches had revealed that the Allies had not wasted the time of the armistice. They had come together in an agreement, the Trachenberg Plan, that struck at the very heart of Bonaparte's grand strategy. They would decline battle with the general, no matter how favourable the odds for fear of being over-matched by his military genius. Only when they could bring to bear a concentration of force of crushing proportions would there be a confrontation.

This way, the old strategy of defeating the Allies severally, one by one, would not be possible. Their individual formations would fade and vanish as Bonaparte appeared before them, leaving him to lead his huge and increasingly exhausted army seeking battle this way and that across the country in forced marches.

The combined strength of the three monarchs at the heads of their armies would shortly be greater than anything Bonaparte could command. Could he reverse their fortunes by a daring *coup de main*?

Chapter 9

The outskirts of Dresden

As Moreau and his little band of staff engineers approached the old town he had his answer. In the fields and small settlements the French soldiers lay in extreme weariness – but in a state of jubilation. Just two days previously, before the Trachenberg Plan could come to fruition, Bonaparte had won a victory of impressive proportions: Dresden was safe and in his hands.

But there was a deadly postscript.

'An intelligence, sir, that I think you will not welcome,' Moreau said, handing over his carefully scripted interpretation of what he had learned from the captured dispatches.

The emperor grunted, closing his eyes. 'Tell me.'

Moreau laid out the essentials.

Like a volcano, Bonaparte erupted. 'The miserable worms! Those devious barbarian swine!' He leaped from his chair and began pacing furiously. 'They seek to rob me of my victory. While I'm still in the field they'll learn they can never beat us!'

Moreau waited patiently. Bonaparte had every reason to vent his rage but it did nothing for the situation. He left abruptly but Moreau guessed where he'd gone. Increasingly, the great man was given to bouts of ill-tempered sulking and was now out of touch in his quarters.

Amillet approached apprehensively, clutching a fistful of papers. 'Such a tantrum in the hour of victory?'

Wearily Moreau told him.

Amillet shook his head in despair. 'See these?' he said, in low voice, holding up the pack of maps and scribbled instructions. 'It tells Marshal Oudinot to take a full hundred and twenty thousands and lay siege to Berlin. Sir, he's dividing his forces in the face of a combined enemy. He's never done that before.'

So that was the surprise he'd prepared for Blücher. And he'd been caught out. In theory, a swift hook around to take Schwarzenberg in the rear was a battle-winner, but without cavalry reconnaissance to locate the opposition, it was madness.

'Er, what shall we do, do you think?'

The emperor could not be disturbed, and in the absence of direction, Headquarters staff-work petered out in despair.

Then news came of a disastrous deterioration in the position.

Lacking warning of Prussians in hiding, General MacDonald and a whole division of Bonaparte's army had been defeated in the most comprehensive way: in one day thirteen thousand had been killed or drowned, twenty thousand taken prisoner and two eagles, regimental pennons, lost.

It had been the worst of conditions. In pelting rain, muskets and other guns were useless, bringing on a vicious hand-to-hand struggle by bayonet, sword and lance that ended with the French routed and driven into the river to drown.

On the other wing Marshal Vandamme's command was trapped and annihilated, he himself suffering ignominious capture.

The losses were great but in the face of the half-million strong numbers in Bonaparte's army they were not catastrophic but for one thing. Raging across the country to bring the Allies to battle was exhausting and ruining the fitness of an army that badly needed rest. Also, the soldiers were suffering from hunger and increasing cold.

Bonaparte roused himself and decreed a retreat to the Elbe, his field forces to lie beyond the river barrier.

It was too late: the position had already been turned and there was nothing for it but to fall back on Leipzig, where he'd set up winter quarters outside the town.

But the Allies did not rest and as autumn laid its chill miasmas over the ground they probed and harried, thrust and vanished. It became clear that Dresden had been a distraction and the main target was Leipzig. And, within reasonable marching distance, all Allied columns were converging there.

Bonaparte would have his fight, in the old style, and on the grandest of scales.

Chapter 10

It couldn't be hidden from Moreau, who had the full state of affairs as far as Bonaparte and his Headquarters staff could know it. Within days a million and a half men would be locked in battle and Moreau had no illusion that this would be anything but a fight to the death.

The first news was confused: rapid traverse and feints, skilful disentangling and clumsy deceptions at places the maps had only as meaningless names. Then, as different parts of the Allied armies combined, battles swelled and climaxed, the ground disfigured for miles with corpses, tramped over by tired troops unable to rest, to eat, to sleep.

It was becoming near impossible for Moreau to account for enemy deployments. Or the sudden movements of artillery and the menacing eruption of whole brigades of cavalry on lines of marching soldiers.

As the conflict thickened into a crucial struggle for battlefield supremacy, Bonaparte often rode out to the front, much as in the old style of Wagram and Marengo. Showing himself, he lashed his men on with taunts and threats, encouraging and exhorting by turns. At one point, so close was he to the fighting that a howitzer shell killed his horse under him, but undeterred, he pressed forward, another legend born.

Moreau saw what it was costing him. Returning, his face would be mask-like, pale and expressionless. The *levret*, a collation of the latest situation reports in book form, would be listlessly flicked over and then depression would deepen, turning into hours of lethargy, galling for those wanting a decision.

There was no slackening of the brutal fighting, often stretching into the night and the following day in an endless, punishing contest. But it couldn't last: battle of the order of millions was unsustainable with the resources Bonaparte had. He was attempting vainly, by rapid march and counter-march, to meet the Allied thrusts coming at him from every direction.

Much of his army was now within the walls of Leipzig with Schwarzenberg's legions of many nations within plain sight. With long, land-bound supply lines threatened, and the need to preserve his army in the numbers he would need for any fight-back, there was only one course left: to fall back beyond the substantial river Elster that bounded Leipzig and regroup.

Summoned, Moreau saw how Bonaparte's cheeks sagged. His corpulence appeared more marked and his movements were slow.

'There's no alternative,' the emperor said. 'Get your men together, find every bridge over the Elster and destroy it – save one, of course.'

The retreat would be orderly, the great army crossing and then the last bridge blown up, the pursuers left on the far bank unable to follow.

'So, be started, sir!'

The procedure was well known and Moreau quickly had wagons loaded with the gear needed, even if items such as powder casks were difficult to source. That night under escort he set out for the north.

It was a journey from the brotherhood of officers to a hell on earth. The encampments they passed held the exhausted rump of Bonaparte's half-millions in fearful condition. They had received no bread or any rations for days and, with the constant marching to and fro, their shoes were worn to ribbons; bare feet bled in the freezing mud. With provisions and clothing lost to confusion and the enemy, greatcoats and warmth were denied them.

It was essential for Moreau to secure their crossing and provide precious rest and security. Trying to ignore the stench and misery, he urged his engineers on, and one by one the bridges were blown while the enemy was kept at bay by heroic feats of sacrifice.

Blücher launched a furious assault on the defenders – the climax was near. It was critical that the final remaining lifeline from the far bank, the last bridge over the Elster, was kept clear for what would be a retreat behind the fast-flowing waters.

Moreau took charge at the near side of the bridge. He posted a strong outward-facing defensive line on each side, three deep, directing between them the retreating columns in an orderly fashion across the bridge to blessed refuge. That rearguard would then be released to make its own way to safety.

What had to come next kept him on the last yards of soil on the east bank, which the French would hold. At the exact moment that the remainder of the rearguard was securely on its way but before the first attackers set foot on the bridge it had to be blown up. Not before, or the last defenders would be trapped, and not after, or the attackers could get to the charges and defuse them. Moreau was responsible for the laying of charges and the timing.

And for the deed itself he needed a man of cool head and utmost courage: Sergeant Didier Corbineau. The greying old campaigner had been with Moreau since the glory days of Austerlitz and Friedland. A miner and rock-splitter, he had a pair of sons proudly in the ranks.

Moreau would verify the charge location, climbing awkwardly among the stone piers above the rapidly surging river to inspect, peering up at the casks daisy-chained around the column heads, ensuring that the match length to each was equal to bring about a simultaneous detonation.

It was not enough to bring down a width of roadway – it wouldn't take long to construct temporary bridging over it. A major section, complete with the massive stone pillars, had to be reduced to rubble on the riverbed.

'I'll be with you, sir,' the old soldier rumbled, as the final act was explained. Moreau would remain to judge the moment: on his signal Corbineau would touch match to fuse and the crossing would be no more. In the confusion Moreau would take boat for the opposite bank, bringing the sergeant with him.

The first of the army corps came up and began pouring across, a scrambling welter of men and equipment, their horse-drawn guns abandoned. They were in all manner of colourful uniforms reflecting the many nations and tribes that Bonaparte's net of alliances had provided.

In stabs of anxiety Moreau raised his head and sighted the distant figure of Corbineau, loyally staring his way, waiting for the crucial signal.

As if in realisation of what was happening, the enemy changed tactics, recklessly storming the massing French. But even after three days' fighting they were a formidable army and with ferocious discipline they faced back and blazed away at their tormentors with everything they had.

Moreau crouched down. Sleeting bullets found flesh to tear and men to slay on all sides as they fought to funnel into the constriction of the bridge. He hunkered lower.

Then he was struck by a sickening thought: Corbineau was enduring the same. What if he was brought down, leaving none to obey his signal?

He raised his head and saw the sergeant's loyal figure – upright and unflinching in the lethal hail, steadfast in the face of death, patiently awaiting his fateful signal.

Frantically Moreau gestured to him to get down, take some sort of cover but the man seemed not to notice. He rose to his feet, ignoring the *whuuup* of bullets around him and, with exaggerated flattening movements, repeated the signal.

At last there was a brief wave of acknowledgement and Corbineau disappeared from view. Moreau dropped prone again, watching their precious army pushing forward to the vital bridge. There were tens of thousands to cross and it would take time before—

In a cataclysmic split second the world turned demented, his brain telling him of a vast, deadly explosion – and then he realised what it meant. The bridge had been blown. And in the same moment he understood why. His staunch and devoted sergeant had mistaken his movement to flatten himself as a signal to carry out his duty and . . .

The reality pierced his soul. It was a blinding catastrophe. Some had been torn to pieces by the explosion. Screams and shrieks came from the press of men at the river's edge as they saw their escape cut off and were inevitably driven to their deaths in the pit that had opened up before them.

Moreau could only watch in speechless horror as men fell to their doom, their heavy breastplates and equipment causing them to drown in minutes. Others were cut down by Cossacks who had ridden into the seething, leaderless mass of desperate men, laying about them mercilessly with their heavy sabres.

Pulling himself together, Moreau looked frantically for his waiting boat but couldn't see it in the hopeless confusion. Eventually he spotted it, bottom up, carried away by the current. Only those who made it to the far bank would live to see another day.

It was a *sauve qui peut* – no officer could make himself heard in the uproar and confusion. Jostled and struck by panicked men desperate for escape, Moreau looked about helplessly.

A sudden blow sent him slithering down the bank into the writhing turmoil of drowning men and horses. Threshing around in the icy water at the edge of reason, he grappled for a floating corpse, then let it go to seize an empty cask and was carried along, clear of the nightmare.

Chapter 11

'Pay no mind to it, Old Crow. War is war and things happen.' His voice was muffled but there was no mistaking the emperor's commiseration as he sat by the fire, head in his hands.

In that moment Moreau could have worshipped him. He had just been informed that his great army had been half destroyed, routed in a single stroke, and the man who had caused it was standing before him.

There was little that could be done: Leipzig was now abandoned and Dresden must inevitably capitulate later. There was nothing for it but to yield the battlefield, with its mountain of dead, and fall back – but to where?

The army was shrunken and in disorder, the countryside alive with uprisings, and the combined Allied host was closing in remorselessly. There was no alternative but to retire to the Rhine, to the very bounds of the sacred soil of France, and concede Germany to Blücher and the enemy.

It was inconceivable. They were no longer to be legions of conquest, simply defenders of the homeland.

*

At the traditional crossing point of Mainz, they took up positions along the great river and settled into quarters for winter.

'*À votre santé, mon brave*,' Moreau said, lifting his glass. It was a very acceptable Bourgogne, a bitter-sweet reminder that even while they'd fallen back on France they were now able to indulge in the choice produce of their native country.

Amillet gave a wry smile. 'Whatever the future may bring.'

'You have doubts?'

'Of winning against the horde at the gates? As long as Bonaparte stays at the helm, no. Only that it's going to be a devil of a toil uphill for a donkey's age yet.'

'You don't yet know what he's planned for the spring campaign.'

'Will we have the men?'

'I would think by then we will. The Allies have stopped at the Rhine, reluctant to face us on our own lands, I'd fancy.'

Amillet looked up, his expression troubled. 'It won't last, of course.'

'It will if His Nibs plays his usual card.'

'Oh?'

'Goes for a peace for as long as he can while we regenerate.'

'Ha. Then we have to say it's now in the hands of the diplomats. God help us.'

Chapter 12

Brooks's, London

'The *Post*, if y' please,' Kydd asked, after he'd settled in a high-winged chair and secured his whisky.

The club steward obliged and Kydd opened at the continental news of the day. Although he was now a senior captain, his interest in the endless shrill talk of allegedly vital clashes between unimaginably large armies left him bored and restless, but he felt it his duty to keep up with the news.

'Good to see you back, old fellow.'

Kydd lowered his newspaper in something like relief and saw it was Malone, a mild and unassuming but exceedingly wealthy Kent landowner. 'Oh, Frederick, draw up a pew. A snorter of something warming?'

'Just passing by.' He pulled over a chair and looked at Kydd quizzically. 'Wondering if the view of this damnable war is clearer from a quarterdeck by any chance.'

'Not from where my stout barky's been spending her days.'

A plump, familiar figure crossed to them. 'Why, ahoy there, Tiger!'

It was his old parliamentary friend Peregrine Fookes – known to all as Prinker – who had given him that nickname, a play on the name of his former ship *Tyger*.

Fookes was a prime man-about-town whose nose for the curious was exceptional. 'Shall I join you? I've heard this hour that Boney's been beat again.'

'Oh? Hanau, was it – or was that a win for him?' Kydd offered.

'Who cares?' Fookes grunted. 'The tyrant was soundly beaten at Leipzig and thrown back to the Rhine is the core of it all. What we want to know is where it's all going. We can't continue like this for much longer.'

'They're calling Leipzig the Battle of the Nations,' Malone came in. 'Does this mean it's the end for the beggar at last?'

'Not as I've heard anyone say it,' Fookes said peevishly. 'We now have the entire Coalition at a stand, staring across the Rhine, knowing that if they venture to cross into France they'll turn the whole nation into myriads of raving martyrs, out to defend the sacred soil.'

Kydd hadn't thought of that and briefly pictured the spectacle of an entire population rising to slaughter or be slaughtered. Even in these modern times it was hard to comprehend.

'Bonaparte has a card left him,' Fookes went on. 'Why not try for a peace? The world's weary of all this war and he stands to keep most of the empire he still holds, if he plays it well.'

A peace. What would that be like? Kydd wondered.

'If there isn't a solid move to stop the fighting we'll face big trouble,' Fookes continued. 'Harvests failed, machine-breaking in the north, continental markets for our goods ruined as they can't muster up the needful, Prinny needs his debts paying off and the Yankees won't give up. And there's talk of the income tax going above sixpence to the pound. It'll be a revolution o' sorts before long, mark my words.'

'There is another possibility,' Malone added pensively, his fingers steepled.

'What else is there?'

'That the French turn on Boney, he spending lives like pennies, all for his own glory.'

Fookes sniffed. 'He's naught to worry on – has all the state and people under his thumb as will brook no opposition. It'll never happen, gentlemen.'

Kydd leaned forward, a cynical smile spreading. 'So there's always the last answer.'

'Which being?'

'Nothing changes. The war churns on.'

'If it does,' Malone said heavily, 'then we're looking at a fight to the death for all eternity.'

Kydd nodded slowly, but he was thinking of the sea and its mastery, which ensured that powder, shot and all else, thanks to the Navy, was getting through to the Allies but being comprehensively denied to the French. 'Excepting we're getting stronger while Napoleon gets weaker. Could it be . . . that if there's no peace we go on to win in the end?'

'You're talking Jack Tar and his sweeping the seas clean,' Fookes said, chuckling. 'And I'm inclined to believe that there's nothing they can't do in this world.'

'To win?' pondered Malone, as if the notion had only just crossed his mind. 'As will take us to the gates of Paris?'

After twenty years' warfare it was a near impossible concept to take in, and an appalled silence descended.

'There'll be much to settle,' Kydd said.

'Such as?'

'We can't leave Boney at large to menace us again – and

our allies will agree that some kind of vengeance for his years of bloodshed would be in order.'

'So that means . . .'

'Yes. A proper trial and so forth.'

'And . . .'

'At the end, is it to be hanging or shooting?'

'For a born commoner, hanging. For an emperor a silken rope, of course.'

'Tricky. Only one thing to do in the circumstances.'

'What's that?'

'Leave it to the diplomats. God help us.'

Chapter 13

The French encampment, Mainz

Moreau woke, startled. But it was only a wolf, hungrily down from the mountains after fresh corpses. A muffled cough outside the tent reassured him that the sentries were alert. At the same time he knew that his master, the emperor, would still be awake and at work, piecing together his picture of what faced them and conceiving of a plan to pluck victory from despair.

He looked at his fob-watch: an hour to dawn. He lay back, taking in the last moments of warmth, then reluctantly arose.

Bonaparte greeted him, yawning. 'The only way to frustrate the rogues is to take the punishment to them by individual portions. Have a glance at these, my ever-loyal Old Crow.'

It was a carefully constructed table of regiments, painstakingly arrayed by function in operations – infantry, artillery, cavalry. It must have taken long hours to produce.

Moreau inspected it closely. It made sense, given what lay against them: a two-fanged thrusting lance at the centre and a wide, sweeping but unseen force hooking about to their enemy's rear. And the force chosen for this daring foray – no, it couldn't be! The Ninth? Savagely mutilated at Bautzen and the one he'd flagged to Bonaparte as unfit for the field until it had been at least rested and fed?

And another. Cold foreboding crept over him. The emperor was fantasising: he was manoeuvring phantom troops, their numbers conjured from the recesses of his mind in memories of the glory days.

As a wan dawn strengthened into daylight, a messenger under cartel arrived at Imperial Headquarters bearing an offer of peace from the Allies. France would retain its natural frontier of the Rhine, the Alps and the Pyrenees, and in return she would stand down her armies where they were at the Rhine.

For Bonaparte to give up his empire was intolerable and, relying on disorder in the ranks of the Allies, he played for time.

It was a mistake: the Coalition tightened their terms and not only restricted the frontiers offered but made a joint declaration stating that their argument was with Napoleon Bonaparte, not France.

The mood at Headquarters was tense and sombre. Moreau found himself going through the motions of preparing field maps and diagrams, as if the big river was part of a defence in depth, while at the same time knowing the defenders were in part mythical.

The reality was almost too much to bear. Since Leipzig, making no secret of their dispositions, the Allies had increased their horde to hundreds of thousands in each of four columns now being poised for . . . what?

Then one day towards evening a starving prisoner, a Russian lieutenant under Count Bennigsen, was brought in. Under sympathetic interrogation he disclosed that Tsar Alexander, well known for his mystical views, intended to break with the Allies and their watch on the Rhine and cross the border into France, regarding Bonaparte as the Antichrist and he the sword of justice.

His declared intention was to march directly for Paris with his untold reckoning of swarming Cossacks and peasants. He himself would be the holy means to bring down the entire ungodly nation to fulfil his sacred destiny.

'Before we fought for honour and glory. Now we fight for our very lives,' Moreau said, over a frugal supper.

Amillet picked at his bread. 'We've beaten the Ivans before.'

'You don't see it, do you?' Moreau replied pityingly. 'It's not to do with Alexander and his ilk. Among the Allies, would you fall in behind the tsar and yield the glory of taking Paris to a barbarian Russian?'

Amillet stared at Moreau helplessly. He was clearly dumbfounded by the other's cold acceptance of certain and unavailing collapse.

Unrelenting, Moreau finished, 'So we see now a race between nations for the honour of being first in taking our native land and putting an end to our adventure of empire on the world stage.'

'We'll fight and—'

'Do you really think that the nations we've trampled in our twenty years of victories will go home after taking our capital? Not at all. There will be scenes of destruction and looting on a scale not seen since Rome fell as they wreak their vengeance upon us.'

Moreau gave a tired smile. In a way it seemed madness to be talking of such while they stood firm, and hundreds of thousands in their divisions were set resolutely against the tide from the east.

Chapter 14

E ven as the December snows arrived Blücher struck out, setting his column to the march, crossing the Rhine at Koblenz, while Schwarzenberg stolidly marched his quarter-millions up from the south.

For the first time in those wars foreign boots tramped into *la belle France* as uncomprehending peasants watched their progress with fear and hatred. Bonaparte reacted swiftly and threw in his legions where he could, knowing at the same time that a major battle would see him crushed, but it was to little effect. In the face of four inexorable columns of the enemy, retreat was the only course. From differing directions the Allies pressed in, the ancient civilities of winter quarters and consequent recuperation no longer respected.

And Bonaparte still fought. While the Allied Army of Bohemia marched through Switzerland, the emperor and his last divisions stood before the combined weight of Blücher's Prussians and Schwarzenberg's Austrians, a two to one impossibility.

Then news came of the slow but sure advance of the English commander, Wellington. He'd descended from the Spanish Pyrenees to the soil of France and was making his way towards her heart. As if this wasn't enough, the army of Italy under Bonaparte's stepson, Eugène de Beauharnais, found itself fighting for its life against a flood of Austrians.

Moreau was now in a haze of sleeplessness, trying to cope with preposterous orders from the emperor against the stark reality he was receiving from many quarters. Desperately, he began doctoring the directives and petty orders. His family was safely in the Dordogne in the south-west, which would be among the furthest removed from the final cataclysm – but what of the others, the countless mass of common folk who could do nothing but trust their emperor and his battalions?

The promised recruits after the last *levée en masse* did not arrive. Supplies dried up, stocks were depleted and the country suffered.

By now Moreau had certain knowledge that the tsar and Blücher were deep into France, contemptuously bypassing Bonaparte's despairing stand and relentlessly closing in on the capital with nothing to stop them.

He took receipt of terrified dispatches from the Paris minister of police telling of empty powder stores, hunger and misery. They described a population in panic with agents stirring up terror of a brutal sack and burning of the city by ferocious Cossacks. These were in clear, not ciphered, and therefore the Allies would know that Paris lay prostrate.

Scribbling as fast as he could, Moreau detailed Bonaparte's orders that had Marshal Marmont detach from the line and march to the relief of Paris with many of the precious guns and horses. If he was swift he'd place himself before the great city before the Allies could consolidate for a last lunge. If Napoleon's desperate swing to catch them in the rear succeeded there'd be a chance for them all.

Then word came of the battle of Montmartre. On the eastern heights of the city, Marmont faced a massive Allied army.

Red-eyed and emotionally drained, Moreau went to Bonaparte with his evidence. He knew that the emperor had secret police information that might transcend what he had to say based on his own military dispatches and dispositions.

Napoleon was controlled, hard-faced and impatient. He received him in the map-room with legs a-brace, his luncheon napkin still in place.

Moreau heard how Marmont had stood and fought with what he had on the heights and that Marie-Louise, Bonaparte's wife, had fled Paris overnight with his son and heir. At the same time King Joseph of Spain, his elder brother and in command of the defences, took a royal carriage out of the city, with most of the government officials.

In the morning Marmont had set his battalions to arms on the move down the heights to the plains to confront the tsar and his immense host. But there was no final cataclysmic scene, no fight to the death. The entire performance was fakery. Surrounded by the numberless Russians, he'd ordered his army to put down their weapons and capitulated on the spot.

It was treachery. Marmont had secretly engineered an agreement with the Allies and the play-acting was only to remove his troops from the capital and show that Paris was now undefended. Given the keys to the city by Talleyrand, a former foreign minister, the tsar and his holy army triumphantly processed through the gates.

Paris had fallen.

'*Mon seigneur*, should this be so—'

Bonaparte's face hardened to savagery. 'I've information they've set up a provisional government, and there's muttering about finding the Bourbons and setting 'em on the throne again.'

'But Paris, our capital, is—'

In a ruthless snarl the emperor demanded that a council

of strategy be called for that very hour. Before long set-faced marshals of the Empire filed in, the room cleared of any less senior and the usual campaign maps laid out.

'My loyal and devoted servants.' His expression, harsh and pitiless, did not fit the words. 'You've no doubt gathered that Paris has been betrayed and is in temporary occupation by the enemy.'

Not a word was uttered by the still figures standing about him: Ney, Oudinot, Culaincourt, others, all heroes of the emperor's past triumphs and each with a grim, determined face.

'This cannot be allowed to continue, else—'

'It is so, it will be thus, and there's nothing we can do about it,' growled Ney, belligerently. This was unlike the staunch and true warrior of Eylau and Friedland.

'We can and we will,' snapped Bonaparte, venomously. 'We shall devote all our strength and efforts into retaking Paris and putting an end to those vile turncoats.'

'Damn it all!' exploded Lefebvre. 'How much longer must we bleed? There's two hundred thousand of the bastards! We can't just—'

'Hold your tongue!' Bonaparte shouted. 'Who's to make judgement on the fate of our country? You?'

'Lefebvre's right,' pronounced Oudinot, in his slow way. 'Only a complete slaughter awaits us there. I for one cannot see it as the right course for France and will not move against Paris.'

'You . . . you . . .' spluttered Bonaparte, his hand writhing on his sword hilt.

'Nor me,' Moncey came in quietly.

'And you?'

Culaincourt shrugged expressively.

Then Ney stepped forward, his face granite. 'Sire,' he

declared stiffly. 'Know for a surety by this that the army will not march on Paris.'

Bonaparte paled. 'Sir, the army will obey me, of that you may be sure.'

Ney was unmoved, his arms folded. 'Sir, the army will obey its generals.' He waited for a response from the dumbstruck emperor, and when none came, he turned on his heel and left.

One by one the others made their exit, some with mumbled politeness, others avoiding his eye and marching out painfully upright. They left His Imperial Majesty, the Emperor of France and the Empire, quite alone, except for Moreau, in crushing grief, bereft.

To see the man who at one time or another had conquered nearly the entirety of the civilised world brought to this, abandoned by the highest and grandest that owed their very status and position to him.

'And you, Old Crow?' Bonaparte muttered. 'Will you . . .?'

Stifling the tears that came freely now, Moreau choked, 'As Your Majesty commands, I will ever be at your side, sir.'

'Very well. We must work together then on this last grievous duty.' The lines in Bonaparte's face were deep and careworn but he spoke gently.

'Th-this is?'

'Give them what they want. I shall abdicate, I believe.'

It didn't take long. The instrument of abdication was worded with the same care and dignity that Moreau brought to every task and after it was completed, while Bonaparte waited patiently, he created a fair copy and handed it to him.

Bonaparte took it. 'As of this moment I'm emperor of the finest empire that ever was.' He folded the paper once, carefully. 'And now I'm as much account as the humblest peasant – but a peasant of France!'

Chapter 15

The North Sea

Another whipping rain squall came heartlessly out of the grey mizzle to larboard, the early-morning cold adding spite to the misery lashing *Thunderer*'s huddled watch-on-deck. Kydd was with them by the wheel at daybreak as was his practice, hearing from the officer-of-the-watch his litany of course steered, sail carried – and a night utterly without incident.

He found some words of commiseration and, taking one last look at the scene of uniform doleful grey, made his way below. How was it that the North Sea had a devilish quality that meant, no matter how tightly hauled one's oilskin, the watch always ended with an icy runnel of water trickling remorselessly down the backbone?

Today, like yesterday and all the days before, was likely to be of the same tedium, the same prospect of the distant hard leaden line of the enemy coast reaching out between a sullen slop of muddy-green sea. But who was he to complain? There were officers whose careers had been spent entirely on blockade, some in the far more frightful conditions of the Brest squadron, with merciless crags of granite rock under their lee day and night in all weathers.

His last spell of leave with Persephone and little Francis had been enchanting, and its warm contrast with now was particularly affecting, but here was where his duty lay. As he sipped his coffee and allowed Binard to fuss about him, his thoughts idly turned to the coast he'd just observed.

Somewhere in its interior, armies were locked in a titanic struggle for domination – and the future of the world. Uncountable millions of soldiers were trudging this way and that, and who knew which battlefield would enter the history books next?

The Navy's age-old task had to be as it always had been: to ensure a raging Napoleon Bonaparte was securely locked into his continental prison, leaving England to its peaceful existence, free from the fear of brutal war and rapine.

He sighed again at the tendrils of memory that were all he had of his other existence and turned to the day's tasking, the employment of the ship's company: how to keep their interest, their loyal involvement in the ship's well-being. Roscoe could be relied on to find them work, but something more challenging was needed.

But what? There was the fore topgallant yard that was said by the boatswain to be possibly sprung – sway it down on deck for closer inspection? Hard work but not in any sense a challenge. End for end the leeward tacks and braces? The same and without the satisfaction. Well, then, if it was not—

The faint, measured cry of a lookout interrupted his thoughts. He couldn't make it out but it was neither urgent nor excited so was not an important sighting, which was to be expected in these waters, held in thrall to a battleship.

He picked up his pencil and doodled while he waited for

events. If it was of significance the officer-of-the-watch would send a midshipman with a report. Otherwise he'd handle it himself.

Then, oddly, he felt the deck gently level and at the same time the swash of wake under the stern fell away. *Thunderer* was heaving to?

Throwing on his coat he hastened on deck. The watch were calmly at their stations, still and untroubled. Ambrose, the officer-of-the-watch, came over with his telescope under his arm.

'Sir. *Advice* cutter, our pennants.'

Probably just the admiral with some pettifogging dispatch requiring him to render a report on remaining water held or some such. Kydd watched as the cutter showily shaped course to round their stern. The watch took their place, standing by as the fore-and-aft-rigged vessel passed by, slashing perilously close to *Thunderer*'s ornate after end.

An oil-cloth package sailed across on a line, was deftly seized and the line cast off.

'Dispatches, I believe, sir,' Ambrose said, without expression, as it was delivered.

Kydd courteously acknowledged and returned to his cabin. Should he deal with it now or have breakfast?

They were official so he really should acquaint himself with them first. He'd open the package just to be sure there was nothing pressing, then get on with his eggs and toast.

Inside he found a single sheet with all the standard flummery, but, unusually, signed by Admiral Cotton himself: 'Cease assignment immediately upon receipt of these instructions and retire to Portsmouth, there to await further orders.'

Kydd blinked in astonishment. To raise the blockade and fall back from the enemy coast was tantamount to a betrayal of duty – it had to be a cunning forgery!

Craddock arrived half dressed with an expression of polite worry.

'An odd one, Harry. Cast a glance at this. Do you spy anything wry?'

As his confidential secretary Craddock sighted all communications handled by *Thunderer* and could recognise the hand of every clerk at duty in the flagship.

'Er, the content is singular but all else seems square and honest.' He handed it back with no further comment.

'Ours not to question. Ask Mr Joyce to lay a course for Spithead, if you please.'

Only a day or two's sail but long enough to allow part of the French Antwerp squadron to sally.

Kydd ignored the incredulous gossip and accusing glances from aft as all plain sail was set for Portsmouth.

The sudden break away from station had the officers exercised too, and when Kydd disclosed the single bald instruction, he was met with more distrustful looks.

Passing along the south coast there was nothing to suggest that any kind of fearful threat had caused their recall. If anything, the shipping lanes were even more crowded than usual. By the time Selsey Bill emerged into view through the dismal rain curtains, the decks were lined with interested spectators taking in the last dozen miles of the entry to Portsmouth harbour.

As they rounded the low shingled point and the wide vista of naval anchorage opened up, half a dozen telescopes rose – and Kydd grunted, 'I see *Culloden*, others.' But Admiral Cotton's flag was not evident so he was evidently ashore.

The Antwerp blockade being withdrawn altogether? It was passing mysterious . . . and then he noticed the unmistakable bulk of the old *Spartiate* and just astern of her *Theseus*, both of the Brest blockade. What were they doing here as well?

A creeping sense of unreality stole over him. Was the entire siege of the enemy coast to be abandoned in order to create a frenzied concentration of force against some dire threat?

An outer watching frigate threw out the challenge and *Thunderer*'s reply soared up. Then from behind it a launch emerged, heading for them.

'We'll heave to,' Kydd said, to the white-faced officer-of-the-watch.

The boat neared. She flew an ensign indicating an officer aboard, who stood up as the boat closed to hook on to the main-chains.

His hail was quickly answered and he slowly mounted the side. He gravely saluted the quarterdeck and approached Kydd, visibly disconcerted by the still figures watching him closely.

'Captain Kydd? Herne, flag-lieutenant to the port admiral. We're all ahoo here after the news so I'm bid give you these mooring instructions before—'

'Mr Herne. Kindly enlighten me. What news?'

The officer stepped back in surprise. 'You mean you haven't heard? Why, I'm persuaded all England must know by now!'

'The news, sir!'

'Ah. Then, Sir Thomas, I'm to tell you that Paris has fallen and the emperor Napoleon Bonaparte has abdicated. The war is now over.'

After a long moment of appalled silence, those out of earshot behind erupted in a rising bedlam of noise as the unthinkable word spread like wildfire.

'Mr Herne, tell us more, damn it! When did—'

'Gentlemen, gentlemen. I know very little of the details and, if you'll excuse me, I must be about my duty. God's blessed us with a victory and I've no doubt you'll learn all about it in a short time.'

Stunned, Kydd simply stood there, unable to bring his racing thoughts to order, then remembered his mooring instructions.

'Third astern of *Orion*,' he said distantly, to Roscoe, 'if you can get those villains back to work.' There were additional orders, which included that no liberty was to be granted to the hands, and all ships were to remain at immediate notice for sea.

His entire existence was now dream-like, unreal. Was it true that the ogre that had haunted every English soul was now laid low? No more to bathe the world in blood, visit war on the helpless?

Kydd made a conscious effort to pull himself together, focusing on proceedings as the stately sway of the deck told of their taking sail again for the last run to their rest at mooring.

Chapter 16

'Sir! *Culloden* has hoisted her flag,' the signal midshipman piped, eyes round and awestruck. Admiral Cotton must have returned, probably with high-level intelligence.

After a short delay there was another hoist. 'Sir, all captains to repair on board, negative frigates and unrated.' All ship-of-the-line senior captains. This would answer all of the questions.

Roused, Kydd snapped to Roscoe, 'I want to see my barge in the water the instant we secure from sea.'

Below, Binard hurried to lay out his full-dress uniform, and in a fever of impatience, he drew it on and returned on deck to see the fo'c'sle party conclude the moor.

Roscoe saw his expression and bit his lip. The time for chat was later.

As the boat swashed along Kydd saw that more and more warships were crowding into the anchorage, many from the more distant stations, the case if there had been a general recall.

Laying alongside the flagship, Kydd took the side-steps in agile leaps, a pipe pealing at the bulwarks.

'Welcome aboard, sir,' an elderly lieutenant said, with a bow. 'The admiral begs pardon, but he has to prepare matters below and asks me to meet you in his place.'

It added to the unreality but Kydd returned the civility and joined the group of captains at the after end of the quarter-deck. Each officer wore the same look of bemused shock and there was little small-talk.

'Ho there, Charles,' he called affably, to Coles of *Melpomene*, a frequent acquaintance in the boredom of blockade. 'A singular affair, don't you think?'

The big man turned slowly and pierced Kydd with a look of ferocious intensity. 'I want the answer to just one question,' he grated. 'And that is, is this true in its particulars or another of Boney's false-hearted ploys? Just answer me that before I dance on my own quarterdeck!'

Unable to give a reply Kydd fell back on the state of the weather, which had cleared.

To his credit Admiral Cotton did not detain them long and they filed one by one into the great cabin, taking a chair without regard to seniority. There were no charts spread, no packs of orders, nothing that resembled the usual operational conference. Cotton sat impassively in the centre regarding them sombrely.

'Thank you for your attending,' he opened quietly into the cabin, which held utterly still. He gave a guarded acknow-ledgement at the thin smiles this produced, then went on in more decided tones: 'By now you'll all have heard of events on the continent, which the Devil knows are hard enough to hoist in, and you've a reasonable need to know whether it's Boney at the hookum snivey again.'

He paused just long enough to give a wry grin. 'I can tell you that he's beat is true enough. That this makes the war over is not.'

From several places around the table incredulous protests arose.

'Understand my source of authority – at base a series of riders from Paris to the coast through a nation turned arsy-versy. That is, enough to learn the bones reliably but the details at variance with each other.'

He paused again, then continued briskly, 'The state of affairs in Paris, gentlemen, is this. After a series of battles, some won, most lost, the four columns of the coalition laid siege to the city. There was no great mortal defiance, for Boney's marshals betrayed him and went for peace. And therefore we find the tsar and his masses entering it peacefully as victors.'

What followed could only have been the traditional end to a major siege – the brutal sacking of a once-beautiful city. Grave looks were exchanged as each pondered the fate of those caught up in the mindless chaos of drunken Cossacks and—

Cotton continued: 'The tsar, however, was faithful to the Coalition agreement, which stated that the war in which they've been engaged has not been against the French nation but against the monstrous genius of its emperor, Bonaparte, and therefore they did not allow pillage and plunder.'

'What'll happen to that foul abomination?' called one.

'As at the nonce he's under guard in Fontainebleau. His wife has fled and he has no powers left to him. The Coalition, however, is in conference in Paris for the purpose of deter-mining his fate.'

'Hanging's too good for the monster,' rasped Coles, with unbridled venom.

'If I might ask it, why do you say the war is not yet over?' Kydd said, troubled at the implications.

'Because it is not. You may beg reason why we are all retired from blockade of the French coast. A good question

60

easily answered. The deliberations in Paris have come only to a trifle of peace, an armistice of sorts. No treaty has been signed and, indeed, with whom? Therefore we are still in the act of war – suspended.

'Given this circumstance, as an act of faith and pledge of sincerity, and in return for a cessation of hostilities, we have released our hold on the coasts and fallen back.' His face tightened. 'There being an act of falsity of any nature we stand at a moment's notice to resume our regular course. Hence my orders forbidding liberty of any kind until developments allow their lordships to permit it. Is this clear, gentlemen?'

It was, but Kydd was left with a burning desire to know more. Would a newspaper from ashore tell it, or would it be nothing but grotesque rumour?

'Do take your opportunity to powder and victual. I rather fancy if there's to be a resistance it will be a no-quarter fight to the death. I'll ask you to leave now. I've a hill of work and—'

'Sir?' the elderly lieutenant said hesitantly, from the door.

'Not now, James, I've a deuce of things to do.'

'Sir, it's a telegraph from the Admiralty just now signalled to the port admiral for distribution to sea commanders as may be present. It's to say—'

'Give it to me.'

Cotton snatched it, his eyes moving over the paper. Then he put it down with an intake of breath, smoothing it out as if in doubt of its existence. He read it again, slowly, then looked up with a twisted smile and said softly, 'Gentlemen, it seems we have our treaty. By this I learn that an act of peace was signed with the Paris Senate that does satisfy in the particulars. As of this hour, my friends, Great Britain is no longer at war with the French Empire.'

The assembled captains broke into a dazed babble. Then they noticed a small smile playing.

'Additionally the signal gives me leave to order you to stand down sea watches, assume harbour routines and . . . to grant liberty to whosoever desires it.'

'Damme!' breathed Coles. 'And which watch steps off first? A pretty teaser!'

'Be warned, sir. My observation when ashore was of an increasing unbridled merriment, not to say licentiousness,' Cotton retorted. Then, primly, he added, 'Therefore I remind you that your ship remains in commission in all respects but your liberty arrangements are none of my business.'

Satisfied chuckles were interrupted by his ringing of a small silver bell. 'Before you make your departure may I beg your indulgence in a certain matter.'

Servants arrived bearing bottles and glasses.

'Shall it be that we here are the first in His Majesty's Navy to raise a glass to final victory in the great war just concluded?'

Chapter 17

'Not a word until I've addressed the ship's company,' growled Kydd, to his coxswain, Halgren, and the barge crew as they foamed speedily back to *Thunderer*. 'If any does, I'll stop their leave for a month.'

The line of deck was crowded end to end with eager seamen, who knew better than to shout down to the barge crew, and Kydd mounted the side-steps with appropriate dignity. Something impish made him feign a dismal, resigned expression at which the noisy gossip fell away.

'All officers – my cabin, instanter!'

He beckoned Craddock and, without changing expression, softly gave instructions.

Staying in his full-dress regalia he awaited the procession of officers, each blank-faced but tense as they took their places.

He looked from one to another, their grave expectation and wariness hard to ignore.

Kydd's features contorted and, with a smothered snort, a dazzling smile broke out. 'The war . . . the war is in detail quite over, gentlemen.'

The tidings penetrated in different ways, the unbelievable now a fact brought to them by their captain.

Kydd waited for a long moment, then called for silence. 'You shall know now as much as I. Allow me to detail proceedings.'

In the tense hush he outlined what he'd heard. What had happened in the last days of the war and the negotiations that had led to a form of peace that had satisfied the Admiralty was not known but the fact was indisputable. The war of Bonaparte was at an end.

'I won't detain you. Stand down sea watches, harbour routine, all else to carry on as usual. I will address the ship's company with details of liberty and so forth in one hour. Tonight, I hope you will honour me with your company at a dinner, which I believe in the circumstances well warranted.'

They rose slowly, varying expressions conveying something of the storm of emotion brewing in every soul.

'Oh, Mr Roscoe, would you remain, if you will?'

'Sir?' His first lieutenant clearly wanted to be on his way.

'Shore leave.'

'Of course, sir.' There was little conviction in his tone at the realisation of the burden of the responsibility.

Kydd had given it thought in the boat returning, however, and had come up with an idea. 'Which watch should step off first? Larbowlines or starbowlines?'

Whoever went off ahead would be the first to taste the ardent delights of a grateful citizenry. Was it fair to restrain the others while wild carousing was within earshot at Portsmouth Point?

'Well, er, perhaps the—'

'I rather think not. Ponder on it – a watch consists of a side of guns, enough to repel boarders, a full crew to attend to set any sail or douse any canvas in time of a squall. But, as well, a cook and his mates, some officers' servants, the purser's steward to—'

'I understand where you're heading, sir,' Roscoe said, energised. 'Only a very few o' the watch will actually be at work, the rest . . .'

'Quite. I desire you make up a notional harbour watch, consisting of only those idlers that can keep the vessel alive – a cook, carpenter's mate and so forth.'

'So—'

'Yes. The rest can join the watch ashore – open gangway.'

'An . . . admirable notion. But . . .'

'Well?'

'What of this dwarf watch of idlers? When will they get their liberty?'

'Well noticed, Mr Roscoe. The answer is that this watch will consist of volunteers. The rule will be that any who volunteer for duty in the first night will the next day be granted double liberty – two days on the frolic – when the others return aboard after their only one night ashore.'

Roscoe shook his head in admiration. 'I stand well tutored in the art indeed. Your squiddy watch in minutes.'

Judging by the uproar the decision was not easy for some but by evening Kydd was captain of a ship that was, to all intents, quite empty of humanity.

The dinner proved as memorable as it was possible to be. Binard and the officer's cook had elected to be volunteers, as had some of the marine servants, and with the officer's cook one of their number the evening promised much.

Strangely, to begin with, Kydd was not in attendance. Craddock explained that he was raising a glass with the volunteers below decks before he felt able to return to his fellow officers.

When he appeared he wore a thoughtful look and did not

immediately join in the chortles and happy babbling. The volunteers he'd just spoken with were older, steadier, and he'd heard opinions from those who recollected the last peace – a dozen years ago at Amiens when, within weeks, ships were paid off into ordinary and a hundred thousand seamen turned out to roam the streets unemployed. What would this peace bring?

Kydd took his chair bowing left and right as his officers rose in respect. When all were settled Kydd gave a discreet signal and two ship's boys bore in a tray of the wardroom's precious gold-chased glasses, glittering in the warm candlelight.

Faces brightened: it was well known that Kydd kept a bountiful table, and who knew what fine drop they would taste now?

'Gentlemen – fellow officers and shipmates.'

Politely they sat forward, ready for the words.

'This day shall go down in the books of history for one reason – the end of a war that has endured more than twenty years and has left us the vanquisher. I feel it right and proper that before we go on to enjoy ourselves, we in our tight little ship do first solemnly toast this fact.'

Eyes strayed to the door to catch a sight of which fine wine it would be.

To the astonishment of all it wasn't the lordly Binard who entered but Bull Opie, their broad-shouldered boatswain. He was cradling a well-weathered standard rum cask, which he deposited carefully at the end of the table, then stood by it with a secret smile.

'I believe that all here must hold that His Britannic Majesty's Navy owes its triumphs not to the quarterdeck alone but to those whose being is before the mast. Our toast therefore joins with that which I've just had the honour of sharing with our volunteers. In our hour of rejoicing we will take our libation in good honest rum – Nelson's Blood!'

As the astonishing spectacle unfolded the boatswain took up his cask again and, followed by the two lads, carried it away to the open air to pour away from the candle flame.

Shortly, with every man around the table equipped with a generous tot, it was time to raise their glasses.

Kydd led with the loyal toast and in order of seniority each of his four officers proposed his own. Then all at the dinner tried to take hold of the idea that war was now a memory, that every action was to be governed by a different set of rules.

The meal began quietly, the dish of elvers received with due respect for the efforts of the few remaining cooks' crew and then it was the roast beef.

Faraway stares and conversations that trailed off indicated where thoughts were leading and the usual boisterous give and take were absent. Then the quiet second lieutenant, Martyn, ventured to enquire of Kydd concerning their future.

'You mean for this stout barky?' he replied, realising he had not given it much thought. 'Who can say? There must be hundreds of sail in want of employ but it would be a rash government that thinks to throw 'em aside.'

He pondered then sat back. 'You've naught to worry of, Mr Martyn. While *Thunderer* remains in commission, her flag aloft, it means we continue life as before. You and every man aboard will receive your full pay as if Boney was still on your tail.'

'Until we're cast into ordinary,' muttered Clinch, the surly fourth. 'All then to be paid off and on to scranny-picking for ever.'

'Not so, old trout,' Ambrose, second lieutenant, drawled. 'We'd be on half-pay at once and the leisure to see the world ahead of us to choose our course.'

'Oh? So to be a crabbed dominie or some such?' Clinch sneered.

'I'd rather think to ask my papa to find me a berth in an East Indiaman,' Martyn said dreamily. 'Regular passages in a ship of size, personal freight, good naval discipline – and a chest of rupees at the end of it.'

'Or if you can't find a berth, the Bombay Marine,' offered Clinton, captain of marines. 'I know three of my ilk who've done main well in India.'

Kydd felt for Clinch. Of humble birth, he'd not felt able to rise in the ranks and could never aspire to such openings. 'There are positions nearer home, Mr Clinch. Think of the coastguard, perhaps, or the Falmouth Post Office packets. And . . . and—'

'Hey! This is a celebration, we've won the greatest war that ever was!' Roscoe burst in, holding out his glass for recharging.

'So it is!' Kydd answered happily. 'And here's to us all on a day we'll not soon be forgetting.'

Chapter 18

It was strange – unnatural – to take the morning air without a soul in sight. Kydd could see the whole stretch of the decks completely deserted. No early-morning scrub-down, hands busy becketing up gear, watch-on-deck with telescope-carrying officer-of-the-day.

Had he been right to let *Thunderer*'s people flood ashore? Now, one by one, his officers had found reason to take their leave and he'd let Roscoe join them, remaining himself as the required officer aboard.

The noise from ashore was even less restrained, church bells pealing joyfully at the news of the war's end.

He couldn't absent himself, so should he send for Persephone? Better to let things settle a trifle and see where *Thunderer* ended up.

Soon the midshipmen would be back with a thick bundle of newspapers and his morning's activity would be spoken for. Still pondering he paced on, distracted by the gleeful racket drifting across the water.

At his desk, temporarily without a ship's clerk, and with Craddock gone too, he was at something of a loss as to what to do. Admiral Cotton had spared his captains the usual run of reports and statements consequent on a fleet's return and he had little to occupy him until later in the afternoon when the dockyard dispatch cutter handed over the day's official mail.

In it was a letter, clearly from a naval person as it was included in the official bag. To his delight Kydd found it was from Essington, the captain of *Triumph* at the battle of Camperdown and the instrument of Kydd's elevation to the quarterdeck. Now a retired admiral, he was issuing an invitation for him to be present at the grander celebrations in London to be mounted by the Palace and civic notables. Kydd could trust they would be historic in scale.

It resolved his restlessness: he'd send for Persephone and they'd travel to the capital, perhaps stay with his closest friend Nicholas Renzi, the Earl of Farndon and his lady, who happened to be Kydd's sister, Cecilia.

Some days later it was all put in train and a thrilled Persephone arrived at the same time as a delighted affirmative reply to a hurried message Kydd had sent to his sister.

Roscoe was content to be acting captain of *Thunderer* and could be relied on to keep the ship in good fettle. Admiral Cotton had already left for London and could therefore raise no objection.

As they bowled along the London road in a post-chaise decorated with flags and sprays of laurel, they took in the countryside, which was in a ferment of joy – almost continuous ringing of church bells, the crackle of musketry of the local militia, dancing on village greens, bonfires everywhere.

They entered the great city towards evening. It was alive with excitement and in an endless deafening commotion. Near every house was illuminated: transparencies of patriotic fervour, lit from behind, were in lower windows along with effigies of the defeated and mortified Bonaparte on rude display.

It was crowded beyond belief. Inching along, buffeted by the surging masses, it was well past midnight when they finally made Renzi's townhouse.

'Dear fellow! You prevailed against the mobility and now are here. You must be famished – Cecilia has ordered a collation to take the edge off.'

'Nicholas,' his wife scolded, 'do let them take off their cloaks and rest after their journey. There'll be time enough to gossip at breakfast.'

Strangely, breakfast did not seem the right time to talk about the titanic events that had so suddenly taken place. Kydd and Renzi's friendship had begun in the first days of the French wars more than twenty years previously, and memories of their shared adventures at sea would never fade. Their destinies had diverged – Kydd crossing the line from common seaman to the quarterdeck, then command, and Renzi inheriting an earldom and becoming a valued secret agent of the Crown.

What was to be their fate now?

Chapter 19

Next morning

The ladies had taken special care over their appearance, and with the gentlemen in the gayest dress they could find, all four stepped out into the hullabaloo.

They strolled through the choked streets instinctively heading for the river Thames, which had figured so largely in England's history, and was now lively with every conceivable craft decked out in celebratory extravagance. Some even had bands aboard; others responded with hearty roystering on deck as they passed.

They found a spot on a grassy bank and spread a rug. Cecilia had arranged suitable refreshments as the servants had been allowed to venture out to find their own delights.

Kydd turned idly to his friend. 'Old chap, have you knowledge of a reliable kind about what's afoot in Paris? I find the newspapers a sorry lot, so mired in rumour.' Renzi, of course, was close to the centres of intelligence in Whitehall.

'Not so dependable, my friend. We owe it to the tsar, I believe, that there's no blood running in the streets.

He's insistent that the French nation's been beguiled by Bonaparte, whom he supposes to be the Antichrist and he alone is to be punished. No revenge on the French people for the burning of Moscow, and as he's first to enter through the city gates his example is to be followed by the rest of the Allies.'

'So . . .'

'The French are leaderless. Bonaparte was central to their rule and administration and now he's removed there is only one thing that can be done for them that will satisfy all the Allies.'

'Appoint a ruler of our own over them?'

'Not really. Can you imagine the disarray when it comes to a choice of who among them will take the honour? No, old trout, there's one easy solution.'

'Which is?'

'Restore the Bourbons, revert France to its situation before the war. Rouse out the old king's brother and set him on the throne, everything *status ante bellum*.'

'The fellow I carried off from Libau ahead of Bonaparte's finest?'

'Just so.'

'They get back all their blood-won empire with him?'

'Your friend Metternich of the Austrians is offering a grand conference of the Allies to be held in Vienna where all this will be sorted out. Whether the others will agree to it remains to be seen.'

'And meanwhile?'

'Paris is occupied by many divisions of Allied troops, who, while being on their best behaviour, are no doubt partaking of any hospitality it offers.'

'And Bonaparte – to be hanged or shot?'

'I rather think neither. Given the continued existence of

his admirers, to turn him into a martyr would not be a wise act for the new regime.'

Cecilia pouted. 'Come, come, gentlemen! We're to rejoice and make merry on our great deliverance. Can we not leave the future to take care of itself? Have some more seed cake, Thomas.'

Kydd lay back with his eyes closed in something like wonder: it was only days ago that he had been in *Thunderer*, enduring vile weather on blockade duty. The war had stretched ahead seemingly eternally, as it always had, but now . . .

'Avast there, ye lubber!' Kydd recognised the seamanlike hail instantly. It was Bazely, a salty mariner from years past, recently made a post-captain.

Kydd opened his eyes and sat up. 'Ahoy there, m' friend. What brings you here?'

The jovial merriment fled from Bazely's expression and he stiffened reprovingly. 'As ye tops it the sybarite, f'r some there's sea duty as calls.'

'Duty?' Kydd said blankly.

'Aye. Very shortly an' I'm t' fight to the end in a great battle, I fear.'

Kydd shook his head in puzzlement but, in a commanding roar that stopped all conversation, Captain Bazely stoutly declaimed:

> '*When danger threatens and the foeman nigh*
> *"God and our Navy!" is the cry*
> *But the danger over and the country righted,*
> *God is forgotten and the Sailor slighted.*'

'As none can deny,' Kydd said carefully, 'But, um, battle?'

For a long moment Bazely stood glowering, then broke into helpless laughter. 'Battle indeed – twenty sail-of-the-line and frigates, an' in home waters too, cuffin.'

'Dear fellow, you're not making much sense.'

Bazely drew himself up. 'Y' sees before you acting admiral who's t' see all goes t' plan in the action – we calls it the battle of Trafalgar.'

Kydd was at a loss for words.

'It'll be in Hyde Park,' Bazely explained, 'as the Serpentine makes a grand stage f'r the spectacle. It's to be a fine sight f'r the people, Tom, a thundering great battle of sea-going models as celebration. Shows 'em how a mighty naval victory gets won and reminds 'em who they owe it to.'

'When will this be?'

'A brace of shakes, shall we say? Leave me your address an' I'll see you get special seats. Oh, an' there's a damn sight more entertainments afoot, all t' be seen in the *Gazette*. I'm t' spread more sail, much t' do.'

Kydd scribbled the address and waved a farewell.

There was indeed a great deal about the celebrations in the *Gazette*, much of it to take place in the royal parks: a balloon ascent, several levees, illuminations making cunning use of carbonic gas – and any number of victory parades and military appearances.

There was much spirited talk between Cecilia and Persephone about which would see their attending and in what mode of dress.

Chapter 20

Brooks's, London

On impulse, that evening Kydd thrust his way through to his club, to take a sounding of what the feeling of the hour was among higher society. It was more crowded than he'd ever seen it.

As a publicly acknowledged sea hero lately returned to his native shore, at this time of victory he'd been most warmly greeted by many he barely knew. It wasn't long before Fookes puffed up, obliging a steward to bring chairs.

'Tiger – you're in Town.' He guffawed.

'As last I noticed.'

'I won't ask how you are, victor of the vanquished. Although I have to say at the moment Nelson must yield to Wellington for the public eye.'

'I'll try to bear it.'

Fookes regarded Kydd indulgently. 'Do so, old fellow. And be understanding that as a bona-fide lion of the field you should expect to be indulged atrociously.'

'Um, quite. So these vast entertainments, I do worry – who's to foot the bill, as it were?'

'Yes. Well, a majority it has to be said are mounted by the Prince Regent. He's no warrior and has not played any part as I've heard in the wars but does have a call on the people's acclaim.'

'Oh?'

'You'll know, of course, that good Queen Anne died in the year—'

'Yes, 1714.'

'Of which this year is the hundredth since. He claims it as the jubilee of the House of Hanover, and Parliament is thus to endow the jubilations. That it's coincident to the end of the great wars is merely fortuitous.'

'Then surely—'

'Tiger. Let me be candid. It would not be meet and proper for you to be seen further in Prinny's company. Since you've been so long at sea smiting the king's enemies you're not to know the people have taken against him. He's a spendthrift beyond believing, his amours and dalliances are ugly and notorious, and as a bloated putrescence he's . . . revolting.'

Kydd flinched. He knew Prinny from the past as a jolly, hard-living but well-meaning king-in-waiting, but to have the people turn against him was . . . unfortunate. 'Not to hob-a-nob?'

'Never!'

'Then so shall it be. To ignore His Royal Highness the Prince Regent. What else is of significance?'

'Ah. Another prospect entirely.' Prinker gave a satisfied smile. 'Not for the public knowing at this point, but I have it on the best authority that in homage to the never-failing bankers of the battlefield, the chiefs of the Allies are to visit England together to pay their respects.'

'The money-men who—'

'No, Tiger. I speak of kings and emperors, commanders of legions, victorious marshals. All wanting to lay their admiration at the feet of the British folk who made it all a reality.'

'So . . .'

'They land at Portsmouth from the continent very shortly. If I'm right, there'll be Alexander, Tsar of all the Russias, the King of Prussia, that of Austria, their chief battle commanders and quantities of others all come to do their devoirs. This is the kind o' company I'd rather you keep, old horse.'

'I'll do my best for you, Prinker.'

'They're calling them "The Concert of Europe", who together are going to settle the continent's future. We're going to keep out of it, according to Castlereagh, let 'em sort out their own destiny while we go on to better things.'

Talk around them rose and fell, and Kydd let it all flow past him while he heard the latest gossip from Prinker. Then, satisfied that he knew enough to hold up his end at the dinner table, he returned to Persephone with his news, but she had her own.

'And you've no idea in the world what we're going to see tomorrow, darling!'

'A mermaid?' he teased.

'No, don't be silly. We're off very early in the morning to the park. There we're to be witnesses to Monsieur Jean-Pierre Blanchard make ascent in his Charlière balloon!'

During the long war the only talk of balloons had been at the time of the threatened invasion, when they'd been rumoured to be on their way to drop infernal machines from the sky on helpless citizenry. It had never happened but this was a chance to see the balloons for themselves.

From where they stood it was difficult to make out details of the enormous egg shape painted in lurid colours. On a nearby plinth a barker with a speaking trumpet was urging the crowd to avail themselves of the souvenirs on sale – and never to underestimate the bravery of the man about to board the open conveyance suspended beneath.

A flourish with a horn brought the spectators to a state of attention as the aristocratically dressed man climbed in, bowing respectfully to right and left. Then, with excited commentary from the barker, the entire apparatus shuddered and moved upwards.

Kydd saw a stout line attached to the balloon eased out by five men on a large winch. He'd heard of valiant escapades in balloons raised by roaring fires but this was rising in perfect, uncanny silence. Higher and higher – above the tallest tree and even higher. The man was just a figure now, waving jauntily down. Gasps of disbelief and delight came from the crowd.

'What makes it rise up, Thomas dear?' whispered Persephone, awed.

'Ah. Your phlogiston gas, I've heard. Or is it to be the gas feeding our new lights on London Bridge?'

The balloon was now like a toy floating just below the clouds and was clearly restless, tugging at its tether, which the men at the winch were hard put to control. A musical figure then sounded from the horn, evidently the signal to descend and the winch groaned and creaked as the men fought it to the ground.

The man sprang down lightly, instantly mobbed by a baying crowd. The two couples stood for a space, still rapt in the wonder of it, until Kydd felt his arm convulsively gripped. 'Darling! Did you hear that? They're calling for any of an intrepid and audacious character to volunteer to accompany Monsieur Blanchard on his next ascent!'

'No.'

'For a trifling fee only.'

'No.'

*

They wandered back to their carriage but as they did so a disturbing sound came from outside the park – a dull roar that Kydd's experience told him came from a mass of humanity on the move, not necessarily with the best of intentions.

'Quick – into the carriage.' This was poor hiding, but the flood-tide of people was getting close and clambering up a tree the only alternative. The coachman, nervous and swearing, got the horses stamping and swerving towards the park gate.

Bursting through from the outside a laughing, cheering and noisy horde was gaily escorting a well-found barouche – with not a horse in sight. The traces had been cast off the horses and taken up by willing hands who were hauling the vehicle themselves. On the seat in great good humour sat two splendid figures in ornate continental uniform.

The crowd swept on with their prize, passing Kydd's now stationary carriage, which from its windows gave the occupants a good view of the distinguished passengers. 'One's Alexander, the tsar, but I don't recognise the other,' Kydd said.

'Ah, the Tsar of Russia,' Renzi muttered darkly. 'As I'd never think to meet him again. I'd wager therefore the other must be Frederick William, King of Prussia.' They had not been noticed as the big carriage ground past. 'And I'd think the tsar's escort will be all of a tizz about this,' he added drily.

'It does tell us one thing Nicholas,' Kydd said, brightening.

'Being?'

'It reveals the Allied sovereigns are now in Town and we can expect a definite lift in the tenor of entertainments. My friend assures me of this.'

Whether or not he himself was rated as of the quality was to be seen.

Chapter 21

The question was answered when they arrived at the Farndons' home in the form of a beautifully inscribed invitation from the Court of St James's desiring the attendance of Sir Thomas Kydd at a grand military review in Hyde Park before the Allied sovereigns now present in the kingdom.

This was no mere spectacle. Kydd was expected to take his place of honour with the eminent and distinguished of the realm, and he felt a surge of pride at the recognition. He was accounted one worthy to stand with the highest, a name of repute.

'My felicitations, old bean,' Renzi said softly, seeing its effect on Kydd, 'which must place a mere earl as myself at a remove from such glories.'

The day dawned bright and beneficent. Kydd was togged up with the help of Binard and Persephone in his full-dress uniform, with sash, stars and all the flummery of his distinguished achievements. This was set off by his handsome sword, its blade with blue chasing glittering in the sunlight, and at the extremity of the scabbard a discreet pair of Cornish choughs to remind him of sterner times.

With Persephone on his arm he stood with a growing multitude of notables at the entrance to the park. Here and there he saw gallant figures from the past, those who had won for themselves and the nation the glory it deserved, and from their distant greetings he realised they were as affected as he.

An obliging colonel with service in the Peninsular conflict pointed out some of the more illustrious foreigners. There was Blücher, the fiery Prussian, who'd impetuously thrust across the Rhine into the French heartland; Schwarzenberg, paramount leader of the four columns; Platoff, the gorgeously attired Hetman of the Cossacks, whose rampaging wild men had plunged fear into the bravest French infantryman but whose behaviour in the capital was now beyond reproach. Others, with names that meant little to Kydd, were apparently figures to conjure with in the great continental war.

They formed up in strict order of grandeur. On caparisoned horseback the Prince Regent of Great Britain was flanked by crowned heads at the fore, followed closely by their foremost and illustrious veterans. As this was a military occasion, civil notables were discreetly held back.

As the first passed, Kydd had a prime sighting of the principals. The regent, corpulent and puffing but wearing an outrageously flamboyant and near-theatrical uniform, was talking animatedly with the tsar, who all but ignored him.

The Russian monarch was much as Kydd remembered: tall, his moon-face still with the feverish, detached look of imminent destiny that had led him from the ashes of Moscow to the gates of Paris. Wearing a simple bottle-green tunic, well padded in the right places, and with a splash of gold epaulettes and high laced collar, his presence as a mystical potentate was unquestionable, riding in the place of honour at the prince's right.

The King of Prussia was on the left, an altogether different figure. Since his country's dismemberment at Tilsit, he was much diminished, a touch of melancholy never far distant, his polished top-boots over white pantaloons lending nothing to a military appearance. By his side Blücher was mounted bolt-upright on a magnificent pure-black charger, his close-cropped snowy hair in heroic congruence with his implacable face and austere dark Prussian blue uniform.

Others pressed forward as the cavalcade approached the entrance gate. At precisely the moment that the head of the procession appeared, the thunder of massed artillery sounded off a full twenty-one-gun royal salute. As it passed through the straining crowds, a military band briskly struck up the anthems of each of the victorious Allies.

The sight was stunning – overwhelming. An ocean of faces, waving hands, and above all a continuous roar of cheering, the multitude extended back to the limits of the park. Even the trees at the boundary were thick with spectators, all determined to show their feelings for those who had brought down the ogre Bonaparte.

Proceeding to the dais and staging, the Allied sovereigns took their places in the centre, bowing and gesticulating in return while lesser mortals in the procession found their places. Kydd estimated there to have been close to two or three hundred, most of whom fell back before those eminences entitled to a named seat. To his secret delight, he was among them, seated quite close to the pre-eminent.

Not far away he spied Sir Sidney Smith, whose languid acknowledgement probably belied envy at his successes. Kydd didn't care: those heroic days when they had both trium-phantly faced Napoleon Bonaparte at the bloody siege of

Acre had to be set against the swirling rumours of his present high life, which included the seduction of Caroline of Brunswick, the wife of the Prince Regent.

More to his satisfaction was the muffled hail from the officers standing below. One was Charles Brisbane, whom he'd last met at sea in the Curaçao action that had seen him and Kydd knighted and was that Graves of . . . Where was it? Copenhagen? There were other naval uniforms about, nearly lost in the sea of scarlet, but most he did not recognise.

The soldiery marched on in fine order, a helpful colonel pointing out the difference between a yeomanry and a rifle regiment as they took up immaculate ranks before them. They watched as the line was inspected by the three sovereigns, accompanied by the continuous roar of a gleeful crowd before they returned to the dais, which they mounted again, standing stiffly to attention.

The raucous cheering fell away and bellowed orders could be heard that had every man shoulder his piece, then present it. On command, in a ripple from one end to the other, came a *feu de joie*. It brought on a renewed frenzy of appreciation from the vast multitude, who raised a din of storm proportions as the march-past began. In review order, picked line regiments of the army stepped out proudly in impeccable discipline, knowing they were under eye from some of the most famed battlefield heroes of the age.

The day ended well, the principals and guests escorted off by a squadron of Cossacks, whose barbaric splendour received from the crowd the most delighted roars of all.

Kydd arrived back at the Farndons', wearied but exhilarated by the experience, with one question in his mind. Why had he been singled out as distinguished enough before the public that he should be seen with the highest?

'Your reputation goes before you, dear fellow.' Renzi

chuckled. 'No one has really forgotten the gallant frigate captain Tom Cutlass, and it would be a sad crew in power who didn't at this time flourish you before the people as in some way their creature.'

'Someone put my name forward. Was it Prinker, do you think?'

'Perhaps someone more in the naval line as understands your shining parts.'

Persephone lovingly topped up his whisky and said complacently, 'Does it signify? He will parade before his admirers as though born to it – won't you, darling?'

Chapter 22

Three days later a grand banquet on a prodigious scale was held by the Corporation of the City of London at Carlton House, the Prince Regent's mansion of wildly extravagant wonder. With its rooms in a cascade of silver and velvet, marble and gold, exotic trophies and relics, elaborate glassware and tapestries, it was a *folie de grandeur* that, it was hoped, would reflect a becoming splendour on the first gentleman of Europe.

Kydd had been there once before, guest of the prince. He remembered the vast banqueting hall entered from a sweeping double staircase.

With Persephone on his arm, he emerged into its Gothic immensity, the heat and light from the phalanx of massive chandeliers beating on the senses. As did the sight of the tables, their glittering silver and table motifs stretching into the distance soon filling with suffocating numbers of resplendently dressed guests.

The banquet proceeded heavily, the dictates of state protocol vying with language incomprehension bringing polite discourse to a speedy end. Attempts at speeches with the toasts were embarrassingly awkward. Kydd was pleasantly surprised when a printed sheet was given out with the port. The poet Keats had been prevailed upon to mark the occasion with a sonnet, 'On Peace', which was declaimed from behind the Prince Regent's chair:

'O Peace! And dost thou with thy presence bless
The dwellings of this war-surrounded Isle;
Soothing with placid brow our late distress,
Making the triple kingdom brightly smile?

. . .

Let the sweet mountain nymph thy favourite be,
With England's happiness proclaim Europa's liberty!'

As the dinner came to an end the prince made presentations around the hall. Kydd shrank to the back of the group but it didn't save him, and echoing loudly in the stifling room he had heard a commanding cry: 'Tiger! So glad you're here, m' good friend.'

The eyes seemed to pop from a reddened, dissolute face and the waist strained perilously under his waistcoat but Kydd saw the prince's delight at seeing him was sincere.

'Do meet my warrior partner Alex, resting now after his honest labours.'

The tsar's intense boredom was evident at the muttered translation of 'sea devil' and 'mariner true'. He slowly focused on Kydd, whose last meeting with him had been the desperate times when, with the wild rumour that Bonaparte had invaded the Russian homeland, he'd transported him and his retinue in *Thunderer* safely back to St Petersburg.

The eyes widened but there was no sudden recognition. Instead, there was a low staccato jabber of Russian in an aside to a concerned aide, who swung away to intercept another glass of champagne. There would be no reminiscences of those long-ago scenes, and as His Imperial Majesty moved purposefully on, the prince flashed Kydd a lop-sided smile.

It ended at last but while guests crowded outside with indecent haste to await their carriages, they were firmly displaced by the official escort of a hundred Yeomen of the Guard in full regalia.

Chapter 23

Further days gave little opportunity for idleness. Persephone felt this was an occasion that would happen only once in their lifetimes and was determined to immerse herself in the frenzied atmosphere.

She pleaded to be taken to the royal parks where she had heard that Grand Duchess Ekaterina Pavlovna, the outstanding beauty and sister to Tsar Alexander, would promenade on horseback every morning, much to the ecstasy of the crowds. However, the press of devotees had made it a disappointment.

Then there was an event in Green Park, where a medieval castle had been erected.

'I've been told that Colonel Congreve is to be in charge,' Kydd announced. He knew the man well and had witnessed the frightful contribution he'd made to the devastating bombardment of Copenhagen with his war rockets. But this scene was tame indeed, with siege being laid to the old castle with mock artillery, feeble fireworks and much running to and fro by 'adversaries'.

It seemed that the climax of storming the castle had been reached when, in a stroke of high drama, the drab walls tumbled down in a melodramatic conclusion to reveal the 'Castle of Discord' transformed to the 'Temple of Concord'.

The noble edifice had the singular property that it revolved to display transparencies and illuminations from within. Amid a storm of ingenious multi-starred rocketry, spectators were transfixed at 'The Triumph of England'.

For Kydd, the highest point of the jubilations was an invitation to a dinner. It wasn't until closer to the time that he discovered it was to be in his honour.

'Really, Seph, I can't—'

'Dear man, you haven't noticed. Every hostess in London would ache to be able to sport a true hero of the wars to celebrate at their entertainments and in this case, knowing the dear old soul, I did accept on your behalf.'

And that night, at a modest address but in the smartest part of the West End of the capital, Kydd led Persephone in to polite but firm applause.

'You should've warned me!' he hissed at Persephone. Unsure whether to be delighted or intimidated, he saw that not only was Admiral Essington beaming from his chair but others from his past. Not the least of these was the formidable figure of the Earl St Vincent, Old Jarvie, who'd so figured in his early career and was probably the most lionised naval character of the age.

It passed most agreeably, the sincere esteem of those fine seamen bringing Kydd to the verge of tears.

In a matter of days the grand visit came to a conclusion. Respect and gratitude had been shown by the continent's most illustrious beings, who had to return whence they came.

As a fitting climax to the ceremonials and in recognition of the true fount of English power, their departure was fixed for Portsmouth. In culmination, there would be a grand naval review of the concentrated sea might of the nation.

Kydd hurriedly made his way south and took boat to Spithead and *Thunderer*. His inspection of the venerable ship showed him that Roscoe had faithfully kept her trim and, with some primping, she could well stand in a line of review.

'Glad to see you back aboard, sir,' the officer said sincerely, aware that any blunder during a review of such spectacular importance would have serious consequences on the career of the officer in charge.

'I'll have your report in one hour,' Kydd threw at him, as he made for his cabin and a change of rig. Binard and Craddock were following, and at this time he had only the services of a knowing old marine to take care of his worldly needs.

Roscoe arrived promptly with a written list and what looked unusually like printed orders. But Kydd needed to know the state of *Thunderer* first.

Ship's company: in short, it could have been worse. Open gangway had worked, a good rollicking had by all . . . and then the coin had run out. All manner of prize money, gun money and, not the least, pay in arrears had to wait for their lordships' eventual attention. They'd been given tickets on the Admiralty for a small amount and had immediately sold them at a ruinous discount to the sharks ashore, but then had had nothing.

In the age-old way, they'd straggled back aboard to where their bed and board was to no cost and the calls for labour in a ship peacefully at anchor were at an agreeable level of idleness. They would so remain until the vessel prepared for her next venture to sea.

The officers were in little different state. Roscoe was living aboard to fulfil the standing order that at least one officer must remain with the ship at her moorings, thereby allowing others to step ashore. Kydd didn't need telling that this would be at the cost to those others of finding the favour hauled in at times of the first lieutenant's choosing. At the moment the only other officer aboard was the quiet, married third, Martyn.

Thunderer was in good fettle. Roscoe had wisely sent down topmasts, and with only half her rigging abroad, wear was kept to a minimum, but how could he have foreseen the sudden declaration of a kingly review?

For the first time in a while the pipe 'All hands – *aaaall* the hands!' sounded loud and piercing about *Thunderer*'s decks and frowsty seamen heaved themselves up the hatchways.

Kydd left Roscoe to do what he could with the men he had, while he studied the printed review instructions.

It was to be under the charge and command of the Duke of Clarence, whose flag would be flown in the three-decker HMS *Impregnable*. He was the brother of the prince regent, and should anything happen to the latter, he would become heir to the throne. In the past he'd been a serving naval officer, rising to command a ship-of-the-line in the Caribbean. The instructions reflected this, robust naval language spelling out the entire day for each of the vessels nominated to take part.

It was a well constructed exercise. The fleet would be drawn up in two lines between Spithead and the Motherbank agreeable to the prevailing wind direction on the day, and *Impregnable* would ceremonially proceed between them. Smaller, unrated vessels would act as gatekeepers in a discreet outer ring.

This arrangement had a hidden purpose. The inshore line was to lie imposingly at anchor. The outer would have their ground tackle buoyed ready to slip at a moment's notice.

Aboard the flagship the principals, at the end of the review, would be asked if they wished to see the Royal Navy at its war-winning pursuits.

It would be nothing out of the ordinary, but on an affirmative, captains should hold themselves ready to obey any hoist of signals thrown out in *Impregnable* in much the same way as they would have done on blockade off the French coast. To his swelling satisfaction Kydd noted that *Thunderer* had been chosen for the outer line, somewhere near the middle and therefore under the most critical eye.

Her crew appreciated the honour and *Thunderer* was scrubbed and painted from stem to stern, her bright-sided hull deep-varnished and brass-work polished to an unearthly gleam.

Two days later came heavy thuds from artillery on Portsdown Hill as the royal party of sovereigns processed into Portsmouth to a rapturous reception, parades and levees lasting all night.

Next morning an excited signal midshipman was first to see *Impregnable*'s masts suddenly leap with colour as the Board of Admiralty house flag broke at the fore with a huge Royal Standard at the main. The prince regent had boarded and the other regnants were presumed to be with him.

Kydd sniffed the wind. A westerly with a touch of the north in it. The reckoning of the captain of the fleet the night before had been well reasoned and the lines stretched impeccably to the south-east, leaving *Impregnable* an easy cast from the northern end, then down through the lines. As the big three-decker put off at ten precisely to begin her review, the entire foreshore broke out in an eruption of adulation, assisted by the best efforts of the militia artillery. The inner line answered with a shore-directed disciplined salute of twenty-one guns erupting one after another from every ship.

Kydd was otherwise engaged. As *Impregnable* passed, it was necessary to have the bare yards manned and official cheers thrown to the skies. His yards were soon crowded with seamen, but would they cheer or would only a feeble croak result?

The flagship processed slowly on, gravely receiving from both sides of the impressive lines of men-o'-war the honours due to three reigning monarchs, the vivid splash of colour on her quarterdeck a wondrous sight.

As she passed, *Thunderer* gave of her best and ringing cheers sounded. *Impregnable* loomed, then moved impressively on down the line. At its far end, the battleship faultlessly put about at a stately pace and stood out to sea – there *was* going to be a species of manoeuvre!

At her mizzen, halliards broke out a first signal: fleet to weigh and proceed in order of sailing on a specified line of bearing.

Ready buoyed, they slipped moorings and loosed sail for the short trip to sea, the westerly breeze a comfortable brace.

The flagship hove to and then another hoist: fleet tack in succession about the stern of the flag. This would give a prime view of the brisk efforts at sheet and braces on each ship in turn as they stayed about to pass from one side of *Impregnable* to the other. Knowing *Thunderer*'s every inch in far harsher conditions, her crew made a brave show of it and the elegant old ship swashed around in fine style.

Straightforward, with no frills or ceremony, this powerful fleet was displaying what it had done in brutish weather day and night, close in to the hostile French coast for the entire twenty-odd years of war – and which had given it unchallenged mastery of the seas.

Kydd wondered what those who had never left the dead earth of the land must be feeling. Could they conceive of going to war in a trackless wilderness with nowhere to hide for miles, the only recourse to engage with the enemy full on? And to take the awesome complexity of the largest moving structure on the face of the planet and turn it into a battle-winner of geographic significance?

The fleet formed again but this time in two opposing battle lines and on the mark opened fire on each other. Only five rounds of shot-less charges but almost at once the intervening space became a churning, towering, flash-stabbed, powder-smoke-grey mass, the combined thunder of guns a visceral sensation.

It was a fine end to the performance and, ready for the next order, Kydd saw instead an 'all ships' hoist soar up and next to it 'manoeuvre well executed' – the highest measure of praise in the signal book.

Impregnable then ponderously took the wind and returned to Portsmouth to land her visitors, now to leave the English shore for the continent.

Chapter 24

'And then the poor little creature cried when all those guns went off,' Persephone told Kydd, fondly ruffling Francis's hair. She'd come to Portsmouth to be with him, suspecting that he could be there some time but had not been permitted to be on any vessel in the active line.

'I've no idea what's to do,' Kydd admitted, charmed as always by her presence in his cabin, her grace, the scent of her. 'At the least we know *Thunderer* is still part of the Antwerp blockade and at a readiness to sail.'

Rumours swirled – *if* negotiations failed, *if* the French people desired Bonaparte as their ruler come what may, anything could happen. There was no option but to remain at vigilance where they were.

Then advice came from the Allied occupiers that the French Senate was inclined to agree with them in respect to Bonaparte's fate. He was to be removed as head of state and replaced by the refugee king, Louis XVIII, brother of the guillotined Louis XVI.

Appropriate signing made it formal and conclusive: the war was over.

*

For an unreal couple of days there was no response from the Admiralty. Keeping the entire fleet in being at Portsmouth was putting an intolerable strain on the victuallers and the rest of the support structure.

It was decided to disperse the ships evenly among the seaports of Britain and orders were sent out. Not to retire or decommission – who knew if the peace arrangements would hold? – but remain at rest for an unspecified time until called for once more to defend the kingdom.

To his great satisfaction Kydd saw that *Thunderer* was ordered to fall back on her home port, Plymouth.

As the ship readied for sea he let it be known that officers' wives would be offered passage to Plymouth by way of appreciation for standing by their menfolk. They would have a right to the quarterdeck and wardroom and could grace any occasion they chose.

Kydd did not ignore the seamen and decreed that the men could invite their 'wives' similarly, with the strict rule that they be kept out of sight. And while they had the run of the ship, the quarterdeck was beyond the pale, and any lewd or drunken behaviour would swiftly find them locked away.

Persephone found herself queen of the afterguard and took pride in her duties. There were only the two officers' wives, the retiring Mrs Martyn and the hard-faced Mrs Clinch, but she charmed them both at the first-night-at-sea dinner at which Kydd presided.

It went off pleasingly, and Kydd found reason in the fair easterly to make a leg across to within sighting distance of the French coast, which threw the ladies into a thoughtful silence and ensured a second night at sea for them all.

Chapter 25

Plymouth Sound

Eventually *Thunderer*'s anchor found rest in Cawsand Bay, with two or three others, and as soon as Kydd decently could he was off to Knowle Manor with Persephone. As soon as he'd had wind of the dispersal he'd sent a note of invitation to Renzi and Cecilia to stay with them and enjoy the rustic festivities that were sure to be afoot.

It gave them time to prepare and for Kydd to perform his solemn duty as returning hero at the big end-of-war parade of the South Devonshire Militia.

Appropriate gunfire salutes and the sounds of no less than three military bands thrilled the crowd, and bursting with pride at the recognition by a noted public figure, the soldiers marched smartly past.

Renzi and Cecilia arrived, happy to have quit the madness of London. Kydd exercised his squire's prerogative and decreed that his hero's welcome should not be a grand municipal dinner but a day's outdoor merrymaking at

Ivybridge, to include an ox-roast with dancing at the maypole.

The event was blessed with sunshine and a warm breeze, and Kydd could not think of a more enjoyable occasion. He and Renzi reclined companionably under the shady trees while a picnic was set up.

The sight of wildly excited children and pleasantly befuddled farm folk was diverting, but Kydd's mind couldn't help wandering to the scenes he'd witnessed that this bucolic world had never known: the fear and terror of a conquering army, the horror of a retreating horde.

With a sigh, he stole a glance at Persephone and vowed to stand ready to do his duty as long as his country needed him – but for how much longer would that be?

The next morning at breakfast the paper had only one story – the end of Napoleon Bonaparte, the arch-conqueror of Europe, was now settled. The Allies, in rare concert, had determined that he should not be hanged or shot but exiled to Elba, a minuscule island off Italy, there to reign as pathetic an emperor as ever was, over a realm that was as tiny as it was ludicrous to such a figure, which, of course, was what was intended.

The newspaper had another breathless story. Since Louis, the Bourbon king pretender, had fled from exile in the Baltic, he and his entourage had been hiding in England. Now he was hearing calls for his restoration. Bonaparte had been safely banished so it would appear there was no reason why he shouldn't comply. The king had now only to reach Paris and lay out his claim. It was reported that the gouty monarch had been received on French soil with somewhat muted enthusiasm by a war-wearied people who wanted little beyond a lasting peace.

Further reports had it that Louis had occupied the Tuileries palace and had agreed to take the throne of France, but in a country much changed from the absolute rule of the past. Quickly, the apparatus of administration was taken up in his name, and blessed order descended on Paris.

An epoch was over: with the return of the Bourbons the old certainties would surely apply.

As they sat companionably in the garden, Persephone gave Kydd a winning smile. 'You'll think me deluded, Thomas, but I had a thought.'

Kydd raised an eyebrow but remained silent.

'If we're now at peace with France and the king is restored, do the old ways count?'

'What do you mean, Seph?'

'Can we not make visit to Paris as we used to, or should I say as they did before?'

Kydd was taken aback and glanced at an amused Renzi, who realised what was being said. After endless years of war the ladies were weary of fashion that was handed down, out-of-date and suspect of counterfeit, and wanted once more to sup at the well.

'Bonaparte's Paris? I don't believe that—'

'It's not his any more, my dear. How do we set about going, do you think?'

Chapter 26

Paris, France

Kydd, Persephone, Renzi and Cecilia stood together, almost protectively, on the vastness of the Place de la Concorde. Here, the nobility of the *ancien régime* had met their end in a welter of blood at the hands of the mob, and despite the flowery sculptural improvements, their presence could still be felt.

It was strange and moving, but at the same time there was the frisson of a foreign capital. Until so very recently this had been the chief abode of the enemy and the curious figures moving about them were then their sworn foes.

Wandering slowly along the Champs-Élysées they watched red-capped Cossack guards sauntering past the glorious new edifices raised by Bonaparte. But nowhere to be seen was the revolutionary tricolour Kydd knew so well. The Bourbon flag, golden fleur-de-lis on pure white, flew everywhere. Images of eagles, bees and the 'N' cipher of the cast-out emperor were crudely painted over and token white cockades masked others.

The shopping did not disappoint. From the same devious sources as before, the Parisian couturiers managed to enchant and bewitch with their creations for the increasing flood of visitors, and Persephone and Cecilia went away well satisfied.

Renzi seemed to know Paris well and, as evening approached, insisted that they go with him to rue St Honoré.

He stopped and regarded the drab stone exterior of one establishment for a long moment. Then he gathered himself. 'Friends, this is a restaurant of my acquaintance.' He didn't elaborate on the desperate days when, on a secret purpose and needing human company, he'd found himself inside.

'Restaurant?' Cecilia asked, in puzzlement at the term. There was nothing by that name to be found in England.

'A place of restoring, perhaps?' Kydd offered.

Inside it was not as Renzi remembered. At least half full of excited foreigners – English, he realised, probably like themselves visiting now they had the chance. A surreptitious glance about did not reveal any familiar features.

With linen cloths on the tables set with flowers and silver-ware, chandeliers and an attentive host, it was unlike any honest English chophouse. One's choice of viands was from a sheet brought personally by a *garçon*. Grilled fish or bouil-labaisse, veal and poultry were on offer, as was an endless choice of iced champagne and liqueurs.

On Renzi's recommendation all chose duck. The sauce had a piquancy of heavenly fragrance, the wine – a red burgundy – the perfect accompaniment.

The next day they visited the Musée Napoléon, marvelling at the looted Egyptian *objets d'art* and other precious articles originating in a score of lands across the continent. Hastily they were assured that the name of the museum would revert shortly to its original – Le Louvre.

Kydd saw it all but was not swayed in admiration. There seemed to be a note of falsity, of defiant self-worth, that was not in keeping with a nation laid low by an aggrandising dictator. He kept it to himself but saw in Persephone's expression her own distaste.

'Shall we see the other side of the Seine?' he asked Renzi. 'That is, if you know what course to steer.'

'There are sights to be seen, brother, but not as I'd desire the ladies to view. Shall we not—'

'Nicholas, you've rollicked here in your youth, pray allow us to take in our fill.'

That night Renzi consulted his invaluable under-steward, Jago, and in the morning the party, escorted safely by four well-paid Russian grenadiers, set out to explore the other side of the City of Light, leaving young Francis with a maid.

The quartier de St Antoine was narrow, foetid and running with ordure, its crumbling medieval haunts a stark contrast to the tree-lined avenues further down the river.

But in the epics of the revolution it was glorious: it was from this spot that the nearby Bastille was stormed, and to here that Bonaparte's veterans had returned: weathered, bewhiskered and ferocious, glaring at the interlopers, swaggering as if they still wore sharp steel. Other ragged, swarthy men stood about, a tiny part of the mass of humanity uprooted by the continental war, drawn to the now calmer centre of the storm.

Renzi found the most respectable-looking tavern and they went inside to a far different experience. The rough talk of the patrons died away at the extraordinary appearance in their midst but the earringed Cossacks stilled any objections.

In his stilted patois Renzi ordered absinthe for all, his *'Citoyen'* instead of *'Garçon'* going far to ease the atmosphere. They sat uneasily, aware that, with its age-darkened wood and coarse smell of a foreign cuisine under pungent tobacco smoke, this was quite another side of Paris.

The waiter reached for a bottle but Renzi intervened. *'Non, M'sieur. La Bleu, s'il vous plaît.'*

His evident familiarity ensured there would be no sly profiteering at a foreigner's expense and the wide-eyed English gentlewomen were able to join in the ceremony with spoon, sugar and the green wormwood-fragrant liqueur.

'A taste only, *mes braves*,' Renzi cautioned, not mentioning that the last time he had taken absinthe he'd drunk himself quite unconscious in the line of duty. On a secret mission for the British government, it had been imperative that he had the French believe he was not a spy but a harmless, if foolish, fop.

The arrival of the drink brought over several curious onlookers and Renzi shared the absinthe with them, desiring perhaps to hear what they had to say about their nation's change of fortune.

Two had the hard, cynical look of the old soldier but the woman among them couldn't hold back her curiosity, eyeing the quality of the ladies. Asked about the downfall of Bonaparte she shrugged, but then to grunts of agreement from the men she scornfully regretted that the rule of France had passed from Napoléon le Grand to Louis le Gros, a sad day for their noble country.

'What of the future, Madame?'

She gave a tired smile. *'Vive la bagatelle, M'sieur.'* Success to the chancer . . .

*

They returned to their *pension* thoughtful and quiet. It was against these sons of France that Kydd had directed the anger of his great guns, but the glories of Bonaparte, celebrated all around, signified an arrogance not justified by what he'd seen at sea.

He watched Persephone dandling Francis on her knee, the maid joining in the undignified cooing, and caught her eye. 'An . . . interesting time, Seph.'

'I suppose so.'

'You'll be revisiting soon, then.'

'I don't plan to, Thomas.'

She cupped the child's face and looked at it with a frown. 'I rather think that the poor mite is a trifle off-colour. It must be the diet – or worse.' She bit her lip and added offhandedly, 'To leave so soon would seem rude but his health must come first, don't you think?'

Kydd knew she'd been affected, too, by what she'd seen and raised his eyes to Renzi, but it was Cecilia who cut in. 'You're right to be concerned, my dear. As it happens there's a trifle of unrest near the estate – nothing to worry on but I'd rather not delay in our return.'

Chapter 27

Addlestone estate, Surrey

'Another o' this fine drop, old trout?' breezed Brodrick, a comfortably placed Treasury commissioner, hovering a crusted port over the glass of his table-mate, Yorke, a more than usually influential under-secretary somewhere in the Trade division.

'Thank you, I will, Charles,' Yorke answered, in his reedy, precise way.

The cloth had been removed so brandy and cigars had made their appearance as the ladies left the snug, smaller dining room in the ivy-covered country house, the ancient pile of Rosslyn, the third earl.

'Been in the family cellar a damn sight longer than I've had years,' Rosslyn called mildly, from the head of table.

The evening was passing amiably, the carefully chosen guests, all at an elevation in government or industry, knew each other and at this private dinner were able to talk freely at any level.

There was Erskine, the London correspondent of the

powerful Rothschild banking clan. Opposite him Hookham, retired ambassador to Portugal, had been recalled for consultations prior to Castlereagh's forthcoming talks in Paris. And further down, Pelham had been tipped for the post of secretary of state after the prime minister Lord Liverpool's adjustment of his administration to a more peace-time complexion.

'Well, now, and here we sit like boobies without we think of Boney safely under hatches in his new kingdom,' boomed Crespigny, Admiralty receiver of droits, who'd been in office since the old King Louis's day.

The brandy bottle quickly found its way to him and he lifted it thoughtfully, 'And we must admit therefore that the war is, by all reckonings, indeed over.'

'That may be so, Biffy, but the peace has not yet begun, I'm moved to say.'

Heads swivelled to Yorke, a hint of irritation in their expressions, as though he was deliberately trying to break the hearty mood.

'How so, old bean?' Brodrick said, humouring him.

'You should be the one to tell us, Charles.'

'Oh?'

'Pray how does the national debt stand now, might I ask?'

The table fell silent.

'The figure is known,' Brodrick said heavily, all traces of levity now gone, 'but kept from the common knowledge as being beyond their understanding.'

'Come now, dear fellow. Are we your common herd?'

Taking his time, he replied, 'We've subsidised every country that ever dared stand against the tyrant for some twenty years now. This must be accounted pure expenditure with no return.'

'The debt, sir,' rapped Russell, an ex-army comptroller in the War Office, leaning forward in emphasis.

Brodrick raised his eyebrows in surprise at the importuning but said evenly, 'Assuming a capital outflow set against our—'

'The debt!'

'Not above . . . eight hundred and sixty-one, I'd believe.'

'Eight hundred thousands? Not so—'

'Millions.'

There was a perceptible tremor of shock as the figure sank in.

'Nearly a thousand of millions?' Crespigny said faintly. 'Do we even have a word for that, sir?'

'The Treasury recognises a million as the highest conceivable number,' Brodrick said stiffly.

Yorke frowned, with heavy patience. 'Then are we to understand that every man, woman and child in England now bears a sum owing an equivalent to ten years' labour in the fields?'

No one spoke, and Yorke took it further. 'This sum is monstrous and well kept from the ordinary sort. Do tell, what is the per annum interest on this?'

'Thirty-two.'

'Millions – in itself double the budgetary line for the entire navy, sir, and all to pay for past fiscal extravagances.'

Erskine, the Rothschild banker, intervened. 'This is neither here nor there, gentlemen,' he said smoothly. 'The debt, and of such magnitude, exists. My thoughts as an interested observer – we should not be over-exercised by it as it's perfectly well serviced by the instruments at hand. Tax, excise, Consols. These will keep penury at bay until the richness of peace-time trade yields up the necessary funds.'

'Tax?' Brodrick grumbled. 'The sainted Pitt's income tax at two shillings has been voted to a cessation and what must we do now? Already we've permitted the Bank of England to issue their odious paper currency without we find gold to put behind it.'

'And, my dear Yorke, do we not find your Trade crew well vexed by grave happenings among the northern iron-folk?'

Yorke leaned back and fiddled with a spoon, before admitting defensively, 'As is not our fault – this arises from the fact that war being past there's no big government orders for cannon and the like, still less for expensive steam machines to manufacture same.'

'But you should soon be in a pretty enough place, Charles,' murmured Pelham, an intelligent but somewhat unworldly man. 'Very soon the armies will return, the navy set their crews on land, and there, you have enough labour to double all your manufactories in one.'

'Never so.'

Heads turned to Deane, the quietly spoken but well-respected civil commissioner. 'Consider – a vast increase in labour, no mill-owner will pay war-time wages. Those who hold fast to their jobs, those seeking desperately for one, all must be satisfied with a pittance.'

Over the mutterings around the table he continued calmly. 'Which is not the worst of it. If we accept this, we face a higher quandary. The great proportion of this nation's population will not be able to afford as before the output of our top-class mass industrial manufacturing, be it textiles or tin pans. The merchantry at all levels will fail and fall – mass producing requires mass consuming, gentlemen.'

'Ha! You're all wrong.' This time it was Hookham, known as a dabbler in exports to Portugal in the wake of Wellington.

'Am I? I think not,' Deane said acidly.

'You've overlooked the navy.'

'The navy?'

'As has cleared the seven seas of vermin to allow honest trade to flourish and bloom. Our ports will flow over with released merchantmen bearing fortunes in our exports as the world has been crying out for all this time. Excise on that alone will take care of this damned debt.'

Yorke grimaced. 'In Trade we've been in trust that it'll be so, but I can't see anything like it to date.'

'Why, you've not been counting true, old fellow. We've been trading thus for more than two months now but find we're beaten by one hard fact. The biggest, widest war in mankind's history has been raging up and down the continent, leaving it, after Boney has been defeated, a sad ruin. The worriment is that we can find no one with the means to afford our goods. No payments, no exports, no revenues.'

Deane gave a twisted smile. 'And all the time the people, after putting up with so much during the French wars, now expect a dividend for peace after a war they won. Reasonable, I would have thought, and I rather fancy they should be satisfied or we'll face a mort of discontent.'

Unexpectedly Erskine broke in: 'Should ever I be consulted – as your privy man of business, naturally – there is but one prescription I can give that will meet your fears.'

'Tell on, stout fellow.'

'Reduce your outgoings to a minimum is all.' There was a snort of derision from Brodrick but Erskine pressed on, unperturbed.

'The chief of which is your war-related expenditures. It strikes me that as of weeks past Great Britain is an ally of every power in Europe. Who then need you defend against? No more subsidies to coalitions and, above all, a stop to the madness of endless building and purchase necessary in a war to the death.'

'You're saying that . . .'

'I probably am. An army of twenty-five thousand is all that we have at the present in these isles. It will suffice for the future too, I believe. We should allow each man in Wellington's legions to go his way upon returning to these shores.'

'But the navy. We can't simply—'

'Are you aware, sir, of the expense of keeping a ship to sea?'

'Hear, hear!' Crespigny grunted loudly, raising his glass in mock toast. 'Not to mention all eight hundred of the beasts.'

'The biggest sink of expenditure in the kingdom by far,' Erskine said, shaking his head as though in disbelief. 'Reduce your ships and *pro rata* you will reduce your costs. I cannot think there's any enemy in sight as requires fifty ships-of-the-line to lie in readiness, can you?'

'The navy's been our sure shield since I was a boy. We always slept safe in our beds,' Pelham said, troubled. 'There'll be a howling if it's touched at all, I'd wager.'

'Howl or no, it must be done,' Erskine replied firmly, and appreciatively finished his brandy.

Chapter 28

Knowle Manor

'My goodness, and it's pleasing to a degree to be back at our dear home,' Persephone said, with a sigh, as she stepped down from the carriage.

'Appleby, the baggage!' the housekeeper instructed her husband. 'And how was Paris, milady?' she added, wide-eyed.

'A caution to us all,' Persephone said, smoothing her dress. 'As to contrive never to be conquered, is the way of it.'

They were fussed inside and the grizzling Francis set to rights.

'Mail?' asked Kydd, mildly. There was nothing of consequence except a brief note from Roscoe in *Thunderer*: he desired Kydd's presence aboard at his convenience.

It was not like his first lieutenant to ask for him. He took a dogged pride in dealing with things on his own, so perhaps it was better to go sooner than later and see what was in the wind.

The gleeful countrywide celebrations had now faded so Kydd was puzzled by the crowds still in the streets as they passed through Plymouth, but these were nothing compared to the sullen masses outside the dockyard.

This was no carefree gathering. He sensed an underlying resentment, a simmering ugliness in the mood. By appearances they were mainly seamen, whether the king's or merchant service it was never easy to tell.

At the top end of Fore Street a large knot of men were in some sort of altercation, but as he neared he saw files of militia drawn up to give him passage.

The militia called out? This was alarming in Kydd's experience of Plymouth and he settled uneasily in the wherry sternsheets to his ship.

Roscoe met him at the side and followed him silently to his cabin.

'Rum do ashore, Kit,' Kydd said quietly. 'The militia?'

'We've a mort of trouble, sir. The men are restless, idle, given to disorder at the slightest chance.'

Kydd nodded. 'They've won the war, spent their cobbs and can't see what to do for a rollick. As might be cured in a trice by some bracing sea-time, which I can't see coming this way for an age.'

'Sir. Do be aware we're sadly at a stand if we get orders, nearly a third of our ship's company absenting themselves.'

In normal circumstances this deficit would cause *Thunderer* to be stood down from the line-of-battle.

'How so?'

'Those married claimed tickets on their pay and left, at least sixty deserting—'

'So many?' At this point by their action they'd abandoned all claim to pay and prize money. No doubt there'd be more than a few straggling back later.

'Yes, sir. Seems there's bad blood 'tween decks. Some say we're to lie here, nothing to do until the next war, all forgotten.

Others fear they'll be served like those ashore, turned out of the ship when it goes into ordinary.'

Then, basically in reserve, they would join the ever-lengthening line of stripped-down hulks moored at the centre of the Hamoaze.

So that was what the trouble ashore was all about, Kydd mused. These were newly unemployed seamen who, without warning, had been ejected from what amounted to their homes of the last years to fend for themselves.

'Anyone to go before my table?' Kydd wanted to know if there were any matters of discipline that needed his attention.

Roscoe gave a sour smile. 'Yes, but they won't front you, sir. I've seen to that.'

There was no point in exercising full naval discipline in view of the much relaxed harbour routine and Roscoe had wisely taken care of it. How much the ship was affected overall he'd no doubt discover very soon. In a further concession to the informal state, Kydd joined the wardroom mess for common meals, which had the advantages of company and warning of any complications seen to be boiling up.

The chief difficulty was in keeping the men usefully employed. Harbour routine had them turn to, part-of-ship in the forenoon and liberty in the afternoon, but day after day of listless inactivity sapped energy and humour.

Worst was the fate hanging over *Thunderer*: there were now more than a dozen hulls lying in ordinary in the Hamoaze. Who was to say that the same destiny was not in store for her? To consider such an end ate at the pride in one's ship and was insidiously destroying the common bond Kydd had brought about that had taken them into battle as an invincible team.

*

'Mr Clinch,' Kydd said, at supper that night, recognising the man's lowering depression, 'have you had your fill of the celebrations, then?'

His fourth lieutenant looked away, clearly disinclined to share his burdens.

Kydd left him to it and turned to Roscoe. 'Mr Ambrose not aboard?' he muttered.

'I gave him leave to go to London,' he replied shortly, 'on account he desires a post in the Hellenic Navy – that is to say, the Greeks.'

Ambrose, the mature, reliable second lieutenant. Now presumably to be lost to *Thunderer*. It must have been a hard decision: to do this he'd be required to resign his commission in the Royal Navy, losing his half-pay and all other entitlements.

'A lack of faith in *Thunderer*, is what it is,' Roscoe growled. 'Who knows? We could be sent tomorrow to Ameriky – they haven't surrendered yet, in course.'

There could be no blaming the man, however, for he'd seen a prospect that would see him secure in the time not so long ahead when large numbers of officers would be flooding out, looking for a future.

Even Joyce, the jolly peg-legged sailing master, was showing signs of gloom. If *Thunderer* was paid off into ordinary, at his age it would most certainly be the end of his sea career. Then there would be yet another well-tended cottage above Spithead with a polished brass plate on the door announcing that here resided a doughty mariner, once the pride of the King's Navy, who'd swallowed the anchor at last.

'Mr Martyn,' Kydd chided his third lieutenant, 'why so lively at all, when all about is sorrow at the damned peace?'

The young man had the grace to blush before he admitted, 'I've just this day received word I'm to be considered for Arctic exploration – in the Ross north-west passage expedition, that is.'

All talking ceased. That one of *Thunderer*'s company was shortly to go on to glory in the much-talked-about mission was difficult to credit and Kydd fought down an unworthy stab of envy.

'When do you sail, pray?'

'Ah. The enterprise is under planning at this time only, but if I'm successful I'll be asked to hold myself ready for a prompt leaving.'

Clinch stirred himself. 'An' who do y' know that gave you the berth, then?'

'My father knows Mr Barrow, he it is that does Arctic at the Admiralty.'

There was no topping that news and the supper came to a polite ending.

The next day the gunner, Mr Lawlor, returned aboard. He was bent and slow, the ague that had come upon him in the chill seas off Antwerp now even more pronounced.

Kydd asked him to report to him in his cabin. 'Mr Lawlor, you're a standing officer and, I'm obliged to remind you, with a duty to remain with the ship.' It was hard to say but the man was a warrant officer and was paid well for his charge of the ship's armament.

The unsmiling old sailor lifted his eyes and said woodenly, 'Sir, I don't reckon on being use t' anyone soon. I'm here to tell ye that I'm resignin' m' post aboard the barky, as starting now.'

This was a disaster. No man-o'-war might put to sea even under direct orders without its full complement of qualified warrant officers. To replace a standing officer was a drawn-out process involving the Navy Board, Somerset House and, in this case, the Ordnance Board.

At the present time of uncertainty and confusion they were

unlikely to move fast on the matter, making it probable that a forcibly idle *Thunderer* would be moved towards the top of the list for paying off.

'You'll not consider staying a trifle longer, Mr Lawlor? We do regret your going, sir.'

The gunner drew himself up. 'No, sir,' he said quietly. 'I made up m' mind – too old in the bones, I is, an' my good lady needs me about the cuddy.'

'But, er, we . . .'

'Aye. Without ye has a gunner y'r hook stays down. Here's a thing, sir. Can I beg ye'll consider m' gunner's mate f'r acting gunner? Ver' reliable, been learnin' his letters all the while, he'll make a fine gunner.'

Kydd didn't know if he had the power to so rate the man. And promotion to a warrant officer was out of his hands as a captain. Then, of course, there were examinations and technical proofs to pass – was he up to it?

'Mr Stirk – do come in.'

The big man padded in and stood respectfully, expressionless, his dark eyes glittering, the brass earrings a-gleam. Kydd saw before him the very best of the breed of deep-sea mariner, they who had taken Britain all the way to lordship of the ocean.

The purser's clerk made his excuses and left them alone. Kydd rose from his desk, offering Stirk an armchair.

'Thanks an' all, sir, but I got work t' do later.'

'Toby, I've got a proposition for you.'

'A – a prop– . . .?'

'As will see you secured in your later years.'

'If ye says so, sir.' Stirk was suspicious – there was going to be no 'old times' about this conversation.

'You'll know our gunner is a mite . . . unwell.'

'Aye.'

'I've asked you here, Toby, to see if you'll fill his place. Acting gunner.'

Stirk's eyes flickered. 'Y' knows I haven't m' figuring.'

'I understand you've been working at it for some time and—'

'I found I ain't fitted f'r book-learning, is all.'

In all probability the study had tailed off into boredom for a sea warrior of Stirk's history.

'Toby, think on it. A gunner – a uniform, small sword and respect – and do I need to say it, a standing officer looking to a fine pension when . . . when . . .'

He had Stirk's interest, he knew, but the man on his own had failed. Why should he try now?

'I know you can do it, old friend – so I'll tell you how. If I can swing it that you're an acting gunner, you'll give it one tiger of a heave with the figuring and letters, then up to the Admiralty for your warrant examination.'

'Sir, you're kind in all but . . . but . . .'

'I can guess. Well, I've midshipmen by the handful with nothing to do. They'll take it in their turns to teach you what's in the books. No, hear me out – they'll get their portion in coin, but only if you pass as gunner. But it needs for you to do your part. Are you game, Toby?'

As it happened, a harassed Admiralty hastily fell in with the thought of a local replacement, subject to the appointment of a qualified gunner as available.

Stirk had a chance – as long as *Thunderer* remained in active commission.

Cheered by the small thing he'd achieved for his friend, Kydd briskly paced his sad and deserted quarterdeck and tried to concentrate on the future.

Chapter 29

The old, proud essence in the snug petty officers' mess on the lower deck forward was missing. The canvas screens painted with heroic scenes of battle and tempest were now rolled up to the deckhead as though in embarrassment at their ship's shiftless sloth.

Quartermaster's mate Doud sat cradling his pot of grog, staring gloomily into the distance, opposite his inseparable Portuguese shipmate, Pinto, who was whittling a wooden sailor figure with his deadly knife blade.

'We got t' do something, mate, else go knaggy in the wits,' Doud muttered. Along the mess-deck were similar scenes of listless forms with little to do, some quietly occupied at scrimshaw or mending clothing.

'What, as doesn't cost cobbs?' Pinto said.

'No, it ain't that, mate. I'm talking as how this barky is right soon f'r a mooring with th' others in ordinary. Stands t' reason, too many ships, not enough wars.'

'So?'

'Then we're off ashore an' be like those other poor swabs y' see outside the dockyard, ye knows why.'

A sudden burst of ill-tempered shouting broke out at the hatchway, bringing an irritated roar from the next petty officers' mess and it subsided.

'Well, what c'n we do about such?'

'Only two choices, mate. One, we stay where we is until it happens, or two – well, do something about it.' He saw Pinto's face darken as it did when he wasn't keeping up with the English.

Doud leaned forward earnestly. 'Do something, yeah. Sign aboard a deep-sea hooker voyagin' to the east or somewhere and b' the time we gets back it'll all have settled down, sorted itself.'

'We can't – we're navy!'

'Listen, if the navy can't take care o' the likes o' we, then we has to take care of ourselves, savvy?'

Pinto sat silent, concentrating on the whittling.

'We steps ashore, goes across t' Cockside. Should be enough merchant hulls in Sutton Pool as wants crew, now the sea's free o' privateers an' same.'

'Then . . .'

'Then we signs on, an' when she's cleared for sea, they tips us the wink and we gets aboard an' takes our leave of all this, y' chuckle-headed bastard!'

'I want t' see what Toby says about it.'

'Stirk? None o' his business, bless 'im. He's in the gunroom, acting gunner an' set fair to get his warrant. Won't want t' be part o' any plan else.'

'It's still deserting, Ned,' Pinto pressed in a low voice.

'As is no distress f'r the navy – they've got a gallows sight more seamen than they've ships t' set 'em on. They won't care, mate.'

It would be easy enough. They were both tough, seasoned mariners with good reason to see through a hard passage safely and reliably, the best class of seaman.

On liberty the next afternoon they made their way to the opposite side of Plymouth Hoe and the old town above the Pool. King's men didn't mix with merchant seamen and the two would have stood out without donning plain foremast dress before they left.

Narrow lanes with medieval buildings led down to the waterfront. A dense forest of masts crowded below, as Doud had predicted, their bowsprits overtopping the congested waterfront roadway in a delicate tracery of rigging.

'We takes our choice, cuffin!' He chortled, and they passed down the cobbled ways to the three-sided wharf, eyeing the sea-worn vessels.

'Easiest thing is t' ask about,' Doud suggested, and stopped a passing wharf labourer.

'Know of any barky sailin' east – India, China, the Dutchy Indies?'

The man gave it thought, then said, 'I heard *Hibernian Packet* was off t' Batavia,' he admitted. 'T'other side, English barque o' six hundred ton, Fowles master.'

'I thank ye,' Doud said, pressing a coin into his hand.

They stepped out blithely and came up with the vessel, a trim enough craft, varnish still bright, rigging hove taut, yards crossed in seamanlike squareness.

There was no activity aboard, probably awaiting cargo to arrive alongside.

'Looks well enough. Does we visit?'

From the fo'c'sle there was a narrow brow, a planked gangway, and they mounted it lithely. Inboard a plainly dressed officer stood with folded arms, his eyebrows raised interrogatively.

'I hears you're about t' shake out canvas for a passage east.'

'Aye.' The voice was mild, almost kindly.

'As we're in need of a deep-water berth both,' Doud

explained. 'Anythin' in the foremast way of it. We've sea service since before these wars.'

'Can't help,' the man said neutrally. 'Crew filled days ago.'

'We does understand.' Doud fumbled in his belt and came out with his fist closed on something. 'Ye'll want t' be sure they presents 'emselves when ye sail. Here's t' say this is an earnest that we'll be there, should you sign us.'

The dull chink was quickly smothered and a smile surfaced. 'Aye, just remembered a couple o' hands I can't rightly trust. You look a likely pair.'

He glanced about and said quietly, 'Burton, mate. Youse?'

'Doud, Pinto.'

'Then when we're cleared an' under orders, get y'selves and your dunnage on board at the trot. Oh, master's name is Fowles. He's shoreside for now. See you both then.'

Hardly believing their luck they made their way back to *Thunderer*, the ship now to their eyes old and dowdy, and prepared for the last act. With no family ties, no obligations and their seagoing possessions in two well-used sea-bags, they took their leave of those they could trust. The actual parting would be under cover of dark, when not too many eyes would be interested in what was happening around the somnolent two-decker.

At the King's Arms they had Burton's word for boarding in only four days and on the due evening they put off in the row-guard cutter, which, after last farewells, left them with a hired wherry for the cobbled maze of the Barbican.

They quickly found their outward-bound barque.

Oddly, for a ship under sailing orders there was no life or bustle around her decks, and as they went up the brow uneasiness crept in.

A tall, bulky figure barred their way. 'What's yer business, cully?'

'Business? We're y' crew as is about t' sign on f'r Batavia,' Doud said importantly. 'T' see Cap'n Fowles.'

'Shipkeeper,' the figure said shortly. This was a man usually hired to keep an eye on an empty vessel. 'An', no, you isn't. This 'ere hooker ain't going nowhere.'

'Where's Fowles?'

'I reckon wi' the new owners tryin' to save his berth as skipper. See, this 'ere scow's been put up f'r sale on account o' debt, the buggers not gettin' any business a-tall.'

Doud blinked in confusion. 'B-but all them others—'

The man looked at them pityingly. 'Yeah, look at 'em. Not one in four workin' cargo, rest jus' rottin'. Now's a rare bad time for sailorin', freights that pay, hopeless t' chase come or go. No bastard has the rhino on the contynong, can't take English fees in any wise.'

A glance around the harbour showed what they'd missed before: the bustle and cries of a working dock area were mainly absent, only a listless activity here and there.

'Pinto, mate. If it's like this before the rest o' the fleet's paid off and gets ashore no beggar is goin' to get a berth.'

'So we . . .'

'Yes, mate. We un-deserts while we can.'

Chapter 30

The letter was brief, albeit with precious endearments. It was from Persephone asking Kydd, when convenient, to return to Knowle Manor for an unspecified reason.

This was not like her: she knew the duties pressing on the captain of a ship-of-the-line and wouldn't ask unless . . .

The spavined horse made much of the final incline to the manor with Kydd in a stew of impatience. He leaped off to see Persephone emerging.

'Darling! You came so quick – it's nothing, really.'

The dark-rimmed eyes told another tale entirely.

'Seph – what . . .?'

'Thomas, things are not so bright here, I'd have to say.'

'Come inside, let's talk.'

It was the wash of worried prattle that set Kydd's senses to full alert but this soon fell away and it all spilled out.

The rich Devonshire land was no longer the never-failing source of agricultural wealth it had always been. For varying reasons farms were failing and, in a shocking sight for the county, twice a tipstaff had been seen on his way out into the countryside.

'And I'm so sorry to tell you, dearest, that Mr Davies and Mr Lawkins have defaulted on their rent and I fear old Johncock will be next.'

This was the reality: whatever was gripping the country was now having an effect much too close to home. To maintain Knowle Manor and the Combe Tavy village in his duty as squire he needed the rent income. If this hardship spread it would be difficult all round.

And Persephone was here on her own, coping with it all.

'Thomas, I have to tell you . . . the taxes and imposts are now outrageous. Pitt's odious tax on income is voted out but won't stop until next year and our property tax has been increased for the third time – disgraceful! What with a monstrous cartload of other taxes it's . . . it's awful.'

Her sweet eyes glistened. 'I have to tell you, dearest, that if this is how things will be I cannot see how we can maintain an estate of consequence merely on your pay as a captain. In these hard times past with those unexpected defaults I confess to you I couldn't see any other way than to realise on our Consols – please forgive me, Thomas.'

These were their savings held securely as government bonds. There was also prize money, salvage, parliamentary grants, the tidy but small income due a colonel of marines. How long must they live on their capital? And if the worst happened and *Thunderer* was condemned he'd be on half-pay for the rest of his active life.

'You did right, Seph,' Kydd said briskly. 'We'll go through the books of account together later.' That she'd kept it to herself while he dealt with the ship was just like her, intelligent, loyal and loving. His heart went out to her and his eyes pricked.

He held her hands. 'The first thing – what is certain about the future.' He stared into space, trying to bring together all of the morbid thoughts he'd so lately had.

'I'm for the nonce post-captain, *Thunderer* seventy-four. As long as she's in commission I'm in receipt of all entitlements amounting to some six, seven hundreds a year. I'll dun that rascally agent to see how much more in outstanding payments, grants-in-kind and so forth are owing.'

'That's for now. The future? It may be that she could be sent on some kind of venture. After all she's had a recent refit and the stout hooker could stand in a line-of-battle with the best of 'em. But then again for a sail-of-the-line there's few scenes of action at a fleet scale as I can see looming.'

His face tightened. 'If I was a betting man I'd be obliged to put my money on that before the year is out she'll be condemned and I shall be looking for employment among those that are left.'

He gave a fond, twisted smile. 'You shall have my confession now, my love. I did have my hopes, Seph, doing so well at sea and then, damn the blackguard, Boney throws in the towel a mite too early.'

'Hopes?'

'Of flying my flag as admiral that you could show off to the world as the man you wed.'

'Oh, sweetheart! As if it matters to me – but I know it does to you, my dear.' She caressed his chest, looking deeply into his troubled eyes. 'I do so understand.'

'I'm well up on the captains' list and in the end – trusting in a healthy death rate – can look to rise to the top and then be made admiral, but I'll be an old man by then. Without we have fleets needing men with a flag, it's thinkable to be an admiral but without distinction of fleet – what we call a yellow admiral. These spend their days on shore strutting their lace but will never smell powder again.'

She saw him smother a gulp and crushed him to her. 'So unfair! You, the greatest sea hero this age!'

'It doesn't count any more, my love. I'll wager Melville at this very minute has crowds pressing him with petitions and interest behind 'em why they should hoist their flag, each with a reason why I should not.'

Mrs Appleby entered with refreshments, her set face a sign that she was aware of what was going on. She hesitated for a moment as if she were about to say something but remained silent and with a wan smile left them.

Persephone crossed from the sideboard with a glass of whisky and pointedly sat opposite.

'Sweetheart. My love, we can't sustain any longer without we make plans.' Her voice had changed, a firm, businesslike tone he'd never heard from her before.

'Proper plans. And, Thomas, I want you to promise me you'll give each your best thoughts, not to cast them aside as inconvenient to your preferring.'

'Yes, dear.'

'Then the first. You will stay aboard *Thunderer* as long as you're able, to the day she's condemned.'

'Of course.'

'At which point you step ashore to unemployment and half-pay.'

'Well . . . I suppose that will be true.'

'You admit that promotion in any form is then closed to you, admiral included.'

'Um . . . yes, Seph,' he said humbly.

'Here in Combe Tavy the times are hard and getting worse. If you're obliged by your half-pay commitment to hold yourself ready for a sea appointment it forbids you taking up any other employ – and we shall slowly consume our means while you're held in forcible inactivity.'

Kydd said nothing, his head bowed.

'It's cruel what I have to say but there's our whole future in it.'

He looked up slowly, his face stricken. 'Say it, as I know what it'll be.'

'Thomas,' she said softly, 'I want you to leave the navy and become a man of the land, owner of acres, magistrate, squire. Someone of the highest consequence here and as far as Ivybridge and Cornwood.'

'I don't know land and vegetables and cows and . . . and such things,' he replied wretchedly.

'You've a fine mind and daring with it,' Persephone said quickly. 'There's quantities of astonishing new inventions coming out now you'll want to introduce – you wouldn't credit their genius. One I saw was just a single horse pulling a machine that not only mows the wheat harvest but bundles it up into stooks ready for the collecting – all in one day.'

'But—'

'You'll never want for advice in these parts, I'm sure. You're very popular as you've always found it to be. You're still young and all you're doing is changing the direction of our life.'

'I'll think on it.'

But she was absolutely right. An active man of his age held in endless idleness as his powers faded was a pitiful sight – and one more probable than not.

A wild thought came. 'Seph, I heard Captain Ross is going to make a try at the North-west Passage. He's looking to make up a tight crew as will keep 'em safe and alive in the frozen Arctic Sea. Exploring, discovering – wouldn't it be something to be part of that! I can volunteer immediately and—'

'Dear, I agree it would be admirable to be a sea hero twice over, but I have my doubts that the good Captain Ross would desire to have a famed sea warrior at his elbow as he navigates through the dreadful hazards. Rather more a husky able seaman on the ropes.'

She hadn't mocked his idea, merely destroyed it with logic.

He downed the whisky rather more indecently than he should, feeling her gaze on him. 'I stay in *Thunderer* until the last moment,' he said thickly.

'Of course, darling.'

He had to make some gesture of interest, if only to allow him time to digest the convulsion of visions that was rushing in. 'I'm still squire.'

'Yes, you are, darling.'

'Then I'm to make visit to Mr Davies, I believe,' he said, with dignity, 'as discovering what ails the land that brings us to such a pass.'

'Good idea, my love. I know the way—'

'Tomorrow.'

Chapter 31

The seamed and white-haired old man lived, as his fore-
bears had, in a low wattle-and-daub cottage on the
greensward at the southern flanks of the Beacons, well down
from the bleak moors. There was a neat kitchen garden to
either side of the ancient door, with its sheep-figure knocker.

The man was prompt to answer but when he saw who it
was his weathered old face under its thatch of unkempt hair
screwed up in suspicion.

'Sir Tom – ye've come for yer rent an' I have t' tell you
that—'

'Not so, old man. What I've come for is a steer on what's
amiss at all. I've been at sea these last months and may have
omitted to keep abreast of things. Can we come in?'

'Oh? Aye, sit y'selves down an' I'll get us a brew.'

The Devonshire cider was refreshing but heady. They sat
at the little table. Mrs Davies had passed away some years
ago and the cottage had the look of a capable but unimagi-
native man.

'So. Two farms gone, another on its way if we believe the
rumours,' Kydd began. 'Is it something in the soil or—'

'No, it ain't!' snapped Davies, slamming his mug down. 'Nothin' wrong wi' good Devon tilth.'

'Then?'

'Prices. All is prices, these shonky days. I'm in sheep, an' I can't find the coin for winter feed, nor yet new livestock at the market.'

Kydd was confused. 'But why not? You've been doing well these last few years.'

'You're in the right, S' Tom. An' you don't know what ye're talking of – I beg yours, y'r ladyship,' he said, in an exaggerated aside.

'I came here to get an idea what's going on, Mr Davies.'

'Oh, aye. Well, it's the same f'r all on us. Prices. My fat-lamb price don't reach the place where'n I can afford to lay in the hay. No hay, sheep die, I starve.'

'All of you?'

'Them what are raisin' wheat and such are in the same – price they gets is terrible, doesn't cover their fertiliser or the labour to sow and reap. Sheaves stay in the fields, rot, nothin' for a year's hard sweat, so where's the new-season seed coming from?'

'Same with pigs, goats and, er, other?'

He nodded miserably.

'Mr Davies. You say prices are the trouble – why so?'

'Y' don't know? It's cos we've won the poxy wars. Before, we worked hard and long but England needed us an' our harvests. Now – why, if ye wants to see it with your own eyes, get down to the Exeter markets. There you'll see barley and wheat by the cartload – but most of it is off of y'r foreign Johnnies at half our price. They can do this cos their labour is slave prices while we have t' pay our lads a living wage.'

Kydd didn't need much more. The flood of cheap grain

and other foodstuffs was ruining England's agricultural heritage. What could he do to help the people of Combe Tavy, his tenants?

From his hazy understanding it was political at base. The cheap imports were reducing the cost of a loaf of bread to a point at which the masses flooding into London and the manufacturing cities of the north could be saved from starving. To go against this life-saving actuality would not be what was wanted.

Kydd returned to Knowle Manor in a deep depression.

Chapter 32

'It's worse in the north,' Persephone said, pointing in the newspaper to a lurid headline about rick-burning. They'd seen the tales of the wild midnight rides of Captain Swing and the machine-breaking Luddites but it hardly applied to them.

'As I can take it from their view,' Kydd murmured. 'If you know things are going to rats, you don't understand why, then the most obvious is to strike out at what you can see before your eyes as does the deed – the machines.'

Persephone put down her paper as Mrs Appleby brought in the post on a silver tray. On it was a municipally stamped sheet, which she plucked up immediately. 'Oh, no!' she whispered.

'Seph?'

'The Revenue – they're going after old Davies. Salt and farm-horses tax not paid. We're to witness the bailiff going in to destrain property to the value of . . .'

'Good God!' Kydd spluttered. 'We can't let it happen to the old man. He's on his own, and couldn't—'

Persephone took his hand, squeezing it hard. 'All his family's in Norfolk, I don't know where,' she said softly. 'He's got no one.'

'They can't do it. I'll tell him directly, his rent due is wiped off. That'll give him something to throw in their faces.'

'You're very kind, darling, more so than I, if I'm to be truthful. Dear love, it's not going to be as easy as that. For one, he's probably had to use the rent money on something else and hasn't got it to hand over. For the other . . . there is something we have to face – together.'

'Seph?'

'If we pay off the Revenue for old Davies, what about Lawkins and Johncock? They're probably in the same situation. And others who are too shy to come forward. They probably think we're flush in the fob with prize money and are a soft touch.'

'Your meaning is that if we help the old man it will bring our other tenants around begging for the same.'

'It will be so, mark my words.'

'Then what you're saying is we must stand meekly by and see old Davies thrown on the parish?' Kydd said, horrified, both at the moral dilemma and the realisation that Persephone had seen it and taken the decision out of his hands. 'Well, Consols at three per cent yield with our holdings—'

'We've gone through all that, Thomas.'

'But—'

'Sweetheart,' Persephone said, with an edge to her voice. 'How much capital can you promise me shall see us safely prosper into this entirely uncharted new age? You can't, and it would be foolish to try, dearest. The answer is that, until things are much clearer, we guard our pennies closely.'

'And let old Davies—'

'I'm so very sorry for him but we're not charity.'

There was little point in going further. She was right. Should he plead 'unwell' so as not to have to witness the whole sordid act?

*

On the day, they waited down the lane for the tipstaff and bailiff with their assistants who, without a minute's delay, marched up to bang on the cottage door.

It was over quickly. After the tipstaff had read out his warrant to the set-faced Davies and flourished his little wooden rod of office, the bailiff pushed past and into the cottage.

He was out with a despising frown. 'Nowt there as I'd set a good value to.'

He looked about and saw the sheep in their pen. 'That'll do. I'll 'ave them.' He motioned his assistants forward while the old man's face crumpled, stoically keeping his silence through brimming eyes.

Kydd couldn't take any more.

With a mighty quarterdeck roar that startled the group into stillness he ordered venomously, 'Hold! Here's a note of hand for the man's debt – stand fast that thievery!'

Not a word was spoken as they rode home but when Persephone dismounted, she went to him and kissed him soundly, without a word, and they went in for supper.

They'd hardly sat down when a soft knock at the door had Mrs Appleby crossly answering it. It was the one-eyed innkeeper, Jenkins.

'Sir Thomas is 'aving his victuals, sir,' she said loyally.

'Oh, s' sorry but I've got an urgent matter for the squire as can't wait.' Jenkins was the proprietor of the London Inn at Ivybridge, a substantial staging inn but as well the accepted tavern meeting place and taphouse for the district.

The urgent matter, it seemed, was that, with the serious fall-off in custom in these parlous times, he'd run up a debt that must occasion the sale of the inn. At this very moment some undesirables were wishing to close a purchase with a view to reverting the premises to one quite objectionable to the good folk of Ivybridge and—

Kydd growled something to the effect that he'd think on it and firmly shut the door in the face of one he'd counted before as a friend.

Not much later another knock was Lawkins, his cap in his hands.

'Sir. I heard on what ye did for old Davies. Now I've been y' loyal tenant f'r years now, always pay rent on time up till that there distemper o' me cows. This is t' say that should y' see y'r way clear to . . .'

Kydd looked up from the breakfast chair, his face lined and tired, and tried a smile for Persephone.

She knew instinctively what was ailing him and reached across the table to squeeze his hand. 'Thomas, I know what's on your mind, my sweet love.'

'You do?' Kydd answered, with a wry smile.

'Of course. You're fretful about your *Thunderer*, aren't you?'

'Why, yes, Seph – Roscoe is a good hand but he goes too hard to do things his way, and these are calamitous times as would try the patience of a saint. And to be true to my duty she's still in commission, according to orders, ready to put to sea on His Majesty's occasions – which she's not, I'm grieved to say.'

'Then you must go to her,' she said decisively. 'You'll only stew and fidget if you don't.'

'No, Seph – I can't leave you here alone in all this.' Even as it came out he knew this was nonsense for she'd quickly taken charge of the distressing scenes at the door, he was unable to find the words to sympathise and deny.

Chapter 33

At Ivybridge excited passengers leaned from mail-coaches telling of the unnerving and dismaying spectacle of crowds thronging aimlessly by the dockyard.

Kydd boarded the Navigator coach, exuberantly staging its way from London to Plymouth. He stared from the grubby window, noting empty fields, corn wilting for want of harvesting – it had never been like this before.

He alighted above the Mill Bay docks, thinking to show himself to the port admiral. Then he noticed at least half a dozen utilitarian ships alongside the quay, which he quickly recognised as military transports. He stopped to watch the stream of passengers leaving. This was no organised disembarking: it was a flood of soldiers and baggage spilling on to the waterfront.

'Wellington's heroes, just back from the Peninsula,' a bystander offered. 'Liberty in England, it must be sweet for 'em.'

Tucked in behind the waterfront were the Mill Bay barracks. Most of the soldiers pressed on up the hill with shapeless packs of precious belongings humped over mountainous miles in an alien land. They were making for the towering gates inside which they would find the order and security of army life they'd not known for years.

Strangely, some men were slowly going in the opposite direction, aimlessly heading for the grog shops further along, sitting in small groups and staring about them as if in a foreign land.

'Ahoo! Ahoo there!' The cry came from three or four soldiers nursing their pots, their faces turned his way.

'Ahoo, Cap'n.' The older in the middle bore the marks of a foot-regiment sergeant. Kydd, nonplussed at the unconventional 'ahoy', went to pass on but the man rose from his bench and came over to him.

'Cap'n Kydd – yez doesn't remember me? Off th' ice in Bergen-op-Zoom, a miracle ye served us!'

The heavily tanned and weathered man, grinning widely, resolved into one of the few in the disastrous Antwerp expedition that Kydd had been able to take off the icy shore under gunfire.

Kydd paused. 'Ah – Sergeant Hoskins, the 33rd of Foot, unless I'm mistaken?'

It caused a flush of pleasure and the man hesitantly held out his hand. 'It is, sah. Jus' today returned from the war. How has it been f'r you an' yours since Boney chucked in his hand, could I ask?'

'A lot quieter,' Kydd admitted. '*Thunderer* is moored in Cawsand Bay,' he added, for something to say.

The man's scarlet uniform was immaculate but Kydd's practised eye saw it had been cunningly patched and sewn innumerable times and the boots, though sagging with wear, shone as though their owner was on parade.

'Tell me, Sarn't, what happens to an old soldier when the war's finished?' He meant it in a jocular way but saw clouds darken the other's expression.

'Ah, not anythin' as would interest ye, sah.'

'Nonsense,' Kydd said, rather more sincerely than he'd expected of himself. 'You're the warriors who put down the tyrant, after all.'

Hoskins blinked once or twice as if to reassure himself of his memories, then told his story without bitterness or rancour.

Marched hundreds of miles to the coast, bivouacked in the open until the transports arrived, the 33rd thankfully boarded, only to find that a contrary nor'-westerly kept them at anchor while the foul wind played with them. The soldiers were condemned to the lower deck in an old and leaking vessel for days on end.

Aware that they were the heroes of Wellington it was not unreasonable to expect an ecstatic welcome in the land of their birth but, they having been hopelessly delayed by the march and adverse winds, all celebrations had long since concluded, and they disembarked at a dusty, indifferent dockside with no one to see the conquering heroes land.

The worst quickly followed. Marched into Mill Bay Barracks, they were high-handedly informed that the 33rd of Foot was herewith disbanded. Clutching tickets of claim against back pay, they were free to go, no longer in the employ of His Majesty's forces.

With very little to show for years of bleak service they had to join the hundreds of thousands now flocking into every town looking for work of any grade.

'Sarn't, what will you do? Where will you go?' Kydd felt so helpless – there was no question that he could find the man a job. He was just one of the swarms of anonymous souls who'd risked blood and death for their country and been callously let go to find their own fate.

'I? Don't worry on me, sah. I'll be off north, bound t' be

work in those there 'factories. Besides, here's one t' look after me – c'mere, Simon lad!'

The drummer boy Kydd remembered from the Antwerp debacle happily leaped up and raced over. He'd filled out and was now a strapping fourteen-year-old. He gave Kydd a quivering salute.

There was little Kydd could think of to say. This was unquestionably a political decision to be rid of the expense of an active army at the earliest opportunity, cynicism at its worst.

He fumbled in his fob but then, realising that to offer money to a proud soldier was not the thing to do, he came up with an idea. Finding a visiting card he took out his silver-chased pencil and carefully wrote:

Harry, I'd be infinitely obliged should you be able to find a situation for the bearer, Mr Hoskins, and his companion. His qualities raise him much above the ordinary, you'll find.

Kydd handed it to the sergeant who gravely accepted it. 'Do take this to Mr Lucius Craddock of the house of Haydon and Woodstein in Manchester, remembering me to him. Clear?'

He knew Craddock was there for he'd given the man leave to visit his family.

Chapter 34

Slipping aboard *Thunderer* without ceremony Kydd went to his cabin and put on his sea rig, the feel of the well-worn fabric oddly comforting.

He rang the little bell and, after a pause, Binard bustled in. His surprise at seeing Kydd was amusing to witness.

'Oh, sir, sir – I did not hear you aboard. Do you wish—'

'Some whisky.' It was early, but he had a lot of hard thinking to do.

His time at Knowle Manor had been difficult. With a twinge of guilt he realised that right at the moment he was seeing *Thunderer* as a refuge from life on his little estate.

He thrust aside the thought and tried to concentrate. More ships had taken up moorings with the lengthening line of hulks in the Hamoaze, and there was every reason to think that *Thunderer* would not be long in joining them. What was his future then? Immediate half-pay with all it meant in straitened circumstances, so what he should be doing, like his officers, was using the time gainfully to find a future.

He went over the possibilities yet again and all ran against the same problem. He was a senior captain of a sail-of-the-line and couldn't be expected to take on a command of trivial proportions or a post ashore similar to the one he'd had while recovering from the wound he'd received in the American conflict.

He was a sea animal, the shore and its ways not his. Neither was he of the nature to make himself noticed about the centres of power, exploit whatever interest he could muster at the Admiralty or press for a position with the highest.

Was Persephone right? Should his energies and intelligence now be devoted to the estate to make a success of the land? Was his fate to join the list of seamen who'd settled down on their own domain after a distinguished career at sea?

He got up and wandered out on deck. There was no sudden snapping to attention, slapping of muskets, officers' hats doffed, lines of men at their deck-scrubbing. The ship had lapsed into a torpid lethargy, movements slow and meaningless. It tore at his heart.

The officers largely went about their own affairs – Ambrose struggling with a Greek grammar while Martyn was lost in an account of the far north by a whaling captain.

Clinch appeared only in the wardroom for meals, churlish and hostile. As a married man it was peculiar that he wasn't sleeping ashore, as was his right, but it was said he'd run into some sort of predicament and didn't wish to. The others left him to his petulant fretting.

Some had found a calling: the hulking boatswain, Bull Opie, had discovered a talent for craftwork and was well into a three-foot-long meticulous model of *Thunderer*, complete with the most elegant ropework.

The ship's fiddler had a school of earnest students who shared his three violins while a marine loftily took classes in flute.

But of all those turning time to account there was one he

was particularly interested to see. In Craddock's empty cabin, away from curious eyes.

Kydd gently opened the door and saw sitting at his secretary's desk a hard-bitten gunner's mate peering at a book – Burrows's *Theory of Gunnery and Doctrine of Projectiles*. He wore a pair of small round spectacles, which he whipped off instantly. 'Why, sir, an' you gave me a start.'

'Oh, do carry on, Mr Stirk, don't let me interrupt your studies.'

It was apparently the turn of Eames, the tall and gangly midshipman, to sit with Stirk, and his boredom rapidly vanished at his captain's presence.

'How is Mr Stirk progressing, do you think, Eames?' Kydd enquired.

'Main well, sir. Er, do you wish to hear him on the subject?'

'I would indeed.'

'Mr Stirk – how do we point a gun?'

Kydd stifled a sudden snort at the question, which at any other time would have had a short and pithy answer from the gun-captain.

'Ah. That's rule six, an' it says, given the direction and impy . . . impetus of the projectile t' find where th' curve described thereby meets a plane passin' through th' point of projection, I reckon.'

'I think so, don't you, sir?'

'I couldn't express it any better myself.'

Stirk tried to hide his pleasure at the compliment and braced for another question.

'Mr Stirk, how long does it take for a thirty-two-pounder ball to carry to a man-o'-war a mile in the offing?'

Kydd remained blank-faced: if Stirk didn't know the answer on the spot, his twenty years at the breech of a gun had all been wasted.

'Ah, an' there I need m' workings.' He fished out his gunner's notebook and licking his pencil began figuring.

'An' that's the time o' flight contrivin' – rule eight. Now that's as y'r radius is t' the tangent of elevation, so's th' given distance to th' object – our Frenchy two-decker – in feet to a number, one fourth of its square root is y'r number of seconds, right?'

To Kydd's awe the big gunner bent to his task. Laboriously, tables were consulted, and mumbling to himself all the while and, refusing any assistance, he finally had an answer.

'I makes it nigh on four seconds an' a rat's whisker.'

'Well done!' Eames exclaimed, impressed.

Stirk leaned back triumphantly, then ferociously turned on the young man. 'Well done? Now you 'ave a go at this'n. You tells me . . . why does it get to be a "square" root? Hey? Nothin' I can see about it says all square an' a-taunto!'

Chapter 35

Time passed slowly and it was a welcome interruption when late one morning the ship had a visitor. He came up the side-steps clumsily but Kydd was not going to turn out the hands simply to rig a boatswain's chair.

The man had a nameless look of petty authority in his black brass-buttoned coat and low-crowned hat. 'Soper, clerk o' the court, Exeter Assizes.' He sniffed. 'Am I addressing the captain of this vessel?'

'You are – Captain Sir Thomas Kydd. Have you any business concerning this ship, sir? Else I must ask you to quit the deck. As you can see, we are well occupied this afternoon.'

'This boat is HMS *Thunderer*, is it not?'

Kydd winced. 'This *ship* has the honour of that name, yes, sir.'

'And you have on board an officer . . . Let me see,' he said riffling some papers.

Instantly alert, Kydd tensed, aware that the other three men in the boat had remained there, probably at hand to enforce whatever Soper's business was.

'Ah, yes. Mr Nathaniel Makepeace Clinch, lieutenant, Royal Navy.'

'What is your interest in Lieutenant Clinch, may I ask it?'

'Kindly produce the person, sir. He's wanted to answer the court on . . . certain charges.'

'I am his captain. I've a right to know, sir.'

'Very well. There's a considerable debt in his name owed to a certain gentleman who, after an unfortunate altercation, demands that the full weight of the law be exercised to recover it.'

So that was what had turned the already crabbed officer into a recluse, hiding aboard. Rising from the lower deck he was proud of his elevation. A common seaman would shrug off such difficulties – 'paying it off with a flying fore-topsail' was the careless salty phrase, referring to a timely escape to sea. A gentleman would see it as a debt of honour.

Kydd thought quickly. 'Well, Mr Soper, I fear it may be a wasted journey for you. I haven't seen this officer for some time,' he said truthfully. 'Er, Mr Roscoe, have you?'

'Lieutenant Clinch? No, sir, not in the wardroom or on the quarterdeck.'

'Then, pray, where is this officer? I have documents requiring his person to be detained this very day, sir.'

'The man is married, Mr Soper, and, while his ship lies to moorings, he has every right to step ashore how he pleases. Hence his present whereabouts are no concern of mine. Good day, sir.'

He turned on his heel and resumed pacing as the boat put off.

What more could he do?

Bitterness flooded back. Why had this grand triumph of the greatest war in history turned to such chaos and confusion?

The boat was out of sight – he'd see now if there was anything he could retrieve from the wreckage of the man's life.

He quietly made his way to the officers' cabins and the end one, the smallest, intended for the most junior. He listened outside. There was stillness. How could the man stand endless incarceration in this tiny space? It smelt rankly of human occupation and he guessed the messman had been regularly chased away.

For these humble cabins there was no door, only curtains, and announcing himself apologetically Kydd drew them aside.

The sight of the hanging body slammed into his consciousness, like a mortal blow. Swaying slightly with the motion of the tideway there was nothing that could hide the staring eyes, the distorted, blood-gorged throat and clenched fists.

Choking and gagging, Kydd fought to escape the nightmare and hurried out to the sweet, crisp air of the upper deck.

Roscoe stared at him, then hurried to his side. 'Sir? You're not well?'

Kydd's world was now his cabin and the empty quarterdeck. He couldn't in all conscience return to Knowle Manor and be absent when the blow finally landed. And yet, when it did, where was he to go?

His thoughts raced back and forth, nothing to plan for, nothing to expect. And pressing in on him was an overwhelming urge to act – to do something to ward off the inevitable fate awaiting.

Chapter 36

On the London Road

The coach rattled and swayed. With so uncertain a future there was no paying over the odds for a post-chaise, and Kydd was tired, dusty and sore when he finally arrived.

Even as he painfully descended into the stink of the capital he still had no idea what he would do. He'd stay at a traveller's inn for now and, for want of a better plan, would make visit to the Admiralty in the morning. Not to the august offices of state but to the Captain's Room he knew so well from former days when begging for a ship. At least there he could hear the latest rumours and shape a course accordingly.

The room was full to the point of discomfort with newly unemployed captains and despairing commanders who sat about in a disconsolate silence, almost as if it were a funeral parlour.

He had no right to be there for, at least in theory, he still had a ship to command but he kept this to himself.

He recognised one or two but didn't approach them, for besides being obliged to hear a tale of woe worse than his own he would have to explain what he was doing there.

He eased himself next to an intelligent-looking officer he did not know and, in a very short while, learned of the situation.

The Admiralty did not seem to know what was afoot politically, whether or not prudently to stand fast on numbers in these unknown days of peace or bow to the strident calls from the Treasury for relentless and single-minded slashing of expenditures.

It appeared that some kind of compromise was in progress, the casting into the outer darkness of – to begin with – the older ships, continuing until some unrevealed cost level had been met.

Either way, prospects for a loyal and long-serving naval officer were dim and fast receding. It was patently clear that if there was a course to take to secure a future, it would have been discovered by these men long before now.

The more he heard, the lower Kydd's spirits sank. He made his excuses and left, trying to think of some clever move that would save the day, but the noise and crush of the streets made reflection impossible.

Bazely? He quickly found his friend was not in town. His club, Brooks's? He hadn't the heart to mingle with the fortunate and successful and, in any case, he could not afford the reckoning.

He didn't wish to appear needy or in difficulties so wouldn't drop in at Renzi's, but who else would understand what it was for a deep-dyed mariner to leave the sea at the height of his powers?

Inevitably, he found himself back on the West Country road, moodily taking in the hills and dales of lush greenery, with nothing to show for his visit but the small comfort that he'd at least done something.

Thunderer still lay in something like the offended dignity of age and he quickly slipped aboard to his cabin. Roscoe had a crop of stubble and red-rimmed eyes: the cheerless time to come had laid its dead hand on him, too.

Chapter 37

Some days later their fate was sealed with a single pack of orders. These were not for far seas and adventure: it was the demise of His Majesty's Ship *Thunderer*.

The end of the month would be considered the vessel's last day in commission. She would be paid off as she lay, her inescapable destiny to join those in ordinary, later to be broken up. Kydd stared at the simple words, willing them to change but they obstinately remained, the melancholy epitaph of a once great man-o'-war.

His eyes stung – just days were left to him to take his delight in his spacious cabin, the martial but comfortably appointed space that had seen so much drama and adventure. Then he would be ashore for the rest of his life.

Gulping, he began listing what had to be done in a ship going out of commission. There would be a monumental accounting. Then she would be stripped of powder and stores and . . .

And what of his men, his noble crew? What would it mean for Stirk?

Stirk would leave the navy as a common seaman among

the horde condemned to the streets, would see no pension and would have only his memories of Kydd and *Thunderer* to take with him.

At his age his scholarly achievements were truly admirable. The more practical aspects including maintaining the books would be child's play to one who'd served as gunner's mate for so many years in so many ships, and he would go with Kydd's warmest possible certificate of service and recommendation. While in London he'd used what influence he still had to accelerate his examination for gunner, now set for the following week. At least this would secure a future for his old friend.

And the midshipmen: as apprentice officers they were mustered in a particular ship, not the navy. They would be cast ashore with nothing, half-pay denied them and, in a navy with far fewer ships, little chance of finding another berth. There was precious little he could do for them.

He pulled himself together. The first item was in all fairness to let the officers, then the men know their future . . . but he would tell them all at the same time. Reaching for his well-worn cocked hat he called for the first lieutenant – who by loyally staying with Kydd and the ship had lost his entire expectations.

'Mr Roscoe, kindly clear lower deck. I have . . . news to tell.'

There'd been no shock, no outcry. It had been long expected and now it had happened. Papers arrived, the long process of mustering gear carried put in train; the purser and then the boatswain began preparing for a third-party survey.

The dockyard clerk-of-the-cheque would come aboard at a date to be arranged to pay off the ship's company. They would go their many ways and *Thunderer* would be an empty, echoing shell, himself and the standing officers the only ones to inhabit the sad, lifeless craft.

There would be the final indignity, of course, the lofty masts stripped of their sails and rigging, stores landed, then the ship towed to the gun wharf and deprived of her guns, those that had spoken so nobly in battles too numerous to count. Finally *Thunderer* would be hauled mid-stream of the Hamoaze and secured in her final resting-place.

He'd sent a quick note to Persephone that she and Francis might expect him home, this time for ever.

His life, from now on, would take a much different course.

Chapter 38

Parliament, London

With practised jabs of the elbow, Peregrine Fookes – known to all as Prinker – eased himself to the front of the public gallery at the House of Commons.

He closed his eyes, willing the man speaking to sit down, as the drone of his voice went on and on against a hum of conversation and restless movement. He wasn't there to be persuaded of the no-doubt-glorious merits of the proposed Tewkesbury canal. He was there to hear the bent, slight figure who waited patiently below.

As Parliamentary under-secretary to Earl Bathurst, long-serving secretary of state for war and the colonies, Fookes had a duty to alert his superior to any motions of the House that could disturb the even tenor of governance in his department.

And this potentially could. Loudly proclaimed by the luminaries of the Clapham Sect, a group of evangelical Christians with powerful friends among the officers of state, the next speaker was said to be about to make the very thunderclap of a speech. His words on a previous occasion had swayed this house into a surge of emotion that had had men weeping and, in an avalanche of cheering, pass a law that for moral daring had left the world in awe.

The current speaker at last sat down and in a stillness that stole to every corner of the chamber the waiting figure got painfully to his feet and, for a few moments, looked about him as if to fix the sight of the packed house in his memory.

Then the Right Honourable William Wilberforce began his address.

'Sir, the man's weak and ill but he had 'em in his hand from the off,' Fookes reported.

The Earl Bathurst frowned. 'So, what did the beggar say? And keep it short, old man.'

'Made sense, an' it had the Tories spluttering and the opposition howling.'

'Get on with it, man.'

'In fine, he says that as the war's ended an' peace declared, what a capital time to get together all the spare ships the navy must have left over and put an end to the slave trade for good an' all.'

Since 1807, when Britain had made illegal, at his leadership, its lucrative trade in slaves, Wilberforce had been known to desire as well the complete end to slavery in all its forms. He'd become a champion of destroying the trade at its source in Africa as a means of denying the slave-owners world-wide their iniquitous labour.

'Same ranting then – but with a bite. It won't fadge, of course,' Bathurst replied irritably. 'Expense. The Treasury's in debt to its eyebrows in sums that stagger belief. They'll put it behind 'em as they always do.'

But Fookes had more to say. 'I took the trouble of lingering afterwards. There's no doubt but the sentiment's with him.

I overheard a Whig design to table a motion of censure, that the administration hasn't the wit or the intention of doing a thing even when now they have the means to do so.'

Bathurst harrumphed without comment.

'And the crowds outside, all of a tizz declaring they'll chair him home. And this with the by-election due before—'

'Yes, yes. So it's your sense o' the matter that we should do something.'

'Anything as shows us alive to the issue, yes.'

'I'll think on it.'

'Sir, I'd rather you act on it, if you catch my meaning.'

Chapter 39

The Cabinet Office

The prime minister, Lord Liverpool, had seen what blazed from the newspapers. Not happy, he'd called an immediate meeting of his ministers.

'Sidmouth,' he called, to his ponderous home secretary. 'Will this blow over?'

'Er, I rather fancy not in the shorter term, my lord.'

'Why not, pray?'

'It all sounds so . . . plausible, if I may make free. To the generality of the voters there seems no earthly reason why something should not be done now we're free of the encumbrances of war.'

'Rubbish!' Liverpool snorted, then added quickly, 'As I didn't mean you, sir. The mobility, they've no notion of the fiscal burden we labour under at this time.'

'Nevertheless, Prime Minister, the risk of being seen to do nothing is not to be borne.' The youthful secretary at war, Palmerston, had a point and as usual would be ready with every reason why he was right.

'Do something? Then what?'

'Punish the scoundrels. Dispatch a fleet to bombard and—'

'To Africa? A rank nonsense, Pam. Er, someone do see if Castlereagh is available – I know he's back in the kingdom, for he's to tell me what he's been about in the treaty negotiations.'

After a small adjournment the cabinet reconvened, this time with the pale, noble face of the secretary of state for foreign affairs present.

'We've been presented by a vexing desire of the excitables to make a flourish in reply to Wilberforce's speech. In view of our dire financial standing, do you think it wise?' Liverpool asked aggressively.

Castlereagh looked thoughtful. His face was a mask of fatigue but he was clearly giving it every consideration. 'My lord, my own belief is that any hasty or precipitate act at this point would not be in the interest of any.'

'There!' snorted Liverpool triumphantly, glaring at Palmerston. 'Temporise, let it settle. All in good time!'

'Sir. I do however raise an awkward objection that is not so easily put on one side.'

'Which is?' the prime minister growled, suddenly guarded.

'At the moment, at this Parliament's desire, I'm working towards the inclusion in the final treaty and settlement an expression of commitment by the entirety of the Allied Powers to the principle of the condemnation of slavery as a repugnance to the dignity of all humankind.

'Should Great Britain be seen to hang back in its practical application I rather fear we shall lose all moral authority in the matter.'

Eyes shifted uncomfortably and heads dropped. What had been brought forward by the peerless minister was in essence unanswerable.

An awkward silence lengthened until Liverpool slapped down his papers and rapped, 'A select committee as shall answer to me on the question. Lord Chancellor?'

Eldon looked up, a small smile briefly appearing. 'Yes, Prime Minister. You shall have an answer within the week.'

'Two days.'

'My lord.'

Eldon rapped his gavel to indicate the start of business.

'My lord?'

Vansittart, the chancellor of the exchequer, was in no doubt. 'Quite frankly, gentlemen, we have no choice in the matter. The strain on the public purse is even now intolerable. What is a pleasing moral stand set against a rupture of finances?'

'Rather a lot, I would have thought,' murmured Westmorland, lord privy seal, snatching a glance at the still figure of Castlereagh.

'You haven't considered the question enough, then, old man,' said Vansittart, cuttingly. 'Have you not thought that this sets us fair to be constable to the world in the matter of slavery? This is asking a damn sight more than a single nation should bear.'

Eldon coughed irritably. 'Gentlemen, we're taxed with producing a response. This discussion is neither here nor there.'

'Don't we have some kind of deterrent force in Africa already?' Sidmouth asked mildly. 'I seem to remember in 1807 when the bill went through we dispatched a fleet o' sorts.'

'Ah. The West Africa Squadron,' Melville, the first lord of the Admiralty answered, a little uncomfortably, 'who might say, a slight accession to force in the area. Grand fellows, but with little chance of making a difference I'd be obliged to admit.'

'Then if an action there won't answer, a fleet to the Caribbee to blockade the slave-masters in their home waters?'

Melville shook his head. 'To achieve that would stretch the limits of any men-o'-war I have left to me. No, sir, it is not the way.'

Eldon's expression firmed. 'Lord Melville, I'm of the opinion this committee believes that any movement on the question must centrally involve the navy. To this end, I'm requiring you to confer with your people and return with a form of positive action that meets the prime minister's demands in the matter.'

Chapter 40

The Admiralty

'Those, gentlemen, are the elements,' Melville finished. He watched the variety of reactions reflected in the expressions of the Admiralty committee, from the glowering of the old sea-dog Yorke, current commissioner, to the smooth intelligence of Devereux, a rapidly rising figurehead of the new scholarly sea-officers.

'Which is t' say, the PM wants from us something noisy as will show to all the world he's done something,' Yorke said heavily.

'Not in so many words,' Melville said, clearly pained. 'Shall we agree that there has to be a move of some kind bold enough to calm the masses? Charles?' He glanced hopefully at Barrow, second secretary, known for his fecund imagination.

'Ah. Sir, it does cross the mind that what is needed is a demonstration of intent clearly visible to the uninformed – a fleet-scale operation of sorts?'

'As will incur expenditure not to be contemplated,' the acidulous first secretary, Croker, retorted.

'Quite,' Melville said quickly. 'Yet it has to be recognised that this entire manoeuvre – being as it is at the behest of the prime minister's office – will be on the books of the Treasury, not to our account. We're entitled therefore to set aside fiscal concerns as being outside our remit.'

'Very well, my lord. It still leaves us with a debate as to the nature of this . . . motion.'

'If I may . . .'

'Walter?'

Devereux arched his fingers and spoke as if at an academic lecture. 'It would appear we must consider one of two forms of reprisal. The first a punitive stroke by a potent force against the sources of the slave trade, namely the slave coast of Africa.'

'A folly and foolishness!' cried Yorke. 'Any with service on that coast knows it's a mud-trap and surf-bound as will keep any vessel above a brig far offshore. How then will you get guns of size close enough to cast their shot at the rascals?'

'The second action is to send a considerable fleet of smaller vessels to penetrate the rivers and lakes to find the slavers and destroy their places of embarkation,' Devereux continued calmly.

'May I remind Mr Second Secretary that we already have a squadron in that region engaged in such a manner,' Croker snapped sarcastically.

'The West Africa Squadron?' Melville mused. 'A contempt-ible enough force, two brigs and a handful of cutters, as I remember.'

'Which as our grand gesture we augment by a considerable number – perhaps even a frigate,' the one-eyed Admiral Ibbetson broke in with warmth. 'This way we need do no more than divert and attach whatever number of the lesser craft as we may to an existing command.'

'That's true,' mused Melville. 'I've found we have the commodore of the squadron well placed in Freetown, which, as you know, is the chief settlement of Sierra Leone.'

Dawning understanding followed: the country had been established some thirty-odd years earlier as a haven for slaves freed by the West Africa Squadron and others. Building a proper naval base there even now was being talked about.

Yorke slammed his fist to the table. 'A grand gesture? A trickle o' shrimp boats seen on their way to do battle with the enemy?' He snorted derisively. 'What they want to see is a fleet with pennons a-fly going out to grapple the foe.'

Before any could comment he added, 'And there we find ourselves well confounded – men-o'-war of size can't close with the coast so this is all athwart our intentions.'

'Er, not necessarily so,' Devereux intervened, earning himself a fierce glare, which he politely ignored. 'Assume we combine the two – send some heavy metal at the head of a reasonable flotilla of the lesser. This way we get our fine show and at the same time useful craft on station to put to the task.'

'Augment the West Africa Squadron? Mooring a sail-of-the-line as guard-ship in Freetown harbour?' Yorke grated.

'Not at all. Any talk of augmenting will not impress. What we need is a fleet of sorts that's imposing and goes by another name for the public to conjure with. One with a flagship and named commander.'

'In the same station as the West Africa Squadron? I think not,' Croker said briskly. 'They'll quarrel like monkeys on a barrel – be aware there's a full commodore in Freetown who won't take kindly to outsiders poaching his territory. Remember, prize money is involved.'

'I was not proposing that. An independent command,

whose orders are to cruise over the entire coastline while the West Africa Squadron continues on its usual ways.'

'If we have a commodore at sea and one ashore they'll come to blows, be sure of it,' Croker persisted.

'Then elevate the sea post to one of admiral,' Devereux said easily, 'as will assure the people that we mean a full war fleet.'

'Two squadrons?' Melville muttered. 'I'm not sure this is wise.'

'Sir, one on independent cruise, one on close blockade – as we did in the Mediterranean in the late war.'

'Mm. An expensive proposition.'

'With an attractive advantage. The West Africa Squadron is allowed to continue under its own line of authority and expenditure but the independents are funded directly by the Treasury. It means, that should anything untoward happen, it might be, as independently, dissolved at a stroke.'

'Anything happens?' rumbled Yorke, incredulously.

'Not for me to top it the Cassandra but I can foresee at least two possibilities – the one, that the cruise achieves its object and returns in glory to be then dispersed as the job having been done. The other, that the whole is a futile gesture having achieved nothing of consequence, the squadron is dissolved and its commander disgraced. For either contingency we are relieved of its responsibility and the grateful Treasury the expense.'

'Well done, Walter. I do believe we can sight blue water ahead. Now what shall we call our new fleet? How does the Preventive Squadron sound?'

'Proceed along those lines?' the officious chief clerk said, pen poised.

'I believe we do, pending the concurrence of the prime minister's office in the matter.'

'My lord.'

'And prepare me a public announcement, if you please,' Melville said primly, clearly satisfied with the day.

'There is the question of properly constituting the squadron as fit for an admiral,' cautioned Croker.

'This we'll leave until the officer has been appointed,' Melville said absently. 'He'll know what he wants, I'd imagine.'

Chapter 41

Knowle Manor

'Darling, I understand, truly, dearest.' Persephone unobtrusively slipped a glass of whisky by Kydd's side. 'But life must go on, you have to concede.'

Her voice was low and charged, for her love's crisis of existence had affected her more than she'd trusted it should.

Kydd said nothing, moodily staring into the fire, leaving the whisky untouched.

'When you're settled in, we'll talk some more about what you shall do. You are the squire, remember,' she added.

'The papers, sir,' Mrs Appleby said, bobbing respectfully.

Kydd seemed not to notice and, confused, the housekeeper turned to Lady Kydd.

'Thank you, Agnes,' she said softly. 'That will be all.'

She left him to his mood and took the armchair opposite, shaking out *The Times*. The advertisements on the front page held little interest for her and now, without dire pieces from the war, the news was thin.

Passing across the paper, she said, 'I see they're planning to do something about the odious trade in slaves, Thomas. Even going so far as to send a fleet to sea to go after the villains. And with an admiral to be appointed in charge as well.'

Kydd came to a sudden alert and scanned the article. In an unprecedented act in a time of peace the Admiralty was to create a new command with the sole purpose of pursuing the African slave-traders.

Vague in details of the fleet's composition, it was nevertheless a flag-officer's charge and a new appointment. And nothing whatsoever to suggest that an appointment had yet been made.

Colour rushed back to his face. It was foolish, lunatic even, but was it entirely out of the question that he could be chosen?

The paper shook as his mind took hold of the thought.

He was a senior post-captain now but there were others ahead of him on the list who should be promoted before him. If the Admiralty really wanted him in post there were ways – usually to 'yellow' those unfortunates in front – to promote them to admiral, then retire them out of the way, as had been done in the case of Nelson before the Nile. And a fate Kydd might very well be made to suffer.

The hope guttered and died. He hadn't the colourful and thrusting personality of the great hero; he was known as a daring frigate captain but that was probably not what was needed in this instance.

Yet he had a few friends in high places who would put in a word where it counted, but only if he were there to be seen and discreetly appraised.

What was he thinking? There were many fine seamen who could be brought to the fore in his place and many others canny enough to have accumulated favours to be paid back at the right time.

The odds were lengthening to ridiculous proportions and he was doing himself no service by hankering after what could never be.

'Dearest,' he said offhandedly, throwing aside the paper, 'I've remembered a brace o' things I need to tidy in London. Shouldn't take too long but I need to be on my way in the morning.'

Roscoe would take care of any last-minute vexations in the final paying-off procedures, and if he missed the inevitable bleak and stiff final dinner, it would be a mercy.

Dear old *Thunderer* – taken to her final rest. His eyes pricked – for as long as he lived, he'd never forget the old lady and what they'd been through together. Perhaps he'd commission a stirring portrait of her by Pocock or one of the other fine painters, or was that to be counted as an extravagance in this new landed reality?

Chapter 42

London

Almost light-headed with a defensive devil-may-care attitude, Kydd alighted the coach at Brooks's, which, for pecuniary reasons, he'd been reluctant to visit.

It was not long before Prinker Fookes found him out in his favourite chair and drew up next to him. 'Tiger! So long. What have you been about these days, you son of Neptune?'

'Ah. *Thunderer*, my ship of the moment, has been condemned. As of days' time I shall be without same and employment by His Majesty.'

'I'm so sorry to hear this,' Fookes said, the shock in his voice betraying the sincerity that lay beneath. 'Have you, er, prospects of any kind?'

'Persephone sees me to be retired upon the land in the character of squire, mustering my potatoes and visiting justice upon the village miscreants.' He downed his drink with uncharacteristic speed.

'Good God!' Fookes breathed. 'I'd heard these are uncommon strange times but . . .'

Kydd gave a sour smile. 'I've taken a cruise around the City but have learned it has nothing to offer a new-minted landlubber home from the sea. I fear my ocean-girdling days are done, old friend.'

Speechless, Fookes stared at him helplessly.

'There is a matter I'd be grateful if you'd give me a steer on.' Kydd's casual manner did not fool Fookes, who looked at him sharply.

'Prinker, I know you're now a nabob of consequence in Downing Street. I'm wondering if you'd give me the drum about this fleet to be sent against the slave trade. Sounds as if it could interest me.'

Fookes pulled back in embarrassment. 'Tiger, that's cabinet business as I'm bound not to give away.' He hesitated. Then his face cleared. 'But a fellow sharp in his own interest could probably work it out for himself.'

'So . . .?'

'Naught but a move by Liverpool to pacify the mobility, they having been stirred up so unconscionably by the Wilberforce speech.'

At Kydd's look of incomprehension he added, 'You probably didn't get the details in your rustic hideaway, but it was the usual polemic against the slave trade with an added sting. Now we're at peace it's thought there's a superfluity of men-o'-war floating about with nothing to do. Why not send 'em against the slave trade once and for all?'

Kydd shook his head in disbelief.

'Tiger, don't dismiss the angry voice o' the people in full cry – they're not to be denied. The fleet will sail.'

'Um, did they say who's to hoist their flag – which is to say, who will command this great fleet?'

'Command? Cabinet doesn't lower itself to such murky details, I'm joyed to say. This is rather the bag of your first lord, Melville. He's to return a complete proposing, including all those petty details.'

'Ah, yes.'

'I don't envy him the exercise.' Fookes chuckled. 'The fleet's all very well, but every jack tar worth his salt will be on his doorstep – you know it's for a full admiral's hat, prize money and all.'

'Prinker, I have to tell you now that's to include me, old fellow,' Kydd said quietly.

'Tiger – you?'

'How else can I hoist a flag? Every admiral that flies his now will hold fast to it until it's snatched away by the angels or devils. This is the only new placement reachable this age.'

Fookes hesitated and said slowly, 'M' honest an' true friend, know that this is a move of politicking, not against an enemy. Should you fail in any wise your fate will not be a kind one.'

'It calls for duty in a rousin' good cause. I'll not be wanting.'

'That I can believe, Tiger,' Fookes said warmly. 'But to go on the slave coast . . . It's a graveyard of the fever-struck. Should you—'

'What are my chances, do you think?'

'Um, not good I'm bound to say, Tiger. You're not a political animal and I'm sanguine this requires you to be much seen. I know not much more than a spit about your Admiralty and its ways. Its chief, Melville, is not a sailor but is well favoured in cabinet. Do you desire I tactfully ask him what he thinks of you?'

'That would be very kind in you, Prinker.'

If only Bazely were back but then this was all at an elevation the sagacious old sea-dog could not be expected to be privy to.

Chapter 43

Within remarkably short order Fookes came back with news. It was not good.

'Old fellow,' he began gravely, 'I'd put all thoughts of high-seas baubles behind you. I was right in the particulars.' He helped himself to some salted nuts. 'Melville's put sentries on his offices to keep away the hopefuls but, worse, it's turned ugly for him, being now a larger fight of the titans.'

'Oh?'

'The sainted Wilberforce has taken undue interest in the expedition, demanding the merciless extirpation of the ungodly while the plantocracy is hot to oppose any interference in its commercial dealings.

'So we have on the one, Wilberforce and his tribe, the Anti-Slavery Society, and on the other the planters with their West India Committee. Wilberforce has the public with him but the committee has something like seventy-odd MPs in opposition. Each wants to dictate the terms of employment of the fleet, and the character of its admiral is central to that.'

'And me? What does he . . .?'

'A mite difficult to plumb his sentiments, he all of dither with the whole affair but I can tell you it seems he looks kindly on your warrior qualities and undoubted rectitude but rather fears that the delicacy of the task is beyond you.'

Kydd's heart sank. With something like sick dismay, he mumbled, 'Then there's no chance for me, Prinker.'

'Well, he didn't say that. If I remember rightly, his very words were "not under active consideration at this time", old trout, he having so many names of note before him.'

'Names?'

'Tiger, I'm desolated to say that it would be a breach of confidence for me to reveal what was said on the matter, you'll understand.'

'I'll hear about it later, Prinker.'

'That's true. Well, without going into details the most attractive it seems is James, Earl of Conyngham. You may have heard of the gentleman, in naval service since the first, getting long in the tooth now, inactive since Copenhagen but with impeccable political and social plausibility. He's an MP and knows his ropes, you may be sure.'

Kydd vaguely remembered the man: wealthy, rather precious in his great cabin decoration and with a superbly practised personal manner. But a not unduly distinguished sea career.

'A keen churchgoer and well known to Wilberforce, his diplomatic skills would be seen as prime.'

'Any others?'

'More than you could shake a stick at, apparently,' Fookes said, with a wry smile. 'Oh, there's one you'll be sure to know – the Swedish knight.'

'Sidney Smith!'

'Just so.'

Memories rushed in. Acre, the incredible siege that had pitted a motley crew of sailors from Smith's squadron, including Kydd, against the battering hordes of the French Egyptian Army led by Bonaparte himself. He'd been soundly defeated, and fled the scene at the only occasion until then that he'd faced the British in open battle.

And Kydd recalled the petulant Smith at Duckworth's shambles of the Dardanelles, cannonballs six feet in size fired at his ship from giant guns and never even noticed. A complex, gifted man, always seemingly in the public eye, if Smith wanted the post there was little the relatively unknown Kydd could do.

'Then there's Dyer, Percival Dyer, the swell. Knows all the fancy and everyone he should – well in with the Evangelicals and . . .'

There were clearly others in the fray and it was becoming unlikely in the extreme that he would be plucked out from among them.

One morsel of hope was left.

'Do you think Mr Wilberforce would take my part if I met him?' he asked meekly.

'Dear Tiger, I don't think so – why should he?' Fookes said kindly. 'And, in any case, he'd say that if you aren't known for speaking your mind to the godless, you haven't the fire in the belly as would see you at the forefront of the crusade.'

They lingered over a brandy but Kydd's spirits were low and he made his excuses. It was now a lost cause, he had no earthly chance, and what was the point of staying any further in the capital at ruinous expense?

It was over – he would quietly take his leave.

Chapter 44

Ivybridge

The London coach at last clattered on the hard Dartmoor cobblestones outside the London Inn, the bray of the horn fetching out the ostlers and footmen. He was nearly home.

He was impatiently handed down, his baggage thumped out of the way against the wall. He entered the gleam of brass and comfortable smell of the tap room, acknowledging the precious few drinkers still supping there, and ordered himself a toothsome West Country ale while old John and his trap were summoned for the trip to Knowle Manor.

He picked up the local newspaper, the *Plymouth Dock & Herald* and went outside with his pint to the bench with its better light.

It was full of the usual gossip and Kydd relaxed in the balmy air. Turning the page he saw a familiar column.

Our intrepid spy, Lookout, must do his duty by his readers even in these parlous days of peace and so he hauls himself duteously up to his all-seeing crow's nest eyrie. He lifts his glass and peers about, far into the cryptic distance in his never-ceasing search for the curious and informative, and lights on the abode of Plymouth's Port Admiral at Mt Wise. There are flags and pennants a-flutter as if in frantic converse with the fleet, lying in idle somnolence below. It can only be the talk of the hour – a new admiral, summoned into being to sail a great fleet to darkest Africa to put paid to that meretricious tribe, the slave-traders. Lookout's own spies reported to him from the depths of Admiralty in London that there are many and varied contenders, chief of which is Captain the Earl of Conyngham, much cried up at court. Closing in for a broadside though is the famous Sidney Smith whose reputation need not to be rehearsed further in this column. And others – it is rumoured that even our own brave Captain Kydd is flaunting his honours before them in the hope that his will be the flag that proudly leads the fleet. As events unfold, as they will, Lookout pledges his close attention to allowing his readers the first . . .

Kydd put down the paper, a wave of desolation threatening his manliness, and went back inside for a consoling further pint but the sound outside of a hard-driven horse approaching stilled all conversation.

The unknown rider pulled up and dismounted. Seconds later the door was thrust open. To his astonishment it revealed a figure in the blue and grey of a dockyard messenger.

'Ahoy, m' hearties,' he threw into the room. 'An' where can I find Tom Cutlass? Got an urgent for 'im.'

'An urgent message for Captain Kydd?' stuttered Kydd, bemused at the use of his lower-deck nickname.

'Aye. Jus' came in b' telegraph from London isself.'

'I am he.' It came out more ponderously than he'd intended.

'Oh. Here y'are, Cap'n. Sign?'

In the pouch was a single folded sheet, a fair copy of the

telegraph message. It required him to present himself to the first lord of the Admiralty in person without delay.

What did it mean? The leaping suggestion that it was the best of news was quickly subdued by the knowledge that this was equally the wording given to those summoned to explain themselves after an unfortunate and particularly public spectacle.

Luckily, the return coach to London was due very shortly. It needed little effort to load up again and head back over the miles.

Chapter 45

The office of Lord Melville

'Sir.' Kydd took his seat before the grand desk, careful to tuck his sword clear of the legs of his chair. 'You asked to see me?'

'Yes, dear fellow, yes. I apologise for this unduly abrupt manner but I was caught unawares by your unannounced departure for the country, and we have matters to discuss. Do forgive.'

Kydd felt a lurch of unreality. All his other dealings with the first lord had been respectful and cordial but this was different. What was behind the friendly tone?

'Of course, sir.'

'You see, we have a crucial decision here at the Admiralty concerning the forthcoming motion against the slave-trading fraternity.'

'Sir.'

It couldn't be!

'Your name has been under consideration for appointment as flag for the enterprise for some time now, and I'm gratified to say that, after due consultation with my colleagues, it has been decided to offer the post to you.'

Kydd stiffened in shock.

'Should you accept, it would give me great pleasure to confirm you in rank as rear-admiral and desire you to hoist your flag with no further delay.'

'I . . . I . . . You're so kind, it's . . .'

'Do I take that as an affirmative?' Melville said innocently.

'Sir.'

'Then we shall discuss the details. Now—'

'If you'd be so good, sir . . .'

'Yes?'

'Why was I chosen when so many are more noted than I?'

'Ah. We'll be seeing more of each other so I'll be frank with you. If you're referring to Sir Sidney Smith, the answer is that he was too ambitious by far, desiring to change the object of the mission to heights not contemplated by their lordships. An international descent, no less, on the Dey of Algiers in the Mediterranean, with the goal of liberating Christian slaves, to the plaudits of the entire world.'

So characteristic of the man's hubris, Kydd reflected. 'Sir, the others?'

'The others, hmm – shall we leave it at that, Sir Thomas? Now, to details.

'It's intended to sail the fleet at the earliest possible opportunity and there's little scope for niceties. I'll be short with you. For certain reasons of state it's important that the fleet gets under way before very long, for which you'll be held responsible.'

In a bright fog of wonder and joy Kydd's mind raced and he struggled to come back to reality.

'Um, fleet?'

'Ah. Well, squadron. Its name is officially the Preventive

Squadron and will consist of two sail-of-the-line, two frigates and a number of lesser, to be decided.'

Hardly a mighty battle fleet but far greater than any slave-master could think to face.

'At the first we shall need a flagship, for which as Admiral of the Blue you have the first choice.'

He regarded Kydd mildly and waited.

Kydd was still breathless with shock, from contemplating professional ruin to being required, as an admiral, to making his desires known in this way. He forced himself to concentrate.

Flagship! One of those colossal three-deckers he'd seen at Trafalgar, an entire admiral's quarters of size and with its own stern gallery, ornate entry-port . . . Nearly delirious, his mind explored what it must be like, until the flights of fantasy were interrupted.

'Of course, a first-rate is not in contemplation, Sir Thomas.'

So *Victory* was denied him then.

'Rather a stout seventy-four, handy in tempest and battle, entertainments and impressive in presence. Have you . . .?'

'Sir, I would be more than satisfied to take up *Thunderer*, my present command – that is to say, as was.'

'No admiral's quarters? She's of the common class of seventy-fours – could I suggest a craft better equipped? I'm sure we have . . . Yes, there's *Centaur*. She has appropriate accommodation for a flag-officer.'

Centaur – Kydd knew her well. In a ferocious action in the Baltic he'd seen her take a Russian ship-of-the-line perilously close inshore at grievous cost in men and devastation.

With her other claims to fame she would certainly do as the first ship that would wear his flag.

'I know her from before, sir. She will suit me admirably indeed.'

'Good – you shall have her.'

Then, with a sharp pang, Kydd realised what he'd done. Nothing less than condemned dear old *Thunderer* to a mortal end. By taking her as flagship he could have sent her back into the bracing sting and surge of the open sea.

'Er, where does *Centaur* lie at the moment, sir?'

'Um, as I remember, in the process of being cast to ordinary in Portsmouth. I'm sanguine her company will be more than relieved to find employment in such a distinguished manner.'

It could have been *Thunderer*. Kydd crushed the thought and heard him continue, 'She will receive my early instructions to re-store for sea and make passage to Plymouth where she's to be fitted out as flagship of the Preventive Squadron. Do hoist your flag as convenient, if you will.' He meant after the appropriate papers and orders had been forwarded. 'I do believe that all this could be arranged in accordance with your wishes, Sir Thomas.' In some way the first lord seemed relieved, jovial almost. 'Meanwhile, we have your acceptance of the post and need to get certain procedures complete. You'll naturally wish to acquire the necessary dress and appurtenances due your station and prepare yourself for the command. For both our sakes a modicum of leave is indicated, I'd think.'

Kydd had a short time to get together a comprehensive list of needs and duties that would transform him into a sea-going admiral – and then there was his position aboard *Centaur*.

Melville leaned back amiably. 'And it would be gratifying to flaunt to the world my newest flag-officer. Admiral Kydd, would this evening be convenient? Say, Boodle's at eight?'

Chapter 46

In a daze of happiness Kydd stumbled from the office, oblivious to the looks from those not-so-fortunate petitioners below, into the bright noise and bustle of the street.

He had to tell someone – the passing pie-seller would probably not appreciate that he'd just encountered one of those heaven-born entitled to fly his flag and rule all men-o'-war under him on the high seas.

There was one he wanted to confront with the news and he made his way in haste to Brooks's.

Prinker Fookes was standing by the fire. A peculiar expression played on his face causing Kydd to hesitate.

'Ahoy there, Admiral,' Fookes purred.

Still in his full-dress captain's uniform, Kydd gaped. 'How the devil . . .?'

'Ha. And who would have smoked it.'

'Prinker,' Kydd said, with slight annoyance, 'I'm fresh come from the first lord of the Admiralty with my flag under my arm. How did you—'

'Saw it coming. No – heard it coming.'

'Prinker?'

'You're famous now, Tiger. The story's even this very hour rushing out to the streets.'

'Tell, damn your blood!'

'Well, as I was told, it's yet another meeting of the manning advisory committee. There's an unholy roar about who's to lead the fleet, those of the Wilberforce blood agin the plantocracy. Passing by is old Jarvie – the Earl St Vincent, bless him. He hears and rages in like a bull, bellowing to all who would hear and many who'd wish they couldn't, something like "To hell and damnation with all your souls! Who dares to tell the navy how to run its ships?" and orders 'em to their faces to find someone without a taint of politics in his veins as the only being worthy to take the tiller. Someone like Tom Cutlass . . .'

Kydd reddened with pleasure. The crusty old earl sailing into battle on his behalf. The world was now turned on its head – to the exalted plane of existence that he now inhabited and where he would find his being for the rest of his life.

Chapter 47

Ivybridge

'Mama – look! Isn't Daddy pretty?'

In the bedroom trying on his full-dress admiral's uniform, Kydd looked fondly at his child from what seemed such a height. The serried rows of glittering gold lace and epaulettes with their precious star told the world that all the majesty of a flag-officer was arrayed before them.

'Francis dear,' Persephone said firmly, 'your father is an admiral now and this is what he must wear.' At the news of his mission to the slave coast, Persephone had been concerned but supportive, she being an admiral's daughter.

Kydd looked in the mirror. It felt odd to be back in kicks – knee breeches – after near a dozen years in pantaloons. And in these highly polished light pumps, so light and flimsy with their glinting buckles, how would he stand a-brace the quarterdeck in anything like a blow?

He fastened his fighting sword and clapped on his tall cocked hat with its cockade and even more elaborate gold, remembering too late that admirals wore theirs athwartships.

And then, one eye a-squint, he snarled, 'Avast there, m' hearty, an' tie me a bowline!'

Francis fell back in terror, clutching his mother.

'Thomas! You should be ashamed of yourself!' Persephone scolded, but her shining eyes and adoring look took the sting from her words.

Kydd doffed his hat and sword and picked up his son, kissing him, which he knew would vex the little man but bring him back to a countenance.

He was well on with the instruction he'd been given to prepare himself as admiral and flag-officer. The dress was the easiest – there were many tailors in Plymouth vying for the honour of rigging out a new-found admiral.

More to the point was the social aspect. That an admiral was quartered in their midst was a wondrous event for the good folk of his parish but he had to show himself for it to have any meaning. As a local squire he had duties – as a sea-going admiral he had many more.

Should he introduce himself to the port admiral in person or fall back on the delicious fact that he was a sea-bound admiral with all the independence that implied?

His flagship, *Centaur*, was on her way from Portsmouth, without doubt her company diverted by the knowledge that a new admiral would board and impart his presence and puissance over them when they cast anchor in Plymouth.

He'd been there not so long ago, as a post-captain taken in fear and expectancy at the prospect of a new admiral with everything that implied – orders, eccentricities, dignity, expectations. And now he was the object of this naval transition.

His official orders arrived with commendable promptness. Melville clearly wanted him on his way as soon as practical.

Sir – His Majesty having been pleased to order a promotion of Flag Officers of his Fleet and my Lords Commissioners of the Admiralty having in pursuance thereof signed a commission appointing you Rear-Admiral of the Blue Squadron known as the Preventive Squadron, I have the honour to acquaint you herewith . . .

It was the authority he needed to hoist an admiral's flag. Later there was another:

By the Commissioners for executing the office of the Lord High Admiral of the United Kingdom of Great Britain and Ireland, etc. You are hereby required and directed to repair without loss of time to Plymouth and hoisting your Flag on board His Majesty's Ship Centaur *at Cawsand Bay to there remain until you do receive further orders . . .*

He hugged the wording to him, especially the 'most humble and obedient servant' that ended the instruction, signed by Croker, the first secretary to the Admiralty – an augury of his new status.

Chapter 48

D ressed in his splendid new uniform, Kydd boarded the open carriage that wafted him to Plymouth. He'd received word that *Centaur* had arrived and had let it be known that he would be boarding his flagship that forenoon.

The Sound was overcast and the seas choppy but Kydd was in another existence. 'Stonehouse Pool,' he ordered the driver.

The journey didn't take long. Handed down, he quickly spied his waiting boat.

It was similar to his captain's barge in *Thunderer* – but much more splendid. He admired the embroidered awning, even if it was of little use, given the grey skies. Neatly rigged from four brass gunwale stanchions, it was restricted to the after end. And there were cushions, curtains, all manner of other comforts due an admiral. Blank-faced, he took his seat.

They drew alongside *Centaur* and strange faces appeared – characterful, strong, individual.

No doubt he'd get to know them before long. Or would he? An admiral would never stoop to chatting with lowly lieutenants, let alone barge coxswains, unless on formal inspections. With a poignant twinge Kydd realised he'd progressed so far through the ranks that he was now all but out of sight of those who were once his shipmates.

Like those under Nelson, who, too, had started his sea career before the mast as an able seaman, they'd shared the same enduring values and qualities of the seamen who manned England's ships.

Centaur was proudly at anchor in Cawsand Bay among a number of other sail-of-the-line, yards squared to perfection, a large red ensign at the taffrail in token of her unattached voyage from Portsmouth to join Admiral Sir Thomas Kydd's squadron of the Blue. He could make out a side-party assembling, and prepared himself.

In absolute silence, broken only by the bump of their alongside below the side-steps, he stood, grasped the red velvet covered manrope and hauled himself up.

Precisely as his hat became visible to the upper deck, five boatswain's calls split the air with the cadence of a piping of the side, his first such as a flag-officer.

He gravely doffed his hat, turned aft and acknowledged the quarterdeck before pacing forward between the inward-facing lines of the side party where at the end waited the one he assumed to be the captain of *Centaur*.

'Sir Thomas? Captain Tippett. You are most welcome aboard.'

'Thank you, Captain.' Kydd felt for his orders inside his waistcoat and pulled them out with a flourish. At this moment *Centaur* was this man's ship and in the next, after Kydd had declaimed his rights to the assembled multitude, Tippett would be flag-captain to an admiral and under his orders.

Both men knew what had to happen and waited a pause

188

as in the stillness, far above at the mizzen-mast truck, a small bundle was jerked free and a blue flag floated out on the breeze. At that precise moment a gun thundered out – the first of thirteen in salute to their admiral and notice to all the world of the fact that *Centaur* had been imposingly set above them all as a full-blooded flagship.

How far had young Tom Kydd of Guildford come in life!

Centaur's officers were introduced – their tallies would settle later but he did make a point of asking that the sailing master and boatswain be named to him, a request that would not be lost on the rest of the ship's company.

Admiral Kydd was then graciously conducted to his quarters – gleaming and spacious. He dared a sniff – every ship had its own individual smell, compounded by its experiences, but this was a not unpleasant new-timber underlay. It told him instantly that it had been the captain's practice to sweeten the bilges nightly by pumping out and then refreshing from the sea, preventing the sometimes foetid pickling effect of long-lying bilge water.

The quarters followed the usual pattern of a great cabin the width of the ship, and with a stern gallery, but the space was notably empty of furniture. The same with the bedplace but he was agreeably struck with the peacetime absence of guns in both compartments.

When Tippett quietly appeared, Kydd informed him he would take residence only after domestic arrangements had been satisfactorily completed.

This would include a personal valet, quantities of servants, not to mention a flag-lieutenant to be found on-board accommodation by the as-yet-unknown first lieutenant, in addition to an admiral's secretary and any other staff creatures that would be wished on him.

*

Persephone was at her best in these circumstances, quietly finding her way aboard and making the acquaintance of the first lieutenant and through him a hard-bitten petty officer and five men detailed to assist in her task of outfitting the admiral's quarters.

Kydd left her to it. His time of liberty was nearly up and he was due at the Admiralty to collect further orders.

While there he'd make very sure that he learned as much of the art of admiral-ship as was possible and also choose himself a flag-lieutenant.

A manservant was another matter. Binard had returned to the bosom of his family and his wines, no doubt with tall Gallic tales of life as a prisoner-of-war of the English. To find another with his panache, suitable for the majesty of an admiral, would be difficult.

He'd ask for recommendations.

Chapter 49

London

Melville was distracted, able only to give him the barest minimum of time. Enough to enquire of Kydd's health, readiness for his flag and an assurance that he would sail the Preventive Squadron at his earliest convenience. It left Kydd free to seek out his objectives, most of which were satisfied in one.

'Dear fellow!' Admiral Essington boomed, eagerly rising from his armchair to greet Kydd, whom he'd first known as a smoke-blackened young seaman in *Triumph*, when the frightful carnage of the battle of Camperdown had died away. He'd then sent him on his way as an acting lieutenant to the quarterdeck.

'Sir!' Kydd said, sincerely touched that his hesitant note asking for a meeting had been returned instantly with the demand they get together that very day.

'Huzzahs of the heartiest on your elevation, as we must all allow.'

And in the next hour or two Kydd hoisted in what was lying ahead for a new admiral.

Servants. In a splendour born of another age he was entitled to the princely number of fifteen, a figure wildly more than Kydd could think what to do with. The secret, it seemed, was to ship the bare Admiralty minimum, five, and quietly sequester for himself the wages of the rest. The more useful part of his retinue, the secretary and his clerk, could then be entered as servants on the ship's books, their pay incremented as desired and the three left over would be found useful employment.

He was expected to entertain, on occasion lavishly, but for this purpose he was allowed 'table money', yet another allowance, all of which added up to a sizeable sum.

He should expect to be feared rather than loved, to spread dismay and terror wherever he appeared and not to seek out any who could in any wise be accounted a friend for fear of favouritism – to be left perfectly alone therefore in all he did.

His territory was the quarterdeck only. The rest of the ship would be unable to function if it were thought that an admiral was lurking beyond the next bulkhead. Even the wardroom as the repose of hard-worked officers was forbidden him; his princely quarters would also be his prison.

A mere word from him was regarded as if spoken from God, not a soul in either the ship or fleet able to gainsay it. It was a power that even the King of England did not possess. It also meant that it had to be the right one or it would hang about his neck for ever.

Essington unexpectedly smiled. 'Kydd, don't despair, old chap. There's ways past this, too.'

And as it was explained, he began to understand much of what he'd seen in the past. An admiral had one great solace. It was not only recognised but even expected that the great man would have his quirks.

The flagship would quickly fall in with any odd desire or

behaviour and, within the limits of sanity, the admiral could do anything he wished to entertain himself.

It left interesting possibilities.

There were many more polished gems of advice that Kydd was careful to note down but the most precious was Essington's grave advice concerning the Admiralty.

Kydd's god-like powers inevitably lapped below the ramparts of the most holy but if he was at one with their thinking he could in the main rely on a quiet approval of his conduct. The catch was that in foreign seas he was weeks, even months, away from communications with their lordships: should any unforeseen crisis loom and his handling of it was not to their liking, their displeasure would later be made known.

Professional matters, such as the signal code in force with the squadron were still his to decree, but he would do well simply to adopt what had gone so well before, as with the complexity of the fleet Fighting Instructions, which in the circumstances was prudent.

'My flag-lieutenant?'

'Many new-stranded ashore after their admirals have been superannuated, you may take your pick. Could I suggest a strapping young fellow, eager to please, from a good family and with experience in the post?'

'Do you happen to know . . .?'

'I'll find one for your approval. You'll also need a damn good secretary as possesses a sound headpiece to sort the wheat from the chaff as to what crosses your desk. Not so easy but for the same reason there's a quantity of these gentlemen sculling about. I've one or two in mind. Shall we meet at my club tomorrow eve and you'll cast your eyes over 'em?'

*

Melville was in a better mood when Kydd came to him for a final meeting. Yes, he could have *Topaze* 32 as one of his frigates and, yes, *Melampus* 74 was even now on her way from Yarmouth to join. The rest of the unrated vessels were specified and had been ordered to make their way to the squadron anchorage in Plymouth in the near future.

Kydd hugged to himself the thought of his old friend Bazely in *Topaze* receiving stern orders from on high to sail his frigate and place himself with all dispatch under the orders of none other than Admiral Sir Thomas Kydd for an immediate foreign-going commission.

The prospective flag-lieutenant, one Augustus Lovett, took his chair gingerly, a handsome young man with a fashionable quiff of hair at his forehead. Kydd warmed to him immediately, his youth and animation, even as he disclosed that Kydd would be his second admiral, following service on the North America station, now approaching a shadow of its former self.

His table manners were faultless, and discreet probing revealed that he was a younger child of an ancient Warwickshire family and could well be relied on in questions of protocol and formality.

He would do.

The potential secretary, one Ralph Dicken, was another matter. Older, showing a tinge of grey and with studied manners, his cautious solemnity was quite the opposite. More mature, and with experience at one time with a commander-in-chief, he was unquestionably qualified but would Kydd, with his open ways, get on with this man's reserve and discreet bearing?

What decided him was his response to questioning. The replies were careful, considered and, even when pressured, never hurried.

Chapter 50

Plymouth Sound

It was time to get to work.

Back on board *Centaur* Kydd was greeted with transformed quarters. Persephone had done him proud and they
were fit for a potentate. Now secure in their affairs she'd not
stinted to produce fitments of the very finest – sideboards
of dual purpose, a demountable table with extensions, and a
splendid carpet to dazzle the eye.

His bedplace stateroom could bear comparison with that
of a country estate, were it not for the gimballed cot with
its patent self-lowering tackle, much to be preferred in any
kind of sea.

There was a personal provision-room for his private delicacies. And all about him, evidence of a woman's touch,
perfectly executed miniatures of herself and Francis, larger
wistful pieces of the Devonshire countryside and pleasing
decorations and ornaments.

It was palatial.

'Come!' he called in response to a discreet knock.

'Sir Thomas.' It was Tippett.

'Oh?'

'While you were at the Admiralty a person of some quality did make mention to me that he believed you to be without a personal valet of distinction due an admiral. Having served in that capacity himself he petitioned me to allow him to pay his respects to you with a view to—'

'Very well. What is his name? Sankey? Do produce him then, Captain.'

The man entered as though to a throne room and bowed. 'Sir Thomas? Should you be in want of a manservant at this time I find I'm in a position to oblige directly, sir.'

The voice was throaty and low but the man's bearing was magnificent: calm, statuesque almost, and with a dignified gaze. He was dressed plainly but well.

'You have a character with you?' If his previous employer had not seen fit to equip him with a certificate of good service that was the end for him.

He passed across a carefully creased paper.

'Vice Admiral Codrington,' Kydd noted, impressed. A fussy, wealthy and pettifogging creature.

'Sir.'

'And you're able to start in service as of this hour?' It was asking a lot but Kydd knew that unless he got the domestics out of the way at the rush it would make trouble for him later.

The requisite details were settled and he was set to stowing Kydd's baggage.

'Captain Tippett, I desire to see something of *Centaur*. Would you be so kind . . .?'

He was in civilian plain clothes and it would be clear to officers and crew what he was doing this once. A quick acquaintance with his flagship and he would then revert to inhabiting only his own quarters.

Centaur had been specially fitted for a flag-officer, most of whose flagships were three-decker first rates with the whole of the middle deck aft set aside for their apartments.

For a 74, a two-decker, other arrangements had had to be made. In effect, Kydd's quarters occupied the space on the quarterdeck aft under the poop-deck, normally in a 74 where the captain had his being, with the wardroom on the deck below on a level with the men's mess-deck.

As they descended he saw what had been done. The entire wardroom had been shifted forward by just enough to afford a remarkably capacious captain's suite, much of a size with what he would have had on the upper deck, a firm bulkhead preserving his privacy from the wardroom.

Kydd was fascinated. Both spaces were the same capacity as before, the only difference being that the captain had sole ownership of the old-style decorated stern windows. He was further impressed when he saw that a passageway, rather like the carpenter's walkway leading along the side of the ship, was provided that enabled the captain and his visitors to move to and fro hidden from the private spaces of the wardroom.

The rest of the ship from his hurried sighting was much the same as other 74s, such as *Thunderer*.

He returned to his cabin to find it squared away, and with the first touches of domesticity. Sankey stood there politely, a cloth over his arm, and had changed out of his breeches into a creditable version of a sea-going butler.

'Sir, you'll appreciate in order to discharge my duties to your entire satisfaction it would be better I learn your inclinations in the matter of . . .'

'Certainly.'

His preferred times for meals and, indeed, his preferences in food, time of rising, presence of servants, all the rest of his daily habits were duly passed on.

By the evening his life was in an acceptable form of order. Gear stowed, dress laid out, a single glass of whisky perched primly in the exact centre of his compact side table – and ahead the evening with its solitary dining to digest the day.

It had already been noted that he was an early riser, attuned to the dawn and its attendant weather, never far away in a ship.

After a good breakfast Kydd set out his day. Feeling increasingly confident, and more like an admiral, he rang his silver bell and, on cue, a servant appeared. 'Desire my secretary to attend on me at nine.'

The man bobbed and disappeared. Where did they go when they weren't needed?

He had the great table set to its smaller configuration in preparation for the meeting.

Dicken knocked quietly and slipped inside the cabin without fuss. Seeing the table, he sat without comment, placing a notebook and loose leaves expectantly in front of him.

'Ahem.' For some reason Kydd felt uncomfortable, conscious that in a peculiar way he was on trial as much as his secretary. 'You've taken up quarters in your cabin satisfactorily, um, Dicken?'

'I have, Sir Thomas, with my clerk Fredericks.'

That would be the cabin handily close over to the larboard side, forward of Kydd's quarters.

The man regarded him calmly, not saying a word. It was somewhat unnerving.

'I've called you here . . .' Kydd realised this was not a good opening – an admiral didn't need to explain himself.

But there was a mountain of answers he needed before he could function in an intelligent way. Where were the confidential papers stowed? Was Dicken up to the latest code transcriptions? How could he discover Kydd's private circumstances in order to handle personal correspondence with discretion?

He could not ask such questions outright of the man, or reveal his profound ignorance of the plethora of accounts and transactions now his to deal with as reigning authority.

With time pressing Kydd decided he'd make a start and let it develop as it may.

'Er, I mean to muster up all vessels in my squadron here present and inform them of a captains' conference on Friday forenoon.'

To his surprise Dicken made no move to jot down the order or to acknowledge it – just the same patient, poised attention.

'Well?' Kydd snapped, with sudden impatience. If he had to spell out the implications of every order . . .

'Sir,' his secretary said gently, 'do you not think that more properly directed at your flag-lieutenant?'

He was right, of course. Kydd frowned but a small smile of embarrassment escaped, to be returned with a fleeting, almost shy grin.

He was human – and Kydd was going to trust him.

'Mr Dicken, I'll remind you I'm a new-minted admiral of days only and I'd appreciate a steer in many things as are unknown to me.'

The rest of the morning was spent in putting order and structure into their relationship and preparing an admiral's office for the fray to come, not the least of which was the quiet discovery of strengths and weaknesses on either side.

He dealt with the flag-lieutenant in another way. 'Mr Lovett, do find somewhere quiet and render me a written account of how you see your day.'

In a short while Kydd had in his hands a detailed list of duties of a flag-lieutenant, which could now be meshed with those of his secretary.

Within days there was a pleasing tidiness and system in place and Kydd began the monumental task of opening the books on his Preventive Squadron.

It was tiresome. In some instances the work appeared pointless and others required a great deal of effort for little reward. Halfway through the morning Kydd left Dicken to it, and walked out to the brightness and breeze of the quarterdeck.

Men froze, others scurried off, but he was getting used to this and turned aside to take in the sights of Plymouth Sound. It was a fine day, glittering breeze-ruffled seas, and he breathed in the bracing fresh briny air with relish.

This was what it was to be a sailor – not to be shut away with dreary paperwork all day.

He went to the ship's side and glanced down. Further along, a lower boom was rigged outwards, where the ship's boats were secured, clear of sight of his stern gallery. A launch, two cutters and pinnace – and a jaunty cock-boat bobbing with them, a gig and the smallest carried aboard.

Two thoughts came together in a flash of inspiration. The first was Essington's shrewd advice: it was no sin for an admiral to have quirks. And the other . . . He spun on his heels and raised a finger at the motionless group around the helm, the current watch-on-deck.

Instantly the worried officer-of-the-day hurried over to him. 'Sir Thomas?'

'Have the jolly-boat rigged for sailing, manned by a lieutenant and crew of midshipmen.'

'Aye aye, sir,' the officer blurted, although clearly confused. Kydd didn't care: it was not unusual for a flag-officer impulsively to demand some action to exercise and test the mettle of a ship's company.

Kydd frowned. 'At once, sir!'

By the time he'd shifted his dress into a nondescript mariner's sea rig, the boat was hooked on alongside, to all appearances ready to face the waves. Pale, anxious faces looked back at him, turning by degrees to expressions of horror when it became clear that he was about to board the little craft.

Like all warship boats there was a plain but heartening sturdiness in its build and, even more pleasing, an odour of canvas and Stockholm tar that spoke of the sea.

The lieutenant was older, suspicious but manifestly a seaman. Kydd thought he recognised the first lieutenant. 'Mr Cawley?'

'Aye, Sir Thomas.'

'Take this boat in a circular motion about *Centaur* at a distance of one cable.'

'Sir. Let go forrard!' he roared.

Sails unbrailed, the main hauled out and they were free to sheer away in a wide sweeping curve. Cawley snarled at the forward hand and the unfortunate midshipman fearfully shrank out of sight but he'd wisely put the strongest at the sheets and his brisk handling at the tiller was rewarded.

It was thrilling to take in the big 74 from so intimate a perspective and Kydd warmed to the sight. However, all too quickly it was over and they secured to the lower boom. His mind was made up.

But just as soon as he reached the deck he was waylaid by Tippett, shocked to be caught out at tea by a zealous admiral.

'Sir Thomas, if you'd directed me before—'

'A fine body of midshipmen, Captain Tippett,' Kydd said quickly, 'who I see are well instructed in their profession.'

'Th-thank you, sir.' As flag-captain he was completely at the mercy of his flag-officer. This was craven fear.

'I do believe it a sovereign cure for afternoon lassitude in the young and therefore am requiring you while at moorings each day to provide the jolly-boat rigged for sailing ready at the lower boom at noon.'

'A lieutenant . . .?'

It was asking too much of the hard-working officers to give up their leisure time so Kydd said indifferently, 'Not necessary, Captain. I shall take the tiller myself.'

Quirks – as easy as that!

Returning to his cabin to change back into the majesty of the greatest officer aboard he noticed Dicken hovering, standing before him when surely he had yet more documents to put in order.

'Ah, Sir Thomas.' He seemed perturbed, excited almost. 'Can I speak to you?'

'Why, hasn't that what we've been about all morning?'

'Sir. Sir – I didn't know you were a – a sailing gentleman as we must say.'

'I'm supposing that is a fair description,' Kydd said, amused.

'Sir.'

'Please get to the point, Mr Dicken, we've much to do before evening.'

'Sir. When I began my secretarial studies I had the choice of army or navy. I've adored the sea since a bantling and chose the navy in which I've served above a dozen years but never – never, sir – did ever I taste the sea! The physical, corporeal reality!'

He gulped, his eyes shining. 'Always in a vast flagship or

admiral's barge – and I see you today as naturally as a swan taking wing for wherever your spirit moves you.'

Kydd didn't know what to say. This was a vastly different creature from the one he'd been immured with. 'I'm not sure I follow you. What do you—'

'Sir Thomas, I beg you – do allow me to go with you. I shall not incommode, I do promise.'

Kydd was amazed at the transformation of the quiet, steady secretary into this eager fellow. 'I regret there can be no passengers, Mr Dicken.'

The face comically fell.

'So if you were to accompany, you would be required to pull your weight as one of the crew – foresheets, perhaps.' Kydd hid a soft smile. He'd got through to the man – and hopefully could look forward to sharing confidences as time went on, as he had with secretaries of old.

It was as well: his squadron was increasing by the day from all over the kingdom, and apart from the need for closely figured orders and the inevitable admiral's inspections, it was all building up to that most glorious of events: taking his very own fleet to sea.

Chapter 51

The Tyrrhenian Sea, early spring, 1815

T he Elban sloop *Inconstant* stank of bilge and overcrowded humanity. In his tiny cabin below decks Moreau, until the war had ended for Napoleon Bonaparte, a very senior adjutant-commandant in the Imperial General Staff, felt claustrophobic and chilled by the cold.

He was much moved by the emotional burden of his mission. For the first time since those long months ago when he'd accompanied the emperor into his direful banishment to Elba he was going to visit the great man. He'd been ordered to leave him to his fate, told his sharing of miseries a waste of a talented life, perhaps to return in the spring, if he so desired.

And here he was, on his way from Leghorn back to Elba with a baggage of the best delicacies to be found in the South of France and a heart full of pity.

What would he find? A broken half-man, a piteous shadow of the world-striding colossus he'd once been – with whom he'd shared so much imperial glory and defeat? It promised

to be the hardest thing he would have to endure in this existence and he shrivelled within a little more.

His mind wandered back to that voyage into ignominy –
the inexpressibly wretched hours in an English frigate just
weeks after Paris had fallen and the captive emperor speedily
dispatched to a cruel exile. To do so under the triumphant
colours of the enemy had cost Bonaparte much, and then to
arrive at such an ignorant and uncivilised land to spend the
rest of his life mocked as the grand emperor of a tiny island.

Unbidden the images of those times rose yet again, as in
his imagination he relived those dark and pitiful days . . .

It was spring, 1814. The early-morning quarterdeck of HMS
Undaunted was busy, the frigate preparing for her arrival in
Elba some time that day. Seamen squared off, ran lines along
the deck and becketed up gear while her captain, arrayed in
his finest uniform and sword, stood by the helm, the group
at the conn subdued and wary.

Moreau had stayed by the mizzen shrouds where he'd
been since the funereal boarding from the last soil of
France, Fréjus, halfway between St Tropez and Cannes.
Unnoticed by any, he was left to his thoughts. He had every
right to retire to his family estate but had vowed to follow
his master. Still in the threadbare uniform that last he had
worn on the field of battle, he was now carrying out his
resolution.

Quite unaccountably the industrious activity around him
slowed and stopped. Then everyone from the captain down
stood stock still, gazing at the hatchway.

A figure was slowly emerging: Emperor Napoleon
Bonaparte.

From the newly risen sun a low beam of sunlight caught
his face and he blinked in bafflement at the glare. Then,

clapping on his bicorne and pulling his grey redingote tighter against the morning chill, he stepped out on deck.

Nobody moved, seized by the reality of the man who had dominated Europe and had now fallen as far as it was possible to go.

Moreau's heart wrung. Visibly exhausted, his corpulence more noticeable and the lines deeper, Bonaparte nevertheless thrust his arms behind his back and began a measured, dignified pacing about the deck.

Contemptuously ignoring the watchers, his features grim but firm, he moved on. One by one activity resumed until it was as it had been before.

There were snatched sly looks, and the four Allied commissioners stood together forward in open curiosity but not a soul dared approach the lone figure.

The sun rose higher, a slight chop setting in, but the pacing continued.

And then there was a sudden cry from aloft.

Moreau's poor English made out the word 'land' but it caused no flurry of action. In fact there was no land ahead that he could make out in any direction.

The figure paced on.

Of course, Moreau realised – from the sailor's height above the deck he was seeing over the curvature of the earth. He bore himself in patience until hands were raised to point out a thin, rumpled blue-grey line on the horizon.

Moreau went quietly to the only officer he could recognise, the captain. '*Monsieur le Capitaine de Vaisseau, est-ce que cette terre . . . Elba?*'

In schoolboy French he received the answer that this was correct.

Moreau approached Bonaparte and waited respectfully.

Stopping at last the emperor rounded on him. 'What is it, Old Crow?' he asked, clearly distracted.

'The land that lies ahead, sire. It is Elba.'

Bonaparte stiffened. Slowly he turned and gazed out over the waters and, for a long moment, held the sight, shielding his eyes against the strengthening glare of the sun. Then, without a word, he turned on his heel and went below, leaving behind a breathless silence.

Robbed of their diversion the seamen returned to work and the hum of conversation again took the air.

Eyes filling, Moreau didn't notice a form appear beside him.

'Général Moreau?' he was asked gently. It was one of the British commissioners whose name had escaped him. The man's French was passably good.

'*Oui.*' Moreau pulled himself together in a manner to be expected of a holder of the Légion d'honneur.

'Campbell – Colonel Neil Campbell. Sir, I cannot but notice your evident distress. You have known the emperor long?'

'Since His Majesty first took the field as a paramount leader of the French, sir. Since Marengo,' he added defiantly.

'A famous victory to the cost of the Austrians,' Campbell observed drily.

'You are a soldier.'

Campbell shook one leg painfully. 'As has left me with a souvenir of Fère-Champenoise a little earlier this year.'

Moreau smiled in embarrassment. In this particular battle from which he'd helped extract Bonaparte before an over-whelming Allied advance but a sudden rainstorm had put paid to this last-ditch defence of Paris.

'I'm sorry to learn of it, Colonel. Yes, I'm desolated to witness the straits to which *Sa Majesté* has been subjected. Think on it – master of the civilised world reduced to this.

Commander of millions and now a paltry hundreds of infantry. High admiral of hundreds of the line with now a navy of a single brig, ruler of half the earth now to rule—'

'My friend. Do believe it could be much more severe. If the Prussians had their way your master would have been ceremoniously and instantly shot. If it were the Austrians he'd have been hanged high and equally ceremoniously in some Tyrolean Schloss, while if it were the Russians he would answer for his burning of Moscow in the vilest manner.'

'But instead we are prisoners of the British.'

'Not at all. I am a commissioner, true, but all this means is that I and my colleagues jointly must satisfy the Allied Commission that the great fellow is safely and securely immured in Elba.'

'Sir. Why Elba? Why must it be such a God-forsaken island?'

Campbell scratched his head. 'Sir, I cannot answer you with facts. My situation is too lowly. But perhaps as a soldier I can satisfy you. An island. If confined on the continent he would – do forgive my direct talking – he would act as a focus for all the disaffected and rebellious to flock overland to his banner. In an island I would very much like to see who might seek to pass any ring of iron the Royal Navy sees fit to throw about it.

'On the other hand, to be ruler of an island is its own guarantee of permanence, for his realm must end at the shoreline, no marching across the border to extend an empire.

'And not a foreign territory and distant? This has the distinct merit of placing the gentleman within easy distance for the purpose of scrutiny and inspection. And corrective action if need be.'

The logic was faultless – Napoleon Bonaparte would thus be monarch of Elba and remain there until he died, as therefore would Moreau.

'Thank you, Colonel,' Moreau said humbly. 'That was well put.'

Some hours later Elba firmed into view. An undistinguished scrubby coast, dashed with the dark green of pines and ever-green oaks, and inland, bare grey bluffs and ridges. Past the first headland it nevertheless opened into a sizeable harbour.

This was the main seaport of Elba, Portoferraio, an ancient walled town, which was the drab cluster of buildings on the inner side of an extensive enclosing arm. There were a few ships alongside at the wharf but in the lazy sunshine the sprawling waterfront gave an impression of ageless apathy.

The emperor was still out of sight below, but Moreau knew he wouldn't be thanked for telling him that if he came on deck he'd be able to take first sight of his kingdom.

The frigate glided in cautiously, reducing to topsails. 'I'll anchor, I believe,' the captain rumbled, eyeing the untidy length of waterfront. The anchor tumbled down from the bows and the frigate came to a rest. He turned and looked meaningfully at Moreau.

It was time for Napoleon Bonaparte to step forward and claim his realm.

But this was a momentous event and could not be hurried.

On the one hand the new King of Elba would want to land with due ceremony. Was a reception being planned? Did the inhabitants even know that they'd been chosen for the honour?

And on the other there was the very real possibility that in the wash of patriotism so soon after the end of the war there might be resistance – assassination attempts, even. Was it wise to send Bonaparte into the unknown?

An advance party? It couldn't include himself or any other Frenchman for that matter, or any officers from *Undaunted*. Then who?

The commissioners would stand to lose much if there was a scene, threatening the safe landing of Bonaparte.

'It places me in a strange position, Général,' Colonel Campbell said stiffly, when he was approached to go ashore. 'As you can see, I have no authority in the matter.'

Excusing himself Moreau left and returned quickly with a small package.

'Sir, this is the King's Letter by which His Majesty expresses the authorisation for his dominion in the land. Be so kind as to place it in the hands of the civil power.'

Unsaid was the need to discover whether or not to risk the life of Bonaparte in a vainglorious gesture that might very well end in tragedy. If that occurred it would unquestionably resound around the world and all present would be blamed.

Agreeing, the captain ordered away a boat under a lieutenant, and a set-faced Campbell disappeared ashore.

It wasn't until evening that he returned with a weary smile. 'There will be no revolt or scenes, my friend. Mayor Traditi and his town council are in a spin of excitement at the honour done them and theirs, and have spent tiresome hours arguing over the nature of their welcome.'

He shook his head in disbelief. 'To see the squabbles as to how high the triumphal arch must be, who shall bow first, where shall stand the ceremonial altar – a consummate moil.'

He grinned. 'It was then agreed that they should surrender the keys of Portoferraio to the Emperor Napoleon but none could be found. So the town clerk was summoned to yield up the keys of the largest civic building, the Palazzo Municipale. But these proved small and paltry, throwing the good folk into a tizz. Fortunately they were delivered of their plight by the night watchman who handed over the stout black-iron keys to the town wine cellar. As we speak they are now being handsomely finished in gold paint and tomorrow the King of Elba shall accept the wine-cellar keys as a token of his possession of the kingdom.'

Moreau had the following morning to prepare the new king.

Napoleon Bonaparte chose to array himself in the uniform of the *chasseurs à cheval* of the Imperial Guard.

At the last minute it was discovered that no flag of the King of Elba existed but His Majesty was prevailed upon to design one – a white flag with red diagonal bearing three golden bees. Working frantically, *Undaunted*'s sailmaker produced one in time and a small flotilla of every boat the frigate possessed set out for the shore.

In the lead was the launch, with a file of impeccably accoutred Royal Marines. Then, the captain's barge, in a fair imitation of a regal conveyance, Bonaparte sitting rigidly upright under a borrowed canopy displaying his royal colours.

It was closely followed by the pinnace, Moreau and the four commissioners wedging into its sternsheets. Bringing up the rear the longboat and gig carried as many of the kingly retinue as could be packed in.

Boats of every description began closing in, the gawping occupants taking their fill of the spectacle and obliging the launch to force a passage through them.

At last the Emperor Napoleon, King of Elba, stepped on to the soil of his realm.

In a breathless hush from the crowd Mayor Traditi diffidently conducted the ceremony of the golden keys. After graciously accepting, Bonaparte moved in procession to the Duomo di Portoferraio for thanksgiving.

At the Hôtel de Ville he met the waiting notables of Elba and, with the greatest civility and elegance, exchanged a few words with each.

The day ended in a warm evening, but when Moreau politely enquired where the emperor would be laying his head he found only confusion among the worthy councillors. In the agitation and fluster of the discussion of triumphal arches and speeches no thought had been given to this and once again they met in emergency session.

Thus it was that Napoleon Bonaparte, king and emperor, spent his first night in Elba in none other than the dusty municipal offices of the town hall, in the civic meeting room on a camp bed, while attended by his devoted valet Marchand and a dozen liveried servants.

But soon Moreau saw how the emperor was suffering. After the absurd events of his ceremonial welcome and the series of grotesque contrasts he drew into himself, a black depression taking hold.

Moreau agonised for he'd heard that, soon after abdicating, Bonaparte had made at least two attempts at suicide and now there was wild talk that he expected to be rescued at any time.

Campbell recognised his condition and made it his personal concern to engage the fallen emperor in military talk, sharing informed reminiscences from both sides of past battles and French glory.

He and Moreau explored the heights above the town for any stately house or estate that could serve as a king's palace. They found one – the Villa dei Mulini, well above the noise and squalor of Portoferraio. Two storeys in a yellow finish with green shutters, it had a most attractive feature: there was a view not only on to the town and harbour but, on the other side, the limitless expanse of the Ligurian Sea, somewhere across which was *la belle France*.

And then Bonaparte's mother arrived to look after him.

Madame Mère, as she was to be known, was an active, autocratic and exacting lady, who moved into a nearby residence and took charge without delay.

Relieved, Moreau tried to suggest diverting occupations for the past ruler of half the world. Elba was a poor, small island but it had a new king who now needed to lay down laws for his kingdom.

And there was his beloved army. At only six hundred veterans of the Imperial Guard, a detachment of Polish lancers and irregulars quartered at the edge of the town, Bonaparte never tired of inspecting, exercising and marching them in imitation of the millions he had wielded not so long before.

His navy consisted of the brig-sloop *Inconstant*, a crew of sixty Elban seamen and a broadside of just nine of the smaller carronades. After a single visit to the ship, however, Bonaparte lost interest and found other matters to attend to.

Unexpectedly, a rather shabby French general appeared from the interior, General Dalesme, who commanded the garrison in two small forts over by the harbour entrance.

The man was in a degree of mortification for, as one of the forgotten outposts of empire at war's end, he'd received no orders or direction of any sort, let alone concerning the arrival of Napoleon Bonaparte himself.

Elba was Tuscan, seized by the French in 1802 but, on the liberation of conquered territories at the end of the war, how did it stand now? And a King of Elba: did this make the island a sovereign and separate nation, neither French nor Tuscan? If so, was it neutral or did it ally with one side or the other?

The general had troubles enough without these distractions. His garrison was pathetic, most of the French long replaced by untrained Elban militia, but it would still stoutly stand to arms if ordered. Yet on whose behalf? This self-same Bonaparte was the one to whom he'd originally sworn allegiance, who had placed him here in trust to safeguard the empire. At the same time it had to be accepted that his devotion now had to be to the Bourbon King of France, Louis XVIII, who would most certainly frown on any relations with the previous despot.

He decided to retire behind the walls of the forts until things became clearer.

Sometime later in a tiny cove of many in the lonely southeast of the island a boat crept ashore. In it a young veiled woman was carrying a child. She was met with every motion of secrecy, led up the steep bluffs to a deserted hermitage in a grove of chestnuts and concealed there.

This was the Countess Maria Walewska and she had been Napoleon's mistress. Now, in the absence of his wife, Marie-Louise of Austria, she sought to accompany him in his exile.

Bonaparte received the news with shock and delight and, in the night, hurried to her side – with the greatest discretion for Madame Mère would most certainly not approve.

In a day or so Moreau saw a transformation and, with mixed feelings, wiped away a tear as Bonaparte told him to return to the bosom of his family, his duty by his master now done.

Chapter 52

Moreau looked out over the balmy sea as his mind came back to the present. Now he would discover what remained of the great emperor he'd parted from those long months before.

He'd left the man grasping for anything that might keep him in touch with the world he knew, and had not departed until Bonaparte had assured him that his duty was done. But after he'd returned to France he had discovered that the one love of his life he knew still held Bonaparte in thrall, Joséphine, had sickened and died at Malmaison just two weeks after he'd been taken into lifelong exile.

That he could rise above the torrent of adversities afflicting him so grievously was more than could be expected of any man and Moreau prepared himself.

Elba appeared to him just as it had then, nondescript scrub and bare hills, with a wide harbour opening up around the point, and he waited patiently to disembark.

The Elban brig *Inconstant* had been slow on passage and with a cramped and cockroach-infested cabin the trip had been far from pleasant, but now they were coming alongside the government wharf at last.

The close-mouthed coachman on the way to the Villa dei Mulini – now dignified as the Palazzina dei Mulini – allowed that the king was well and often to be seen about the island, but beyond that could say little.

Moreau kept his business to himself and before long they'd topped the rise and drawn up outside the yellow washed building, impressively cleaned and improved, builders apparently still at work inside.

'To pay visit to His Majesty,' he told the servant, passing across his card but from behind a familiar figure appeared.

'Sir, it's Général Moreau, is it not?' Marchand, Napoleon's valet, asked.

'It is. Is he . . .?'

'Why, sir, this is the Palazzina, the public seat of the king. It is under improvements. His Majesty has a private residence.'

'May I believe he's, er, well?'

Marchand gave a warm smile. 'You shall find out for yourself, sir. He will be pleased indeed to see you again.'

The Villa di San Martino was quite unlike the sun-touched Italian styled Palazzina. A stern, porticoed edifice in dark stone, it was also busily under renovation.

Marchand went in ahead and, after only a short time, emerged with a familiar figure. Moreau's heart skipped a beat: advancing on him with arms wide in welcome, was Emperor Napoleon Bonaparte, his liege *seigneur* of more than twenty years.

Moreau bowed low and was swept up in an unrestrained embrace.

'Old Crow, you came to see me, you rascal!'

This was a different man from the cruelly lined, burdened

soul he had seen face the end of his dominion with such dignity.

His features were smooth and serene, his body held bolt upright and dressed in plain green with pantaloons and stout top-boots, almost casual and spontaneous. His expression was mild and engaging, eyes bright and amused.

'It pleases me immensely to see Your Majesty in such fine fettle,' Moreau said softly, with another bow, 'as is my assurance that he is nobly and auspiciously bearing his durance.'

Bonaparte gave a satisfied guffaw. 'Not such a burden, Moreau. I've the time to set the island to rights, get it in some sort of shape fit for an emperor. Would you care to see it?'

Moreau recognised the old impulsive ways and secretly smiled. This was the Napoleon Bonaparte he knew.

A swiftly summoned open carriage ground up in a flurry of gravel and, with Moreau still in his travel garments, they were borne off.

There was no question. Portoferraio had been greatly improved. There was now an avenue of sorts leading away from the Piazza Lungone, the main square, in a straight line inland, admirably suited to martial parades.

Many other roads had been paved, widened and straightened, but Moreau was most impressed to learn of a hidden but effective drainage system against summer storms that lay beneath.

On the way to the iron-ore mines he learned that, besides a municipal code of impressive detail, there was now a tax system to support health measures and impose control over maritime trade.

The mines dated back into the prehistoric past when Elba had been a major producer to the ancient world. Now Bonaparte was seeing to their industrial development, the purity of the ore ideal for the forging of the larger species of artillery.

Bonaparte beamed at Moreau's obvious admiration. 'You'll stay in San Martino, in course.'

'That is most generous of you, Your Majesty.'

'I do hope your business does not call you away too soon, Old Crow. I've heard my sister Pauline is to visit me shortly and I would so like you to get to know her.'

'Just so, sir.'

'And tonight we shall sup together. Not in a field tent on short rations I promise you,' he said, with a chuckle.

The repast was served in a sumptuous banquet room that would not have shamed an English duke. Under the candle-light it was warm and convivial but held only three – Madame Mère on her son's left, Moreau to his right.

Their host still retained his campaign habit of eating rapidly and with his fingers. What other unthinking relics of a warrior past were there still? Moreau wondered.

'We regret that Colonel Campbell cannot be present,' Bonaparte said archly. 'He's in Florence having his leg treated. Stays with his "cousin", the Contessa Miniacci, who, we may understand, is more in the line of a . . . comforter.'

It chilled Moreau to hear it. Not the casual divulging of a confidence but the proof that Bonaparte had already a network of informers out there in the old style.

'Old fellow, what I'd most wish to hear is what you can tell me about France. Under the detestable Bourbons, how does it fare?'

It was said rather too eagerly. Was an enthusiastic condem-nation of his supplanters called for, or a rather more balanced picture such as before when he'd provide forthright appraisal of the battlefield?

Moreau considered for a moment and decided to tell it as

he understood it. 'Sire, society is riven. The old regime are the *arrivistes* now and are resented. Many fear that the Bourbons will demand property be returned to them, their previous owners, and that the positions of power will soon be taken by returning idle aristocrats over those of talent. As well, the Church is returning to secure its influence over the people.'

'The king?'

'Louis le Gros? A vapid, timorous creature unable to control his lackeys and incapable of enlightened rule. It's thought that he's naught but a puppet of the Allies and that France will live ignobly in subjection for evermore.'

Napoleon's eyes hooded but he made no comment. Then he looked directly at Moreau. 'The army. How does it in these times, pray?'

'Sir, as you'd conceive, garrisons in far places, never having tasted defeat, being told to lay down their arms and march back to barracks, not understanding why. Most thrown on the streets to exist how they may and the worst . . .'

Moreau was having difficulty keeping the bitterness at bay.

'The worst, sire, is the fate of the prisoners-of-war,' he continued thickly. 'Released out of the gates of their prison with naught but the rags they stood in to straggle up to a thousand miles back to Paris. And there . . . and there to be despised as beggars and thieves is their reward.'

He could have added more – the contempt and hatred that seethed beneath the surface everywhere he'd been, the arrogance of the returning nobles, the feckless spending on restoring symbols of the *ancien régime* and the moral cost of the toadying necessary to achieve any kind of position.

Bonaparte glowered sightlessly away for some time. Then, with a visible effort, he faced back to Moreau and became a charming host once more.

'A glass with you, Old Crow – to times past, *hein?*'

Chapter 53

A week later a commotion at the seafront signalled the arrival of an honoured guest for the emperor. It was La Principessa Paolina Borghese, otherwise known as Pauline, Bonaparte's younger sister.

Moreau stood clear of the rapturous welcome she was given and it wasn't until later that he made her acquaintance at the villa.

She was every bit as he'd heard her to be, beautiful, and with a sexual charge that could be intimidating. Married to the Prince Borghese, she'd been rumoured to take her pick of a stable of lovers.

Moreau could well believe it for, even as he was introduced, the twitching fan and fluttering eyelids were at work.

Vivacious, animated, and adorned with the latest fashion, she could fill a room with laughter and delighted chatter, and Moreau felt the whole mood of the Palazzina lightening.

'You will be visiting long, m' lady?' he asked politely.

With a fond glance at her brother, she answered sweetly, 'As the emperor makes decree, I believe.'

*

In a whirlwind of engagements she swept up the social scene – even the staid Colonel Campbell was affected, often to be seen in the circle of admirers who followed her everywhere.

While she attended at court Moreau saw that his master seemed happily settled in his situation and it was probably time to take his leave of the great man.

He found it difficult to broach the subject for, in all probability, they would never meet again and he fell back on trying to compose a farewell note but the words wouldn't come.

Despairing of the task, he heard footsteps approach and a soft knock at the door.

He opened it to see a blank-faced Marchand. 'The emperor desires that if you are at liberty at this time it would oblige him greatly should you attend on him.'

This was not the usual kind of summons into the imperial presence and his senses snapped alert.

They passed down the outside path to a small pavilion where Bonaparte was wont to pass the time taking snuff while leafing through old campaign accounts.

It was also a place well suited to any privy exchanges and he entered cautiously. Pauline was sitting at the table opposite her brother, looking ravishingly lovely but with an unbecoming frown in place. Between them were scattered some papers and maps.

'Sire?'

'Dear Moreau, I've explained to Pauline that of any on this island there's only you I can truly trust with any confidence.'

'Majesty.'

'You see, she has brought more to Elba than her wit and beauty. Much more.'

Money? News?

'Old Crow, she has brought me hope!'

Baffled, Moreau waited.

'These papers could be the means whereby I shall be set free of my chains to reclaim my rightful empire.' There was a sudden energy and tension in his manner.

'Before embarking on the venture I desire you cast your eagle eyes upon it – I will not stir until you declare it possible. Will you do it?'

A plot to set the emperor free, even to wrest back his legacy. Either a ham-fisted and under-resourced rebellion or, on the other hand, a cunning and rapier-like move while the Allies continued their ill-tempered bickering?

'Sire, of course I will do this for you.'

'Very well,' Napoleon said, in a sudden deadly tone. 'We three are the only ones who know of it and it must be kept so. Pauline as my relative requires no pass from the Allied commissioners to land on Elba and will act as my courier. All we need now is your appraisal and we start the planning. Agreed?'

While the two sat back impatiently Moreau read the papers.

They were from Joachim Murat. A flamboyant but brilliant cavalry general given to acts of insane heroism but unthinking impulse, he was also remarkably vain, glorying in theatrically ornate uniforms, the pomp and glitter of high command.

Married to Bonaparte's sister Caroline, Murat was now family, and had been made King of Naples. It had gone to his head and, after the catastrophic battle of Leipzig, he'd agreed with the Allies that, should he not dispatch troops to the desperate Bonaparte, he would be allowed to retain his crown.

This betrayal had embittered Bonaparte and estranged the family, but here was a plot apparently instigated by the man. Aware of the eyes on him, Moreau read and reread its substance.

It was simple enough. If the emperor could contrive to

cross to the nearby Italian coast, Murat would muster his entire cavalry of forty thousand horse to come rapidly to his side and openly declare for him.

Within a short while word would spread and frustrated veterans from far and near, by their hundreds and thousands, would flock to the banners well before the Allies could think to react and reconstitute their previous battalions.

From there, a triumphant march on Paris, with overwhelming numbers, would be the crowning act. The metropolis would be ready with its welcoming crowds, anxious to throw off the canker of Bourbon rule and raise Napoleon Bonaparte back to his rightful throne.

It was a daring and beguiling vision and, despite himself, Moreau felt his pulse quicken. Nevertheless there were many questions to be answered first.

'Not impossible,' he found himself saying. 'But guns? Field kitchens for the march? Baggage trains?'

'Ha!' Bonaparte leaned forward in his intensity. 'Our first move is to march on Rome. This is in sovereign French territory and I'm sanguine my old comrades will quit their barracks and stand by their eagles as in the old times – guns, equipment, all I'll need for a swift and conclusive campaign.'

Further on there were the great plains of the north where a vast army could grow quickly into a military juggernaut and, with a speed of march for which Bonaparte was well known, the whole business could be over very soon.

In fact it was looking possible. The shores of Italy were less than a day's sail away – even Naples could be reached within a couple of days.

'Then I conclude, sire, that there is every chance it could succeed . . .'

The frown left Pauline's face and Napoleon sat back in ill-disguised satisfaction.

'. . . providing certain points are settled.'

'Say on, Old Crow.'

'How certain are we that the King of Naples will ride to your side when you land? If he does not, you're helpless, left to the Allies to lay hold of and banish to a far worse internment.'

'The vain peacock knows the Bourbons can at any time demand his crown for themselves,' Napoleon said, with a cynical snarl. 'And he needs to secure it. It's clear that in my triumph this will be so, but even more he wagers that in my gratitude for liberty I will be generous in the matter of spoils of war.'

It made sense and undoubtedly Murat as King of Naples had at his command regiments of untouched soldiery to call upon to form an immediate nucleus to the host.

'Any further . . . objections?' Napoleon asked silkily.

'Just one, and this threatens to end our venture conclusively.'

He hadn't meant to let slip the 'our'.

'Oh?' There was a touch of impatience, of imperial displeasure close beneath the surface, and Moreau proceeded carefully.

'Sire, as so often to the hurt of the French nation we find that we're beset by the might of the British Royal Navy, who at this very minute have no doubt a ring of iron set around us. To remain undetected at sea, even for hours, is too much to expect of the Fates.'

'You forget one thing, M'sieur,' Pauline threw into the gloomy silence. 'We're not attempting to send ashore an army – only one man who must make the immortal journey, and if he cannot be concealed in some way then I pity our cause!'

'Do I take it we have a plan, Old Crow?' Napoleon asked lightly. 'Or not?'

Chapter 54

Moreau could not shrink from the implications of what he was about to do. His old imperial overlord needed him and he could not refuse, but it meant therefore that he was now guilty of rebellion against the lawful sovereign of France, King Louis XVIII, and if discovered he would suffer the consequences.

The escape of Napoleon Bonaparte from his exile would echo around the world like a thunderclap. The rapid massing to his colours of an untold horde would strike fear and terror into the Allied camps. With soldiers sent home, navies laid up and all the delicate cross-national command formalities dissolved, it would be far too late to come together to prevent the return to glory of Emperor Napoleon Bonaparte.

Unless, in the initial critical period of the break-out for Italy, he was stopped, intercepted by the Royal Navy or even the French – Bourbon – Navy, which had been seen occasionally off Elba.

Constrained by the vital need for secrecy, Moreau knew he must work on his own, stitching together a foolproof procedure, faultless in its detail while the emperor continued his public appearances and acted as though nothing was afoot in the sleepy seaport that could interest Campbell or others.

Leaving aside the crucial smuggling out, there was more familiar territory to deal with. The constitution of the avenging army: everything from campaign maps covering northward to command structures flexible enough to allow rapid growth. Murat would want a glamorous and ostentatious leading position, but what of the individual divisional or even regimental commanders? Battles – wars, even – had been lost to incompetents or weak-willed leaders.

Moreau would leave that to Bonaparte and concentrate on other business, the usual complexities of artillery-company deployments, provision for the wounded and supply-train requirements when numbers to be served were unknown.

But before all that, of the utmost importance, he must verify that Murat had indeed the military assets he claimed, else the whole affair would collapse before it began.

A spy must be dispatched without delay, a reliable and sharp-witted agent, who would as well be in a position to spell out precisely and in detail what the King of Naples could field when the time came.

He found Bonaparte scratching away furiously and realised that it was not only himself who was working all hours.

'Sire?' he asked softly.

The emperor raised his head and looked at him coldly, in the old way that no longer intimidated him.

'I need assurance that the King of Naples has indeed at his command what he alleges. First-hand knowledge would be gratifying.'

The cold look eased. 'Already in train, Old Crow.'

'And, dare I say it, have we specie of some kind as will be payment for fodder, victuals, other? The men will answer the call to arms but without . . .'

Bonaparte got briskly to his feet. 'Come!' he commanded, and strode to the far side of the room where his library still remained in its packing chests. 'You see?' he said, throwing open a lid revealing learned books, which had not been disturbed, full to the brim in neat piles. Moreau selected one – the Montaigne essays, in their original middle French.

Then his eyes strayed down. Beneath the empty slot he could just make out rows of silken bags, lying snugly together. As he picked one up it gave out an unmistakable heavy chink. It was full of gold francs and he supposed that beneath the rest of the 'library' there were many more.

The weight of the chests would be put down to the heft of books in bulk and there would be little incentive for casual theft.

Now remained the most vital part: the furtive crossing to the mainland. With their hidden resources they'd have no difficulty in bribing a passage but the risk of being boarded and taken by the Royal Navy was near impossible to ignore. With scores of warships, from battleships to war schooners, just out of sight circling the island, there was no reliable solution.

Frustrated to a degree, Bonaparte paced up and down, like a tiger in a cage, but while the campaign formed tidily on paper no practical first move suggested itself.

Chapter 55

Some days later in the calm airs a ship-sloop lazily eased into the harbour. Three-masted and of a class that in the French Navy would be termed a corvette, it was a Royal Navy ship-of-war, often taken as a miniature frigate.

Wondering the reason for its presence, Moreau wandered down to the waterfront and took in the trim, purposeful lines. Seamen were coiling down ropes, squaring yards to perfection and looking to a fine harbour stow.

On impulse he mounted the brow and, on her quarterdeck, was stopped by an officer. 'Sir, your business?' He was a pleasant, open-faced young man marked with authority.

'Ah. Your good ship is pleasant to the eye, sir. I'm M'sieur Moreau on the staff of the King of Elba whom you will understand as being the Emperor Napoleon Bonaparte. I've a marked desire to see more of her.' His English was rusty but seemed to pass muster. The mention of Bonaparte he could see had gripped the officer's attention.

'Commander Adye, and I would be pleased to conduct you on a tour of my vessel, *Partridge* ship-sloop.'

'You are very kind.'

'Hoping that I might be granted a sight of the great man himself – at a distance, naturally.'

'I'm sure that could be arranged, Commander.'

It was an investment well worth making, for by the end of the visit he'd learned a very great deal. The vessel would not normally visit these parts but had granted an indulgence passage to Commissioner Colonel Campbell at Leghorn and would be leaving shortly to resume her cruise of the western Mediterranean.

But the morsel Moreau hugged to himself was his innocent query concerning the boredom that went with a continual circling of the island as part of the ring of iron.

Adye hastened to assure him that there was no such ring of iron and instead his cruise agreeably took in the north parts of the western Mediterranean with its many diverting Italian and French ports. It emerged that the powerful Mediterranean fleet under Admiral Pellew had been drastically reduced and was therefore unable to provide the protective cruising it once did.

The impression Moreau gleaned was that there was no formal guard patrol and Campbell was only in a position to request aid should there be unrest or similar on Elba where the fallen despot lay in despair.

This was entirely a different situation: with only the friendly *Partridge* to be expected at sea, and she shortly to weigh for Genoa, the risk had been drastically reduced.

The escape planning intensified. A ship was selected, a Genoese brig trader of the commonest kind with the usual Customs hidey-holes. It would sail innocently alone at night the trifling fifteen miles to Piombino on mainland Italy. There, the emperor would step ashore and hasten to the interior plains where Murat would await him.

A tense excitement grew, and it was now only a matter of

time and the final piece in the jigsaw: the covert but firm commitment by Murat to begin the enterprise.

Several days later Princess Pauline slipped away on a mission to bring back this crucial pledge.

Chapter 56

Early the next morning Marchand diffidently approached Moreau. 'Sir, he does insist and is most stubborn.' Behind him was a sullen figure, a barefoot Corsican seaman with colourful sash and bandanna. 'Says he has important news for His Majesty but will not declare what it is. I told him there'd be no audience with the emperor for the likes of him.'

'*Où nidifie l'aigle?*' Moreau said carefully. It was a courier challenge from the last stages of the war.

'*Où aucun homme ne pourrait suivre,*' came the reply correctly.

'Dispatches, or verbal?'

'For the ear of Napoleon Bonaparte only,' the man stated flatly, in execrable French, folding his arms.

'I am his deputy, you may inform me.'

The man remained silent and hostile but, for some reason, Moreau felt it was important to follow through. The seaman was taken into an anteroom to be searched, then brought before Bonaparte.

'Sire, this man claims news for your ears only,' Moreau announced.

Bonaparte, at his desk, looked up stonily at the man, who

was taking his fill of the sight of probably the most notorious figure of the age. 'So?'

The man hesitated then crossed to a table and, from his shapeless Mediterranean bonnet, extracted a tobacco pouch and emptied it. He retrieved a very small square of paper and handed it to Bonaparte, ignoring Moreau.

Bonaparte smoothed the tightly folded single sheet and read aloud:

'We, the chief citizens of Orléans, do desire herewith to extend our condolences to our Emperor in his exile and pray that his ordeal is diminished even in so small a part in receiving this, our homage . . .'

'A brave expression of loyalty,' Moreau murmured.

'And unsigned,' Bonaparte said sourly. There was nothing in the document that could incriminate any person in Orléans of a treasonable utterance. He thrust the paper back at Moreau.

'Pay?' The seaman held out a well-creased hand.

The paper was thick and elegant, the calligraphy first class, but something triggered a ghostly thrill from the past. Impulsively Moreau snapped to an alert and rapped, 'Clear the room! All leave if you will!'

It left him alone with Bonaparte, who smiled wolfishly. 'What trickery is this, Old Crow?'

'A candle will soon tell.'

Positioning it at the centre of the desk, Moreau looked at him intently. 'You'll take down the message, sire?'

'Of course. Know this isn't the first clandestine message that has passed by my hand.'

'Majesty. This may not be your common lemon juice – if it's kitchen soda and the juice of grape it will show only the once and then be gone for ever.' This ensured that it could never be used in evidence later.

'Then march on, Old Crow.'

Reversing the paper Moreau positioned it at a distance over the candle. Very faintly pale brown lines began to appear, spreading as he carefully held it.

'Are you seeing the message, sire?' He had to keep the heat equally over the sheet: if it was soda-based and the heat died, it would fade and disappear for good.

'I have. And interesting it is indeed,' he whispered, in something like wonder.

It was nothing less than a declaration that, should Napoleon Bonaparte raise his eagles on the soil of France, some of the most powerful military figures in Paris would rally to his side bringing their disaffected battalions with them. It was boldly signed by names that resounded from of old. It was a courageous – and possibly desperate – act.

In effect it told Bonaparte that in France a significant proportion of its army was prepared to join his colours, if he was there to lead them to prevail against the hated Bourbons. It was not a serious prospect, of course. Bonaparte had no invading army and Italy was not the soil of France. Further, the very real plot that was developing with Murat had much more potential, even if it was more protracted.

'What do you think?' he asked.

Moreau told him of its practical impossibility and added that, while it seemed to ensure the key to the city of Paris when they arrived, it was the Murat plan they should concentrate on.

Bonaparte said nothing, his face a mask. Moreau decided discretion was called for and, making his excuses, left.

Chapter 57

In the early afternoon Moreau was called for again and found Bonaparte pacing energetically to and fro as in the old times before an intricate battle.

'Ah, Old Crow, I've made my decision. Now hear this. I don't trust Murat further than I can spit. Far better to put my fate in the hands of my loyal countrymen.'

'Sire?' There was no concentration of anti-Bourbon sentiment that he'd heard of close by.

'I shall make landing somewhere in the south, and let the people come to me. Then we shall march north on Paris and, with the aid of those stout loyalists, I may then regain my throne and honour.'

Moreau was appalled. 'Provence is royalist, sire. You'll be arrested on sight and taken in chains to the Bastille!'

Bonaparte's lips thinned. 'Have a care, sir. You saw that pledge. I have but to raise my sacred standard and the citizens will give me an army.' He eased slightly and added, 'Besides, I have my Elban army – and navy.'

Staring at him in consternation, Moreau stammered, 'Majesty, you cannot be serious! Six hundred of the Guard, a detachment of Polish lancers without horses and the rest mere militia – not far above one thousand! The population of a small village – and no guns! We'd stand to be encircled and wiped out by a single regiment.'

Bonaparte stopped pacing and turned to give a cold glare. 'Moreau, recollect to whom you're talking. It is my imperial decision, after careful deliberation, and looks to loyal Frenchmen knowing what is right for their country and duly rising to the colours. If this is something you don't understand let me release you from any further obligation to service.'

Moreau bowed but said nothing. It was wildly improbable. There would be risings among the few who heard about it but they'd be greatly outnumbered by those who saw fidelity to the Bourbons as the safer course. And the credit for seizing the rebel emperor in his insurrection would be irresistible to most.

'Then we tell Murat to stand down?' he said quietly.

'No. Keep the brazen fool on edge until we have our triumph, then watch him beg.'

The pacing began again until Bonaparte stopped and, with a tiny smile, said impishly, 'Then you're game to stand with your emperor in his great gamble, Old Crow?'

Chapter 58

In the utmost secrecy plans were put in place for the earliest possible descent.

Much consultation of maps dictated their route – a landing at the closest point of France to Elba, somewhere between Nice and Cannes, followed by a march around the fringes of the Alps to Grenoble and then directly for Paris.

This time of the year would see the mountain passes still under snow, but leaving it too long would waste the best campaigning weather later in the interior, and who knew when the climactic confrontation would come to pass?

In scale the mounting of an expedition of a bare thousand men was nothing like that of the colossal armies Moreau had dealt with not so very long ago. He soon had the requisite tables and lists to hand for everything from victuals to powder and shot.

An invasion fleet was put together: the Elban Navy brig *Inconstant* and an assortment of six feluccas, small lateen-rigged trading vessels only just sufficient to carry the emperor and his force, with minimum rations. As a precaution *Inconstant* was painted in the famed Nelson's chequer to disguise it as a cruising Royal Navy sloop.

Tension mounted. Improbably, it was all looking possible and the last arrangements could be made.

Timing was everything, chiefly the movements of the only remaining commissioner, Campbell. He had to be kept ignorant of the plot unfolding under his nose, which implied the last acts had to take place with him off the island.

After nearly a year on Elba, Colonel Campbell had become thoroughly bored and was spending more and more time with the Contessa Miniacci in Florence, making shameless use of *Partridge*. When the sloop called at Elba to convey him to his latest tryst Bonaparte and his band would take it as their signal to flee: it guaranteed the absence of commissioner and warship.

Chapter 59

One morning, in wan sunshine with a light, fluky breeze, *Partridge* made her way slowly into harbour. For her, the view was much as it had always been: a lazy waterfront, the odd morning tradesman and, further inland, the Imperial Guard in fatigues doing nothing more military than planting a second row of trees before the town hall.

Without ceremony Campbell hurried aboard to disappear below. The vessel set sail and departed.

Instantly, the scene ashore burst into activity. All sentries, replaced by Elbans, joined the line of men transferring stores and materials to boats out to *Inconstant* at anchor offshore. With just two horses and two light guns there was no need for elaborate loading procedures. Well before evening the soldiers had returned to their barracks and the sounds of the *retraite* drifted down on the sleepy town.

At nine, well after dark, troops noiselessly wound down the main street and, with minimum equipment, embarked in boats for *Inconstant* and the smaller ships. It was expected to take the best part of the night and Bonaparte ostentatiously retired.

To onlookers it was fairly clear what was going on. There'd

been a recent insurgency of some kind in one of the smaller Elban islands to the north and they were about to suffer a surprise descent, which at that level had nothing to do with their emperor.

And in the morning the King of Elba was seen about to lay supplication at the chapel of the Misericordia, a private visitation requiring that his route be cordoned off by garrison soldiers. General Dalesme left it to a subordinate, having decided that he was not interested in anything to do with Napoleon Bonaparte.

In minutes the emperor, well wrapped against the chill morning, had taken boat and, in a short while, was being welcomed aboard *Inconstant* by her captain, Lieutenant Taillard.

'The weather?' Bonaparte grunted, squinting at a grey haze at the horizon.

'Fair to calm, Majesty,' the older man said evenly. 'As I'd say too calm for my liking.'

'All the way to France?'

'Sire, it's only a couple of days' sailing, a little more if this calm persists. I see no reason to fear it worse.'

The anchor won and yards braced round, the brig took up the slight south-easterly and made for the open sea.

Moreau caught his breath. In the face of all that stood against him, Napoleon Bonaparte had escaped Elba. It was now a matter of winning through to the other side of this alien element and the adventure could begin.

Away from the land breeze their progress diminished to a lethargic ripple. Bonaparte's impatience grew and he blurted, 'And all the time the English are combing the seas while we float about waiting for them!'

'Majesty,' Taillard soothed, 'while we suffer they do so as well. They're out there somewhere and also are going nowhere in this calm. We'll make it through, sire.'

A chill breeze picked up in the early afternoon and *Inconstant* made better way, the smaller transports bunching astern as if they were ducklings eager to stay with their mother.

Bonaparte did not leave the deck. Frowning and silent, he stood unmoving, his gaze firmly ahead as if expecting France to emerge at any moment.

The ship's bell clanged, there was disciplined activity on deck as the watch was changed, and still Bonaparte stubbornly kept his watchful station.

And then came a cry from the masthead.

A man-o'-war had been sighted off to the starboard bow, to weather. Had it seen them? If it had, it meant that, upwind, it could race down on the unwieldy flotilla with flight impossible.

Every telescope was up, waiting for it to come into sight at deck level.

'Majesty, I'm sorry to inform you that she's seen us and has hauled her wind to come down on us.'

'What will you do, Taillard?' Bonaparte asked quietly.

The captain was unable to answer. If it were the usual course of events he would decide whether to stand his ground and fight or cravenly flee.

With the Emperor Napoleon Bonaparte aboard, any action that put the man in peril of a man-killing broadside was unthinkable. On the other hand to attempt to make off would in effect be an admission of guilt.

That left only one thing to do. 'We bluff. Hold our course.' He lifted his voice and roared to the deck in general, 'Down! Every man not on watch, lie down on deck!'

His apologetic glance at Bonaparte was answered with a sour grin before the emperor lay down elegantly to await the outcome.

In the freshening breeze it wasn't long before the distant

warship had come into view and shown its colours. These were not English but nearly as menacing. It was a naval ship well enough – Bourbon French, and with a very clear duty.

In a pretentious manoeuvre it swashed around until it was running along with them a hundred yards apart, the glint of telescopes on its quarterdeck an indication that they were under close observation.

Taillard recognised the sloop. 'She's *Zéphir*, thirty-two-pounder carronades,' he muttered. 'We wouldn't stand a chance.'

The blare of a speaking trumpet came over the swash of their wakes. 'What ship, where bound?'

'*Inconstant*, a resupply run from Genoa.'

Now would come the demand, with a shot across the bows, to heave to and be boarded.

Oddly there was a pause and then, in a different tone, a baffling question. 'The Man – is he well?'

It took some moments before Taillard realised what was happening. 'He's never better!' he hailed back. As an Elban vessel *Inconstant* would know if anything was amiss with the famous exile.

There was a pause. Then, with a jaunty wave, the sloop paid off to leeward and took up on a diverging tack. They'd been discovered but spared a stop-and-search. Taillard suspected that, as with many Bourbon men-o'-war, *Zéphir*'s secret allegiance was not to their king but to Bonaparte and they had every reason to be concerned about his health.

Even more likely something about *Inconstant* had given away that they were about the emperor's clandestine business. Possibly *Inconstant*'s attempt at disguising herself as a British ship with a Nelson chequer.

Clear of Elba and its offshore islands, course could now be set direct to the north-west and the French coast. In the open sea *Inconstant* picked up speed, pleasing in its eagerness to touch at France and deliver its fabled cargo.

When sail was sighted again to weather and altering towards, it seemed so unfair. No merchant ship would take time to investigate another so it had to be a warship.

Familiarity resolved her identity from afar and it was not welcome news. The English ship-sloop *Partridge* was on a cruise and the lords of the sea would take no nonsense. They could outrun the bigger vessel and there would be no sympathy with their purpose.

This was the beginning of the end for the whole adventure. Taillard could only order everyone flat on deck again and wait for the inevitable.

Chapter 60

Aboard HMS Partridge

Captain Adye was alerted to a scatter of ships in something like a convoy, not something he'd expect in peace-time. He was duty-bound to investigate but with Commissioner Campbell on board, expecting a rapid passage back to Elba, it was exasperating. Fortunately, the good colonel was below, as usual, in the throes of seasickness.

He raised his glass. A brig-sloop was in the lead with half a dozen smaller craft in a haphazard gaggle following. It flew no flag but it was not unusual for captains in the open sea to save wear and tear on expensive bunting.

Then he took notice of a peculiar fact: the sloop was painted with a Nelson chequer, but he knew that there were no British ships at sea in this part of the Mediterranean. No doubt this was a French royalist vessel: an increasing number, in open admiration of the Royal Navy, were decorating their ships in like manner.

And the convoy? Probably nothing but a routine supply

run to an outlying garrison with the humblest of escorts against the Barbary pirates that still roamed in these parts. Relieved, he grunted orders that had *Partridge* falling back on her original course to Elba.

The rest of her passage was uneventful, baffling light head winds delaying her arrival, but Campbell was on deck as soon as the calmer inshore waters told him his time of trial was nearly over.

Impatiently, he waited while the ship rounded to and anchored, lowering a boat to take Captain Adye and the commissioner ashore.

'That's odd,' remarked Campbell, as they neared the jetty. 'See? The sentries are properly posted well enough . . . but they're all Elban, no French that I can see.'

It was a mystery but didn't concern him. There was really only one thing that did, and as soon as he was landed he found the officer of the guard.

'Where's the king?' he asked sharply.

'His Majesty? Um, I believe he's out riding in the mountains, Commissioner.'

'And will be back when?'

Confused, the officer stammered, 'I'm not to be made privy to his movements, sir. I cannot say.'

Cursing under his breath, Campbell stumped up the hill to the Palazzina. Around him the people were going about their business in their slow fashion. All seemed serene and untroubled.

Perhaps he was making too much of little things but then again the door only opened on the third knock and it was not Marchand who answered.

'I demand to make audience with the king,' he rapped. 'Find him.'

'Oh, sir, he's in town inspecting the works to the Liguria road. He'll be back soon.'

Two different stories. His senses pricked. Could the unthinkable have actually happened, that the most notorious figure in the civilised world had broken out, escaped?

Frustration building, he wheeled about and made his way to one who would know the truth, Princess Borghese.

'Why, Colonel! A visit, and so early in the day.' She had recently come back from what rumour held to have been a clandestine mission to Italy but on return there'd been a stormy encounter with her brother and she'd been set aside.

'Your Highness, I beg to know the whereabouts of the Emperor Bonaparte.'

'Oh, is that all?' She pouted. 'I do believe the wretch has sailed for France to raise a rebellion to win back his throne. I'm sure you'll catch him if you hurry.'

Thunderstruck, Campbell raced down the hill to the waiting Adye.

'Nobody knows where Bonaparte is,' he puffed. 'They're covering for him. I went to Pauline and she said he'd sailed for France to seize back his empire.'

'Good God!' Adye gasped. 'Then we—'

'She's lying, of course. No one but a looby would believe Bonaparte such a fool as to land with a bare thousand and expect to win against the Bourbons and Allies both. No – she's trying to put us off course as to where he's really headed.'

'Sir – I would have thought it most likely that Italy is the objective. No more than a day or two's sail, he's welcomed by his brother-in-law Murat and the pair get busy raising a vast army to the satisfaction of both.'

'So more in the south, he the King of Naples.'

'Seems reasonable, in fact the only rational action open to him with his resources.'

'Naples?'

'Yes! Captain, clap on all the sail you possess and get to sea this minute. The world is depending on us.'

Chapter 61

Off the south coast of France

It was not a particularly stirring sight – a hilly coast, dreamily firming out of the morning mists, not so different from other shorelines around the north Mediterranean. But it had one quality that set it above all others. This was the blessed soil of France.

And, wildly improbably, Napoleon Bonaparte was about to land with just a handful of warriors to reclaim his empire. It was an act of daring and defiance that had no precedent, and Moreau had to check himself from thinking his master of unsound mind even to contemplate the deed.

The vista gradually extended in both directions. This was the Golfe-Juan, a curving two-to-three-mile near-uninhabited bay. To the left was a headland beyond which lay Cannes, a fishing village, and to the right a more rugged cape, with Antibes, a larger fortified town, on the far side.

Gliding into the enfolding bay *Inconstant* came to, her anchor tumbling down, the remainder of the little flotilla close by. At that instant the white fleur-de-lis-emblazoned Bourbon flag was struck in every ship and in its place rose the tricolour of empire, an act of outright sedition.

'Captain Lamouret,' Bonaparte ordered, when movement had ceased, 'I desire you should take a party ashore and make reconnaissance before I land. Do visit the Antibes citadel and acquaint them of my presence and my wish to meet them.'

Moreau loosened. This was a prudent move. It was not impossible that traitors had informed the authorities of Bonaparte's planned arrival here and had prepared a welcome. Additionally, once the citadel declared for Bonaparte their numbers would increase greatly, while the artillery and magazines released would be invaluable.

The longboat made for a short, stony beach and the grenadiers formed up. The coast road was quickly found and the party marched out to the right along it to cross the cape and disappear from view.

Through a telescope it was quite apparent that there were no battalions drawn up in the wooded slopes and, apart from a gaping shepherd watching them go past, no others were in view.

The order was given to disembark.

Boats began streaming ashore, Bonaparte watching until he landed, last of all.

Men crowded around, talking in whispers.

Dressed in the deep green and white uniform of a colonel of the *chasseurs à cheval* of the Imperial Guard, Bonaparte strode to their centre.

'Soil of France! Fifteen years ago I decorated you with the name "Country of the Great Nation". One of your children, the most glorious to bear this beautiful title, comes again to deliver you from anarchy. Nothing for me! Everything for France.'

Echoing from the bay, guns fired in ecstatic salute for an

event that would go down in history, and Moreau laid down memories he knew would stay with him for the rest of his life.

An olive grove was the site for their first camp. Not in any way an impressive scene, the entirety of the expedition consisted of eight hundred men, a pair of tiny four-pounder guns and two horses. No baggage trains, no field kitchens, no standard impedimenta.

It would improve when the Antibes citadel came over to them, as Bonaparte had promised. But as the evening drew in, and crackling fires were lit to provide a meal, an exhausted grenadier staggered in with harsh news.

Far from being received with glad shouts and acclamation Lamouret had been left outside the stout fortress unable to deliver his proclamation. After wearisome shouted discussion the gates were opened but it was a trick. After he and his party had marched in, the outer gates were shut behind them and the inner remained barred.

They were trapped and disarmed. Governor Ornano and the garrison had taken an oath of loyalty to King Louis and would not be suborned, certainly not by a returning tyrant with a handful of men.

It was a shattering blow. The entire venture had been based in trust on Bonaparte's assumption that a clamorous welcome awaited the people's deliverer.

More immediately it had been understood that the grateful population would be happy to ply them with food and drink, but now there were few rations.

Bonaparte acted quickly. Captain Casabianca was sent with a dozen men to parley with the governor for the release of Lamouret. Without horses, the hard march on foot there and back was wearying and when they returned they found that the citizens had been roused to lock and bar the town against them.

It was a blow as much moral as physical. They couldn't fight their way to Paris against all of France but what else was there? Moreau could only conceive of one course it could take now – that they should quietly withdraw and return to the safety and comfort of Elba while they could.

Bonaparte, however, was of quite a different mind.

Crisply, he gave his orders. The formidable General Cambronne set off in the opposite direction, over the rocky point to Cannes. Tall, hard-featured and with a coarse voice, if he couldn't achieve something it would be strange indeed.

The next order was disconcerting for the little band on the edge of France. *Inconstant* and her flotilla of transports had been sent away, leaving them entirely alone. Moreau heard that the ships were to fetch reinforcements but he knew there were none. Another explanation: Murat was shipping artillery to them, but this also was false, as the Murat plot had been arbitrarily thrown aside.

The real reason, Moreau knew, was to leave the expedition with no option but to move forward into the interior.

Better news came by messenger from Cambronne. He'd cowed the undefended village with tales of troops flooding ashore and had said that if they failed to declare for Bonaparte or, at the very least, find ways to please him there would be consequences.

That night Bonaparte and his men slept dry and snug, and by noon the next day they'd accepted a total of 3,600 rations, every post-carriage and wagon in town, and as many horses as could be rounded up.

Chapter 62

There was no point in delaying and, with Cambronne and an advance guard setting off ahead, Napoleon Bonaparte's march of return began before the morning had advanced far. Less than half of the company had access to a horse or wagon but the rest were Imperial Guard who stepped it out on foot as well as ever they had across the length and breadth of Europe in the glory days of the past.

The first stage was across the coastal plain to the foothills of the Alps, the town of Grasse. The going was brisk in bracing weather, half moving a-foot, with Bonaparte in a humble two-wheeled calèche. Many of the Polish lancers without a mount heroically shouldered their saddles as they plodded on.

Up in the chillier highlands, the town emerged but not before the sound of bells floated down to the tired column.

'Majesty, if that's the tocsin . . .' A general alarm spread by church bells. They were in no shape to withstand a determined descent by local forces but they badly needed to find food and shelter.

The advance halted. A dispatch rider from Cambronne fell back with details of the situation.

The bells were no tocsin: it was a funeral only, by a population that had been shocked to discover that the villainous Napoleon Bonaparte, whom all had thought banished for good, had come of all places to their modest home in the hills. There would be no acclamation and certainly no defections to his standard. The weary column trudged on into a deserted township that offered little.

Having bargained for every horse and conveyance with their diminishing gold, the next morning they stepped out bravely on the mountain track that led to the heart of the Maritime Alps.

Snow-streaked in bitter winds, they moved along a slush-haunted track that, after hundreds of miles, would take them to the other side – Grenoble.

There, even Bonaparte admitted, unless they were received in something like a victorious welcome, the enterprise was doomed.

Moreau, with only a few, knew more. Secret dispatches sent to them had a dreadful message: even as they toiled into the mountains Marshal Masséna had, under orders from Paris, set out from Toulon along the coast with a powerful formation that had just one purpose: to cut off Bonaparte from where he'd come while presumably another force closed in from the north.

It was turning into a ludicrous charade – a minuscule invading force without guns or horses, never having once been either embraced as liberators or found any willing to support and follow. And with the Masséna thrust coming behind them there was little they could do except press on.

A town was ransacked for transport, horses, anything, and the ramshackle column got under way once more, this time up into the grim fastness that was the Alps. It was ferocious going, snow still blocking the passes, the dozen or so town carriages from Grasse struggling in the icy conditions. Old *grognards* of the Imperial Guard gloomily reminisced about Russia and the great retreat.

They passed through another town – more sullen resentment, barely concealed hostility, white royalist cockades on every cocked hat.

Rugged mountain tracks were now a trial, the only mercy long stretches of alpine country barren of humankind and therefore threat, the bitter wind and snow flurries their only antagonist. And all the time in the knowledge of the dire fate that was in store should Grenoble turn against Napoleon Bonaparte as all others had.

Then the bare track came to an end, intersecting at last with a broad river valley and with it a fine flat highway headed north-west.

Acquiring more horses and wheeled transport, the pace picked up until, with Grenoble just half a day further, past the last of the Alps descending to the plains beyond, the worst of all possible outcomes occurred.

A lathered rider galloped up and passed on a scribbled dispatch from Cambronne. Ahead, where the road passed a lake on one side and a towering ridge on the other, a full battalion of garrison troops, the 5th of the Line, had taken up position athwart the highway to Grenoble.

And these would be only the first, other formations no doubt coming up fast behind.

'Tell Cambronne to fall back – on no account to engage them. I shall present myself to them.'

Moreau took a ragged breath. He knew very well that any man who shot the pretender to the throne of France would be richly rewarded.

With Masséna closing in only days behind, and an army rising ahead, it was the last throw of the dice for Bonaparte.

Around the final bend the Bourbon soldiery came into view squarely across the Grenoble highway – a baleful line of prepared infantry, bayonets fixed, their officers clearly visible.

Napoleon's footsore little band marched forward – proudly, defiantly, until he brought them to a halt and issued his orders.

Would it be a frontal attack, a bloody affair of hand-to-hand fighting to force a path through, or some cunning device that led them around the position?

'Imperial Guard – to the fore!'

The few hundred hardened veterans stepped forward and formed line.

'Present arms!'

A sharp slapping of muskets and they were rigidly at the present.

Bonaparte wheeled about and, facing the lines of the king's men, slowly doffed his cocked hat in salute.

There was no response.

'Reverse arms!'

It was incomprehensible. In a manoeuvre usually seen only at funerals, muskets were swivelled to bring muzzles pointed uselessly to the ground.

'Forward march!'

With Napoleon Bonaparte well to the front the hard-bitten troops marched ahead, no movement betraying that they knew they were heading into what could quickly develop into a storm of fire.

'Halt!'

They were now within thirty yards of the aimed muskets opposite and a false move on either side would see death in seconds.

In the breathless stillness Bonaparte broke the spell. He stepped forward to the open ground between them. Throwing aside his famous grey surtout to reveal the well-known favoured green uniform of the *chasseurs,* he hailed them.

'Here I stand! Soldiers of the 5th of the Line – recognise me. If there's a *grognard* among you who wants to kill his emperor – he can do it now!'

It was a master-stroke.

After the barest hesitation came the exultant shouts – '*Vive l'empereur!*' Throwing aside their weapons they went to the one who in the so-recent past had led them to many famous victories, whose very appearance had so many times inspired them on to triumphs and conquest.

Moreau watched in disbelief, then amazement, then in frank admiration. If this was what lay ahead, there was no doubt that Bonaparte's crazy gamble would succeed.

Grenoble was now Bonaparte's. Its rich industries had suffered much under the Bourbons' heavy-handed taxation and imposts and preferred the wartime profits he had provided.

The mood was ecstatic, whole streets lined with jubilant Bonapartists ready to throw in their means to achieve a return of the emperor to the throne of France.

It was looking quite as if they could win – against any odds.

Chapter 63

Plymouth, England

'And I will certainly make mention of the gift of two hundred Bibles generously donated to *Centaur* by the Right Reverend the Bishop of Exeter,' Kydd said, glancing graciously at the gentleman. How the devil he was going to stow them in a crowded man-o'-war, then hand them out to denizens of darkest Africa who were presumably without a word of English, he was at a loss to know.

The civic dinner had gone well, the candlelight glinting agreeably on his gold-laced admiral's uniform and much respect had been shown him.

'And before I sit I would like you to be in no doubt concerning the esteem I hold for my noble flagship in which I shall be embarking on an adventure in so far a place.

'In my time in the navy I have been to many distant seas. Let me tell you a story – spin a yarn, as we sailors have it – about a meeting with a hulking Russian sail-of-the-line in the ice-bound Baltic.'

Movement at the back of the room caught his eye. It was

Moore, one of *Centaur*'s lieutenants, standing hesitantly at the door. If he wanted to pass on a message he'd have to wait while Kydd finished his tale, which he did in stirring fashion.

'And so once again I have to thank you for so entertaining an evening,' he said, at its conclusion, beaming to this side and that.

'That was wonderful, darling,' Persephone whispered, as he took his seat again.

But before he could take a sip of wine Moore appeared at his elbow. 'Sir Thomas, I'm truly sorry to interrupt your dinner but I've been sent to acquaint you with a circumstance of the utmost consequence.'

'I see. What can this be, pray?'

The lieutenant glanced at Persephone and, with some embarrassment, replied, 'Of a nature as would better be told privily, sir.'

Kydd frowned. If he was going to be informed that *Centaur* had sprung a leak or similar . . . 'Very well. Persephone, my dear, would you excuse us?' He followed Moore out of the hall to the vestibule, ignoring curious looks on the way. 'What is so important that it cannot wait until the morning, sir?'

'Not for the common sort to hear, you'll agree, Sir Thomas.'

'Well?' Kydd growled irritably.

'Boney's out.'

'I beg your pardon?'

'Napoleon Bonaparte has escaped from Elba.'

Thunderstruck, Kydd could only goggle at him.

'No one knows where to, or what mischief he contemplates, but Admiral Keith requires your immediate attendance on him – this hour, sir.'

The commander-in-chief, Channel, needing him so urgently at this particular time?

'Er, is he . . .?'

'He's new arrived from London, and awaits you at Mount Wise.' Moore shifted uncomfortably, as he continued, 'I've taken the liberty of bringing a carriage alongside.'

At such a summons he could not delay a moment, and leaving the lieutenant to handle explanations, he was on his way without delay.

The offices were in a ferment but it wasn't to the operations room Kydd was shown: instead he went into the private quarters of the commander-in-chief, a snug room with a brisk fire. Keith stood before it, hungrily devouring a steak pie with his fingers, and still in his travelling cloak.

It had been years since he'd last seen the man, stern, tough and with more than a touch of the Scottish dour. Kydd remembered with a warm surge that Keith had been the one to set him on the quarterdeck in his first command and—

'Admiral Sir Thomas Kydd, sir,' the urbane flag-captain introduced, then noiselessly withdrew, leaving them alone together.

'Ha-hmm,' Keith mumbled, through the remains of his pie, which he quickly finished, licking his fingers and taking the opportunity to look his guest up and down.

'No need for that full fig, Kydd,' he rumbled, eyeing his full-dress finery. 'We've work to do.'

'Sir. I've just come away from—'

'Never mind. I need first to express my felicitations on your elevation to a flag,' Keith said gruffly. 'Always knew you had it in you, Kydd.'

'Th-thank you, sir.'

'Now, to affairs at hand.' Keith stripped off his cloak and threw it into the corner. 'A dram?'

'That would be most welcome, sir.'

The malt that came from the elegant cut-glass decanter was the very finest.

'Confusion to Boney!' Keith smiled grimly. 'Never thought we'd be toasting the like again.'

'Wherever the devil lurks,' Kydd agreed.

'Now. Here's the griff,' Keith said, taking one of the armchairs and piercing Kydd with a fierce look. Kydd took the other and waited.

'All the world is ahoo with worry about Bonaparte but he's not the greatest danger.'

'He's not?' Kydd couldn't suppress his astonishment.

'Hah! For one who served at sea in the Channel through that brace of years before Trafalgar you'd be first to believe it.'

'Er . . .'

'As we speak, our best word suggests Boney is between the South of France and Paris, in the Alps somewhere I'd hazard. And as he progresses – at his usual pace – he's without a doubt subverting his old comrades along the way. When he gets further to the north there'll be many more, for Louis le Gros is not well liked. All this is bad news for the Coalition but worse for England.'

'Sir?'

'The navy – our sure shield, our wooden walls. What has happened to it, Kydd?'

'Why, saving your presence, sir, much has been condemned into ordinary, the men cast ashore and—'

'Quite. I agree with you! And the French?'

'Um, still in harbour, I'm supposing, sir.'

'Just so. And will remain so while the Allies bicker on about the spoils, who gets how many sail-of-the-line and so forth. In other words, it still exists in its entirety.'

Keith leaned forward with deadly intensity. 'I ask you this, Kydd. What should you believe will happen if the French officer corps decide to declare for their past emperor?'

'Surely . . .' But Kydd suddenly knew it only too well to be a fearful possibility.

'Then I'll tell you. One of their number – and they've a good few thinking leaders – will realise that, with our navy shorn to a sad few, they greatly outnumber us. For the first time in twenty years of war they've a prime chance of getting control of the Channel. And that means . . .'

'Not an invasion?' Kydd said, shocked by his own words.

'Why not? The invasion barges and so forth along the coast have been kept in fettle – only last year just before the peace nearly half a million francs were voted on their upkeep. If they move fast and hard, with the crossing secured they could throw ashore a conquering army while all eyes are on chasing Boney.'

Keith reached out and splashed more whisky into his glass, then Kydd's.

'Thank you, sir,' Kydd answered, hurriedly gathering his thoughts. 'But might I ask why you are telling me this?'

He saw a wave of tiredness pass over Keith's face. 'Because their lordships, well apprised of this, have ordered me as commander-in-chief to prevent it happening at all costs. How? They are supposing that I can get to sea a sufficiency of metal that can deter. I cannot – even those hulls left to me are not in any wise ready for sea.'

Kydd kept silent: there was little he could contribute at this level.

'But more important than the ships are the men. Not just the foremast hands but the commanders – of all stripe.'

'So . . .'

'The sea-going admirals are up-country with their families or elsewhere out of reach. If I wanted to get a squadron to sea at this moment I'm reduced to one, hobbled by his advanced years and gout, or another, who between us both is not best suited to a difficult command.'

'Sir.'

'And you.' A wintry smile broke through. 'With a flagship victualled and stored, complete with its own little fleet near ready for sea. You – a proven fighter, level-headed in a hard corner, and one I know.'

'That's kind in you to say, sir.'

'So this is why I'm appointing you without delay to act in the character of admiral of the Channel Squadron.'

Kydd gulped.

'To put to sea in a small clutch of days with as many sail-of-the-line as I can scrape up for you. To lie off as many ports as you can to make 'em think again.'

Kydd felt a sudden wash of exhilaration. 'Or to stand in their way should they make motion to continue on.'

'You understand the essence of the task admirably, sir. I wish I could entertain my new Channel sea commander more nobly at this point but, as you can see, time presses unmercifully on both us and the French.'

'I'll take my leave, then, sir. Your orders?'

'Will be few and clear. You ken what's at stake for your country. You know what to do. Do it!'

Chapter 64

Admiral Kydd returned to his flagship at the ungodly hour of shortly before midnight, without ceremony and as silent-hours routine rounds were making their way about the ship.

'Desire the captain to attend on me directly,' he ordered, allowing an imperturbable Sankey to remove his boat-cloak and outer full-dress uniform.

Tippett quickly appeared with his frock-coat over his night attire, correctly assuming Kydd's abrupt summons was more important than his appearance. 'Sir?' he said, anxiety written in his face.

This was not Kydd's ship and he had no right to order in detail what he wanted done, but the situation was dire.

'Ugly news, Captain. Bonaparte has broken out of Elba.'

'Ah, yes, sir.'

Kydd cleared his throat. Why did he not feel it in him to address Tippett in less formal tones? And it irritated him to realise that the man was more apprehensive in dealing with his admiral's demands than in absorbing such a shattering revelation.

'The commander-in-chief, Channel, has appointed me to lead a fleet to sea of as many of-the-line as may be found. My orders require me to proceed at once.'

'Sir.'

'I want *Centaur* to put out to sea before nightfall tomorrow or the next day at latest, stored and watered for extended service of which we will be flagship.'

'Aye aye, sir.' Still the nervous uneasiness.

'So do carry on, Captain Tippett.'

'Oh, er, should I turn up the hands at this hour?'

'Yes, sir, you should!' Kydd spluttered, amazed that the man felt he had to ask.

Centaur came alive within a short while of the boatswain and his mates piping 'all hands' at the hatchways.

Kydd's secretary was promptly before him, still buttoning his shirt.

'You've heard, old fellow?'

'They're speaking of nothing else in the wardroom, Sir Thomas.'

He would leave it to the traditional first-night-at-sea dinner to share with them the deadly danger of the French Navy declaring for Bonaparte.

'Your man is ready with a quill, I trust. There's much to be done.'

Kydd's Channel appointment was of far greater moment than that of the Preventive Squadron. With the peace now so precipitately ended, he was now a *fighting* admiral no less.

He was well aware of the task before him. Nothing less than putting together a scratch fleet from the vessels anchored about them: a core of sail-of-the-line, frigates to do what frigates must and as many of the invaluable brigs and cutters as he could pluck up.

And then getting them to sea and formed up into something like a battle disposition. Keith would do his damnedest to lay his hands on more but these would have to follow in their wake in the days to come. Direction would have to be left for them. But for now the most pressing need was for word to go out that, with the commander-in-chief's authority, he took each individual ship under his orders, under his flag. He realised, with a thrill, the blue that was there at the masthead.

They worked through the night and while it was still dark boats put off from *Centaur*. Captains of all species of warship awoke to the fact that they not only had a new master but it was expected they have their ship ready to sail in hours.

With so much paper-wrangling it wasn't until a watery sun ushered in a new day that Kydd was in a position to pay any attention to the vital question of his strategy as a fighting admiral.

Snatching a standing breakfast he stared with reddened eyes at the charts spread over the big table. So familiar but so threatening. Before, his seamanlike concern had been with the lethal rock-fanged reefs and granite crags, the evil bluster of on-shore gales, the massive hidden swirls of currents. Now it was all of those things but with added menace: the threat of a hostile fleet issuing out to crush them by sheer weight of numbers.

His eyes took in all of west-facing France. The biggest concentration of threat would be at Brest, furthest north and closest to Britain. Then there was Lorient, a shipbuilding base but really more of a lair for privateers and similar. Other small harbours. But the next in significance was the complex of ports about Rochefort, near the centre of the long Atlantic coast – La Rochelle and the rest he knew only too well from his part in the action of the Basque Roads.

How in Hades could he watch all of them?

Before, as the captain of a blockading ship, he'd had his objectives clearly assigned. Now *he* must individually task his own squadron for they expected the same from him.

But how long must they stay at sea, watching and waiting? In the twenty years of war until now there had never been a time when the Royal Navy had not maintained a squadron off these major seaports, keeping the sea in all weathers and ready for any break-out. If Napoleon Bonaparte succeeded in a bid for power the blockade had to be restored in its full predominance but now it was his duty alone to face any eruption until he was relieved.

Keith's hurried confidential appraisal of what his burden would be had provided horrifying reading. At the peace some months ago the French had possessed eighty-one ships-of-the-line of *Centaur*'s weight of metal or above, another eighteen on the stocks building – and more than a hundred frigates. If only half of these were in shape for sea, and only half of those went over to Bonaparte they were outnumbered to a ridiculous extent. No wonder Keith had considered it the greater threat.

He looked again at the returns of condition being rendered hourly now. If he sailed at the end of the day – which was looking increasingly unlikely – he'd have no more than seven of-the-line with him and about the same number of frigates. And the only advantage he had was a moral one – the reputation the Royal Navy had built up for bulldog aggression that would make even the most determined French admiral hesitate.

Towards the end of the afternoon he'd call an 'all captains' and lay the whole affair before them. But by then he had to have the elements of a strategy and directions of how he required his fleet to respond in the event of a full-blooded action. Not only that, but signals were strongly related to the manoeuvres specified and generally both were promulgated together.

Fortunately, he had on hand a copy of the Fighting Instructions issued by the last Channel Squadron commander, a thick, detailed tome that he could either adopt completely under his own name or, more practically, change to suit his far-from-typical circumstances and issue the result as amending the Instructions, a far quicker course.

Before midday he prepared to review his fleet – *his* fleet!

Suppressing a surge of pride he picked up the list. Four two-deckers: *Valiant, Spencer, Dictator* and *Hector,* all at decorous anchor around the flagship. None could in any sense be termed new but all were apparently ready for sea and battle if their fitness reports were to be believed. Another two short of complement and not stored would presumably follow later.

Their captains. Nelson had made it his first concern to get insight into their strengths and weaknesses and Kydd knew he should, too. In battle this would mean he could send them into the smoke and fury at the heart of the action in the knowledge that all were aware of what he intended and how to achieve it. He would get to know them in time, but before then he would devise a simplified approach that could be deployed on the spot.

Frigate captains: it wasn't so very long ago that he had been one of them and he understood their character intimately. Their role was inshore reconnaissance, not the line-of-battle, and therefore they did not need his strategic thinking. They could be relied on, however, to take daring risks and would dependably stay with a chase.

Only two frigates were fit for sea service and within reach – *Boadicea* and *Topaze,* lying the other side of the Sound. Four more were promised from outlying ports but would not reach him in time.

Topaze: Captain Bazely, scrupulously correct in his dealings with his old friend and the first to render weekly accounts to his admiral as every ship's captain must. Kydd had a mind to make him some kind of commander in charge of the inshore frigates, to rein them in as they ranged eagerly up and down the coast.

By the dog-watches it was clear that there was no prospect of putting to sea that day, which gave plenty of time for his 'all captains'.

It was very fine to take his ease in his great cabin while above, as the muffled piping-aboard indicated, his ship-of-the-line captains gathered on the quarterdeck. When all were present they would be ushered into his presence by his flag-lieutenant.

His table spread to its fullest extent of polished mahogany was impressive, and an admirable surface for the display of charts and maps.

'Pay no mind to seniority,' Kydd said pleasantly, as they sat uncertainly, 'time being of the essence.'

He felt as if he was inhabiting another body, given the gravity and respect shown by these experienced and senior battleship captains, and it brought him up short. How should he proceed, relate to them? Strict, friendly, cool, demanding? His actions and speech would lay down the nature of his leadership for the future.

'Ahem.' The heads went up, the looks rigid. He felt something being slid under his finger – it was a piece of paper with a rough sketch of the table and a name against each chair. His secretary Dicken was proving a godsend.

'I say time, for there's none to spare,' Kydd said gravely and went on to explain the threat of the French Navy going across to Bonaparte and their task in thwarting anything to follow.

'A hard claw to wind'd, I'd think it, sir.' It was the older one to the right.

'I can only agree, Captain Darby,' Kydd said. Instinct told him that the man was confident and a clear thinker.

'As will stretch our little band a mite tight,' growled Beresford, fiddling with his pencil. One to watch.

'Do you favour the line or pell-mell, Sir Thomas?' From Collier, this was an attempt to open the higher matters first.

'A nice question, sir,' said Kydd, 'and one I believe worthy of discussion by us all.'

He let them voice their opinions and watched them carefully. Darby of *Spencer* was lucid and of few words, favouring a concentrated line, while Hanwell of *Dictator* was more rambling but forcefully going for an all-or-nothing melee. Others took differing positions.

It was an excellent opportunity to size up their characters and to break the ice, and by the end of the meeting he had some kind of measure of them.

His intention was to sail as soon as he could, hoping that by the time they'd reached station his thoughts would have coalesced sufficiently to form a strategy that he could lay before them.

As it was, the need to get some kind of deterrence in place was crucial. He was dog-tired and heartily grateful that he could claim an all-night in, unlike so many on board.

Chapter 65

The next morning dawned dreary and grey, rain threatening, but Kydd was determined to set sail that day. 'I'll trouble you to hoist the Blue Peter,' he ordered Tippett. The flag indicated to all the world that the ship was to sail within twenty-four hours. And for a flagship that meant its fleet as well.

Irritably he brushed aside routine clerking for he needed a solid steer on what was happening in France.

Keith's office was not helpful – the best they had for him was a vague picture of chaos and panic at the highest as Bonaparte advanced on Paris. There was nothing that revealed the situation in the great dockyards and bases on the Atlantic coast.

Under his eye *Centaur* completed storing and watering, and the deadly cargo of the powder hoys was finally hoisted aboard. First *Valiant*, then *Spencer* indicated completion and *Dictator* followed.

He would definitely sail on the tide that day.

There were difficulties, of course. An admiral had duties

and burdens unknown to the common run: clearances, decla-
rations, final dispatches; visitors and petitioners; decisions
high and low.

And then, unbelievably, it was time: 'All ships – prepare to
unmoor.'

Standing on *Centaur*'s quarterdeck Kydd had to hold back
a wide grin as he pictured the bustle and rush on each of
his ships as they raced to obey his order.

'Execute.'

He stood clear in the hurry of activity, conscious of his
imposing figure in silver-buckled shoes, white breeches and
gold-laced cocked hat and knew there would be more than
one telescope on him.

On a whim he took out his pocket glass and swept it around
the anchorage – and stopped. There, high on Plymouth Hoe,
a lone figure, still and erect. With a lurch of the heart he saw
it was Persephone.

As an admiral's daughter she'd known just how busy he'd
be and had refrained from distractions, letting him go
without fuss to do his duty. His eyes pricked. A flag-officer
under public eye couldn't possibly give a shy wave or
acknowledge in any way her devotion, and as the big 74
swayed and took the wind for the open sea he felt a lump
in his throat.

With Devon fast fading to a grey anonymity among the
rain squalls, *Centaur* took the Atlantic rollers square against
her starboard bow in an exuberant thud and hiss, the age-old
rhythms of the sea.

And yet more decisions came for Kydd. The flagship was
leading the squadron in order of sailing as specified by himself
only that morning, the four battleships in obedient line
stretching astern. *Spencer* was observably unhandy in anything
like sailing by the wind and was sagging to leeward. Should

he make public criticism of Darby to indicate that he'd noticed and to demonstrate his character as a taut admiral – or tactfully ignore it?

Ahead, far out on either bow, the frigates were punching through the seas in distant explosions of white. It was not likely in this short time, but a rebellious French force might already be taking position at the chops of the Channel and these eyes of the fleet would be Kydd's only warning.

At a sudden tapping from aloft he glanced up as a matter of course to locate the Irish pennant, a rope pulled loose and fretfully rattling against the board-taut canvas. About to roar admonishment to the watch-on-deck, he held back. Naturally this was Tippett's affair as captain.

Annoyingly it was not noticed, the irritating patter going on and on but as an admiral there was nothing he could do about it. It took a little of the shine off his pride at leading his own fleet out on an important mission.

He took refuge in his cabin. There, he went over what he would do to direct the squadron to best effect but there was no getting away from the enormity of the task.

He'd wanted to be an admiral. Decisions came with the position that were his alone.

It had to be assumed that the Bonapartists would move quickly while the British were still taken by surprise, so he had to be ready for any possibility.

The most extreme: a full-scale fleet action against great odds. This would not be a leisurely forming into line-of-battle but a rapid confrontation. Given the numbers, it was probably better to keep in a single concentrated force that could be led by the flagship against the enemy to where it would cause the most destruction to deter it from its wider purpose. It would call for first-class signal work and resolute conduct by all. In this he was probably contemplating the destruction of himself and the squadron, but with what was at stake it had to be so.

On another level, there could be a confused mix of bluff and bluster, which his far inferior resources would not go far in deterring. This was a game of playing for time in so far as the French could be persuaded to take part and he with no cards of any significance.

Or would it be falling back on a blockade, at the very least off the bigger ports? Yet even this well-tried strategy was in question. In reality the Royal Navy was not set in array against its old foe. In theory at least, the royalist navy under Louis was not the enemy, more a neutral, and any attempt to confine it to harbour or challenge it on the high seas would be seen as a hostile act.

Kydd's orders were flimsy and insubstantial. He was enjoined only 'to detain and send to port all armed vessels entering or leaving French ports'. No mention of actions in support of unwillingness to conform, let alone an open sortie by a battle fleet.

It would all depend on the circumstances at the time that he made the right judgement in the face of the threat. And he knew it stood as read that no one else would take the blame should he fail.

The lesser options were still crystallising when the cheery strains of 'The Roast Beef of Old England' on fife and drum announced dinner.

The brightly lit wardroom was quiet and respectful. Kydd's traditional first-night-at-sea dinner was by no means a ritual common to the rest of the navy. And for the admiral to dine with mere officers and with the captain present was an alarming experience he could remember only too well.

'Mr Dovers?'

The chaplain rose to his feet importantly and deigned to deliver grace.

To Kydd's right was Captain Tippett, to his left the first lieutenant, Cawley. Neither dared initiate an exchange, for the custom of the service was to refrain from speech unless addressed personally by the officer who was the senior. It was hard going, Tippett intimidated by the close proximity of a divine being, and Cawley unsure of what would interest a fighting admiral.

Kydd extended his favours further out and found a fellow devotee of Devonshire lamb in the third lieutenant, Moore, who went pink with pleasure at discovering that in Cornwood he was living within a mile or two of the admiral's no doubt vast estate.

The dinner progressed heavily but in the inevitable speech Kydd was able to try out some of his conclusions, which were lost on many but, to his secret delight, all joined in a hearty desire to trounce the Corsican tyrant, which so many of their past messmates were unable to share.

Chapter 66

Centaur, *at sea*

The so-familiar outlines of Ushant left to larboard, Kydd shaped course south, past the wicked dark red granite of the Brittany coast, which every naval officer knew by heart. His objective was the Iroise, the waters in the approaches to Brest.

If there was to be an irruption of warships in quantity, this was where it would happen. His information was that up to forty sail-of-the-line lay within, but with his few vessels, what could he achieve?

But he had ideas, some of which stemmed from his successes in America, where there had been a similar need for blockade. He'd dispatch his sail-of-the-line in twos, each pair on irregular showings off the various ports so that those ashore would be uncertain whether they were alone or part of a greater fleet that lay in wait offshore. It had worked then, why not now?

At the 'all captains' his orders were ready: *Valiant* and *Spencer* with newly arrived frigates to cast south, *Dictator* and *Hector* to flaunt themselves in the north. *Centaur* would remain at a known sea rendezvous off Brest.

His fighting instructions were received soberly, only Beresford daring comment on their sacrificial role should there be a major sally by the Bonapartists.

Kydd now had the luxury of considering his options.

They were in time! No mighty fleets had been unleashed; no invasion was imminent. It didn't mean that none was intended, and the next move must be to discover whether or not there was.

There could be only one way to be sure. It was absurd, ridiculous even to think it, but he could see no alternative than to penetrate into the fortress base of Brest and see.

At least in theory King Louis still reigned there but even so the presence of a British warship would be provocative.

But it didn't have to be. This English admiral was known to possess an eccentricity – he took to cock-boat sail whenever the scenery looked inviting and what more so than the Goulet and Rade de Brest at this time of the year?

The jolly-boat slipped along jauntily, the little craft not noticed by the stream of mercantile shipping headed through the mile-wide channel, the Goulet, which was the entry-point to Brest.

The three midshipmen kept an awe-stricken silence, but Kydd had ensured he was free to observe by demanding the captain's coxswain, Bayley, take the tiller.

It was strange to the point of uncanny to be roaming free where months before the fleet blockade had been unable to, but paradoxically there was little to fear. If there was to be no traitorous sally, they were passing a friendly port, while if there was, they would not give away their treacherous design for the sake of striking at a derisory jolly-boat.

After an hour, the narrow channel fell away to reveal the

magnificent ten-mile stretch of sheltered anchorage to the right – the Rade de Brest, with the Brest arsenal complex on the northern shore.

Here was where the French Channel fleet took their rest and refuge, a forest of ships at anchor, the weightier towards the middle and others further upstream. Kydd ruefully recollected that his entire professional career had been spent in thrall to the occasional break to sea of battle groups from this very place.

His eyes, however, stayed fixed on his objective. There were uncountable numbers of men-o'-war, which appeared sound and presumably were capable of putting to sea. He absorbed the details. The ships seemed inert. The little activity around their decks gave away nothing in terms of how many crew were aboard – a full complement of gunners or simply a handful of ship-keepers?

Their yards were bare. No canvas bent on meant no preparation for sea, but topmasts were not struck on deck, which implied no intention to remain where they were for very long. All flew the white Bourbon ensign at the staff but that had no significance – if they had surreptitiously taken Napoleon's side they would hardly advertise it.

Kydd replied with a cheery wave to a passing hoy and tried to make out what he could. These ships were there to be handed over in reparations to the Allied victors, who were still arguing over the apportioning.

But then he noted something that did not make sense. Many of the two-deckers and some of the three, peacefully at anchor, sat low in the water. They had to be fully laden, and in a warship this could only be with stores, powder and shot.

What naval power under duress to part with their vessels did so while still loaded with valuable stores?

Until this point there'd been nothing that had given him any cause for suspicion. Their anchorage, on the opposite side to that of the town of Brest, should have kept them from discovery but Kydd had chosen to take a light-hearted sail that had given away their game – unless there was another explanation.

The exploration had shown no immediate squadron preparing to put to sea, but all was not as it should have been.

He put about the little boat and took a long board back, passing to the northern side, to the mouth of the north-flowing Penfeld river. On the eastern bank the commercial docks were busy and swarming with waterfront workers. On the western side the arsenal was in complete contrast, idle and deserted, even though he could make out some kind of Admiralty flag on one of the buildings.

Against the foreshore more ships were in various states of repair and idleness. The whole gave the impression of a sombre melancholy, of abandonment. Offshore moles and dockyard detritus hid much from view, but he'd seen enough and they headed out for the setting sun.

Chapter 67

There was not enough to act on, even if it were within his power to do so. Should he concentrate his squadron here at the cost of deterrence at Rochefort and La Rochelle? Should he send urgent dispatches to Keith that he'd seen ships to their marks low in the water?

But if Bonaparte's break for freedom failed and the people, tired of war, did not cleave to his side, it would be a worry of spirits for nothing.

One thing the navy had taught him: it were better to be hanged for doing something than doing nothing. The decision to be made was whether to break up the squadron or concentrate off Brest. The only way to resolve this was to find out the truth behind the laden ships.

In his youth he might have considered some daring night-time swimming escapade but this was different on many levels. He couldn't in all conscience order another to do it. Neither could he, as admiral, put himself at risk.

The answer came to him so suddenly he laughed out loud, startling Dicken working nearby.

As an admiral of a notionally neutral navy, he had every

right and reason to call on the French Brest commanding admiral to pay his respects.

It had to be done in the proper form. His flag-lieutenant, Lovett, would be sent on ahead to prepare the way, his ship to remain hove to outside the territorial limits of Brest, the number of visitors proposed and named.

But if a plot was imminent, what better opportunity to paralyse any fleet opposing than to rob it of its admiral? Kydd decided the chance was worth taking.

Centaur came to in deep water of the Grand Minou at the entrance to Brest, her guns thundering a salute to the fortresses that stood guard along the Goulet approaches. His barge was lowered and manned and stood off under sail, quickly met and escorted by an elaborately ornamented French craft under a prodigious Bourbon ensign.

A double line of helmeted soldiery stood rigidly to attention, sabres glittering, the officer-of-the-guard in as much gold lace as a British general. A senior naval officer and his equerry stood close by, in cordial expectation.

'*Contre-amiral Armand Picheur, chef d'escadre, la région de Brest,*' Lovett urbanely introduced. The same rank as Kydd, an older and irritatingly more sophisticated-appearing gentleman. Lovett, however, took care to present Kydd as *le baronnet*, provoking a polite bow of acknowledgement and restoring his mood.

Another was introduced, Capitaine de Port Émile Tayard, a gruff individual, less well ornamented. The party moved inside the main building.

'*Quelques rafraîchissements, l'amiral Kydd?*'

The room was lofty and set about with marine artefacts artistically displayed. On one wall a vast painting of a complicated fleet action dominated and on the facing one a blank area showed signs that it had once held an ornate banner.

Picheur was courtly and gracious, clearly keen to set his guest at ease. 'You, an admiral, so young,' he said admiringly. 'And seagoing, too. You have a goodly sized fleet, *n'est-ce pas?*'

'Not as who's to say,' Kydd admitted modestly, without thinking. Then he remembered: his job was to deter, to flaunt the might of the British Royal Navy to discourage rash sorties by any who might be so inclined.

'That is, my greater fleet is further out where there's sea-room to exercise,' he explained. 'As you will understand, sir.'

The *capitaine de port* leaned forward and muttered something.

'M'sieur Tayard believes we may be of assistance in the matter of watering, of victuals. Would you wish to bring your fleet into the Rade to carry these aboard, perhaps? We are of the same taking, sir.'

'You are very kind, sir, but I must decline. Books of account and so forth.' Kydd chuckled companionably. 'A very attractive anchorage,' he went on, 'as I saw for myself in a most pleasing sail about the Rade.'

As if suddenly recollecting, he added, 'And passing by your reserve fleet. A hard thing to have to deliver these fine ships to others.'

There was an exchange of looks between the two that Kydd could not interpret.

'Out of interest, sir, I saw many ships low in the water, down to their marks,' Kydd continued amiably. 'Is it your intention to yield up these vessels fully loaded?'

'Fully loaded? Not at all, sir. I do believe you are in error in believing it so.' The tone was easy and relaxed. 'No, sir, those ships you saw are under schedule to ease bilges. That is to say we admit sweet water to flush them out and at the same time prevent undue shrinkage of strakes about the waterline.'

'Quite.' This was not a regular practice for British ships in ordinary but made sense.

Kydd enquired politely as to the possibility of any disagreeable motions in Picheur's command arising from Bonaparte's escape from Elba.

'*Mais non,*' the French admiral said positively. 'You will see for yourself, the land and the peoples of Brest are quiet and not given to foolish gestures.' He gave a slight smile and added, 'But should I have need of assistance in the matter, you may rely on it that you will be so consulted.'

With a winning smile he stood up and extended his hand. 'So kind in you to visit, Sir Thomas. It warms my heart that our navies now exist in such concord together. Shall we see you again, perhaps?'

Kydd bowed as elegantly as he could and left.

Chapter 68

The French admiral waited for a few moments, then relaxed. 'Well, Émile – what do you think?'

Tayard glowered. 'New promoted, inexperienced, we'll have no trouble from that one. Does concern me he says he has a large fleet offshore.'

'He lies,' Picheur said easily. 'The *rosbif* navy lacks ships to do nothing but keep a watch over us at this time.'

'He took a boat around the anchorage.'

'And would have seen nothing but idle ships. You've told your men to keep strictly below-decks at all times?'

'As would see them at a yardarm else,' rumbled Tayard.

Picheur eased out the papers he had been working on and inspected them. 'So. We have seventeen declared for the emperor. Eleven of them sail-of-the-line. I'd be happier with twenty – and time presses.'

He rubbed his chin thoughtfully. 'We've made the two- and three-deckers priority for storing and powder, I trust?'

'Of course, Armand,' Tayard answered scornfully. 'You'll have enough to flood the Channel with good French oak when the time comes. Which is . . .?'

'When our noble sovereign takes power in Paris and not before, else there'll be many weak-hearted who may take pause in fear of the Bourbons.'

'Have you had word from the emperor as yet?'

Picheur frowned. 'No acknowledgement so far. But remember our purpose – to throw an army across the Channel over the bones of a defeated Royal Navy, like a lance into the belly of England. If this does not cause the Coalition to fall apart, nothing will.'

He beamed at Tayard. 'And under my command we need no complex plans wished on us by Central – I simply take my mighty fleet to sea and within hours confront the English in a glorious crushing defeat, which the emperor can only applaud!

'Émile, we shall end our days in laurels, and laden with lavish rewards, which we'll so richly deserve. Now, shall we leave the dreaming for later and make it happen?'

Chapter 69

Aboard Centaur

Kydd saw that the midshipmen were provided with a brace of claret to assist in the telling of their recent adventure to the rest of the berth while he pondered on the result of his visit.

That he was welcomed so openly at such short notice made it seem that nothing perverse was afoot. The reason given for ships riding low in the water was credible but to verify it would be thought at the least as bad manners.

And while he was no skilled judge of character of elegant and urbane French admirals there'd been no sign that Tayard and Picheur were anything other than loyal subjects of King Louis.

Most persuasive was that he'd seen no activity that resembled a major fleet preparing for sea – or crowding seamen manning the ships in readiness.

Therefore with no evidence to the contrary it seemed there was to be no sudden breakout and thus no need for him to concentrate his meagre forces off Brest. He'd send them south to the other big seaports before it was too late.

*

One by one in the light airs sail was set and the squadron spread out in a gentle run southward. So light was the breeze that they were not out of sight until early afternoon and finally *Centaur* was on her own.

At her station, in the deep-sea approaches where naval ships were more to be expected, it was a surprise when a lookout hailed the deck that a substantially sized sail was sighted heading directly for Brest.

It was not the business of a sail-of-the-line to take interest in a single ship, still less a flagship, but the times were not usual. In his bones Kydd felt he should make some sort of examination and cursed that he'd sent his frigates away with the others.

'Captain Tippett, it would oblige me should you close with the vessel and take a look at her,' he asked. If nothing else it would ease the tedium of their watch of the coast.

Ponderously the big 74 hauled her wind but the calm persisted and it was hours before the chase showed hull-up at the horizon. Telescopes went up in *Centaur*. Judging by its lines and the number of gun-ports the stranger was probably a large frigate but with no identifying colours visible.

This was odd. Kydd knew that all Bourbon warships were, under the terms of the peace, safely in harbour, and as far as he was aware no other nation possessed such strength. And then the mystery deepened. Without warning the vessel backed its foresail to bring it around and made off down wind, essentially fleeing back whence it had come.

Maddeningly, the breeze grew fitful and died, leaving them both becalmed some miles apart. As so often occurred in ocean sailing, one vessel in sight of another in a calm could catch a wafting zephyr while the other remained in a gurgling stillness, this time in favour of the chase.

By degrees the stranger faded into the distance. Annoying

but no disaster – it was almost certainly about its lawful occasions. But why had it made off so suddenly?

Kydd's suspicions hardened. He had to stop the ship – but how could he in this calm? And it was away to who knew where, even if he found a workable air.

He had an answer even before the gentle wafting of the counter-draught reached them. The chase was out of sight but he knew where it was headed – Brest. He would lay a direct course for the Plateau Fillettes, a spine of rocky islets obliging ships on a course to the Brest arsenal to keep to a narrow passage to the north of the Goulet.

If he was wrong, nothing was lost, but if he was right . . .

A cheerful flurry of breeze helped them on their way and well before the Fillettes there was sail – it was the chase.

This time it was *Centaur* to windward and yard by yard she came down inexorably on the unfortunate frigate.

Under her guns there was no arguing and a boarding party led by Lieutenant Cawley was sent across. There appeared to be some discussion on her deck and soon the officer returned. This was the good ship *Marianne*, on passage from Martinique in the Caribbean. Its purpose could not be disguised. A frigate right enough, but one *en flûte*, its guns landed to make room for other cargo: troops.

This ship was carrying upwards of two or three hundred troops sworn to the Bonapartist cause and was headed for Brest.

It could no longer be denied. Kydd had hard evidence that some kind of plot was at work, the extent of which was unknowable but appeared to be centred on Brest – and he'd dispersed the only sea power standing in its way!

Kydd reacted in a frenzy of action. 'Prize crew for *Marianne*, sir, as swift as you may.' He took aside the lieutenant in command and instructed him to make for Plymouth under a press of sail to advise the commander-in-chief of developments. Any reinforcements that Keith could scrape together would, however, almost certainly arrive too late.

And those he'd sent away? He'd not even his dispatch cutter at hand to sail after them until she returned from an errand in the north.

He sniffed the wind. Light and shifting in the north-west, fair for their passage. 'Captain, clap on all sail for the south-east. I mean to pass through the Chaussée de Sein before nightfall.'

'Th-through?' stuttered Tippett, 'Did you say *through*, Sir Thomas?'

'I did.'

A daring but desperate throw of the dice. This was a long, closely crowded chain of treacherous islands and reefs reaching all of twelve miles out from Brittany to which prudent mariners always gave a wide berth, adding thirty miles to their voyage – as would no doubt his squadron headed south.

But for those intimately acquainted with the area there was an alternative. A deep but very narrow pass close to the inner end, the Raz de Sein. Dangerous and seldom tried, Kydd remembered the last time he'd seen it, the gaunt, iron-grey rocks furiously lashed by an Atlantic gale, the white spume whipping far out to sea.

A pale-faced Tippett confronted Kydd. 'Sir, I must protest! As captain of *Centaur* I cannot allow my vessel to be so hazarded.'

'Sir, you have my direct order.' The higher stakes were the defence of the realm, not the preserving of a single ship from danger.

Aware that the quarterdeck was silently witnessing the exchange, Kydd folded his arms and stared the man out.

Abruptly Tippett wheeled about and left the deck. Kydd's hard gaze shifted to fix on the first lieutenant. Nothing was said but Cawley muttered an order to the officer-of-the-watch, who obeyed with celerity.

They were on their way to the Raz de Sein, leaving who was in command of the ship an open question.

'Mr Cawley, the sailing master – my cabin.'

Leaving the watch-on-deck to settle *Centaur* on her new course Kydd went below.

Any who believed they were headed into a screaming hell of seas and foaming rocks needed to be disabused. These airs were still light and playful, far from threatening, even a soft mist at the horizon. But this was far more deadly, as Kydd knew so well.

A fresh gale could be handled with a well-found ship, plenty of headway, bite to the rudder. It was much harder when a vessel had barely enough breeze to keep steerage way on and therefore nothing in hand to take swift avoiding actions.

And the Raz de Sein – the Race, well named for the ferocious tidal currents that churned through the rock-strewn gaps – would require they mustered every ounce of leverage as they entered.

A chill washed over Kydd as he reviewed what he was about to do. The currents in the Goulet were bad enough – three, four knots – but those in the Raz de Sein were commonly seven knots or more, faster than a fit man could run and certainly faster than *Centaur* could make in these sulky airs. If caught by one of the vicious swirls or overfalls, the ship would be carried on to one iron-hard islet or another to be broken to flinders within a single tide.

Was it worth the risk? Given what he knew of the near-certainty of a plot and the consequences if it was carried through, it was.

'Sir – don't do it!' Clare, the master, begged. 'Remember *Séduisant*.'

A French 74, of the same dimensions as they, had been driven ashore while part of the 1796 Irish invading fleet. Only a few dozen were saved out of her crew of six hundred. With the adverse currents, other ships could only look on helplessly.

'I've heard of her,' Kydd admitted. In fact he'd been not far from the event and later had seen bodies washing up.

He'd also been close to the sailing master of his own ship and had taken in much that was useful from that wise old mariner.

'We'll be safe and free if we pay our proper respects to Old Father Tide,' Kydd said, with encouragement. 'The figures you've heard of currents through the Raz are the worst – they're naught but tide-scour. If we can contrive to make our passage on the slack, why, it's only a handful of miles and we're on our way.'

He smoothed out the Iroise chart, conscious that he was acting far from being a feared and lofty admiral, but he couldn't help it. This was honest seamanship. He was in his element and he grinned happily.

'We take our departure from the Tévennec rock, just this side o' the channel and lay it nor'-west-b'-north for five miles and then we're clear.'

'The tide set?' Clare asked carefully.

Kydd nodded but he'd already satisfied himself how it was to be done. 'We stand off and on until an hour before the ebb, then get under way past it. The tide set is to the suth'ard and if we catch it right it'll carry us through at a spanking seven knots. Clear?'

'An' if we don't catch it right?'

'You can call me a Dutchman. Now, Mr Clare, rouse out a tide table for the Chaussée and let's do some figuring.'

*

The moment to make their move was two hours ahead: enough time to finish some business.

Kydd knocked at the captain's cabin.

'Come in.' The voice was low, muffled.

'Captain Tippett, a word if I may.'

The officer did not rise from his chair and looked up at Kydd resentfully. 'Sir Thomas. Do know that I shall be requesting a court-martial on my conduct.' It was the right of any officer to claim a court-martial to clear his name if impugned.

'So you are sanguine that *Centaur* will survive the transit?' Kydd responded quietly. There was no reply, and he went on, 'In any event we are about to do just that. The only question is, shall it by under my orders or yours?'

'You had no right to—'

'I have right of rank, sir. But before we debate this, do allow that your concern for your ship does you credit and I am in no way offended or feel inclined to take any action on its account.'

Tippett stared back, set-faced.

'My judgement is that the preservation of this vessel is secondary to that of recovering a squadron of enough puissance to deter a sortie. To this I will add that my experience in these waters is not inconsiderable and therefore the passage will be made.

'Here is what I propose. The transit will be made, but the log will show that it was done under the advice of the reigning admiral, myself, who therefore must shoulder the blame should anything untoward occur.

'I desire that you should return to duty after your, er, passing disability, and take us in hand. I have spoken to Mr Clare who is now in possession of all he needs to conn *Centaur* through. I rather think we need not take this further.'

Chapter 70

The Tévennec rock was not a hundred feet high and fifty wide, utterly bare and craggy, baleful and sullen to the eye.

The breeze was fluky but thankfully somewhere in the north-west, and their approach was steady. Under easy sail *Centaur* felt her way forward past the landward side.

Kydd was on her quarterdeck standing sternly a-brace and doing his best to radiate confidence. Tippett appeared and, ignoring the looks thrown his way, took up a position within a few paces of Kydd.

Every officer of the ship was on deck, watching narrowly, and seamen were glancing nervously at the dark menace sliding towards them.

And then the currents reached out and took the ship in their power. Nothing dramatic, simply a slight divergence of heading from that set under sail – the bowsprit tracking imperceptibly off, while at the same time the vessel was impelled ahead on an inexorable course of its own, carried bodily forward in a fast-moving mass of water on and past the rock.

The winds were too light to provide enough impetus through the water to give steerage way for the rudder and they were to all intents and purposes helpless. As the currents reached the narrow tide-scoured channels beneath they accelerated and *Centaur* was carried on headlong. Men could only stand in awe as less than a hundred yards off the deadly menaces shot past.

It would have been usual to have boats out ahead to sound the depths but in this tide-race they would have been swept to their destruction. As it was, the sailor at the chains forward could only guess at the sounding as the hand-lead streamed out at an angle.

Kydd tensed. Having placed *Centaur* in the right place at the right time they were being propelled in the proper direction but now was the hardest test. At a point halfway through the Raz the angle of the ship through the water had to be changed to present to the urging current a slightly different profile and induce an edging away from the last cluster of rocks.

It required the fore course, a large sail, to be fully spread and trimmed to take the breeze squarely, levering the forward end of the ship over, but Kydd was not going to give the order.

'As you see it, Captain,' he said mildly.

Tippett took one glance at him and shouted his orders. Obediently the bows edged over and one by one the ugly perils swept past until the currents duly disgorged the two-decker into the wide expanse of the other side.

They had brought it off – but not a minute could be spared. Clapping on all sail, *Centaur* stretched south in pursuit of her squadron and before the end of the day *Valiant* hove into sight accompanied by a frigate and several brig-sloops.

Sending the sloops on to recall those still ahead, the two ships-of-the-line put about and scrambled to take up position off Brest once more.

Chapter 71

Lyon, France

The noise was deafening on the narrow streets. Crowds were pressing in a riotous mob on the advancing soldiery, screaming in hysterical abandon and casting flowers and greenery before the tramping ranks. They fell back at the well-caparisoned staff officers riding by but redoubled their adulation when the figure of Napoleon Bonaparte in his humble calèche could be made out.

Lyon, too, had suffered at the hands of the peace and the predatory Bourbons. Those cheering the return of the conqueror now far outnumbered those mourning the blood-shed to come and the emperor was borne on in transports of delight.

Moreau found himself carried along too, the fevered and exultant atmosphere impossible to resist.

At the evening halt an entire *auberge* was commandeered as headquarters and resting place: the man of the hour was visibly tiring. Throughout the night envoys from surrounding regiments and garrisons came to offer their allegiance while dispatch riders from the capital brought tidings of mutiny and mass defections.

'So what are we to do with 'em?' Bonaparte tore at a chicken leg.

'Sire?'

'Louis and the rest of his wretched crew.'

Moreau was taken aback. But it had to be addressed.

'The last time the people rose up they demanded their king's head. What if they demand it of me? I won't do it, Old Crow. It'll look bad for me in the history books.'

He noisily drank from his wine-cup. 'I know,' he chuckled, 'I'll send 'em into exile. I've got just the place – a little island called Elba.'

Twice more Bonaparte appeared at the front balustrades to the adoring multitudes before he retired for the night, but Moreau knew it wasn't to sleep. As each grand marshal or figure of the old empire declared their sincerity and devotion for Bonaparte they had to be judged and a post found for them at their level of competence in the hourly swelling army. This had to be done delicately, for an affronted dignitary was more of a liability than of value.

Added to which, this was really a campaign requiring all the impedimenta of an army on the march. Where were the supplies coming from? And distributing everything from rations to a form of pay in the field was a nightmare to plan and effect.

The next morning the victorious cavalcade moved off to Châlons. Now only days from the gates of Paris a conclusion to everything loomed.

Chapter 72

The Tuileries Palace, Paris

Raised voices were coming from the inner sanctum of the palace where the gouty old king spent his hours in placid contemplations. A short while later a visibly shaken courtier emerged, convulsively gripping his staff of office.

The waiting Colonel Franklyn, envoy of England to the royal court of King Louis XVIII of France, got to his feet. 'Not a contretemps, not with *sa majesté*, old fellow?'

The *grand maître*, the Prince de Condé, pulled himself together; the two had been friends since the previous year's restoration and understood each other.

'Ah, a disagreement, it's true. I'm at the end of my wits at the vexation it causes me.'

'That he still has not decided his actions in the face of the tyrant's advance?'

'That's the pity of it, *mon brave*. He has decided to remain and defy.'

'A brave gesture but doomed,' Franklyn murmured. 'Why does he think this, *mon ami*?'

'He's taken in that Bonaparte landed with a bare thousand or two and no guns. He won't hear that, since then, the people have turned against His Royal Majesty. And, besides, with his own army he sees past a hundred thousand strong, so he can expect only a satisfactory conclusion to any further trespass into his realm.'

'So I have my answer.'

'He stays.'

'Not as if I—'

'Pray do not judge, sir. Recollect, he was born and raised in the Palace of Versailles in conditions of the utmost extravagance, all his shaping years, only to see it ransacked and his family murdered one by one, his own end a miserable exile.'

'Quite.'

'Then, as in a miracle, to be restored as King of France in substance and reality, only to be threatened within the year with the nightmare again. An uprising of the people against their lawful sovereign with who knows what finality to it all? In truth his mind cannot accept it.'

Franklyn made his excuses and found his ciphering clerk, the close-mouthed and sagacious Johns, and together set up for a confidential dispatch.

Johns waited patiently for the plain text allowing Franklyn to cohere his thoughts. 'So the king refuses to quit the Tuileries. We must accept that, but do we ask the navy to provide him passage to a form of sanctuary on British territory? The prince regent needs to be consulted before the offer is made, of course, but if he's not for moving what's to be done?'

This was straying from his own remit of conveying an appreciation of the circumstances at court – all that the Foreign Office needed to know was the fact of the king's stubborn refusal to leave. 'Just a quick write. We want it to get out as soon as it will.'

*

Franklyn slept late, but in the morning Johns was nowhere to be found, even though living close to the palace.

It wasn't until close to midday that his clerk finally appeared. 'A late night, Charles?' he said acidly.

'More a late morning, as it were, sir.' At Franklyn's glare he went on in a less jocular tone. 'Do not, I pray, think to pass over to the Left Bank – the district is in uproar, a rumour having taken root that King Louis is to defend Paris with giant guns all along the line of the Seine at the cost of ruin and destruction to their homes.'

'Is he? I've heard nothing of this.'

'The mobility has decided it to be the case, sir. They're forming militia bands and parading, for what purpose I'm unable to say.'

Franklyn held up his hand and cocked his head. 'Listen!'

Faint sounds could be heard rising and falling, the far-off thud of a drum.

'We're safe in the palace, but unless . . .'

Louder nearby shouts rang out – of command, orders.

'They're turning out the guard.'

'No, Charles. I do believe we're hearing the arrival of some grand vizier to wait upon the king.'

With a crash the anteroom door was flung open and brilliantly uniformed cuirassiers with drawn sabres marched in to clear a passage through the astonished courtiers. In short order they were followed by two of the highest military in the land: the grim-faced Marshal of the Empire Ney, flanked by a scowling Marshal Soult.

Impatiently they waited while the *grand maître* performed the honorifics and they passed inside.

There were no raised voices but the animal growl of Ney could be made out, with the occasional restless stamp of boots. Before long they emerged as a tight, thin-lipped pair and hurried away in an impatient jingle of accoutrements.

'So?' Franklyn asked the *grand maître* when he could.

'Again, no. He's remaining here in the Tuileries – but the marshals at least persuaded him they should take action against the usurper.'

'Good.'

'Soult is taking his entire division south to confront Bonaparte, while Ney swears he'll do more. He vows to bring him back in an iron cage.'

Franklyn sighed. At last, the Bourbons were stirring to save themselves. And with the full weight of the entire army under some of the most gifted generals of the age, they had every chance of achieving it. There would be a clash somewhere in central France, and Europe would be at peace again.

Two days later he received notice that it was decided to stiffen morale by showing their king to the people.

A review of troops on the Place de la Concorde was arranged. But in pouring rain whitewash ran off the hastily daubed Napoleonic badges and signifiers, and a grossly corpulent monarch required a crane to mount his horse in a grotesque commentary on the reign.

As an inspiring moment it could only have had the opposite effect and that night the noise of riotous crowds outside was clearly heard in the Tuileries.

The next day began badly, with King Louis apparently too affected to continue his duties and the palace a seething hotbed of rumour.

In the early afternoon appalling news came. The opposing armies had at last met – and there before the citizens of Auxerre, Marshal Ney had knelt before the emperor and sworn his allegiance, with that of his army.

Soult, on the other flank, had done the same and now a

triumphant Bonaparte moved forward with an unstoppable host and nothing between him and the capital.

The palace became a fevered, petrified body going through the motions as the reality of the advance of the legendary and notorious Napoleon Bonaparte penetrated. Servants failed to answer their bells, meals were unsatisfactory and chambermaids with frightened faces scuttled to and fro with no clear purpose.

Franklyn had no illusions: in military terms there was no question of the outcome, but the implications were dire.

With a final conclusion just days ahead, and the king showing no signs of weakening his dogged hold on sovereignty, there had to be an end to it all.

Pondering over his urgent dispatch he reviewed the most important matters.

At the first was the simple question: when Bonaparte took Paris, as he must do in short order, what would be his style and title? Would he assume the throne, become head of state and King of France as it presently existed or demand that the empire be re-established in his name? If so, what was the status of the peace treaties that had so recently been signed? Did it then mean that France became the enemy once again?

Bonaparte had reached the headwaters of the Seine and now was on a direct line for Paris through Nemours and then Fontainebleau. If anything was to be done, it had to be now.

'Dear chap,' he opened smoothly on the distracted *maître*, 'a word with you, sir.'

'A very small word.'

'Of my own recognisance, I offer to His Majesty passage in a ship of the Royal Navy to a declared place of safety.'

'Safety? Who in Europe would think to snatch Bonaparte's prey from him?'

'England.'

'Impossible!'

'Pray, why not?' Franklyn asked softly. So much rode on this personal offer for there was no time left to communicate back and forth with London on any alternative.

And if the king was captured the consequence didn't bear thinking about.

'Impossible? Think on his feelings, sir. Once again, a frigate sent to rescue him. As happened before when, in circumstances of great danger, he was lifted at the last moment from the shores of Libau to lonely exile in England. I was with him at the time and do well recollect the gallantry of your fine Captain Kydd. But this is not the worst of it.

'I will tell you – it'll be seen by all that at the first whiff of danger France's King Louis cries immediately for English succour, where before he spent so many years in exile there. In fine, he'll be seen as England's creature well into the future.'

'I think not. It'll be that only Great Britain remains staunch and true to her friends.'

'Thank you, old fellow,' the *grand maître* said sadly, 'but I fear His Majesty will not be moved.'

'It will be cause of a civil war.'

'As maybe, but the king remains in his palace.'

That night, as he prepared for bed Franklyn slipped a horse-pistol into a drawer and tested the locks. Bonaparte was said to be in Fontainebleau, no doubt luxuriating in its quarters – it was but forty miles from where he stood at that moment.

The loyal Johns arrived early, his face set. 'If this were a battle we'd be hearing the guns,' he muttered, a small pair of pistols his contribution.

'We'll be safe, Charles. Bonaparte would be ill-advised at this point to cause offence to the British Crown, I believe.'

A muffled female scream raised his eyebrows. 'Whatever the end may be, it will not be long delayed.'

News spread wildly: Bonaparte was even now entering the southern parts of the capital and not a shot fired. Crowds swelled, cheered, hooted, and the chant of *Vive l'empereur* hung on the air everywhere.

There would be no cataclysmic battle, no heroic last stand. The confrontation was done, overtaken by the tidal wave of acclamation for the emperor.

Still the royal apartments remained quiet, a stark unkemptness creeping into the pristine chambers and an unearthly stillness hanging.

In the early afternoon he heard that Bonaparte had reached the Seine and was now marching for the Île-de-France in an obvious lunge at the Tuileries Palace, at the heart of Paris.

Whatever the consequence, it would all be over in the next few hours.

A stampede of feet sounded outside the door. Franklyn peered out – the entire floor was in agitated activity. It took only seconds to determine what was going on. The palace was making ready to depart.

Baggage was wrestled along, rolled tapestries and favourite paintings stuffed into portmanteaux, all hurried outside.

Franklyn went to the window and looked down on at least a dozen carriages frenziedly loading baggage and to one side a single conveyance, shrouded and still.

It went on until dark. Then there was a flurry of animation and the argosy set off. Shortly afterwards the lone carriage took aboard its pathetic single passenger and, with no ceremony, clattered off into the night.

Shaking his head, Franklyn had to acknowledge that by any reckoning history would declare Napoleon Bonaparte to be the victor and conqueror.

Chapter 73

Fontainebleau

The courtyard, where the year before Bonaparte had taken his moving farewell of his Old Guard, now resounded to huzzahs and heartfelt cries as his soldiers paraded once more before him.

He took his time, noticing this man and that to their intense gratification and then, in imperious tones, bade them to march on to Paris.

Moreau watched as if it were a dream. A bare few weeks ago it had been a wild notion set in the face of all logic and odds. And here a rapidly increasing army was on the last stage of a descent on the capital.

A morning drizzle cleared and before them lay the City of Light. They passed on through the well-known *arrondissements* with their ancient cathedrals, boulevards and grand squares, then across the Seine to the Right Bank. In the evening, by the light of flaming torches, Napoleon Bonaparte reached the very centre of Paris.

Hours after King Louis of France had left, the emperor returned to the Tuileries Palace where, after acknowledging the hysterical crowds several times, he fell exhausted onto his bed fully clothed.

Moreau let himself in and noiselessly tiptoed to his side. He looked down at the insensible figure, the lines and streaked face powder. What this man had endured in the past month was beyond description but it had led to his being set once more to reign over France, a deed of historical dimensions that would resound magnificently down the years.

Tenderly he drew up the silken coverlet and whispered, 'Sire, you've achieved more than is mortal. We do all make honour. But in the days to come the battles you face will be far harder.' He would have to bring together a fractured nation, repair a defeated people, then lead them and their country to their rightful place among the concourse of mankind. And, at the same time, confront whatever the Allies could bring against him.

For a few more moments Moreau stared down at the sleeping emperor, then quietly took his leave.

Up before dawn the emperor was at his desk with indecent cheerfulness, summoning Moreau to share a snatched breakfast.

'So, Majesty, what's first on the list?' he mumbled. He could think of so much – was Bonaparte to be re-crowned emperor or was it to be an understated decree of assumption of the throne? How to handle the fractious Parliament, the status of reopened trade, in short showing their face to the world and—

'First? I'd think you well know, Old Crow.'

'Sire?'

'Settle things with the Allies. They're at each other's throats in Vienna anyway, and don't want to be vexed by our internal arrangements. I need their compliance in a recognition of myself as *de facto* ruler of a stable France in place of that unsainted ninny Louis as much for the sake of our malcontents as them. Then we can get down to business.'

'So in the future . . .'

'Old Crow, our past glory will shine a path to what may be possible then.'

He stroked his chin thoughtfully. 'Fouché. I'll have him send someone he trusts to make discreet overtures to Castlereagh and the rest. Meanwhile I'll put a stopper to that noise in the Assembly.'

'That will be a miracle should it be achieved, I believe.'

'A plebiscite. To form a constitution – providing for two chambers, the peers and the representatives. That'll keep them a-brawling for years.'

He rubbed his hands briskly. 'And now another cutlet to recruit the strength.'

In the days that followed Moreau worked harder than ever before. And it quickly became clear that Bonaparte trusted no one, suspecting infidelity and duplicity on all sides, but by bold strokes and cunning rising to any challenge.

Pardons were granted to all who had erroneously taken the royalist cause. A broader basis for compensation for returning aristocrats was announced, and promises made to appeal to those enduring humiliation and hardship under the old regime.

Gratifyingly, no response was evident from the quarrelling Allies.

Then one morning a statement was issued from Vienna. It was sudden, shocking and clever. The Allies had declared Napoleon Bonaparte an outlaw. They were not at war with

France: the enemy was not the French nation but the person of Bonaparte. And to this end they were forming a fresh Coalition to bring about the final extirpation of the scourge of all Europe.

Moreau found him in his study, scribbling notes he flung to the side, one by one.

'Oh, do sit, Moreau. I shan't be long.' If the emperor was downcast at the news he didn't show it.

'A contemptible blow, sire.'

'You think so? I'd have thought it predictable.'

'Why so, pray?'

'It's but an excuse to open war against France and tear her empire from her. They see how my return has given heart and spirit to the French nation and are mortally frightened that we shall rise again, to their routing.'

'By driving a wedge between our patriots and lost sheep.'

'As you say. Now there's a mort of work ahead. Shall we begin?'

In rising excitement Moreau saw that the danger had energised him – the old Bonaparte had emerged to seize the moment.

His strategy was clear: forget all thoughts of a ponderous defence of, first, Paris and then out in a ring to more distant parts. Instead, a lightning thrust into the heartland of the Allies, through the eastern border into the Netherlands and then Prussia, confusing and scattering them before they could assemble the mighty armies of before.

'Will the people bear another war? It's much to ask of them.'

'If I give them a quick and glorious victory they'll follow me anywhere, Old Crow.'

'We've only a small army – the Allies must number in their hundreds of thousands.'

Bonaparte frowned. 'Yes. For this we have to fall back on conscription.'

'That will not be easy. They call it "the blood tax" on the streets.'

'If they want their glory they have to fight for it. Now let's get our order of battle in shape.'

He'd already sketched out his dispositions and Moreau concentrated to take it all in carefully.

'The main, under my command – I will call it l'Armée du Nord – here, ready to move off before the end of the month. Five corps, artillery, cavalry and my Imperial Guard.'

A sound, balanced force calculated to move fast and require light support.

'And for discouraging a flanking assault, an Army of the Rhine in Strasbourg, a strong showing at the Pyrenees and another in the Alps. Perhaps a separate force near Toulon to put down the royalists.'

There was very little time. To assemble weaponry, horses and equipment in such numbers was a heroic endeavour, as was getting into place the stores of war ready for the march, all with a measure of secrecy.

And their objective? An even more closely kept secret.

Moreau, however, perceived the real plan when he received orders from Bonaparte to head a clandestine band over the border into the Netherlands. There, as an engineer, he was to reconnoitre the crossings possible between Mons and Charleroi for an army and its guns.

So it was Brussels.

Such was the urgency that he set out the next morning and was rapidly up with the border. That night he and his detachment crossed to make their survey.

He discovered that there were indeed adequate bridges across the Sambre for the volume and loads foreseen. And it appeared that the enemy was not expecting them, for the ground was thinly defended, considering that they were less than thirty miles from Brussels.

Moreau's heart beat faster – Napoleon Bonaparte was coming up fast with his main army and, with what was contained in his dispatches, would not delay in throwing his forces into battle.

He was in time. The next day the world would see the beginning of the gigantic gamble that would end in his glorious triumph.

Chapter 74

At sea off Brest

As day followed day the tension subsided from his little squadron outside Brest. If the break-out was imminent there was no sign of it so far, and Kydd guessed that the French were waiting for some triggering event to coordinate their actions. Or, possibly, they'd given up their intentions on seeing a British squadron doggedly back in position across the Brest approaches.

But as time passed Kydd's anxieties took another tack, familiar yet different. They had left Plymouth at breakneck speed and had won the race – they were in position on time. But at a cost: their provisioning and watering had been sketchy. Only *Centaur* had anything like a full hold of provisions and none that had completed with wood and water.

If this was a usual blockade an orderly system of victualling hoys would keep them supplied, and in turn ships of the squadron would fall back on Torbay to water and take fresh beef aboard. But the system, with all its requirements for victualling agents and their contracts, in the field had not yet been restored. Yet his squadron would be looking to their admiral for a solution.

It was out of the question to detach even a single effective ship from the squadron either to replenish in England or to send one of his precious inshore sloops to beg for resupply. The squadron must remain entire, whatever the cost, and subsist on what they had. In the first instance he would signal that all ships go 'two upon one', which the seamen would know as 'short canny', and leave the details to them.

The hardest hit would be the little brig-sloops and cutters, whose sea time was measured in days only before they must re-victual. They would already be pinched for sustenance and could not be expected to endure for long off the iron-bound Brittany coast.

Desperate times deserved desperate measures. At the moment Kydd had six ships-of-the-line in company. He decided to assign to each one a pair of the lesser breed to keep in victuals from their own stores, however that was managed. And he'd address the larger issue of provisions as he could later.

The flag-lieutenant was summoned and left with orders for the fleet accordingly.

Thanks to his dear Persephone, his personal stores were well stocked. He would issue invitations to the short-provisioned wardroom at decent intervals even if he could not to the larger fleet.

Last, he ordered Tippett to hail a passing fisherman and purchase his catch. Sailors did not count fish as anything like as belly-filling as beef or pork and complained bitterly about the resulting toll on the mess kettles, but this was a proven way to augment their victuals.

It had been a generally accepted principle during the recent hostilities not to make war on fishermen, with the result that both sides took advantage of it. The fisher-folk delighted in the trade – offloading their catch right where they'd hauled it aboard meant so much longer on the scene for more fishing without putting back to port.

Kydd had another reason to treat with the fishermen. 'Mr Dicken, I desire you accompany the crew purchasing fish. Kindly hear what you can of their jabber that would be of interest to me.' With as yet no relay of victualling hoys from home he had no feed of intelligence, let alone common news of the day. At least he would hear the latest gossip of the continent and conceivably that which touched most closely his greatest concern: the readiness for sea of the Brest fleet.

The boat put off in a tumbling sea but was soon up with a low-bulwarked lugger. 'You have turbot?' *Centaur*'s master's mate demanded, in execrable French, chinking coins suggestively.

'*Mais non*, but we have cod. You want while fresh from the sea?' The grizzled old skipper was clearly familiar with the barbarian English.

Dicken listened carefully. Regrettably, the patter about him was in some heathen Brittany dialect that he couldn't understand.

To get closer he eased himself from the pinnace to the fishing boat. '*B'jour, M'sieur le skipper.*'

'*B'jour,*' came a guarded reply.

'Things are quiet for you, *n'est-ce pas?*'

'As can be expected.'

'*Pardon?*'

'You haven't heard – *l'empereur* Bonaparte – he's in Paris, the villain. All the country rises to do him homage. He's back on his throne.'

'So—'

'So we expects another war.'

This could only mean that Napoleon Bonaparte had escaped from Elba and had secured the devotion of the nation. Consequently he had the means to resume his previous conquests.

'How do you—'

'*Salut toi là,*' the skipper growled, at a deck-boy. The lad slipped away, returning with a rolled-up newspaper, which he handed over.

It was the *Moniteur*, the official organ of the French state, which laid out in unmistakable terms that the state of France was now in the hands of an emperor with the avowed intent to raise France high again.

There were details – a new constitution was about to be announced, royalists forgiven . . .

Aboard Kydd took the newspaper impatiently. Bearing in mind that the *Moniteur* had never been famed for truth-telling he could still put together a picture that did not make pleasant reading. In effect the entire situation in the defeated nation had been thrown into turmoil with the end result unknown.

It was fairly obvious that before long Bonaparte would resume his wars of conquest. It made sense for them to time any clandestine actions to begin together. At the same time that Bonaparte marched out, the Brest fleet would make its move.

This was bad enough but a darker thought began to emerge. What if there was a deeper plot – that Bonaparte's march instead was towards the sea, intended to meet a victorious fleet that had swept the Channel clear for an invasion?

In hours the state of the world would be utterly undone and history would take quite another course . . .

And all that stood between Bonaparte and his triumph was Admiral Kydd's tiny fleet.

Never had he felt so alone. As a ship's captain he'd been blessed with those like Renzi and Craddock to whom he could confide his fears and hopes, but as an admiral he was expected to exist in lonely isolation.

Crushing his doubts he sat back to consider the alternatives. There were not many. Another ship-of-the-line, *Brunswick*, had joined the squadron but her captain was complaining of unsound timbers and could prove a liability. Two cutters and a gun-brig were all very well but the greater need was ships that could lie in the line-of-battle – *his* line.

His eyes strayed about the cabin, the most comfortable and extravagantly appointed he'd ever been able to claim as his own. But as yet without the warmth of belonging, which could only come with long sea voyaging. And dangers shared. Much as had happened with *Thunderer*.

Snapping back to the present he reviewed what he'd prepared his squadron to do. It was all very well to order them to plant themselves squarely across the entrance to Brest but in what formation? To form up in line-of-battle needed miles of sea-room and time, and was the classic practice to bring about a fleet action. But in this instance he was expecting to be greatly outnumbered, which if he was in a line would result in the enemy taking the opportunity to double their lines to take them on both sides.

No, it had to be done in another way. A tight concentration, so no ship could be on its own. Yes, some sort of mutual support pattern. As only a new-found admiral he hadn't had time to read the theory and histories – his inspiration had to be that of the imperishable memory of Nelson.

The object of Kydd's squadron was to inflict the maximum damage and casualties to delay and discourage the break-out. He had to concentrate his firepower but at the same time remain manoeuvrable and ready by signal to change tactic.

That was it . . . Two Nelson columns and close together – but each ship leaving a space astern through which its opposite number could direct fire, effectively allowing all guns on all ships to engage on both sides.

It demanded discipline and courage and not a little seamanship to hold position. Did his captains possess these qualities?

'Mr Lovett,' he called.

His flag-lieutenant appeared promptly.

'We exercise the fleet in accordance with these Fighting Instructions.' It was up to Lovett to ensure that Dicken's carefully worded script was copied out, one for every ship, to be deftly tossed aboard each in an oil-cloth package. Kydd would give them the rest of the forenoon to digest the contents and call a captains' conference for the afternoon.

When the time came the captains were courteously welcomed aboard. It was still a thing of awe and satisfaction to Kydd to receive them each in full dress uniform, sword and breeches that they'd had to don, anxious about their appearance before the august admiral in his flagship – and he, Tom Kydd, perruquier of Guildford, was that admiral.

He wasted no time in getting down to the essentials. How he wanted this battle to be fought and what was expected of them.

The idea of a staggered double line was novel but well received. However, it wasn't long before the more battle experienced of them realised its main disadvantage – gunsmoke. They'd be so close that the vast quantities generated by the concentration of firepower would make sighting past the stern of the one opposite a chancy affair.

He had an answer – of sorts. He had the initiative, the enemy columns would be pierced by his two by three concentration. Therefore he had the choice of the angle of penetration, which he would try to ensure would see the wind passing down his columns, not across, thereby clearing most of the smoke from the gunners' sight-lines.

His captains ruminated on the challenge of holding position while seamen were at both sides of guns. This was the case for ships in standard line ahead as well but the manoeuvre would need close watch not only on the next ahead but as well the opposite line.

Kydd was the only one with experience of not just one but two major engagements – the Nile and Trafalgar – and he shared what he'd learned.

Unsaid was the one thing that neither he nor his opponent could command. The weather.

Before they departed Kydd had some final words. 'Gentlemen, I won't dwell on how vital to our country this action will be. I've a belief, however, that we have some little days before we must do our duty because Bonaparte will want to harmonise his march on the world with this menace on England.

'Therefore, beginning tomorrow, we spend every hour we have left to us in exercise, practice and more exercise.'

It wasn't much of a paean to battle but that was not his way. Something of his single-mindedness did communicate for they went over the side with grave, committed features.

'*Valiant*'s pennants and "keep better station",' Kydd rapped in a hard voice. The signal soared up – not so much an order as a public rebuke. It was not a serious infraction – the 74 had strayed by yards beyond the two-cable separation he'd laid down, noted by an eager lieutenant with a sextant taking angles.

It was going well, he had to admit. The trick with the staysails, which could be handled from on deck, had been readily adopted by them all and *Centaur*'s gunner had pronounced a fair sight-line in each case.

Rather less satisfactory was the signal-handling. Kydd

needed to see a fast response to some of the less well-known orders, the tack-in-common or tack-in-succession, and he was going to get it.

'All vessels, "Assume inverse order of sailing,"' if the enemy line turned back on itself to rescue the centre as had happened at Trafalgar.

'*Spencer*'s pennants – "Why are your larboard gun-ports closed?"' Thank goodness for Popham's telegraphic code.

It went on relentlessly.

Kydd sniffed the wind. It was damn near summer but this meant nothing to the Bay of Biscay. A sullen slop was on the waters and the sky uniformly hazy, something evil lurking out in the west.

It took the zest out of sail-handling, a listless sag to the lines to leeward and a sultry flap in the upper rigging. In these waters it could well change in a very short time to a snarling blast – or not.

They continued their exercises and, as if obliging Kydd for a variation, the winds shifted from the customary south-west to veer more in the north, strong and chill.

In the morning they met their affable fisherman and his friends, for to keep a fleet supplied, even one as small as Kydd's, needed tons' weight of fish.

'News?' asked Dicken politely.

'You wan' news? I have!'

It was there in the *Moniteur*, probably dictated by Bonaparte himself, Kydd reflected sourly. In response to hostile moves by the Allies an army was being formed to defend the sacred soil of France and it was about to strike out against its tormentors. Its leader would be none other than the emperor himself, Napoleon Bonaparte.

The time had come. Bonaparte was making his move – and so must the Bonapartists in Brest at any time from now on.

An all-ships signal was thrown out to come to full readiness, and obedient to his orders all drew together in their tight formation ready for whatever they would face.

As the afternoon wore on, the seas and winds firmed into a spiteful bluster, white caps appearing and the inevitable rain squalls coming down on them. It was not pleasant but that was what the blockade squadrons had endured since the wars had begun.

Then the light began to fade. It was beyond belief that a large body of sail would attempt a sally in restricted and dangerous waters during the night hours in threatening weather. With something like relief, Kydd signalled to disperse and lie off until daybreak.

There was little more he could do, not even to award the men an extra tot of rum, for this was the captain's prerogative and he doubted that Tippett would have the imagination.

Restlessly he sat wedged in his armchair flicking over the pages of a worthy book but his mind couldn't stray far from the thought of the battle to come. Did every admiral fret like he in the night before or . . .

His eyes caught the miniature of Persephone dandling Francis, a lively, light-hearted likeness that always lifted his spirits. What was she doing at that exact moment? Intelligent, an admiral's daughter, she would be under no illusions and was probably trying to find something to occupy herself.

He would write her a letter!

Now, what should he say? There was the possibility that they could join action tomorrow and the outcome in his case . . .

He nibbled the end of the quill. A last letter? She wouldn't in the least want a maudlin life confession or an artificially patriotic declaration, more in the way of . . . putting down just what love he held for her, what she meant in his life . . .

His eyes pricked and, with a start, he realised he was in precisely the same position as his hero Nelson on the eve of Trafalgar. He had written what he must have suspected to be possibly his final thoughts to his loved one. But did Admiral Kydd have such noble, majestic and powerful words at his command?

In the pre-dawn murk and cold, driving spindrift on the quarterdeck no one noticed the figure in the well-worn oilskins quietly appearing to stand behind the group at the conn, their heads down at the whipping blast.

'How's the glass?' Kydd heard the muffled, ill-tempered voice of the officer-of-the-watch demand of the slight shape of a midshipman. The lad clumsily crossed the deck to go below dutifully to consult the barometer.

He was back quickly, skidding and falling once on the wet deck but gamely picking himself up to report, 'Still above twenty-eight an' three-fourths, sir.'

So no real blow in store for the moment – Kydd had suffered far worse in these waters. At the same time it was not particularly fair to appear on deck without announcement, but for some reason he needed to be here to see in the new day as he had countless times in the past.

By slow degrees darkness lifted, revealing a tumbling white-streaked waste of Atlantic nastiness stretching out to a wan grey horizon.

Four of the squadron were in sight and it re-formed as Kydd slipped below but not before he'd noticed something. Patiently, he waited for it to become evident to the watch-on-deck and was well into his toast and marmalade when a breathless lieutenant presented himself.

'Cap'n Tippett's respects and desires you to know the wind's backed more into the nor'-west-b'-west, sir.'

'And?'

'Er, and it means the Frenchy is headed?'

'Very good,' Kydd said drily. 'I shall be up on deck when my breakfast is finished.'

All the time the wind was in the west no sortie was possible through the Goulet except at the cost of throwing the entire granite coast into a lee shore for themselves – hellishly dangerous for any square-rigged ship caught between headlands and unable to tack out against the wind.

For the moment they could safely lie further out to sea, but not too far: if the wind shifted back into north it was then fair for the break-out. If they were slow to return, the French could slip by unharmed for their Channel onslaught.

The weather had not improved by the time he made his – official – appearance on deck. He looked about imperiously and addressed Tippett. 'Signal, "Ships to stay in sight of flag at all times."'

'Aye aye, sir.'

Over to larboard it did his heart good to see the light frigate *Topaze*, loyally keeping station, taking seas in white explosions on her bow, her motions frisky and energetic. His good friend Bazely was aboard her. Kydd had last seen him in much more civilised company, but before that in places as wild as the Arctic, and there they'd not been strangers to a blow.

Guiltily he realised there was no need for an admiral to keep the deck in the filthy weather and, after acknowledging the respectful morning greetings, ducked below and allowed Sankey to towel him down.

He allowed a grin to surface at the thought of Picheur cursing the wind foul in the west. If he was under orders from Bonaparte he would have some explaining to do to the notoriously sea-blind emperor as to why he hadn't left the comforts of port.

As it happened, two, then three days passed with the wind stubbornly in the west. Kydd guessed that somewhere far out in the Atlantic one of those infamous giant revolving storms was making its passage, its reach extending a thousand miles or more, its effects long felt.

After five days there was a marked increase in the ferocity of the rising gale. Flogging canvas was taken in before it tore, preventer tackles rigged, and on the tiller relieving tackles secured, all well-known tempest precautions.

It was all Kydd could do to stop himself stamping about in scrutiny of the procedures but, yet again, it was the task of lesser mortals and he was obliged to hold himself aloof.

The gale flattened to a hard blast and the big ship began to stagger at the driving succession of combers from out to sea, a fearful thing on such a cruel shore.

If this was his ship nothing could have stopped him seeing it through on the quarterdeck with his officers but in the flagship that would rightly be construed as lack of confidence in the ship's command team. He had no alternative than to keep out of sight and let them get on with it.

His instincts told him the situation, even before the lieutenant's insistent knock on the door brought the dismaying news that the gale had veered more to the north.

It was now approaching fair for Picheur to make his lunge seaward.

This was a serious concern for, in respect of wild seas on a lee shore, they'd kept well offshore into the deep Atlantic. Now they had to close with the coast with all speed. If Picheur was quick he could choose to make his exit before they arrived, then a sharp turn to one side or the other and vanish.

On deck it was clear that nothing had changed apart from the wind more in the north and as hard, the seas still in a restless charging towards the out-of-sight land. Now, though, there was no other recourse than to head for the deadly waters inshore to seal off the Goulet.

Kydd knew he was throwing the ships and their crews into fearful hazard so close to the lethal coast but the higher purpose must be served – if Picheur made his sortie unhampered the Channel would be open to him and Kydd would have failed.

With the signal hoist to follow quivering board-taut, *Centaur* led Kydd's ships in, doubled lookouts in the foretop to sight the first sea-mark to fix their position after days of dead-reckoning out at sea. His general plan was to find the Iroise, the wider outer area before the Goulet, and in this near northerly to stay to windward on its north side as this would leave the other side as the lee shore with all its hazards.

This would be the rocky shoreline around Les Vieux Moines – the Old Monks. Tucking in on this seaboard would not only lead them safely along to the Grand Minou then to the narrow point of departure, the Goulet, but its lofty crags would as well give them shelter as they proceeded in.

The disadvantage was the same as everywhere in this hellish seascape. A sub-sea nightmare of rocks, outcrops and reefs on the approach that could, without warning, tear mercilessly the bowels from a ship. The tide at the moment was on the make but this was not in their favour. Much more needed was a low state of tide that exposed the horrors in a wild wash of seas.

As if this was not enough, the first chill squall blustered in, a curtain of white that swept across the wind-lashed waves, cold and spiteful. That it usually heralded a moderating of the blow in some not too distant time was of little comfort as the wind continued to veer. It stung and blinded lookouts and deck officers just when their eyesight was most needed.

There was no need to take up their tight formation at this stage, for play with the guns was impossible in these seas. Far more important was the need to bring the squadron to the broad field of battle.

The squall cleared to leave an empty sea. It was imperative to make a fix before they were up with the Brittany coast and, if at all possible, the tower of the light on Pointe Saint-Mathieu.

Hour by hour they made their approach, pitching and rolling as if demented but not daring to ease sail for fear of being too late. The northerly was still fair for them but Kydd's dread was that the wind could steadily veer even further until it was in their teeth, and after that it would be fair for Picheur and his fleet.

Another squall bullied its way past them, the men at the helm straining at their labours, heads down to avoid the worst of it.

Centaur and her fleet were risking all at his command. It was a heavy thought, not made easier for him with the realisation that it was entirely as a result of guesswork – his guesswork. He'd actually gone into their midst and seen nothing that could definitively state Brest was in a state of insurrection in the Bonapartist cause. Despite their claims the Martinique transport might merely have been on the way to add to the small forces aimed at liberating Napoleon from Elba and not to join a strategic-level plot to aid in an invasion of England.

The whole thing sounded so far-fetched that his resolution wavered. In his captains' conferences no one had contradicted his reasoning but why would they? He was Admiral Kydd, much above their competence to dare question.

Until now it had simply been a matter of a precautionary cruising off the French mainland just in case, but by recklessly closing with the iron-bound coast he was putting thousands of men in mortal danger.

In all humanity he should cease his mad dash immediately and put about for the relative security of the open sea.

If he was right and Picheur was at that moment getting under way it would be a gross betrayal of what he owed his country, but if he was wrong, with the fine seamanship in his fleet to be found after twenty years of war, there was every chance they'd come through unscathed.

They'd crack on.

A little after one in the afternoon a sudden cry from the foretop had Lieutenant Moore mounting the shrouds with a telescope, the officer with longest service in these waters.

To keep focus at the glass took real skill, bracing against a bar taut and thrumming line from aloft but it was done.

'Sir,' Moore reported, when he won the deck again, carefully looking somewhere between Kydd and his captain. 'Three points to starboard, four miles? Weather too murky to be sure, and it being half-tide difficult to make out.'

'Hazard a guess, man,' Tippett urged irritably.

This was a hard thing, for the sailing directions had helpful sketches of notorious threats at low and often high tide states. A jagged rocky group looked very different when fully exposed, but there was never a half-tide view.

'Ah. First took it for the Bozmen, but another squint an' I saw it didn't have a flat an' reef to the east. More like to be the Parquette but—'

'You're saying we could be either side of the Iroise? Come, come, sir, this is of no use to us.'

Kydd took a swift look about them. Three sail-of-the-line were in sight in a straggle astern, *Topaze* fading into thick weather somewhere ahead. In real danger Bazely was there with rockets to warn and Kydd was confident the squadron would read the situation without being told.

'I suggest we leave our unknown rock not so far to larboard, Captain,' Kydd said carefully. Would this be construed an order in any court-martial to follow?

'You do, sir?' Tippett replied, the wind whipping his words almost to inaudibility.

If this was to the south, keeping in with the thing would still give them a margin before the main coastline loomed. If they should be in the north they were in position to raise the land as they chose.

'I do, sir.'

Orders were passed: to lay the rock a half-mile to larboard. If this was near Les Vieux Moines it was a good sign – they'd reached their objective before the French. Kydd had half expected this: Picheur would know he had an untried fleet and would let the weather moderate before risking his ships.

And in that moment it chose to rain. Thin, near-horizontal and salt-tasting it clamped in, a heavy mist obscuring all out beyond a hundred yards, firming into a harder, lashing downpour that made it impossible to locate the evil ledge of rock.

With no other option than to continue ahead it was at last sighted very close fine on the larboard bow, taking Atlantic surf in hammering blows raising smashes of white a hundred feet skywards.

Warily they bucketed past, all eyes on it as it passed to windward, nearly hidden in surf and roiling seas and defying all identification.

They were now inshore of an unknown crag and heading

further in without either a sight of what was ahead or an indication of where to lay course.

Without warning, out of the white mist of spume and rain dead ahead, another, larger, sea-girt rock emerged, more an islet than a reef ledge.

Instinctively Kydd roared, 'Hard up at the helm there!' With the northerly they were close-hauled on the larboard tack and it made all the sense in the world to fall off the wind and leave it to windward.

'Sir! Sir! That's Le Corbin – we're in the south!' Moore's face was distorted with fear and, with a lurch of the heart, Kydd knew why. Not so far ahead of them must be Pointe du Toulinguet, a tongue of land that generations of mariners knew marked the southern reaches of the Iroise.

And below it was the wicked expanse of Roche de Lion, then the awful dark granite cliffs and precipices of the mainland of Brittany.

They had one chance. To weather the point, get past it to the bay beyond. In the rapidly diminishing sea-room there was no space to stay about to safely head out to sea – they could only stay on this board and claw their way hard up by the wind around the bleak point . . . and pray.

The sailing master, Clare, held rigid with concentration, stood by Kydd as if seeking approval for his actions as each sail was individually trimmed to bring about the closest to the wind *Centaur* could manage.

The Roche de Lion emerged in a savage welter of thundering seas but, praise be, it could be left to leeward as they passed. Now there was an even more formidable mark – Toulinguet itself.

Its ugly cliffs nearly hidden in the murk and sleeting spindrift, it loomed as the finality of the land that had set *Centaur* afloat and was now reclaiming its own in the harshest possible way.

Clare knew these waters and swore that from two hundred yards off the point out there would be no hull-ripping peril. All they had to do was round it into the bay beyond and go about to make it safely out to sea.

For a heart-stopping moment, as they closed with the desolate cliffs, it seemed they would not make it. They crept around, every sail and rope thrumming with tension, at less than a couple of ship's lengths off the outer vicious disturbance of a sub-sea rock.

'Just in time, Sir Thomas,' the master managed. 'See – wind's veering still.'

If they'd left their run only a few hours they could not have weathered Toulinguet, and their carcass even now would be battered to splinters somewhere in the desolation of rock and scree to the south of the point.

They were not safe yet. They could ease from their desperate clawing and shape a saner course, but there was still the staying about to gain the open sea.

It would be just as chancy. The bay opening up was clear but only a mile or so long before another craggy headland jutted out to bar their way. They had only this distance to put the helm over and, by a skilled set of sail manoeuvres, put the bow of the ship through the eye of the wind, then had it come in on the starboard side and away.

To tack a large square-rigged vessel needed time and space and they were precious short of both. Kydd looked astern – two sail were distantly following but securely further out to sea than they, probably having seen their developing predicament earlier.

'Ready about! Stations for stays!' The order went down the deck, men leaping for their lives at the commands, the helm easing to fill the sails for best speed and lines laid along for instant use.

Tippett glanced at Kydd who nodded very slightly.

'Helm's a-lee – brace to!'

The northerly hammered in, seas crowding against the hull in heavy thumps of spume and occasionally sluicing across the deck in a powerful rush.

Now was the critical moment as the foresails were braced around to bring them aback and lever her bows over. Timing was the decisive element, and in their current plight they would have only one stab at the manoeuvre. If unsuccessful, it would see them sagging to leeward and in a short time caught up as a wreck ashore.

The Fates decided to act against them. In a chance combination of gale-driven waves and the angle they were constrained to by the shape of the bay, *Centaur*'s bow plunged and took aboard a stampeding flood of green sea. It bullied down the deck, sweeping men off their feet and into a tangle of rope that destroyed the careful sequence of the staying about.

Sickeningly, inevitably, the bows fell off the wind back to the original heading to produce the worst conceivable outcome. *Centaur* had missed stays. And with the headland impossible to weather, their fate was sealed.

'Club-haul?' the master desperately asked Kydd, but there was no time to throw out an anchor and pivot the bow around it by brute force.

Realising what they faced, the seamen had already thrown down their lines and were looking about desperately for any kind of salvation. Only a thin veneer of discipline stood between them and wholesale terror and panic.

Kydd was in a frenzy of desperation. The headland stood immovably across their path and, unable either to weather it or tack about, *Centaur* would be driven with a heavy inevitability into a hopeless destruction.

Their end was now certain.

Glancing poignantly out to sea, thoughts racing of mortality for him and so many others, Kydd caught sight of a grey shadow emerging from the filthy weather a mile or so further out.

It was *Topaze*, no doubt returning to see what had happened to the flagship. Her bearing changed as she spotted *Centaur* and cautiously made to close with them.

It was a touching gesture for there was no earthly chance she could do anything for them in this howling maelstrom. All she could do was stand off and witness their deaths in eerie imitation of Kydd himself. Some years before, off the Danish coast, he'd had to watch helplessly as a 98-gun flagship and another 74 were driven to destruction ashore in a fierce storm, ending the lives of a thousand men.

Now, here, he would be the one to die – so ironic that in clear sight only hundreds of yards off there was a well-found ship with a warm, dry wardroom and captain's cabin.

Centaur, still on the larboard tack, was locked by the winds into ruin ashore while *Topaze* was on the starboard tack and, in this veering northerly, would be granted safe passage out to sea again.

The frigate clearly saw *Centaur*'s fate and, with a pang, Kydd watched her douse sail to slow and drift out on their beam. Kydd spotted the tubby form of Bazely on her quarterdeck, saddened that his friend should be the one to see it all end.

Oddly there was agitated movement about her deck and even more weirdly he made out what it was. Bazely was lifting an object – of all things a rum cask. Bizarrely, he flourished it furiously above his head.

Surely he was not suggesting . . .

Bazely shook it again and then Kydd had it.

'Captain,' he said urgently, 'the fo'c'slemen to stations on the fore-deck – and stand by to go about.'

Tippett looked at him helplessly, plainly at the edge of reason.

'Now!' Kydd urged. '*Topaze* is going to get us out of our moil.'

Even *in extremis* convention must be followed but if Tippett failed in his duty Kydd was ready to take his place. In something like a trance, however, the orders were given and Kydd wheeled around to give Bazely his signal.

Instantly the rum cask was thrown overside and Kydd watched it bob and tug. Then, caught by the wind's blast, it was driven downwind towards them.

Desperate hands grappled it and brought it in – with the coir rope streamed from the frigate, which was quickly made fast inboard.

Another signal. In *Topaze* sail bellied and caught. The line tightened and, as *Centaur* readied again to stay about, there was a powerful coercion at her bows, forcefully tugging them through the eye of the wind to the unspeakable delirium of the starboard tack and escape.

The wind indeed veered still further but, as predicted, the blow moderated, the seas easing their wild onrush, the wind losing its hard edge. By first winning the centre of the Iroise, *Centaur* was able to bring together her scattered squadron and confirm that, mercifully, all had survived.

Still shaken by their near-calamity Kydd focused his thoughts.

There was now no question that Picheur would seize his chance for a run and be upon them in hours . . . if Kydd was right in his thinking that the conspiracy was a reality. He hadn't the leisure to call a captains' conference and could only trust that they understood his unusual fighting formation and would see it through in the thick of battle.

'"Flag to *Topaze* – manoeuvre well executed."' The highest praise that, as an admiral, he could bestow. Later, Bazely and he would raise a glass or two together, and as was the way of it in the navy, nothing more would be said.

But he had more immediate work for the stout little frigate. Another signal hoist had the single-decker on its way to the Goulet, the narrow passage where Picheur and his fleet must issue out, to penetrate inside to give due warning of their approach.

Making his formal appearance on deck Kydd waited for a group of the more senior officers to be grouped together, then loudly called over to Tippett, 'Ah, Captain. Very fine conduct by the Centaurs this day. I congratulate you on a first-rate ship's company and naturally there will be particular mentions in my dispatches.'

A blank expression was returned, and Kydd knew that a very relieved post-captain would retire to bed that night, even if on the eve of battle.

Overnight the blow had mostly subsided, innocent sunshine their reward for their suffering but if Picheur made his move it would be at first light and would be upon them shortly.

'Sir Thomas, I have to inform you that *Topaze* bears down under a press of sail with the signal "enemy in sight" hoisted,' Tippett said grimly, appearing at the admiral's cabin door.

Kydd's heart began to pound. He'd been right. There was indeed a deadly plot and it was taking place before their eyes. It was by orders received and duty to the nation that they must oppose it – at whatever cost.

For long years he'd learned how to deal with pre-battle dread but this was different. The entire outcome hung on his competence and acumen as a flag-officer and the best that could be said about him was that he was untried.

'I'll be on deck shortly,' he promised Tippett, and gave fleeting thought to what dress he should wear. Since Trafalgar it had been the practice for admirals and the like to conceal their decorations and gold lace from enemy sharpshooters in the tops. It would be plain sea-going togs.

He buckled on his fighting sword, which he'd acquired as a junior lieutenant, a gift from his Canadian uncle and a superlative weapon.

And, well, what else could he do?

In a twist of understanding, the words of the seer, the widow Garsen, came back to haunt him. The reference to the fork in the road and great consequences was to this very day. He could choose to retire, wildly outnumbered, or sacrifice himself and his squadron for the higher cause.

His team was waiting on the quarterdeck. Flag-lieutenant Lovett regarded him gravely and Dicken, who he knew had not been in action before, stood calmly, set-faced but steady. Others – Tippett at one pace behind him, the grim-faced captain's coxswain Bayley, with cutlass and a brace of pistols in his belt, and the captain of marines within discreet hail.

He raised his eyes to the horizon for by now *Topaze* had become visible, all sails nobly straining, a marked bone in her teeth, her hoist still abroad and fluttering urgently.

And then the first pale shapes of sails appearing past the point. The enemy.

Was it even possible to think in those terms? The complexity of the situation pressed in on him. The French Navy notionally owed allegiance to the King of France and was therefore not hostile. To open fire on ships flying his flag, even in a mistaken belief, would bring universal outrage and Kydd's disgrace. And if he let them past he was disobeying his own orders.

He knew he'd have to act, and act alone. He ruthlessly crushed his doubts.

'Go to quarters, if you please, Captain.'

They had cleared for action in the last hour before dawn and the martial drumming at the hatchways echoed in a grim silence.

He brought up his pocket glass and trained it on the lead vessel, a first-rate. It wore the flag of a *contre-amiral* but, much more importantly, the white ensign of the Bourbons.

There was now no longer any procrastinating. The decision an admiral alone must make and no other was upon him. If the oncoming armada would not obey his call to return to port he would open fire in defiance of the consequences.

Relieved at the resolution he looked across at the officers around their captain, standing calm and steadfast, ready for whatever the day might bring.

Kydd eased into a smile. There was no doubting: *Centaur* was going to do her duty and this was to obey his orders even if it meant near certain annihilation.

And out on the beam – *Valiant, Dictator* and *Hector* in impeccable station, battle ensigns aloft and scrupulously obedient to Kydd's orders for tight formation. There, likewise, would be hearts of oak and stern obedience to duty.

They were ready.

Mid-channel, under topsails, Kydd's squadron awaited the conclusion.

The French showed no signs of deviating and came on in an ominous line – Kydd counted a dozen at least but then, at half a mile off, there was a diverging, the line beginning to break up.

Sudden hope rose, then died, when he understood what was happening. Alternate vessels were moving out until the line had transformed into two columns advancing together.

They intended at the least to sail past on either side of Kydd's tight little squadron, at worst to surround and crush them.

In either case, within the hour there would be a raging clash at arms that, before the sun went down, would end in carnage on both sides.

Was there no alternative? If there was, only he could provide it. His thoughts raged, then settled. 'A white flag at the fore-shrouds!' he snapped. 'Squadron, heave to. A boat in the water under sail, its own white flag. And a lieutenant. No arms to be carried.'

He was going to Picheur to confront the man, not the battle-fleet. Whether the white flags would deter the fighting would be known very shortly.

Before even he'd boarded the barge an answering white flag was briskly mounted in Picheur's flagship.

But there was no corresponding heaving to. As Admiral Kydd's boat got under way the French fleet continued to advance. It was a provocative and less than honourable treatment of the conventions of a white flag.

As they neared the flagship it pulled out of line and backed sails to heave to, and Kydd's barge came in to hook on at the side-steps of the massive three-decker. The peculiar odour of a French ship wafted over them, the alien qualities that Kydd remembered from more than one capture.

A figure appearing at the entry-port disappeared again.

Gripping the manrope, Kydd mounted up in as dignified a manner as he could. The instant he passed into the middle gun-deck the squeal of pipes sounded in a faultless display of naval ceremony. An expressionless lieutenant approached and requested in perfect English that Kydd follow him as he was expected by Admiral Picheur.

Feigning to adjust his dress – still the plain action rig without decoration – Kydd snatched a glance about. Every gun was manned, the match tubs emitting wisps of smoke, the gun crews clutching their implements of trade.

Like *Centaur*, the vessel was at a split-yarn prepared for action.

'Why, Admiral Kydd! Welcome aboard, Sir Thomas. What do you think we can do for you?' Standing by his opulent desk Picheur, in his far more flamboyant dress, spoke silkily, confidently.

Wrestling with his thoughts Kydd hesitated.

'Oh, Admiral, I'm forgetting my manners,' Picheur added smoothly, 'but refreshments will have to wait, for you see we're rather in haste, sir.'

'Why are your gun crews closed up?' Kydd blurted, burning at the languid contempt in Picheur's tones.

The groomed eyebrows rose in mock puzzlement. 'But, of course, we are even now on our way to gunnery practice, Admiral. You will understand a ship's company becomes stale if in harbour too long.'

There was no use fencing like this and Kydd took a breath. 'Sir, I would not have you in any doubt.' Despite his apprehensions he felt his voice take on an edge of menace. 'The orders from my commander-in-chief require me in these times of insurrection and threat to ensure that no armed vessel enters or leaves any French port.'

He drew himself up and demanded formally, 'I therefore advise that you put about and return to Brest until these uncertain times are past.'

The lazy smile disappeared and Picheur straightened. 'Sir!' he rapped. 'Are you expecting a flag-officer of the Marine Royale to take such shameful orders from an officer of – of a foreign navy?'

'To defer your gunnery practice and return – yes, sir, I do.'

For a long moment a silence hung and Kydd tensed for a contemptuous defiance.

But the smile returned and Picheur eased. 'Admiral Kydd, do consider my position. It is my duty to take my fleet to sea to assure myself of its fitness for battle. Supposing that scoundrel Napoleon Bonaparte sets his ships upon me, should I not fight back?'

He gave an expressive Gallic shrug.

Kydd was taken aback. Why was the man playing with him? It made no sense.

Then it did. Picheur did not want to fight Kydd. He clearly would win but at a cost. He had to preserve his forces for the much more important goal of clearing the Channel for the invasion crossing. It was the only thing in Kydd's favour, and if he could turn it to advantage, the entire crisis would be averted.

His mind raced, but to his despair no solution came.

Noting his hesitation, Picheur went on persuasively, 'Sir Thomas, a little gunnery practice in the Iroise surely is not too much to ask.'

There was only one reply possible.

'Sir, my orders are explicit. I must require you to retire whence you came.'

Picheur's expression hardened. 'And if I stand on my honour as a French officer and continue upon my lawful occasions?'

Any threat Kydd could throw out would only be laughable and he took refuge in a stubborn 'I have my orders, sir.'

'And I mine, sir.'

'Do I understand by this that you intend to proceed on to sea?' Kydd said huskily, with a lurch of foreboding, knowing what the answer would be.

'I shall, sir!'

There was nothing more he could say or do. In a short time the world he knew would be split apart in a holocaust of shot and flame, and there was every chance that before the end of the day Persephone would be a widow.

'Then I shall escort you to your boat.'

Kydd's expression must have told the boat's crew what their future held and they remained mute on the way back to *Centaur*.

Having failed to heave to, the French ships now had come up with Kydd's squadron and lay to within close gun range in unmistakable threat, in their numbers easily dominating.

There could be only one end to it, but they would pay for it!

Chapter 75

As soon as he regained *Centaur*'s quarterdeck, Kydd barked, 'Get down that white flag – the talking's over!'

It would give indication that Kydd was deadly serious in his intentions and was making ready to carry them out.

'Er, you will give the word, Sir Thomas?'

'I will,' Kydd answered, irritated that Tippett had not remembered what he'd said in his orders. The signal to the squadron for opening the action would be the first shot fired from *Centaur*, which he alone would take the responsibility for ordering, it being his considered judgement that there was no alternative.

And that time had now arrived. If he did nothing and the French squadron passed him by on its mission of slaughter he could never live with the dishonour. He must do his duty and may Persephone forgive him.

With a last glance at the expectant men about him he raised his eyes to the enemy flagship. His personal trigger point was the hauling down of their white flag, the first target the three-decker most directly out on their beam.

For a fleeting moment a wash of unreality threatened to

unman him – the knowledge that a single word from him would end the lives of countless men, creating widows and untold numbers of fatherless children.

All in the line of duty.

With only a tiny tremor he raised his pocket telescope to the flagship's white flag and—

A distant crack, and another. Gunfire! And far in their rear. Some trap?

Swinging about, he tried to make out the lone craft that had evidently come down the Chenal du Four passage to emerge into the Iroise under an insane press of sail, firing guns as it came.

Astonished at the intervention Kydd strained to take in what he was seeing. It was a small craft, rigged fore and aft. A dispatch cutter! A Royal Navy aviso of the kind used in fleet communications. And it flew a carnival of flag hoists, unreadable at the distance, but very clearly the craft wanted to reach Kydd urgently.

On the edge of plunging into battle he was torn with indecision but a warning presentiment stayed his hand as the cutter slashed through the seas directly to his flagship, no doubt confused by the French squadron surrounding it.

Rounding *Centaur*'s stern, a lieutenant shouted something incomprehensible and a familiar oil-cloth package made its way up to the quarterdeck.

Not a soul dared intervene as Kydd took custody of it and, impatient to read it, in practised slices soon had the brief contents before him.

He staggered back and, in an unstoppable whirl of impressions, just managed to keep a countenance.

'Captain Tippett. A barge as before, as soon as you may.'

With white flag aloft, the boat made for Picheur's flagship, whose own white flag was still a-fly, possibly realising that the dispatch cutter's sudden appearance could mean a serious alteration in the character of what he might be facing.

He was respectfully received but at the entry-port Picheur himself awaited him. 'Sir Thomas, an unexpected pleasure. You wish to . . .?'

'I suggest we talk in private,' Kydd answered languidly, 'as the substance of our discussion is not so suitable for the lesser kind.'

A venomous look from the French admiral told Kydd his confident manner had let Picheur know he was about to learn something that was not necessarily in his favour.

There was no polite ceremony in the ornate cabin and Picheur faced him aggressively. 'So what is it that seeks to delay the inevitable?'

Kydd gave a lazy smile. 'Sir, our nations are friends and allies at this time. I thought fit to share with you this dispatch, which I'm sure will rest your anxieties with respect to the tyrant, who has recently given so much cause for alarm.'

'Your dispatches – as admiral?' Picheur snorted, disbelievingly.

'The same, sir. There can be no secrets between friends, you'll agree?'

Picheur's eyes narrowed. 'The actual . . .?'

'For which I signed not an hour ago.'

'If this is a jest . . .'

'See for yourself, sir. The signature is that of Viscount Keith, commander-in-chief of the Channel Squadron, of whom you will have heard.'

He let Picheur snatch the hurriedly written pages and hastily scan them.

His features paled as he handed them back. 'It does seem that . . .'

Kydd took them and for emphasis read aloud: '. . . *by the*

Duke of Wellington in a complete and glorious victory for the Allied nations at a place named as Waterloo. It is known that Bonaparte fled the field after his complete defeat and therefore is no longer considered a tenable threat to the civilised nations. You will remain on station until . . .'

'Welcome news, do you not think, sir?'

'Ah. I understand what you are saying, Sir Thomas. Perhaps we no longer have need for our gunnery practice and shall put back to Brest.'

'A stout decision. No doubt you will inform your people of this welcome turn of events?' There was every excuse to wallow in his triumph but he held back his feelings.

Picheur rose and stiffly escorted Kydd to the entry-port. Kydd's duty was done, Picheur's only beginning.

His orders were to remain on station until told otherwise, no doubt in view of the confusion and disorder that must reign ashore. Who knew what the vengeful followers of Bonaparte might try to wreak over a demoralised population?

It was enough to know that in a matter of days his tired but proud squadron would be returning to England, having comprehensively stood the test of courage and resolution.

That night he chaired the celebrations, careful to avoid calling it a victory dinner, but equally determined to let all know how gratified he was at their conduct. But before dressing for the occasion he'd had the lower deck cleared and in an address to the entire ship's company he'd explained the stakes that had been on the table and the consequences of the victory at Waterloo. The seamen then crowded below to claim their double tot.

A more formal occasion the next day was an invitation to the captains of the squadron, Kydd instructing Sankey to ransack the last of his private store of provisions. It was a memorable time for all, and while they could not return to England as victorious heroes, he made sure they would hold in their hearts that they'd been part of a stirring affair they could tell to their grandchildren.

It was tedious waiting for release, and when another two ships-of-the-line, *Theseus* and *Bellerophon*, joined, all he could do was issue them with his fleet orders and take station with the others.

Behind, a dispatch cutter closed at speed, arousing much curiosity. Surely Napoleon Bonaparte was no longer in possession of such an army as to threaten the Allies once more?

It was urgent orders from the commander-in-chief but not at all what was expected. Bonaparte had escaped once again!

After abandoning his army after Waterloo he was rumoured to have made plans to evade capture by taking ship to re-base himself in the United States of America.

At all costs this must be prevented, and again it would be Kydd and his ships that had the prime responsibility. He was to take his squadron and individually place it in blockade of the Atlantic coast of France, boarding every ship to prevent the fallen emperor making good his escape.

And all that anyone could be sure of was that the old foe was at large somewhere in France. Any more than that was impossible to uncover at this time. He drew up a simple list of the squadron vessels and began planning just where he could deploy them.

The most likely was that Bonaparte would head to Brest, the nearest of the Atlantic ports, and therefore that would be his post. How ironic if he made himself guest of Picheur and unstoppably broke out in his three-decker and other sails-of-the-line on a voyage to America, this time past a helpless Kydd.

Or was he cunningly travelling swiftly to any of the lesser southerly ports to slip out in an innocent merchant ship? Kydd had no alternative but to disperse the squadron as widely as he could and hope that his smaller craft would not be overwhelmed by even a single frigate.

Failure would see him crucified by a mortified Coalition and his name go down in history as a notorious incompetent.

Chapter 76

The Élysée Palace

'The *levret*, Majesty.' Nearly toppling in exhaustion, Moreau placed the collation of situation reports on the desk in front of Bonaparte. He'd spent the entire night putting it together following their frenzied return from the field at Waterloo. Bonaparte had considered it essential to reach Paris to steady the citizenry on hearing of the defeat but at the cost of most of his personal baggage, which had had to be left to the victors.

It was unreal, the livid memories of the stink and squalor, corpses and mud, the battlefield shrieks of the wounded, set against the gold-filled opulence of the palace, the peace and order, civilisation and calm.

'You're priceless, Old Crow,' Bonaparte grunted, seizing it avidly. 'Go and lie down for an hour or two while I get among it.'

Moreau could only manage a fitful doze, his mind still ringing with hideous images and the emotional drain of days.

He came back to see Bonaparte sprawled in his favourite chair, lips pursed as he considered what he'd read.

'So. A setback but not an end to it.'

'Sire?'

'Waterloo is lost to us, but since then see how noble General Rapp and his Army of the Rhine took on the Austrians at Strasbourg – and knocked 'em out of the running. And Suchet with his Army of the Alps not only did for Marshal Frimont but went on to invade Savoy, bless him!'

'The Allies are advancing, Majesty.'

'If your appreciation is to be believed, Old Crow, only the British with fifty thousand and Blücher with sixty are on the march. And last time I counted, they're easily outnumbered by our intrepid Marshal Davout here in Paris with a hundred and twenty, let alone when Grouchy, Soult and the others come over to join us.'

Moreau took reassurance from the words. The situation was not one of despair, then. Bonaparte was pointing out that while Waterloo was a reverse, the fighting was going on and with some success in many other parts.

'If we're quick, I smell a counter-stroke as will catch them strung out, giving us a famous victory when we need it most.'

This was Bonaparte at his best – turning a stinging defeat to his advantage.

'And I have a card to play that could be a settler.'

'What's that, Your Majesty?'

'The first batch of conscripts at St Cyr and the depots are ready and at hand. Do you know how many they all amount to? A hundred and fifty thousands! And if I can't do something to restore matters with a quarter-million then I'll hand in my baton.'

'The Senate won't like it.'

'They'd like to see France restored to glory and this is the only way they'll get it. Put this all together in pretty form and see what Fouché makes of it. The false-hearted reptile always wanted to be in with whoever he thinks a winner.'

Moreau saw the red-rimmed eyes, the lined features. His heart went out to his emperor, well-tried in the carnage of war and trials of empire – to be made subject to the moods of politicians who'd never heard a shot fired.

'I'll see they get it, sire.'

It didn't take long. The faction-riddled chambers met and debated but the conclusion they reached was a deep suspicion that if Bonaparte did not get what he wanted he'd dissolve them outright. Therefore they declared themselves permanently in session.

'They're locked in wrangling,' Moreau reported back. 'Without we get an approval there's no funding. We're helpless.'

'Those miserable swine!' Bonaparte raged. 'I'd see them in hell before I go begging.' He began striding up and down the room while calling down every curse possible on the perfidious deputies.

Then he subsided, slumping into a chair, morose and bitter. 'I have them so used to great victories they can't bear a single misfortune. If they don't move on the matter the Allies will be at the gates of the city in a week and then what will they say, the worthless scum?'

'The streets are alive with the people crying out for your cause,' Moreau said encouragingly.

'What use is that when the power lies with those useless pigs? Old Crow, what's to become of this poor France? I've done all I could for her . . .'

There was one last thing he could do for his nation. Moreau hesitated to put it forward, but knew it had to be said.

'Sire. As the chambers are against you and the Allies will

shortly take Paris there is only one action left that can head it off.'

'Yes,' the Emperor of France said heavily. 'Give up the throne – right?'

'Majesty, it can be no other. Time is not on our side.' That he had to be the one to press for the fall of this great man was gut-wrenching but was now his duty.

Bonaparte said nothing, staring into the void for a long time, before saying softly, 'And then what, Old Crow? What do emperors do after their act on the world's stage is over?'

Chapter 77

Château de Malmaison on the outskirts of Paris

Empty, beautiful, echoing, lonely. This was the residence Napoleon had fitted to be the married home for himself and Joséphine, but she'd died while he was exiled in Elba. What memories were flooding back to him now? wondered Moreau. Perhaps Napoleon actually preferred the loneliness, his wife Marie-Louise not prepared to return to him.

There had been no choice in the matter – the Élysée was closed to him, the Tuileries would soon be occupied by King Louis, invited by Fouché to take up his reign once more.

And hanging over all, there was the growing righteous outcry against him from those who wanted to be seen on the right side when the Bourbons took the reins of state. Even to remain in the Paris of a vengeful mob might be unwise.

'Their devotion has turned to hate,' Bonaparte whispered, in his armchair before a small fire, nursing a goblet of Chambertin. 'Should I then spend the rest of my days in this place?'

'Where else, sire?'

'Why, another country that has the grace to take me.'

'Don't think on it, sire. It won't come to that, I'm sure of it.'

'I'm tempted to think of one, Old Crow.'

'Where, Majesty?' Moreau wasn't about to abandon his respects merely on the grounds that others had.

'America.'

'Sire! You can't be serious – it's a raw, untamed nation without the blessings of civilisation as we know it and—'

'Do you not remember we once ruled there – in the south, Louisiana? I should not have let it go in 1803 but I'm sure to find a welcome there, don't you think?'

A chamberlain appeared at the door, irresolute at the sight of the two together.

'Yes?'

'Er, might you receive Major Carnot of your guard, sir? He vows it to be a matter of some urgency.'

The emissary did not waste words. 'The Prussians, sir. General Blücher has issued an order-in-general to his cavalry. They are under strict instructions to bring you in, dead or alive.'

'Um, how far distant are they, Major?'

'Small days.'

'Thank you, you may go.'

He turned back to Moreau. 'It rather settles matters, it seems. I believe we must not delay our departure. The Austrians want to lock me away in some forgotten castle, the Prussians demand to hang me, others will be content should I be shot out of hand. There's only one place where I might feel safe.'

'America, sire?'

'To America. I shall ask Decrès for a frigate or two to convey me.'

*

347

Even before the convoy of carriages had been loaded there was further crumbling of the situation. Moreau had spoken to the shadowy emissary of Fouché's office. His message was brief but unanswerable. Within a short time a warrant was about to be issued for the arrest of one Citizen Napoleon Bonaparte for the crime of treason.

Why let it be known? It seemed that Fouché was allowing Bonaparte to make a hasty exit in order to spare himself the embarrassment of a trial and disclosures.

They had to flee the country.

To where? If to America, Brest was the obvious naval seaport – the closest and best equipped. But Decrès had sworn the only frigates in seaworthy condition to cross the Atlantic were at Rochefort, halfway down the Biscay coast of France.

It would have to be done at the highest level of secrecy, for the spectacle of the Emperor of France in flight from his country would not be lightly tolerated by the people.

It was decided: Bonaparte would proceed alone in a simple carriage to Bordeaux in the centre of the richest wine region; Moreau would follow by a different route through central France with the long-term baggage disguised.

In the darkness before dawn the convoy set forth for a far different exile.

Chapter 78

Off Brest

The 'all captains' had been hoisted, accompanied by a gun.

The flagship, HMS *Centaur*, was hove to in the slackening seas and the boats of the fleet were not slow in complying. The admiral, Sir Thomas Kydd, was not known for being of a forgiving nature as far as obedience to signals went.

One by one they clambered aboard in order of seniority, assembling on the quarterdeck where they were met and greeted by the admiral.

Maitland knew Kydd from when he'd been a sloop commander, like himself, at Alexandria in the last war. The French Army of Egypt had been comprehensively defeated and Napoleon Bonaparte, after a bloody encounter at Acre, had abandoned his troops to return to Paris.

Even then Kydd had been known as a seamen's fighting captain and had gone on to fame as a frigate commander, a reputed favourite at court.

Maitland remembered the strong, open features, now lined

with concerns, but the lithe topman's figure was still in evidence, the direct gaze of the eyes just as strong.

'You've just joined, Frederick,' Kydd said, with a sincere broad smile. 'Glad to have you with us, old fellow.'

It had been some time. Maitland had been prevented from sailing with others to reinforce in the America war. Now, he'd been sent in *Bellerophon* at very short notice to add to the meagre forces Kydd had at his disposal.

The conference was brief and to the point. 'I've received word from the commander-in-chief that the Emperor of the French has been removed from power by the French themselves so we've no more fear there'll be a fleet action of sorts,' Kydd opened.

There were rueful grins about the table. Advancement came from bloody battles, not diligent books of accounts, however well carried out.

'Now we've all hell broken loose and the devil to pay as it were. Bonaparte has left Paris and disappeared and no reliable intelligence where he is now, with or without an army. What concerns us is a report that he's planning a voyage to the United States of America, there to recoup in some way.'

Maitland glanced at the others around the table. Kydd spoke well, clearly, forcefully and on their level. If the rumour that he was a tarpaulin sailor from the lower deck was accurate there was nothing in his manner to betray it.

'I've orders of the utmost importance that require that, for obvious reasons, this cannot be allowed to happen – and it falls to me as admiral of the only active squadron at sea to prevent it.'

Maitland felt a stab of envy. Kydd was most fortunate to hoist his flag when so many others had been superseded to allow it, but he for one would not be the first to grudge him.

'To this end, gentlemen, I can see no other course than to blockade the coast as of old. This squadron will disperse to stations as I'll direct, there to cruise as best fitted to intercept outward-bound shipping. Search the vessels down to the very keelson. Any military contraband found will make the ship good prize. Clear?'

'Supposing His Nibs is uncovered?'

'Treat him as a prisoner-of-war and take him to England.'

'If we're fired upon?'

Kydd gave a wolfish grin, and replied, 'Fire back!'

'Sir Thomas.' It was the foppish Spencer of *Valiant*. 'As our flag-officer where will you be for dispatches and rendez-vous, sir?'

'My station will be here but I could be found as far south as Quiberon Bay. Captain, I expect you, however, to stay at your post most faithfully and not come looking for me.'

He glanced about the table for further questions, his expression forbidding.

'Sir, supposing word comes from any one of us or your intelligence sources that Bonaparte has been seen somewhere?'

'Any with such information is to let me know by their fastest cutter and I'll judge its worth. If such seems reliable enough it'll probably have me desiring all to converge *tout de suite* on the position concerned.'

Maitland knew this to be a most terrifying decision to make. If proven incorrect, the coast would have been stripped bare for the sake of making interception the more certain, very necessary, but thereby allowing Bonaparte to slip out to sea from some other place.

He didn't envy Kydd quite so much now.

'Then, gentlemen, your stations. From the north . . .'

It was fairly done and with each station came an accompanying assembly of brigs, cutters and, with some, a frigate. To Maitland's satisfaction, when *Bellerophon* was posted, it was the Basque Roads, which he well knew, the La Rochelle and Rochefort complex, the second most important French naval base after Brest.

'Not as who should say a difficult operation,' Kydd said, with a wry smile. 'I've had worse – but, as God is my witness, none so consequential!'

Chapter 79

'Your Imperial Highness, do be welcome! I will never forget this honour as long as I shall live.'

The dockyard master attendant could not have been more overcome, bowing and fawning on the great figure he'd served for so many years but never once set eyes on. Now, with not the slightest notice, he'd suddenly appeared before him.

'Yes, yes. You have a frigate ready for sea, I understand.'

'Majesty, not one but two – *Saale* and *Méduse* clearing for the West Indies to sail shortly. Er, is there anything . . .?'

'Where are they?'

'Sire, moored in the frigate anchorage, which is in the Basque Roads. Do you—'

'Arrange a boat. I wish to visit them.'

Moreau and the others – including his baggage – had not yet made their appearance and Bonaparte had to be content with a hastily assembled escort from the garrison for the journey by the dockyard yacht to Île-d'Aix. It was an island at the head of the Charente inlet, within the shelter of which frigates could safely moor.

They were at anchor, demurely facing together into the tidal stream, a brisk westerly bringing white caps in on them in a disciplined succession.

'That one,' Napoleon demanded, indicating the larger.

'*Un visiteur distingué*,' was all the lieutenant could think to reply at the hail from the deck, for fear of disbelief.

From below Capitaine de Frégate Philibert of the *Saale* emerged with a thunderous expression.

'*Quelle est cette absurdité?*' he demanded.

Napoleon threw open his boat-cloak and faced him.

'S-Sire!' Philibert snatched off his hat and bowed.

'Your quarters?'

'We're about to set sail, Majesty, but if you—'

'Captain, I have here a direction from Minister Decrès requiring you to give me passage to the United States of America.'

Philibert did not even look at it. 'This will be both my honour and duty, sir. Ah, when shall you . . .?'

'My baggage is not yet arrived. You'll depart when it's safely aboard.'

'Yes, sire. I trust it will not be long doing so – this westerly is getting lively and, of course, you will have noticed it's foul for our departure.'

'I'm sure you'll take care of that, Captain.'

'Then as I shall need charts, I beg to know where in the United States of America Your Majesty intends to land?'

The Potomac and Washington were mentioned but Philibert pointed out that as the presidential mansion had been recently burned down it could conceivably be embarrassing. He suggested New York as more practical.

'You shall sleep aboard, sire?' Philibert wanted to know.

'Until we leave I shall stay on the land, I believe. Fort Liédot on Aix I'm sure can find me a place to lay my head.'

On the island he was secure from any sudden Bourbon move to arrest him, and his baggage, when it came, would be equally safe.

'I bid you good night, Captain, and do look forward to our voyage together.'

Chapter 80

Aboard Bellerophon

The ship leaned to the westerly, fair for a fast passage south. Maitland had no need to consult the charts: the difficult manoeuvres during the action at Basque Roads were still vivid in his memory.

Admiral Kydd wanted him to cover not merely the Basque Roads and La Rochelle but to the south, the Gironde river. The ancient port of Bordeaux, from which so much commerce flowed, not the least the rich wine trade, stood at its navigable height.

If Bonaparte was going to leave by naval craft, a frigate perhaps, it would be Rochefort where it would happen. If, on the other hand, he was obliged to flee in disguise it would be Bordeaux, where merchant ships departed for destinations worldwide.

On reflection his first call would be Bordeaux. They were reputedly anti-Bonapartist, resenting the effects of the emperor's Continental System as the ruination of their trade and would not take kindly to his presence.

Yet it had to be accepted that, with no intelligence worth the name, Bonaparte could be anywhere in France. The southern Mediterranean ports had an infinity of foreign lands close to hand in which to find refuge but Maitland had his orders and Admiral Kydd would not be one to overlook any wandering off on his own.

Bellerophon anchored squarely across the estuary of the Gironde. Maitland quickly had the boats out, their orders to stop and rummage any vessel of sea-going size, and for the lesser, board and politely enquire whether they'd perhaps seen the Emperor Napoleon Bonaparte while ashore.

There was little more he could do – perhaps give it a day or two, then repeat the exercise somewhere near Rochefort and then La Rochelle.

For now he sent his attached sloop and two gun-brigs to do much the same in Médoc country and up to the ancient Île d'Oléron, reporting at the close of each day.

No sooner had *Bellerophon* secured from sea than Maitland's first lieutenant apologetically leaned into his cabin. 'Boat alongside – wishes you to have this,' he said, handing over a carefully wrapped package.

'Reply?'

'Waiting alongside.'

Maitland took it in irritation. There were many jumped-up merchants thinking to take passage back to England or needing some favour.

It was a simple enquiry concerning his stopping of outward-bound shipping. Did it apply also to British flag registry vessels?

The writing was meticulous but bore no signature or address. Enclosed with the message was a writing quill for the convenience of a reply.

Maitland snorted. As if His Majesty's Navy had not enough of their own. 'Here, take it as a spare,' he said, sending it across the table to his clerk.

'Er, not so useful, is all.'

'Oh?'

'It's blocked up in the channel, like.' The hollow stem was obstructed by a tightly rolled piece of translucent paper. Using tweezers it was carefully eased out and smoothed flat.

'*This is to advise you that Napoleon Bonaparte has escaped Paris and is now hidden in these parts . . .*' Stunned, Maitland took in the remainder.

The writer, a substantial British wine merchant wishing anonymity but speaking with obvious authority, even specifying the lodging Bonaparte had occupied the previous night, disclosed that it was the emperor's intention to leave for America by naval means in the very near future.

Again there was no signature or any means of identification.

It was breathtaking news – if true. If it was, not only did it reveal where the former emperor was but also confirmed that Bonaparte had not yet left for America.

A reply for the boat? He hurried on deck and went to the side. Two unkempt rowers looked up, expressionless. Maitland casually put the quill behind his ear and was rewarded with a cheery wave of understanding before it shoved off.

So! It could only be Rochefort. If he was quick he could be there in time to prevent the greatest catastrophe of all.

Should he blow the whistle – get word to Admiral Kydd that Bonaparte might have been found? Perhaps not: he would want proof of some kind before sounding the tally-ho on the former emperor. Better to get to Rochefort and confirm.

Chapter 81

Off Rochefort

'No, Captain! I will not leave without my baggage,' Bonaparte snapped irritably. 'Do you seriously imagine I should appear before the Americans dressed like a pauper?'

'Sire, these winds are unkind to us. Unless we proceed very soon we shall be shut in against the land.'

'You have my orders, sir. Be so good as to obey them.'

Philibert kept his silence. There were other reasons just as cogent for an early departure. He had seen increasing numbers of smaller craft of the Royal Navy passing offshore, no doubt searching for Bonaparte. A frigate could easily brush them aside but then it would be too late: the secret would be out.

As the morning went by the winds grew more unfriendly until they reached a point dead foul for departing. Familiar with the local weather he realised that now it would probably be a day, two days, before the wind shifted around and allowed them to put to sea.

Sometime in the night the baggage arrived but, given the conditions, it could not be loaded aboard.

Napoleon raged at the delay from the safety of the ramparts of Fort Liédot, but late in the morning into Basque Roads there appeared a horrifying vision not seen since the ruinous battle some years before. A British line-of-battleship, a full 74-gun monster of the breed, gliding in to anchor in the traditional place reserved for ships-of-the-line. It was cataclysmic.

To seaward of the frigates, it effectively held them in its power, and it showed every sign of wanting to stay.

Moreau was appalled. Time was not on their side – the royalists would be getting their orders from King Louis before long, which conceivably would include a cancelling of Decrès's direction to the frigates.

They were safe so long as Bonaparte stayed out of sight in the fort. Without contact with the shore, his whereabouts in Rochefort could only be guessed at and the man-o'-war had no authority to land armed men and search for him.

But how long could it continue? Hastily a meeting was convened to find some alternative way of getting to sea.

There were few alternatives. 'There's *Bayadère*,' suggested the master attendant. 'A corvette, she's light draught enough to make the Maumusson passage.'

A narrow, tortuous and sandbank-ridden channel separating the south of Oléron from the mainland, it would be quite impossible for any ship of size to follow through to the open sea.

'Ah, that's the rub,' murmured Ponée of *Méduse*. 'A corvette. A fine thing to slip to sea but, once there, much too modest in speed. She'll be taken by the first British ship who sights her.'

There was no response from Bonaparte, who sat glowering at the head of the table.

'Why not ship out in a merchant packet? The master's

papers are checked in the cabin while His Majesty keeps out of sight below.'

'Hmm. There's plenty of sail abroad – the season's Bergerac is shipping at this time.'

Moreau had his reservations. Would the great man consent to being battened down below? And the conveniences offered in a commercial ship were few. But if it offered a chance . . .

'I'll go now and see if it can be done.'

The docks area was bustling with activity and he had no trouble in locating a likely craft, its bowsprit arrogantly spearing over the wharf, ready for sea to his untutored gaze.

Feeling more than a little out of place in his army uniform, he mounted the gangplank under the disapproving eye of some kind of boatswain.

He was right: the ship was putting out on the evening tide. And the ship's master was eager to do what he could for the deposed emperor but explained it was impossible. The British admiral had instructed his ships to rummage when boarding – like Customs, to make comprehensive search below. The emperor would have no chance of escaping discovery.

If neither a naval departure nor a merchant ship, what remained? Moreau left the ship disconsolate and distracted, not noticing a figure falling into step beside him.

'*B'jour, mon brave*,' the man said, in atrocious French. 'Did you have any luck?'

'What can you possibly mean by that, sir?'

The man looked shrewdly about, then said quietly, 'Jones, Caleb Jones as is the American consul hereabouts.'

'Jean Baptiste Moreau. What can your business be with me, sir?'

'Ah, now, I was passing by and I see a general or some such going aboard a merchantman, not as if it were a usual

361

thing. So I asks myself what can interest such a gentleman? Only one thing I can think of . . .'

'Sir, you are impertinent.'

'You must be a-looking to smuggling out your Bonaparte and you're desperate in the matter.'

Moreau stopped in astonishment and dismay. 'How can you—'

'So I thinks, why not do a deal as must satisfy both sides? I'll get your emperor out . . . for a small fee.'

He spoke for a short while and Moreau's hopes came flooding back. 'Come with me, Mr Jones. I think we can arrive at some arrangement agreeable to you.'

The hastily reconvened group heard Moreau introduce the consul and add, 'I beg you will hear what Mr Jones has to say.'

'Well, now, and there's no big mystery. I've, um, interests in two fast vessels, *Pike* and *Ludlow* as were corsairs in the last war. Very speedy, has the legs on every English ship as wants to detain 'em. We bundle His Majesty in one and the other scoots off to divert attention, and I guarantee just as before they gets through handsomely!'

'May we know what you'll be charging for this service, sir?'

'Don't rightly know – never shipped an emperor before. Shall we leave it for now?'

'And when can we expect them to be ready for sea?'

'Ah. A small contribution on the nail would speed things, they being laid up this half-year.'

Bonaparte prowled up and down like a bear, unapproachable with a scowl of helpless impatience. Word was coming from Rochefort and La Rochelle of a deteriorating situation, the royalists now distinctly in the majority and on the streets.

'Are those corsairs ready yet?' he growled ill-temperedly at Moreau.

'Patience, Sire. We can't have them sent to sea incomplete, so to say.'

They were trusting this American with everything, but the man was going out of his way to keep from being seen as the agency that had allowed Bonaparte his means of escape.

Then the long-foreseen blow fell. The Fouché warrant for the arrest of Napoleon Bonaparte had finally arrived in the gendarmerie at Rochefort. The next few days would see the final moves take place that would see Bonaparte taken as a criminal to Paris for public trial.

It was inconceivable – but it had happened. The British ship-of-the-line still lay implacably across the path to sea and more and more vessels with the dreaded white ensign could be seen criss-crossing off the bay.

Was this the end for Bonaparte?

In a fury of despair Moreau stalked the battlements of the fort – if only . . . Then he recalled the captain of a Danish cognac trader he'd met who'd said kind things about the emperor. If he threw himself on the man's mercy to devise some means of flight by sea, might there be a chance?

Magdeleine was not capacious, a Baltic-style coastal brig, but was neat and clean in the Scandinavian style. Besson, the captain, took Moreau below and quickly laid out a plan.

This involved an identical barrel to the others in his cargo but equipped with a breathing tube, used earlier in the war to smuggle wanted persons in and out of Denmark, then under Bonaparte's Continental System.

Two ships would independently put to sea, one the *Magdeleine* and the other a more capacious ocean-going vessel. Once through the cruising warships there would be a transfer, then a comfortable passage to the United States of America.

It was, as far as Moreau could see, faultless and he hurried back to where Bonaparte was pacing to and fro.

'Majesty – a plan!'

He laid it out, expecting some kind of eager acceptance, but Bonaparte strode on, a black frown still in place.

'Sire, we should act very quickly, I fear.'

'No.'

It was final, as Moreau had learned to recognise over the years.

'May I know why not, sir?'

The pacing stopped and Bonaparte turned to face him. 'I'd think better of you, Moreau. Consider, should the vessel be stopped and I discovered, the world would learn that Emperor Napoleon Bonaparte was caught fleeing his own countrymen by hiding in a barrel. I won't have it.'

The endless pacing began again but Bonaparte added, in a wounded growl, 'And I'll have you know that there have been . . . developments.'

'Sire?'

'Ask another, I'm wearied of talking.'

Struck dumb, Moreau hesitated, then took his leave and sought out Bertrand, the leading figure in Bonaparte's entourage. He found him in the emperor's quarters with another, whom he didn't recognise, who was weeping copiously into an exquisitely embroidered kerchief.

'General – do I intrude?'

'What is it, Moreau?' the big man said gruffly, clearly disquieted by the scene.

'I've just seen His Majesty with a sound plan for his departure but he refuses to entertain it. He besides mentions developments.'

'His Imperial Majesty is not himself, I believe. And if you call this sorry affair developments then, yes, there have been.'

In obvious anguish the other man sobbed once, tore himself away and left.

'That, Moreau, was the King of Spain as was. Joseph, His Imperial Majesty's brother. Came with an offer to disguise himself as the emperor to distract the pursuit while the emperor slips away.'

'What did—'

'His offer was refused on the grounds of extreme danger to the royal person,' Bertrand said flatly.

'But . . . but the gendarmes will be here very shortly indeed. All avenues of escape have been exhausted. This is . . .'

'We need to take extreme measures, Moreau. You're a better hand at words. Let's be started.'

Chapter 82

Aboard Bellerophon

Maitland gazed moodily through the stern windows at the grey, fretful seascape, pondering the surreality of it all.

The greatest tyrant and conqueror of the present age was almost certainly here – the swirling rumours couldn't all be wrong. He'd duly notified Admiral Kydd. But there were rumours of Brest, too, and the risk of the squadron abandoning its posts for the sake of gossip was too great. He'd been left with strict orders to keep close watch on anything that moved.

The frigates were the obvious refuge, but despite the watch-on-deck ordered to keep a glass continually on them there'd been no sign of Bonaparte.

And what of the hearsay that he was planning an exit in disguise aboard a merchant ship? Or the one about his shipping out as a common seaman in a Danish brandy trader?

Or – hard to take – the firmly held belief that he'd already left and was now halfway across the Atlantic to freedom?

Either way he knew in his bones he'd be blamed in some way. But what else could he do?

He spent the next hour listlessly at his paperwork until gratifyingly interrupted by the midshipman of the watch, who handed him an anonymous-looking pack. 'From a boat just alongside, sir.'

Maitland broke the unrecognised seal and found himself reading, in exquisite French, an astonishing and dramatic revelation:

The Emperor Napoleon having abdicated the throne of France, and chosen the United States of America as a retreat is, with his suite, at present embarked on board the two frigates which are in this port, for the purpose of proceeding to his destination. He expects a passport from the British Government, which has been promised to him, and which induces me to send the present flag of truce, to demand of you, Sir, if you have any knowledge of the above-mentioned passport, or if you think it is the intention of the British Government to throw any impediment in the way of our voyage to the United States.

It was signed 'Bertrand, Maréchal de Palais' and addressed to 'the Admiral commanding the cruizers before Rochefort'.

Shaken, he realised that what he had hoped for and dreaded had indeed come about. In his hands was proof positive that Napoleon Bonaparte was in Rochefort and even more wildly improbable was in active contact with him.

There was everything to play for now. Energised, he concentrated on what to do. First – word to Admiral Kydd, who would need to know instantly, as would London and the Admiralty. Get the dispatches away this very hour.

Next, some sort of delaying reply – the same boat would

act as intermediary, no question of bringing the man himself aboard for discussion.

He whipped out paper and pencil and began sketching out his reply.

Almost immediately he stopped. Think it through, old fellow!

The very fact that Bonaparte – the French – was contacting him directly was satisfying evidence that *Bellerophon* and her little flotilla were successful in their watch and guard. There would be no rapid flight to sea.

The next was the implication that time was seen to be running out, which might well be the case as King Louis would be taking every action possible to run Bonaparte to ground. This letter was a first move, an attempt at a covering of legality to the break-out. The piece about passports was a bluff, of course: the last thing the British government wanted was Bonaparte on the loose.

His reply had better be well worded, no implication of promises made or threats expressed, but at the same time the honest truth on display.

The boat, with a pair of army officers, was waiting for a reply. There was nothing to be gained by delay and he began a first draft.

In only forty minutes he had it complete and read through it one last time.

I have to acknowledge the receipt of your letter addressed to the Admiral commanding the English cruisers before Rochefort, acquainting me that the Emperor, having abdicated the throne of France, and chosen the United States of America as an asylum, is now embarked on board the frigates, to proceed for that destination, and awaits a passport from the English Government; and requesting to know if I have any knowledge of such passport; or if I think it is the intention of the English Government to prevent the Emperor's voyage.

In reply, I have to acquaint you, that I cannot say what the intentions of my Government may be; but, the two countries being at present in a state of hostilities, it is impossible for me to permit any ship of war to put to sea from the port of Rochefort.

As to the possibility of allowing the Emperor to proceed in a merchant vessel, it is out of my power, without the sanction of my commanding officer, Admiral Sir Thomas Kydd, who is at present off Brest, and to whom I have forwarded your despatch, to allow any vessel, under whatever flag she may be, to pass with a personage of such consequence.

I have the honour to be, etc.

Stretching painfully, he rang for the clerk to make a fair copy and ordered a much-delayed breakfast.

The response was immediate. A small working schooner made its way out to *Bellerophon* with two distinguished-looking officers desiring a consultation.

Maitland could almost smell the desperation as they came aboard, and knew the crux of the matter would be reached. If only Kydd was here – but he was on his way and couldn't be expected for some time.

'General Savary, Duc de Rovigo, and Comte Las Cases,' introduced an aide.

'As representing General Bonaparte?' All Allied officers had been instructed never to recognise any other title for the fallen emperor.

'Our authority,' said Savary, handing over a ribbon-bound scroll.

'One moment, if you please.' At the very least he would have witnesses to what followed. The first lieutenant, the captain of *Falmouth*, who happened to be on board, and the ship's chaplain duly filed in.

The deputation began by pointing out that the departure of Bonaparte to America would ensure that any focus for insurrection around his person would be impossible at such a distance. As well it would reassure the Allies that he could never, in any wise, act against them.

Maitland accepted this but reminded them that his orders from Admiral Kydd still stood: he could allow no vessel bearing such an important person to put to sea under any circumstances whatsoever.

There were muttered interchanges before it was allowed that certain factions in France desired to make Bonaparte's trial the focus of what amounted to a civil war, which would most assuredly be laid against Maitland's door for not acting to prevent it.

He waited for them to make mention of the troops of bloodthirsty Prussian cavalry raging through France under orders to take Bonaparte alive or dead but they held back.

It was time to play his own card. 'Gentlemen. It appears that circumstances have conspired against you. I believe that there is nothing more in your power that can save your principal from arrest and the shame of a public trial.'

Their rigid expressions betrayed the truth of what he was saying.

'I do, however, have a suggestion that may spare him such a spectacle.'

'Do state it, sir.'

'That he takes refuge – asylum, as it might be – within the safety of the civilisation and laws . . . of England.'

A sharp intake of breath told him that at the very least he had their attention. The Admiralty orders to the fleet were that if Bonaparte were encountered he was to be brought direct to England. Thus Maitland was only doing what he could to make the process more seemly.

'Ah, what undertaking do we have that Emperor Bonaparte will be accorded the grace and respect due his rank and station?'

'Sir, I cannot give this undertaking in my own name, but His Royal Highness the Prince Regent is known to be an admirer and there are many in Britain who join with him in this.'

'To be scrupulously clear, sir,' Savary said heavily, 'you specify that any action of Emperor Bonaparte to put to sea by any species of ship will be prevented.'

'My orders are clear on the point, sir.'

'Any?'

'Excepting this vessel for the purpose of embarking on a passage to England.'

'And this is your final word on it, sir?'

'It is.'

There was little else that could be usefully discussed and the deputation withdrew.

In something of a haze of wonder and disbelief Maitland sat back and considered. The offer had been made. Given the appalling adversities facing the former emperor, it was more than likely it would be taken up.

In that case the acceptance must be acted on as nothing other than a capitulation.

And Napoleon Bonaparte was surrendering, not to a victorious army but to the Royal Navy, which had comprehensively rendered his plans to stand astride the world for ever out of his reach.

Sometime in the evening another boat bore a final letter.

It was short, to the point and conceded nothing.

Comte Las Cases has reported to the Emperor the conversation which he had with you this morning. His Majesty will proceed on board your ship with the ebb tide tomorrow morning, between four and five o'clock.

I send the Comte Las Cases, Counsellor of State, with the list of persons composing His Majesty's suite.

His Majesty despatches to the Prince Regent a letter, a copy of which I have the honour to enclose, requesting that you will forward it to such one of the ministers necessary that he may have the honour of delivering the letter with which he is charged to the Prince Regent.

I have the honour to be, etc.

It had happened. For a surety the name of Napoleon Bonaparte was now history and its owner would never threaten the world again.

In rising wonder he realised that the name of his ship – and himself – would now go down the centuries as the one to whom the great figure had personally surrendered.

Pulling himself together he spoke to the stiffly correct count and took his list. Sixty-odd in the entourage.

They had until early in the morning to prepare *Bellerophon* to be fit not just for a mortal king but the most infamous conqueror the world had seen.

Chapter 83

'The instant a boat is spotted,' Maitland growled, at the officer-of-the-day, as the delicate light of dawn began to extend over a calm pearlescent sea.

He'd spent a sleepless night on the most trivial matters. How, for instance, was Napoleon Bonaparte to be ceremonially greeted? An officer coming aboard is piped over the side, a captain piped with a side party and an admiral with a guard and band. What therefore did the regulations dictate was the correct routine for an emperor?

It wasn't until the early hours that he realised the answer was there all the time.

For tidal reasons Bonaparte would be coming aboard at about five in the morning. And that was most definitely well before the eight bells signifying the end of the morning watch, which saw the hoisting of colours to greet the day and the end of the 'silent hours' during which no ceremonial, however hallowed, could be permitted to disturb the sleep of the watch below.

Napoleon Bonaparte would not be greeted by any ceremonial whatsoever.

As the light strengthened, a brig-of-war was sighted standing towards, making slow progress in the light breeze. It bore no distinguishing ensigns or pennants beyond a flag of truce but on her quarterdeck there was a tight knot of colourful figures.

It would be some time before it came alongside and Maitland's mind raced with anxiety at what conceivably might still happen to prevent the great event from coming to pass.

'Sir,' the officer-of-the-day broke in anxiously, 'it's the flag-ship come, I believe.'

Maitland swung round. It was: *Centaur* was making into Basque Roads from seaward steadily on course directly for them.

He snatched another glance at the brig. Still under way, it was coming on lethargically as though reluctant to give up its precious burden. And it was clear that *Centaur* would be up with them well before the hapless brig.

He felt a welling up of feeling: if the admiral reached here first, Bonaparte would necessarily surrender to him, rendering Maitland and *Bellerophon* nothing more than a footnote to history.

'Mr Mott!' He rounded on the first lieutenant. 'Do take my barge and fetch General Bonaparte to me.'

'Aye aye, sir,' Mott said stolidly, and roared out the orders that set *Bellerophon*'s barge in the water, stretching out for the brig.

It came back promptly, and at last the figure of Bonaparte could be made out as the boat curved about to come along-side at the side-steps.

The first up the side was Marshal Bertrand who said, rather lamely, 'Sir, the emperor is in the boat.'

Maitland ignored him. Rather guiltily he'd ordered a small guard of marines to muster, but as Bonaparte mounted the steps they did not present arms and, in a breathless silence, the fallen emperor stepped out on to the deck.

This was the man half the world feared and hated and who had come close to being its ruler.

Dressed in the faultless perfection of the undress uniform of the Chasseurs à cheval de la Garde impériale, the well-known wide cocked hat, white waistcoat and breeches, with highly polished military boots and in the famous olive-grey greatcoat against the morning chill, he presented himself with becoming dignity. Pulling off his hat, he said loudly, 'Sir, I am come to throw myself on the protection of your prince and laws.'

The Napoleonic wars were over.

After showing him his cabin and appointments, Maitland apologised and announced that it was the custom for him to call upon his newly arrived admiral. Shortly, he set out for *Centaur*, now anchoring.

Chapter 84

Kydd scanned *Bellerophon* with his glass. It was early morning and there were no colours evident, alien pennants or any other indication that she was successful in the hunt for Bonaparte. Her barge was in the water – no doubt Maitland in the normal way coming to make his number with his admiral.

Nothing could be more crucial than that Bonaparte was in sight: Kydd's urgent order for the squadron to converge on this place had stripped all other ports of their watchers.

He returned to his cabin for privacy in receiving Maitland's report but more to show that he wasn't so anxious to hear and looked up casually at the knock at the door.

'Come!'

'Sir. I have to report—'

'Bonaparte?' Kydd couldn't help it.

'I have him aboard, sir.'

Kydd could hardly believe it. 'In *Bellerophon*, under strict guard, of course?'

'More as a guest, sir.'

'Damn it! Sit down and tell me everything – no, wait, there'll be more than a few would like to hear it too.'

The story came out, his audience sitting enthralled. 'So I sent the barge to bring the business to a speedier conclusion. I trust this is acceptable to you, Sir Thomas?' Maitland concluded.

'A reasonable thing in the circumstances, I'd think. And the beggar surrendered to you on your own quarterdeck. That'll make a story as will keep you in with society for ever.'

In his relief Kydd felt a wash of benevolence to the officer who had secured the squadron's goal. This was ultimately his triumph as admiral, and by rights he could claim Napoleon Bonaparte as his own in the flagship to take back to England and instant fame, but he stopped himself. He had won his flag. Now, in peacetime, the prospects for Maitland were bleak. This was his moment of glory. Kydd wouldn't spoil it.

'How do you feel as to keeping him? Would you like to part with him?' he teased.

The answer was full-hearted, and before long Kydd was leading his squadron and imperial prisoner on the passage back to England.

It was an uneventful voyage. None of the many ships passing could have any notion of who they were conveying. As they rounded a dark-shrouded Ushant during a customary rain-squall it occurred to Kydd that aboard *Bellerophon* Bonaparte would be looking his last on the soil of France.

They came to anchor in Torbay, the traditional shelter and refuge for the Channel Fleet on blockade. Only a few folk strolling on the beach looked curiously at them while Kydd deployed his squadron in a protective arc to seaward – but not before his dispatches were on their way to Keith, commander-in-chief, and the Admiralty.

Keith's answering dispatch was swift. The squadron would remain in Torbay for further orders but on no account should General Bonaparte be suffered to receive visitors, or any person be allowed to board *Bellerophon* or approach in a boat closer than one cable's length.

Within hours the news that Bonaparte was aboard *Bellerophon* had got out and boats began putting off from the shore hoping to catch a glimpse of the fabled tyrant.

He obliged, strolling the deck in his legendary garb and cocked hat, noticing the well-dressed and removing his hat, then bowing to delighted ladies. After a day the concourse of boats held at a cable's length by armed marines was remarkable, shouts and cheers carrying across the water, often acknowledged.

Sometime later instructions from the Admiralty were relayed to Kydd. He and his squadron were to remove to Plymouth Sound where Bonaparte was to be held for the final dispensation as deemed by His Majesty's government.

In a chaotic scrimmage with the crowd of boats, Kydd led his ships around Start Point and on to the Sound in a difficult northerly and then, in the so-familiar surroundings of Devonshire, into the centre of the Sound where he anchored.

This time there were boats from shore to shore, near a thousand or so, someone counted, joyously awaiting the appearance of the person of Napoleon Bonaparte, who obliged repeatedly. The crush increased – there was talk of boats being overturned, even of drownings – and still the madness continued.

Kydd needed to report to Keith but found the formidable splendour of his boat and full dress did not guarantee him a passage and he had to send for a launch of brawny sailors to force a way through.

'A raree show indeed,' Keith rumbled. 'You met the villain?'

'Aye, sir.'

'What do ye think of the rogue?' Keith was notoriously far from an admirer of Bonaparte.

'Rather disappointed,' Kydd admitted. 'Fat living going to the belly, indolent, rather curious where in England he'll be spending his days.'

In truth how could any figure in middle years match up to the legend of ferocity and triumphant conquering? If anything, beneath the familiar dress was a rather ordinary individual, if both amiable and opinionated.

'Well, I can satisfy him on the last. A decision by Government near instant. It's to be St Helena.'

Probably the most isolated speck of land anywhere. Kydd could think of no worse fate for a grand emperor to spend all his remaining years, left with his memories and no hope of release.

'Not to be landed in England or to meet any of consequence before he sails.'

Clearly to prevent any focusing of sentiment to prevent his exile.

'I've instructed *Northumberland* to make ready to embark him, but do leave to me the announcing to Bonaparte. When the transfer is complete you may consider the object of your squadron achieved – and in the most splendid manner – and may stand down.'

With an overwhelming sense of finality Kydd took boat back to his ship and, to his surprise and great pleasure, was greeted by Persephone waiting with the officer-of-the-watch.

'Darling! You're returned – and in glory, too!' she breathed, quite oblivious to the envying looks from the officers.

'Not as who's to say a rollicking adventure,' Kydd answered softly, disengaging himself.

Little Francis squealed to be picked up and the trio left the deck together. In the cabin Kydd told her of Bonaparte's fate. 'Should you want to meet the fellow, I believe I've the weight to persuade them to make it so.'

Persephone shuddered. 'I'd rather I didn't, Thomas. He's the cause of so much grief in this groaning world. Let's move on together into the new one without the brute in it. You'll still be an admiral?'

He smiled fondly. 'I'll still have my flag and my future, Seph.'

Some days later found them hand in hand on deck watching the spectacle that would define an age.

Kydd's final act as his squadron's admiral was to ensure that the transfer of Bonaparte from *Bellerophon* to *Northumberland* was completed without incident. This having been done, the undistinguished 74 heaved in her bower anchor and, without fuss or salute, stood out for the Channel and her long voyage to the south.

Lost in thought, they watched the ship slip away, diminishing and touched with the red of a setting sun, until at last she was hull down – and then disappeared.

Kydd turned to Persephone and kissed her gently. 'Well, sweetheart, it's all over now. And, by any reckoning, the world is going to be a very different place.'

Glossary

absinthe	an anise-flavoured spirit, considered potent to taste
arrivistes	new-established in the local culture
barouche	luxurious open four-wheeled carriage
Boodle's	gentlemen's club established in 1762
cat-blash	a cat's regurgitation, useless for anything
Chambertin	celebrated red wine from Burgundy
coup-de-main	manoeuvre to secure objective by speed and force
crow	iron bar to lever and direct the great guns
cully	cant term for fellow
destrain	the act of seizing movable property out of the possession of a defaulter to compel payment of the debt
dimber	an attractive item
dominie	a tyrannical schoolmaster
eagle	the leading pennon of a French formation
fettling	setting to rights; from to fettle a horse
frowsty	the worse for wear after an evening ashore
greensward	land that is under grass, not woodland
hob-a-nob	close in with, in social terms
hooker	any vessel larger than a boat
hookum snivey	shady dealings
mobility	the generality of crowds, the 'mob'
murrain	ill-defined disease of farm animals
picquet	small military defensive post
quoin	wedge used by gunner to raise/lower elevation
sauve-qui-peut	'save who will' – every man for himself
scow	flat-bottomed boat; pejorative for a despised vessel
scranny-picking	mean pickings in employment

spavined	horse with disease of joints, unable to gallop
stanchion	pillar-like upright support
tipstaff	officer of the court, from the small ceremonial staff he carries
whicker	characteristic short neigh of interrogation in a horse
younker	a stripling youth

Author's Note

Admiral Sir Thomas Kydd Bt, Royal Navy. Who would have thought it? But it has happened, and with this volume his tale is complete as promised – one man's journey from pressed man to admiral in the Great Age of Fighting Sail.

It all started for me in 1999. A software designer, I'd just signed off on my biggest and most fraught project. As I sank into an armchair, my wife thrust a large tumbler of whisky into my hand and looked me straight in the eyes. 'Sweetheart,' she said, 'get a life!' Her suggestion: that I write. And about the sea . . .

Once I'd overcome the initial shock and decided to give it a go, I realised there was a lot of sense in what she said. As far back as I can remember, I've been bewitched by the sea. Attendance at a decent grammar school was wasted on me: on the school bus I'd gaze out across the Channel at the low grey shapes slipping away over the horizon on voyages to who-knew-where, taking my imagination with them.

I'm 'old navy' with a deep respect and admiration for the service, so it had to be the navy I'd write about. I chose

Nelson's time, the great climax of the age of sail and a magnificent canvas for sea tales. This was an era when the sea was respected and wooed by men who didn't have steam engines and brute force to meet the waves. I also wanted to bring the sea itself into a more prominent role, but was as yet unsure how to achieve this.

I decided to take the perspective of the men who actually did the job out on the yardarm, serving the great cannon or crowding aboard an enemy deck, rather than of those shouting orders from behind. So, the lower deck it was – and then I came across some surprising statistics. Unlike the army, where commissions were bought, all naval officers had to qualify professionally, and scattered among them were no more than a couple of hundred common seamen who made the awesome journey from the fo'c'sle to the quarterdeck, thereby turning themselves into gentlemen. A tiny handful became captains of their own ships; remarkably, some even became admirals. How could it be so? Just what kind of men were they? None of them left any written record of their odyssey. I had my book – and my series.

This final book is a climacteric – not only with Kydd achieving his flag at last but set within the exceptional times that saw the final meteoric fall, rise and fall of Emperor Napoleon Bonaparte. As always, I have explored the historical context within which Kydd plays his part and this is especially crucial for a perspective of these last remarkable scenes and I make no apology for Bonaparte's frequent appearances.

It was an extraordinary period, and having to cleave to one narrative has obliged me in parts to simplify and omit some detail. But in essence it did happen as I portray it, Kydd performing the real-life role of Admiral Hotham, even if historically the French never reached the point of actually making sally from Brest.

Some writers have taken the view that if the Royal Navy had done its job it would have caught Napoleon as he left Elba and spared Europe the mountain of corpses that was Waterloo, but I'd rather put it down to a cash-strapped government falling over itself to save money after a ruinous war with an over-hasty, wholesale decommissioning of their greatest military asset. This, by 1815, left the northern Mediterranean the responsibility of a contemptible single ship-sloop, quite impossibly presumed to be blockading Elba as well.

And I take issue with blaming Commissioner Campbell for letting Bonaparte slip away: he was never Bonaparte's guard, and his three fellow Allied commissioners had long since faded away out of boredom. His conclusion, with that of Captain Adye, to go to Naples in pursuit seems to me to be for the time reasonable: a large army a day's sail away waiting for Bonaparte to act as focus for the disaffected masses before marching north – or was it to be the lunatic notion that he would be taking his few hundreds to invade France and face the Allies directly?

The final act following the emperor's fall is shot through with myth and legend none of which answers for me the question of why Napoleon so fatally dithered. He intended to decamp to the United States of America even before he left Paris, and there is evidence that the Madison administration was secretly implicated and must have been irate at the delays.

The affair with Captain Maitland receiving the secret message in a quill pen is quite authentic but much else is little more than myth. One odd occurrence is certainly true. It's been pointed out that the whole business in Plymouth with shipping off the fallen emperor to St Helena in just a handful of days shows all the marks of a hurried political reaction to an embarrassment, but the real reason is far more bizarre.

At that precise time the gifted but intemperate frigate captain Lord Cochrane of Kydd's fighting acquaintance had been arraigned for an alleged stock-exchange fraud. In a typically cunning move he obtained a writ of habeas corpus on the person of one Napoleon Bonaparte to appear as witness at his London trial. To the dismay of authority it was upheld at the highest, and his lawyer sent a bailiff post-haste to Plymouth to serve the summons. The captain of *Bellerophon* was advised and various iffy stratagems were employed to dodge the paper, one of which was to have Bonaparte transferred under cover to *Northumberland*, which happened to be nearby and ready for sea. Just in time she sailed, the bailiff's boat left bobbing in her wake.

It does nicely round off a most momentous episode of history.

The reader may be curious to know where I stand in relation to Napoleon Bonaparte. Whatever else, I find it hard to step easily past the deadly calculation of *The Times of London* in 1814 that, it could be said, every minute of his imperial existence had cost the life of a human being.

So now Tom Kydd's tale is done. I have put down my pen and can reflect on the whole adventure.

It's been an exciting ride. Location research has taken me from Turkey to Hong Kong, the South Seas to Canada, but more than anything it's been a deeply fulfilling task that has been in the close company of my wife and literary partner Kathy.

In the process I've made some lifelong friends – from past president of the Royal Society of Marine Artists Geoff Hunt, whose oil paintings of the covers of my books greet visitors at my home, to Polaris submariner Peter Goodwin, one-time keeper and curator of HMS *Victory* and a never-failing treasury of information.

I owe a debt of gratitude to so many others, especially the legions of local historians around the world who always could be relied on to know where the bodies are buried!

As I've reflected on my journey with Thomas Kydd et al. I've had cause to remember the many publishing professionals who have eased my way over the years. I must acknowledge my current editor Oliver Johnson for his sagacity and editorial sensitivity. However, of the original Hodder crew, there's only one remaining, copy editor Hazel Orme, who's unfailingly seen me safely through the perils of omissions and commissions.

Sadly, along the way two very special members of Team Kydd have crossed the bar. The first is literary agent Carole Blake, founder and director of Blake Friedmann Agency. It was she who 'got' my vision for the series and sold English-language rights around the world and was also responsible for the series coming out in a number of foreign languages. Her role is now ably handled by Isobel Dixon.

The second is audio narrator Christian Rodska, who passed away earlier this year, 2024. To many he will ever be 'the voice' of Kydd.

I've been taken by the sea (you may have noticed) from childhood and left home for good at the age of fourteen to go to sea first as a traditionally trained naval shipwright, ending my time with the Royal Navy as a reserve lieutenant commander, serving as Kydd did before the mast and on the quarterdeck. Through my hero therefore it's been my pleasure to continue my communion with the sea and its inhabitants for all of near a quarter of a century.

Oh, and if you think it's voyage end for my writing, it's not. After a few months' sabbatical I shall be setting sail on a brand-new adventure set in the same period, featuring a certain Lieutenant Harry Wylde.